within

CLEO SCORNAVACCA

Within Six Months

Credits

EDITOR

Mac Bros Book Stuff

COVER ARTIST

Stephanie Hobbs
Steph's Cover Design

COVER PHOTOGRAPHY

Michael Reh
Michael Reh Photography

COVER MODEL

Micah Truitt

FORMAT & DESIGN
Jo-Anna Walker
Just Write. Creations & Services

BETA-READERS

Samantha Talarico
Misty Goulet Yancey (Bookluvin Rose)
Table of Contents

This book is dedicated to my reader's group, The Wild Roses, and to my readers…

For supporting me throughout the very long process of getting this story together.

Thanks for being patient, or even not so patient.

Thanks for loving Tommy Conte from the beginning…

I'm beyond grateful.

prologue

TIME...
We follow it, chase it, work around it, and work with it. We want it to start, and at times, we want it to stop. We have too little of it, or sometimes we have too much. In an instant, it moves too quickly, or not fast enough. No matter how we feel in those moments, time is always there challenging us...holding us accountable, reminding us that we should never take it for granted.

Yet...I did.

It was that point...that pivotal moment, when I realized, that where I was, and what I was doing, wasn't living. It was going through the formal motions that my family, friends, society, and the world expected of me. Yet...it couldn't be any further from my truth—from what I truly desired.

I finally had to admit, for much of this past year, I was preoccupied with everyone's life around me. I, in turn, neglected my own, or maybe subconsciously, I wanted it that way. Perhaps it made it easier to ignore my failures rather than face them head on and fix what was broken.

My breaking point...my moment, came when my lifelong friend Rain found the happiness she was searching for, or should I say, it found her. When she moved forward, I knew it was time for me to move on, and that's exactly what I was determined to do.

Life, as I knew it was about to change.

And...if I had my way, what I truly wanted for myself would finally fall into place this time.
Within six months...

chapter
one

Tommy

MY NEW LIFE started now…

Standing on the deck of the old Long Beach Island shore house I had purchased back in February made me realize how its revitalization went hand in hand with the deconstruction of my inner turmoil.

Its strong frame weathered by many a hurricane still stood firm today. Yet, the interior of the stilted Cape Cod was a different story. Although everything was somewhat functional, it was hardly up to date—forgotten. Not unlike me, who had dealt with several personal storms in my life recently. Though, there I stood admiring the magnificent Atlantic roar in front of me, while my insides churned with confusion, apprehension, and a curious excitement of what lay ahead.

Memories passed through my body as I struggled with regrets. I contemplated whether I should have told my family and friends the truth. Only Daniel knew I'd settled here, while everyone else thought I was off surfing the globe, trying to *find myself.*

I missed my brother, Mike, and my best friend, Rain, the most. Even though Mike and I hadn't been on speaking terms, it gutted me that he wasn't part of my life; my fault, not his. Yet, the daily absence of my best friend hurt even more; again, my doing, not hers. I wished I could've told her my plans, but she was part of the problem. I didn't know how to let go where she was concerned. It was something I had always struggled with.

Shit! Maybe I should just call them and let them know what I was really up to.

A few days back, I turned the rickety lock for the last time on the front door of the New York Brownstone I'd shared with Rain for the past ten years. The strong but familiar reverberation sounded when doing so and reminded me of how comfortable I was in the house. The hollow echo that emanated was an ominous reminder my comfort had become complacency, confirming the finality of my situation and the decision I made for my future.

The physical move from New York City to the Jersey Shore was an easy one and went off without a hitch. Hopefully…a good sign of things to come. Yet, here I was…melancholy, questioning if I was making the right decisions.

Look at you…you're not even here a week and already you want to turn tail and head back to a life you couldn't stand to live anymore.

Enough of this! Frustrated with the reflection in self-pity that didn't help then and wouldn't fix things now, I slammed my hand down on the old railing, cracking the wood even further, as its random pieces flew up and then fell to the patio below, sending sand filled smoke billowing in the air.

Great…one more thing to fix.

My aggravation not only proved I was done working on me and the house for today, it also caught the attention of my neighbor, Viv Marshall. The lady next door who helped broker the deal between me and James Stanton, the original owner of the shore house and her brother.

"Good evening, Tommy, is everything okay? By the look and sound of things, perhaps you bit off more than you can chew." She observed as she appeared on the stairs that led to the front deck of the house.

"Good evening, Viv, I'm fine, with the house anyway…" I said, with a broad smile, hoping to hide my embarrassment.

She gave me a flat, disbelieving smile in return.

Shaking my head, I pushed out a strong breath. "I'm fine, really, just tired. Maybe this is all hitting me now? It's probably a hint I should take a break," I said, waving my hands around at the work I'll need to tackle in the morning.

"Well, we have plenty of entertainment to keep you occupied, especially with the start of the summer season. I saw your surfboards in the car when you arrived. You can head out to the end of the island and grab some pretty good waves," she said, pointing south.

"Fantastic! I think I'll check out some of the surf shops tomorrow. Maybe I can hook up with a few of the locals who surf the island." I faced the ocean; the enormous flowing water before me gave me pause. Mesmerized by the crashing waves in the distance, I took in another deep breath.

Noticing my reaction, Viv joined me in the view. "It's amazing, isn't it?" Viv asked as she came up behind me and tried to read my thoughts. We quietly walked forward in unison, away from the damaged railing, and stared at the magnificent, churning water before us.

I turned to face her and saw that she too was completely drawn in. As a light wind tousled her blonde strands, she stood captivated by the familiar picturesque world that surrounded her daily. As I studied her more closely, the noise inside of me settled down and a welcomed quietness formed.

"You love it here, don't you?" I asked.

Her body straightened and nostrils flared as she let out a long profound breath, nodding in agreement, she placed her clasped hands gently over her heart, where they remained.

"Yes, I love it here." Viv gazed out at nothing in particular, but it seemed as though her focus was on something only she could see, something invisible that held a special place in her memories.

"I have a feeling I will come to love it as much as you do."

"You will. I can promise you that. Everyone who comes here loves it. The sea air gets under your skin. It makes you feel different, completely at peace." She explained simply and definitively. Even though I thought there was more to her statement than that, I didn't press her any further, nor did I want to appear intrusive.

We talked a little more and then said our goodbyes once Viv felt my mind was in a better place. Just as she was about to leave, she turned abruptly back to me and snapped her fingers with an exaggerated movement over her head. "Hey, I almost forgot; my niece, Jade, is away right now, and she's due back late tonight. I wanted the two of you to meet, so I'd like to have you over for dinner tomorrow night. She's your other neighbor, so I think it would be nice for you both to get acquainted. If that's okay with you, I mean?"

"Sure, that would be fine. Thanks for the invite. I look forward to meeting her." I didn't know if excited was the right word, but I did feel relieved to have plans for the holiday weekend. Well, at least for Friday night, that is.

"Then it's all set. Come by around 8. We can have dinner out on the porch."

"Can I bring anything?"

"Nope, just yourself. Jade owns a bakery here on the island. She'll bring the desserts and I have the dinner covered. She'll be able to give you some information on the surf reports and some of the clubs that she and her friends go to."

"Your niece surfs?" Although surprised, I asked enthusiastically.

"Of course, she grew up down here. The Jersey Shore is the perfect place to be a child, and the perfect place to learn how to surf and stay out of trouble." She smiled wide and waved, as she disappeared down the stairs.

Smiling to myself, I turned back to stare once more at the Atlantic, or should I say my new backyard. Yeah, this was definitely the ideal place to move.

The thoughts racing through my head were interrupted by a ferocious growl in my stomach. With my renovation duties being sidetracked by my overactive mind, I decided to clean up and head out to a place down the street that Viv had recommended.

The Palm had a great mix of music, with farm to table foods passing under my nose. The wait proved it was one of the more popular spots on the island. I opted to eat at the outside bar on the street level. While taking in the incredible views of the shoreline, a beautiful blonde with eyes the color of frosted sea glass approached me with my drink. Placing the bottle before me, and with a warm smile, she introduced herself.

"Good evening, I'm Kim Turner… the owner of this fine establishment." She teasingly boasted with a tilt of her hip to one side and her arms opened up wide, as she presented to me the business she was so obviously proud of.

I reached out my hand and introduced myself, "Tommy Conte, great to meet you, Kim."

"You're new to The Palm *and* the island. I can tell." She smiled as she placed her hand in mine.

I met her bright smile with a curious grin. "How's that?"

She turned away to face the Atlantic briefly before bringing her focus back to me.

"It's the way you look at her." She cocked her head in the direction of the water without looking away this time.

"Her?"

"The ocean."

I chuckled. "You're partially right, Miss Turner. I've seen oceans before, but now it's different. I just moved in down the road from here. Plus, with a view like that, how could you not be taken back by it?"

"It's true. I've lived here my entire life and she never gets old. I can attest to that, even after all of these years, I never tire of her."

"You've always lived here?" I asked, wondering if she knew Viv.

"Yeah…always"

"Then perhaps you know my neighbor. Viv…Viv Marshall?"

"Know her? She's known me and my family since I was a kid. Her niece Jade is a good friend of mine."

"Wow… small world."

Kim laughed slightly. "Not really, the long-time locals on the island tend to know everyone, just like any other tight-knit neighborhood."

"As a newcomer, that's comforting to know."

She nodded. "Have you met Jade yet?"

"No, no I haven't."

"Well, you're in luck. Jade and I are having dinner tonight. She's coming home a day earlier than expected, so when she arrives I'll bring her over so you can meet."

"That would be great, thanks."

Just then, one of the waiters brought my food and handed the plate over to Kim who placed it on the bar in front of me.

"I'll tell you what, let me leave you to your dinner. I need to check on some things in the kitchen. I'll come back once Jade gets here."

"This looks delicious, thank you again."

"No problem at all. Enjoy." She left through the beach bar's side opening, leaving me to devour my meal.

An hour or so passed with no Kim and no Jade. I concluded Kim either had her hands full with the enormous crowd, or Jade hadn't shown up as Kim had expected her to. At this point, I'd grown tired. This was my cue to head home. Besides, I would definitely get to meet Jade at some point, and after the terrific meal I just enjoyed, I would certainly see Kim again, as I intended to return to The Palm often.

Heading out, I noticed the crowd on the dance floor had grown a great deal larger since earlier this evening. I maneuvered my way through the mass of bodies dancing to a song I wasn't familiar with.

Finally, I found a small opening that led to the exit.

Then…I found *her*.

A beauty with long chestnut hair, eyes to match, and legs that went on for miles, was walking in my direction. Instant attraction quickly changed into reach and rescue as my reaction was to scoop her up into my arms to avoid her falling face first into the sea of dancers who engulfed us.

Luckily for me, her bashful smile and the force at which she grabbed onto my arms showed she wasn't offended, in the least. Her expression made me think my night was about to change for the better, and I wouldn't be leaving after all.

chapter

Two

Jade

THE HEAT FROM hundreds of engines resonated into a visible blur that floated in the air over the city—holiday traffic…I should've known. Taking the pastry courses in Manhattan just before Memorial Day weekend, and then having to drive home in this, was nothing short of sheer stupidity. Although it wasn't all my fault; Blaze was supposed to meet me at her place, because we planned to travel down the shore from here together.

Unfortunately, meeting up with Blaze didn't go smoothly either.

Before giving up, I tried her one more time.

"Hey, Jade"

Finally, she picked up, but her voice was labored, and I was sure she was running somewhere in the city and not toward home to get ready for our trip back to New Jersey.

"Don't 'hey Jade me'. We should have been on the road over an hour ago," I snapped.

"What are you talking about? Be on the road? Oh…wait…shit! I was supposed to meet you. That was today, right?"

She was forever putting her job before her friends—namely me.

"Yes, Blaze…that was today."

"God, I'm sorry. I got caught up with this house and with this new client, and now I have to meet him for dinner."

"Uh huh," Was all I could say. This new client was an all-day thing? Since when?

"Okay, what is that supposed to mean?"

"It means you are doing way more than talking to him about current interest rates and closing points."

"You know I would rather be with you on the beach surfing than here in the city, but this sale could potentially put my name on the 'who's who' list of realtors in Manhattan. Please understand." She pleaded as she gave no other excuse for dinner with a man she spent the entire day with—over a house.

I suspected if this guy was rich, which was definitely possible based on the house I knew she was showing, and if this guy was hot, which was also a good possibility, then I would be lucky if I saw Blaze at all this entire summer, let alone this holiday weekend.

"Okay, so I guess I'll see you tomorrow then?"

"If dinner ends early, I'll drive down tonight."

"Fine. I'll leave the key in the usual spot."

"Great! Kiss Kim for me, and I'll see you later."

Surprisingly, driving out of Manhattan was far easier than the drive home would be. A Thursday night before a major holiday weekend caused all highways to merge onto the Garden State Parkway, more like the Garden State parking lot at this time of day when heading south from the city.

As I left the tunnel, the beauty of this warmer than normal May afternoon heated my skin. Smiling to myself, I stopped my inner complaints knowing the top was down and the radio was on and currently blaring Demi Lovato's Cool for the Summer.

The drive was long and anticipated, yet thankfully uneventful, as I headed back to Long Beach Island…I was finally home.

Parking my car on the street, I ran into the house. I needed to quickly shower, apply some make-up, and pick out a casual outfit to wear for dinner that was still a bit sexy for the club.

I noticed I missed a call from Kim, the owner of The Palm, where I would be having dinner tonight. She sounded concerned as if she had something important to tell me.

The Palm wasn't a fancy place. It was an older three-story beachfront building in the Beach Haven section of the island. The inside was dark with rustic walls that were decorated with vintage surfboards in an array of lengths and vibrant colors. Besides the boards, there was a huge driftwood bar that ran along the left side of the club on the main floor. The stools were black leather with silver grommets equally spaced around the sides of the seats. In the center of the room was a black bamboo floor used for dancing or mingling, depending on what the entertainment was for the evening. On the right side of the room were turquoise colored couches and black club chairs, also tufted with the same silver grommets that adorned the bar stools.

In the summer season, there were several large potted palm trees placed strategically around the club, inside and on the patio outside, overlooking the ocean. The main floor held a small but state of the art kitchen for light meals and snacks. Kim had a weekly order of pastries and desserts delivered from my shoppe, so her cook's focus could be on making savory dishes, not to be worried about the sweet stuff.

Upstairs, there was another bar similar to the one on the main level, but not quite as big. Kim booked local bands for the small stage on this floor, usually on special nights or holiday weekends. Tonight, no bands were booked, so the music for the evening was set up beforehand as part of a pre-programmed file being run by the club's computer and sound systems. It was a sophisticated set-up, but one which kept costs down. The second-floor patrons had the option of accessing several decks outside, as well as the bar area inside that looked down into the entertainment area on the floor below.

The third floor of the building held the apartment where Kim lived. She was not the first owner of the bar. Her dad and his brother owned it, but they felt they'd had enough and decided to sell it. She asked if it would be okay if she purchased it and paid it off over time. Both gentlemen agreed. She kept the name and updated the look slightly—to go along with the theme.

Kim had placed two large hourglasses at each end of the bars. She would flip them over about an hour before closing. Her regulars knew it was time to place their final drink requests, and new customers caught on quickly. Like many of the bars on the island, The Palm had a very strict policy on drinking and driving. It wouldn't happen on Kim's watch, so she had staff members that worked as drivers to take the locals back to their homes and visitors back to their rental houses or hotels.

She had no problem getting help for the busy summer season. Many of the local college students came home for the summer and needed to work to pay off their ever-rising school loans. The bouncers were local law enforcement that could use the overtime to help support their families. During the off-season, the bar was quiet and Kim ran it with two long-time employees. Her dad and uncle would come in to help out if need be.

I parked about a block away, anticipating a larger than normal crowd for a Thursday night because of the holiday weekend. I was right. The Palm was packed. I walked to the side entrance where the employees checked in before they started their shifts. I knew the drill; I had waitressed for Kim's family when I was out of school for the summers. That's how we became friends. Kim was slightly older than me, but when she would come home for summer break from college, we would work together; as did Blaze and Courtney—a former friend of mine.

Tonight, was different, though. Kim needed to speak with me about something, something that at first I wasn't too concerned about, but now I felt uneasy, and I needed to know exactly what was going on. I found her mixing drinks at the bar on the main floor. The music was great and began to relax me more than I had felt for the last couple of days. Manhattan was amazing as always, and I learned a great deal, but there was nothing like the Jersey Shore. The people, the atmosphere, and of course, the sound and scents I had grown accustomed to as a child made me feel at peace. It was home, and I was glad to be back.

Kim's bartender arrived about 9:30 PM to relieve her and that's when we grabbed our sandwiches and headed into Kim's office. I realized I was more exhausted than I'd originally thought, so I decided as soon as we finished our talk, I would wrap my food to go and head home to my soft, cozy bed and sleep until noon. I didn't have to get up early tomorrow morning. One of my staff members said they could open for me. I had anticipated I would be out with Blaze tonight, so I had made arrangements weeks ago.

We both sat down at Kim's desk, each with a sandwich and a drink. Kim had an ale and I had my new favorite, Sweet Vermouth over ice with a slice of lemon. Taking a sip, the amber liquid engaged my palette with hints of spice, while its subtle sweetness tickled my nose and warmed my body.

"So, what's up?" I asked, as I settled back in my seat and braced myself.

"I know you were originally supposed to be here with Blaze, but I'm sort of glad those plans were canceled."

I straightened in my chair. "Okay, what's going on?"

"I opened tonight knowing the crowd would be huge. What I didn't expect was to run into this guy on the patio who said he just moved here and said that his neighbor was your Aunt Viv."

My heart stopped. "Are you sure?"

"Positive…that's why I called you, hoping you were still coming tonight, so I could talk to you about it. When I didn't hear back from you, I called Blaze and she filled me in." She stopped. "You know as well as I do that Viv can only have one neighbor on one side of her, so apparently, this guy Tommy moved into your brother's old house."

"Viv must have accepted an offer while I was away in New York. I wonder why she didn't call me." It wasn't like my aunt to keep things from me. Although she knew I was sensitive to the idea of selling or even renting the old place, I didn't think I would find out about it from anyone other than her.

Kim leaned forward. "Do you want to know what I think?"

"Oh God…I'm not sure," I paused and apprehensively nodded.

"I think he's single. From what I could tell no ring, so maybe, just maybe, Viv is playing matchmaker again."

"Okay, but that's nothing new. She's always trying to set me up and marry me off, ever since Damien and I broke up. What does that have to do with the house and this guy?"

"When you see your new neighbor, you'll know why." Kim was grinning from ear to ear, like a schoolgirl.

"That good…huh?" I asked, but I knew the answer.

"Better than that good."

"If you think he's that attractive, then you date him." I joked. I didn't want her to think I was angry with her observation.

"No way! When it comes to having a man in my life…I'm with you. Besides, I have plenty of men in my life every day of the week."

"Funny, but they would be called customers, not potential love interests."

"Exactly… and that's just the way I like them." Kim's voice softened as she looked out toward the ocean, which was barely visible this time of night.

"I'm sorry, Kim. Have you heard from him?" I felt like such a shit. Kim's childhood love left several years back to go after a career in the music industry. Apparently, he was doing well…too well to return for her.

"Yeah, here and there, you know the way he was even when he lived here. My life was his revolving door."

I shook my head in disgust.

"Hey, stop… it's not your fault. I knew what I was getting into when I let him get into me." She smirked.

"I know but…"

"But nothing…this is exactly the reason why I asked you here." Kim stated, confidently.

"I don't get it…"

"Listen, I would never want to get on Viv's bad side, you know that, but when your new neighbor explained who he was and that he already moved in, well, I just didn't want you to deal with any more surprises than you have already," she stated, as she extended her hand across the desk to me.

I smiled and reached out to her.

"Thanks, Kim, you know I just had this conversation with Blaze about Viv and her career as my personal love broker. I know she means well, but I'm just not ready to get my feet wet again."

"Hey, you don't have to explain to me. I had the same issues with my family and friends. They felt I was waiting around for a day that would never come. What they still to this day don't get is that if I want to wait…so be it. The truth is that in the beginning, I was waiting, but not now, not anymore. Now, I'm enjoying my life the way it is. You know…without all the complications."

"I know exactly what you mean. I just wish Viv did. She doesn't want me to be alone, but what she doesn't understand is that having a man in my life isn't always the cure for loneliness. Actually, getting Damien out of my life cured me more than I thought."

Kim smiled.

"When we first broke it off, sure it hurt, but I've had plenty of time to get used to it, and I couldn't be in a better place right now."

"So that's a *no* on banging the new neighbor?" Kim squeezed and jiggled my hand, as we both laughed hard.

After we finished our meal, Kim asked me to wait here to find my supposed new neighbor, who was having dinner out in the club, so we could formally meet, but she eventually returned alone.

"He must have left," she shrugged her shoulders. "Well, I'm sure you guys will meet up tomorrow. I mean he *is* living right next door."

It was getting late. I stood to leave, but before I did, I walked around the desk to hug my dear friend.

"Thanks," I said as I released her.

"For what?"

"For the heads up."

With a tip up of her chin and twinkle in her eyes, Kim regarded me with a deep kindness in her warm smile.

I walked out toward the dance floor and yelled back to her, stating that I'd call her over the weekend with the lowdown on what transpired between me, Aunt Viv, and my apparently sexy new neighbor. I disappeared into the crowd that had begun to move to the beat of a song that I wasn't remotely interested in. Making my way through the army of moving body parts somehow had gotten me turned around. I didn't know if it was due to my not so sensible but comfortable heels or because of the drink I had, combined with the warmth emanating off the dancers in the room and my sheer exhaustion, yet out of nowhere I lost my footing.

I was about to slip down into the mass of people when a strong arm came around my waist to save me from imminent humiliation. As this mysterious stranger steadied me, I involuntarily placed my hands on his upper arms to balance myself. Looking up, my breath audibly hitched. There in front of me was the face of my hero. I never expected his looks to take my breath away, but they did. Hopefully, he hadn't heard or noticed my reaction.

He had very dark brown hair, almost black. The same as his eye color. His jawline was chiseled like a stone sculpture with a shadow of precisely groomed stubble. His body was strong and nicely built, although I couldn't see his arms from my vantage point—we were too close. All I could do was feel his ripped strength beneath my fingertips, as I held onto his biceps.

"Are you okay?" He shouted over the music with an uncertain but concerned expression on his face.

Dear God, even his voice was sexy. I pulled myself together and stopped my brief and hopefully not apparent schoolgirl stare to quickly answer him.

Get hold of yourself. You've never been this bashful in front of a man before...and let go of him.

He crouched down slightly and cocked his head to one side.

"Are you sure? Can I call someone for you?" He loudly asked.

"Why would you need to call someone for me? I'm not drunk. I just lost my footing, that's all." I went from shy to sounding off over the noise and onto him...defensive and insulted.

"Hey, I'm sorry. I didn't mean anything by it. I was just trying help." He stumbled on his words slightly as he released his hold from around my waist and raised his hands up in his own defense, which made me automatically let go of him as I realized his arms were still in my grasp.

"No worries. It's just been a long day. I apologize." Miserably, I tried to make amends for acting ungrateful for his help and concern. I guess I probably wouldn't believe me either with the attitude I just threw him.

"I feel bad. I didn't mean anything by it. Can I buy you a drink to atone for my behavior?" He smiled a sweet, yet reserved smile.

His response made him even more attractive. I felt a wave of electric energy surge through my body, and it wasn't coming from the large group of people who crowded us on the dance floor. It was because of him, his voice…his mannerisms. Maybe it was the one nightcap that skewed my normal judgment.

"Thank you for the offer, but I had one drink already and one was definitely more than enough this evening." I wished him a good night and started to walk away. That was when he gently placed his hand on my waist again. My body stilled and tingled once more.

"Okay, no drink, but how about a dance, then? Just one; I promise." He looked at me and grinned. He tried to be shy, but that look was anything but innocent. I must admit, he had me curious, a reaction I hadn't felt for any man in a long time.

I nodded, then smiled, and so did he. Tove Lo's Talking Body was just beginning to play overhead and I hadn't danced all evening, so I agreed. I wasn't a huge dancer, but I felt comfortable at The Palm, and for some strange reason, I felt comfortable with my mystery man…perhaps, too comfortable.

My mystery man? Where did that come from?

He gently brought me to his body, and I placed my arms around his neck, almost automatically. It seemed so natural—as if it was right. We moved together seamlessly, as the rhythm of the music and the sexiness of the song carried us away from the other people in the room. I didn't want to overanalyze it, but it was probably not a good choice of song to dance to since I had no idea who this guy was. I couldn't explain why I accepted his offer, but I couldn't stop myself; he intrigued me. Or maybe it was simply that the situation created the illusion.

It was the beginning of the summer season…my favorite time of year. The Palm was alive with people. My business, Summertime Sweets, was going to have a newly renovated location by the end of the summer, and Blaze would be here on Saturday.

I was admittedly on edge about meeting my new neighbor, Tommy; especially because after Kim described him, I had a feeling this was one of Viv's never-ending attempts to play matchmaker for me. Or maybe it was nothing that complicated. It could have been the combination of the Sweet Vermouth and lemon that proved to be too much for my tired body, which was possibly confirmed by my almost dry dive into the dance floor.

Noticing how our bodies blended perfectly, together we pressed against one another as we continued to move. The crowd masked the intimacy of our dance, as our eyes locked. They held a conversation of their own as the music played on…Who are you? Do I want to get to know you? Is there more after this dance…this night? The conversation spoke of sexual attraction and one I didn't want to revisit in my personal life at this point. Yet, with him… tonight, in this atmosphere, at this moment in time, it wasn't so inconceivable at all any longer.

His hand splayed wide at the small of my back. The heat of his palm emanated through my clothing, allowing my body to relax as I pressed back further into it. I became wet from his small gesture, touching me in places that I hadn't given a second thought to for quite some time. I couldn't understand it. Why now? Why this guy? I hadn't even known him for more than 5 minutes. Who was I kidding, I didn't know him at all. Yet, me and my body were completely surrendering to him.

I wanted more. I wanted him to kiss me. A kiss was intimate, far more intimate than sex itself. It held everything and said so much without saying anything at all—the way his body swayed, and the way his eyes darkened even further, he wanted it too.

Our mouths parted at the same time; he leaned down to let his lips graze my skin. Briefly, he pulled back to make sure the kiss he was about to give me was consensual. I nodded, letting him know I wouldn't stop him. Silent, serious, and with eyes hooded, he leaned in, his breathing deepened, and he proved with his mouth he wanted this too. And for some unexplainable and undeniable reason, so did I.

Our breathing became heavy as our eyes locked; our lips paused and then touched again. Apprehension held him back at first, but only for a brief moment. Pressing forward, his mouth opened, inviting me in. My tongue explored as my emotions spiraled out of control from what was building between us and between my legs.

A bombardment of conflicting thoughts swirled through my mind, questioning and appeasing me all at once.

Why would I allow a complete stranger to intimately kiss me out in public? Was it safer that way? Why would I allow myself to be taken in so easily? This was never me. Yet, the more I kissed him, the more I wanted him. It was as if I couldn't stop—this kiss drove me more and more away from the room and into a world I wasn't familiar with, a world with him. I craved it, and I didn't want it to end, but then…it did.

Shit.

My phone buzzed in my pocket.

Startled, I jumped back, violently breaking our intimate connection. Breathless, his face dropped. I needed to explain, so I held it up and waved it quickly back and forth to show him it wasn't him.

I looked at the phone. Oh, this wasn't going to be good.

"Blaze," I shouted over the noise. "What's wrong?"

"Can you come, please? Wait. How did you know that something's wrong?" Her voice was shaky, she was in tears.

"You know as well as I do that you wouldn't be calling me at this late hour if nothing were wrong. What happened?" I shouted once more.

Silence.

"Blaze, tell me what happened, or I won't come." I was firm.

"You're going to be driving, so I'll explain everything to you when you get here." Her answer wasn't good enough. I looked up at the man who intrigued me tonight and decided to use him as an excuse not to save her this time.

"I'm at The Palm dancing with a sexy stranger, so you're going to have to spill it or I'm staying put."

My statement grabbed the attention of my hot dance partner, which earned me a salacious grin. My body warmed once more from his expression. She really needed a good reason for pulling me from my intriguing evening with this guy.

"I told you I had a dinner meeting with the potential client from during the day. Then we went out, talked business, but then one thing led to another and now…"

"Oh no! Do not tell me you slept with him." I interrupted her mid-stream. I had the feeling she did, but I also had the feeling this story was going to get worse before it got better.

"Okay, I won't tell you, but that's not the worst of it." She confessed. Well, she sort of confessed.

"There's more?"

"We're at Mt. Sinai."

"Blaze." That's all I could say. I didn't know how to respond. It's not as if I didn't know how spontaneously Blaze lived her life. She has gone out with clients before, but sleeping with them was not something she ever told me about in the past, and Blaze told me everything.

I couldn't judge her. She was an adult, over thirty and single. She could run her life and make decisions for herself, without any help from me. Especially since my judgment in my last relationship wasn't all that stellar, and in the last half hour, my choice to kiss a perfect stranger on the dance floor wasn't my best idea.

I looked up as if to see the new song that started overhead. Then I looked at my dance partner and looked back at the phone. I told Blaze to hang on. Approaching my handsome stranger; who made my Thursday night more exciting than my life had been in quite some time, I gently touched his shoulder as I kissed his cheek softly and strongly whispered in his ear so that he could hear me over the song.

"Thank you for a great time. Something's come up." Smiling, I backed away into the crowd once more.

Turning to leave, I heard him call out for me.

"Hey, I had a great time, too. I'm…Tom… When can I see you again?" He shouted, but I couldn't hear his name.

"I live on the island. I'm usually here on and off. Maybe we'll see each other here again soon." I raised my voice.

"Wait! What?"

I tried harder but to no avail. The crowd surrounded him and we were separated from each other. At that point, I couldn't see him any longer, so I started pushing my way out because I had to get to Blaze, who was now pleading into the phone.

Stepping outside, a burst of the coolness from the night air hit my exposed skin.

The icy rush made me feel immediately better—alive, but not more alive than I felt with *him*. Shaking my head to clear my thoughts, I headed to my car. Blaze and I continued our conversation as I started the engine, so I could get back to Manhattan to help her in whatever jam she was in this time.

My pulse surged as I was fully awake, driving back to the city. The strange thing was that I hadn't slept since yesterday, and it was now close to midnight, yet I felt like I was wired for sound. My adrenaline rose and turned my vitality into anxiousness, which made my need to reach my best friend even stronger.

chapter

Jade

FINALLY, I REACHED my destination. With quick short decisive steps, while being cautious not to trip and fall in my heels, I entered the emergency room at Mount Sinai. Approaching the reception desk, I asked for Blaze Morgan's bed. The receptionist behind the desk seemed confused and stated no patients had been admitted to the hospital through the emergency room that evening with the name of Blaze Morgan.

I immediately called Blaze. She didn't pick up. I was just about to tell the receptionist there had to be some mistake and see if she could please check again when Blaze appeared from a doorway that led to the patient beds.

"Jade, thank God! I'm so glad to see you." As she put her arms around me, I met her embrace with additional concern noticing the wash of red combined with a myriad of dark blues and black streaks coloring the skin below her lower lashes, exposing not just exhaustion, but tears.

"Did they release you? What happened?" I was confused.

"Release me? What do you mean? I was never admitted." She looked at me like I had three heads.

"Then why did you call me in such a panic?" I waited for her explanation, yet was met with an embarrassed grin instead.

"Oh no…You mean to tell me you dragged me all the way back here to the city to help you with the guy you slept with tonight?" I raised my voice, realizing I misunderstood her previous phone call and her tears. She wasn't crying because she was injured. She was crying because her little romp caused her client some sort of medical emergency. I didn't want to know, and I knew I was going to regret it, but I asked anyway.

"Well, if you must know, I was the one who called the ambulance. They said he had a slight heart attack and with some further cardiac therapy and medications, he should be as good as new." Blaze seemed satisfied with herself for saving this person's life after she screwed him, literally.

"Why exactly do you need me here? You clearly have the situation under control." I snapped back.

"We need you for moral support."

"We? We who? The *we*, meaning you and him?" Looking her straight in the eyes, I asked her why I would give moral support to a man she just slept with and whose heart couldn't handle the sex, based on the results of this evening. It was apparent my sleep deprivation finally had gotten the better of me. Rather than deal with this, I turned to go.

"Jade, please we need your help. I need your help," she begged to keep me from leaving.

Examining her white knuckles grasping my skin, I turned back with an expression mimicking short on patience and more of shock.

"Why would I help the guy you slept with?" I stopped, I had the answer, but I questioned her anyway. "Wait. He's married, isn't he? I'm right, aren't I?"

"No, no…He's single… I mean divorced, and to answer your question, you know him." She continued to ramble, giving me more than I wanted to hear. "I myself was handling all of this just fine, but he asked me to call you." She revealed more, but still not everything. I thought I was hearing things. Who the hell was he?

"I know him? Who are we talking about exactly?" I was getting more agitated as this conversation went on.

Silence.

"Blaze...who did you fuck?" I was loud and I didn't care who heard me at this point. The people in the emergency waiting room were aghast at my statement. I didn't apologize; I was tired and pissed and wanted the truth.

After she let out a deep sigh and looked around at the people in the ER, she apologized to them while scuffling away with me in tow to hurry into the nearest corner to reveal the name of her lover for the evening.

"Reece" Her tone was flat, low, and somewhat embarrassed.

"What?" I was dumbfounded and shocked all at once.

"I said, Reece." She repeated the name I had already heard her say but wished I hadn't heard at all. There was only one Reece that both Blaze and I knew.

"I heard what you said the first time. Are we talking about the same Reece? Reece Montgomery?" I carefully asked through shallow gulps of air.

"Yes, Jade, we're talking about Reece Montgomery, the one and only." She started to get annoyed by my interrogation, but I didn't care. Especially, now that she confirmed who her lover was.

"So, you fucked Damien's father? Are you out of your mind?" I couldn't believe this happened. Let alone now I had no choice but to face my ex's dad, who was just through those swinging doors. Since he and his wife had divorced, I noticed Reece liked them younger, but *Blaze,* of all people? Being twenty-five years older than her wasn't half the problem...they hated one another.

"Wow! How things change..."

"Do you have to be so shocked and horrified? It's not like I just announced that I slept with *your* father."

I ignored her last comment and must admit, I did get it. That was the point. Reece Montgomery was a very attractive and powerful man. He was a huge food and wine industry mogul. In his early years, he worked as a chef in some of the most well-known restaurants in the country. He made his way up to owning seven of the top dining establishments around the world, as well as acquiring three vineyards—one in Napa, one in Italy, and one in France. I admired his perseverance. Yet, what I didn't admire was that he used that same tenacity to get what he wanted in his personal life—namely women. He treated them like property—disposable property. If they were no longer valuable to him, by that I mean his definition of valuable, then they were gone without a second thought.

When it came to pursuing the opposite sex, Reece went after them with an unstoppable force and a no holds barred attitude. His looks and the way he carried himself made him very attractive to many women, and he knew that and used it to his full advantage.

Although I had to admit I was somewhat surprised Blaze would fall for his undeniable charisma. Especially since she never liked him when we were growing up. I remember as teenagers she threw him attitude anytime we were at the Montgomery home. She never gave a definitive reason for her negative persona when she was around him, but it was palpable anytime they crossed paths. Now she was sleeping with him. I guess she got over whatever was bothering her back then.

"He wants to talk to you. That's why I called you tonight," she announced, pulling me from my thoughts and back into this nightmare.

"Me, why me?" I sounded irritated because I was. There was absolutely nothing Reece and I needed to speak about.

"I don't know. He wouldn't tell me, but you know how he gets when he wants something. I didn't want his requests to further hinder his recovery or worse, so I called you because he demanded you come right away." She was being honest. Reece was demanding to the point of being almost obnoxious. No, let me correct that...he was obnoxious. What bothered me was that Blaze also seemed worried about Reece's request to see me, just as much as I was.

Although so many emotions ran through me at this point, I had to find out what he wanted. I couldn't change what went on between Reece and Blaze, nor did I want to. They were grown people. They could do what they wanted when they wanted and with whom they wanted. They didn't need and I'm sure they didn't want an opinion from me, but Reece summoning me here meant there was more to all of this than meets the eye. It was time I found out what that something was.

I took Blaze by the hand and pulled her close. I gave her a strong supportive hug. Then, we broke our embrace and smiled at each other.

"Okay, let's go see what Reece wants. The sooner we get this over with, the sooner I can get back to the shore to my warm bed."

Blaze nodded and continued to have a firm grip on my hand, as we walked to Reece's room. I think the reason she kept a hold of my hand was more for her than me.

We approached the glass doorway behind which Reece's ER bed was located. We could hear his voice bellow before we even entered the room. Just before we arrived at the threshold, a screech from a young woman's voice came from inside. Then a plastic cup filled with water and that same young woman crossed in front of us. Both our heads turned in the direction of the nurse and the pink, flying object.

Blaze released my hand and rushed in to see what was going on. I took the lighter approach and strolled to the opening. Smirking with arms crossed as I leaned on the door jamb, I said, "Wow, Reece, even a silly thing like a heart attack doesn't stop your antics."

"Jade, come closer and give your father-in-law-to-be a big hug." He smiled widely. Almost as wide as his dramatically outstretched arms.

I paused briefly, then as I walked over to hug the man who would have been my father-in-law, if his son hadn't decided to sleep with my other good friend, or should I say ex-friend, Courtney Reynolds.

"Reece, please give it up. Damien and I are never getting back together." I said in a soft whine, as my shoulders collapsed in frustration.

"He'll come to his senses. I can promise you that. I will not have my son marrying that bleached-blonde twit." He stated with pure disdain for Courtney.

As much as I wanted to ride the wave of hatred for Courtney like Reece did, I couldn't. I wasn't in any way pleased with what had happened, not by a long shot, but after some time to cry, smash things on the walls, and burn the mattress they commiserated on, I realized, none of it had done me any good. They were off fucking one another and I was in the house distraught, feeling sorry for myself and binging on anything chocolate I could find.

"Listen to me, please. Your son made his feelings apparent when I walked into my house and the two of them were in the bed Damien and I shared. He and I are over, now let it be."

"No, you listen—"

This time Blaze cut him off.

"Reece, will you for once hear what Jade is saying? She's done, and if hearing her tell you isn't enough, would you like for me to play the recording of her dragging the mattress out of the house and burning it?" She held up her cell phone and gave him a silly, practical, flat-lipped smile.

I mumbled to her comedically. "You saved it?"

"Of course. I thought if nothing else, we could look back at it and have a good laugh." She smiled and gave me a quick wink.

I smiled back, yet our conversation was not amusing to our cranky patient.

"Ladies, if you're both done playing games, there's a reason I asked Blaze to call you." He looked at each of us to make sure we were through kidding around.

Spoilsport.

We both looked at him and waited for the unveiling of his reason why he needed me so desperately in the city at such an ungodly hour of the night. I should say morning. It was after 1am.

"I need a favor from you."

"Which is?" I knew what was coming, but I wanted validation.

"Well, I want you to call Damien and ask him to fly out here." He was hesitant but unabashed, so that didn't stop him.

"Why would I want to do that?" My question sounded flatly uninterested.

"You would do that for the sole purpose that I asked you to do it and because we *are* family."

Both Blaze and I outwardly moaned in disbelief at the same time, but he didn't miss a beat. What gall that man had. He didn't care about family, as he put it. He wanted to see his son, so he could disrupt Damien's personal life or whatever he had planned in that self-indulgent brain of his. Then he wanted me to do it because he felt it would have more impact if it came from me.

Although, I was pretty sure Damien wouldn't buy it. After all that happened between us, Damien knew I wouldn't pick up and call him out of the blue in the middle of the night. Reece knew that, so he believed if I did call his son, then Damien would be concerned and come out here right away. Reece felt he could use the situation to his advantage, especially since their father and son relationship had grown tense in the past few years.

"And because if I have Blaze call him, then Damien will wonder why Blaze and I were together at such a late hour," he stated in an aloof manner, as he straightened his nonexistent collar, stretched his chin up, and smoothed the front on his hospital gown to visually show the practicality of his motives.

"I see. So, here's what you should do. You should pull out your cell phone and contact him yourself," I stated unsympathetically.

"You know as well as I do he won't come if I ask him to." He mildly snapped.

"You're right. He will probably screen the call, and when he finds out it's his pushy father, he'll shut off the phone for the evening altogether. Better yet, he'll probably block you for good."

"Jade, you don't want that to happen, now do you? Damien is all I have as far as family is concerned." He unsuccessfully played the victim.

"Don't give me that shit. It serves you right that Damien doesn't speak to you, except other than for business. You don't know when to stop."

"And I won't stop now. Please call him, for me?" He tilted his head as he waited for my answer, but knew I would do it for the sheer reason that he would have just continued with his banter.

"Damn it, Reece. You just don't give up." I rolled my eyes at him.

His grin was methodical. "Conceding is for the weak."

"It's also for the tired that wants to go home," I stated as I pulled out my phone.

Blaze giggled.

I called Damien against my better judgment. If it was 1:30 in the morning here on the East Coast, then it was 10:30 in the evening in Napa. I hit the call and waited for Damien to pick up. I tried to convince myself that this wasn't wrong. It's not like we hadn't spoken at all in the last couple of years. He always checked in with Aunt Viv, so on several occasions, I picked up for her. When he and I made small talk, it was always uncomfortable and very, very brief.

"Jade, what is it? What's wrong?" He sounded sincerely concerned, as he answered the call without the traditional greeting.

"Damien, your dad is in the hospital. He had a heart attack." My approach in telling Damien about his father was possibly too quick and not heartfelt...*whatever.*

"Is he okay? How'd this happen? Can he speak? What hospital?" The questions flew out of his mouth one right after the other before I could answer him. The one thing I would admit is that Damien loved his dad, even if they were at odds.

"Well, the doctor stated he'll need cardiac therapy and he shouldn't stay alone."

"I see. How long will he be in the hospital?" He asked.

"He's at Mt. Sinai and he is due to go to cardiac therapy next week on an outpatient basis. He's going to need your help, though." I fibbed slightly. Reece wanted Damien home for reasons that he had not divulged just yet, but I had a pretty good idea he was warming up his matchmaking skills again because of his earlier statements to me.

"Okay. I'll make some arrangements and we'll fly out on Tuesday, sooner if I can get a flight. Many are booked due to the holiday."

"I forgot about the holiday, but I'm sure they'll be keeping him over the next few days for observation, regardless. He's in the ER now and they're preparing his admittance and room," I said, as I saw Reece, with a defiant look on his face, shake his head back and forth. Oh boy, here we go. Reece was going to be Reece...very difficult.

"Okay, keep me posted." There was a pause and then he continued. "If that's not too much for me to ask of you, Jade?"

"Either I'll call you or Blaze will should something change," I added that Blaze would call, that way I would get myself away from this situation and away from having to speak to Damien for anything more than our usual uncomfortable small talk. I wouldn't let Reece control this situation and make me revisit a completely devastating time in my life. A time I had no intention of going back to.

"Thank you. Wait. Blaze is there with my dad?"

I couldn't speak. Damien's grateful tone took me back to happier times.

No, Jade! Don't let him get to you; remember what he did. There was no going back.

"You're welcome. Oh, Blaze came with me, so she knows what's going on as well. One of us will be in touch after the doctor updates his report tomorrow."

Our call ended. I placed my phone back in my bag. When I turned back to face Reece, all I saw was the look of sheer satisfaction, because everything seemed to be going Reece Montgomery's way.

"Happy now?" I asked sarcastically.

"Delighted," he stated with a tone of smug pleasure.

I walked over to Blaze and kissed her forehead, as I place my hand on her shoulder. "Are you staying or are you coming with me? I really have to get back. Tomorrow is the first day of the season for Summertime Sweets."

"I thought you were renovating the new location?" Reece asked.

"I am, but I'm keeping the old shoppe open until the work is done. I can't disappoint my regulars."

"Oh shit! I forgot! I'm sorry." She looked at me, then she apprehensively looked to Reece for what she should do. I found this somewhat odd. She only slept with him for the first time tonight. Or did she?

He looked at both of us and then looked down while his lips were pursed to keep him from saying something that he might regret. This told me that Blaze was staying put and this wasn't the first time they slept together.

"How long?" I asked, and Blaze knew what I meant.

Blaze hung her head to the side and took a deep breath in, which she then exhaled in defeat.

"Six months"

"I see. So, for the past six months the two of you have been sleeping together and the only reason why I am finding out about this now is because Reece had a heart attack? Great Blaze, that's just great," I reprimanded.

"I didn't say anything, because I was afraid of how you would react if I told you," she stated.

"You mean Reece told you not to." They both looked at me in shock. I was right. Reece then decided it was time he stepped in.

"It wasn't like Blaze didn't want you to know. I was the one, you're right, that stopped her. My reason was to give it some time to see where this was going between us and should it develop into something more serious, then, of course, we both would have told you." His voice was like velvet. The words strategically rolled off his tongue as he gave his summation of their romp between the sheets for the past six months. I assumed it was a romp and they were still working things out being six months was too soon to know where *it* was going.

It was true; nothing, not even a mild heart attack could stop that man from getting what he wanted. My only concern was her and her feelings. Reece could and ultimately would fend for himself. He was never worse for wear when relationships he had ended. He would never allow anything to tarnish his image.

Bastard.

"It may not be the most opportune time to mention this, but so help me God if you hurt her like you did to the others you've been with, you're gonna wish this little heart attack killed you. Do I make myself clear?" Timing can be everything and my timing to threaten him could have been better, but he didn't seem all that sick, as evidenced by his screaming at the charge nurse when we came in and his ordering of me to talk to Damien on his behalf. For a sick man, he seemed quite capable, so I felt it was important to let him know the shit he pulled with the other women he screwed would not happen to my best friend.

Yet, he was not one bit moved by my threat.

"I admire your loyalty to Blaze, but I can assure you I have no intention of hurting her. On the contrary, once I'm healed, I would like to take our relationship to the next level," he admitted.

Oh, boy!

Blaze turned to him with a surprised look on her face, surprised, but not excited. "What are you talking about?" Blaze asked, her tone was discreet, disapproving, and slightly jittery.

"Darling, I was saving this as a surprise, but I felt if things kept going as they have been, then perhaps we could move you into my penthouse."

I hid my smirk. If I knew Blaze as well as I thought I did, I knew Reece's statement had commitment written all over it. And Blaze didn't do commitments. At this moment, I almost understood the attraction Blaze had for Reece and why it lasted this long, but I also knew it would never be enough for her. On the surface, he didn't appear to want a commitment of any kind, just like Blaze. He was attractive, older, sophisticated, and had the funds to keep life exciting without being over the top.

For Blaze, it was a nearly perfect relationship to have with a man, but throw the word commitment in, and Blaze would go into panic mode and start preparing damage control in advance.

Tonight, however, she was remarkably calm. She probably didn't want to stress Reece out or cause any further complications with his health. Especially because her creativity in bed was partly to blame for the state he was in at the moment.

Blaze did the only thing she could do. She used me to bail out on him for the weekend.

"Now is not the time to talk about me moving in with you. There is plenty of time to talk about that once you've completed cardiac rehab and Damien heads back to Napa. For now, let's take things one day at a time, shall we?" She said to end the conversation. I had to hand it to her for that performance. Her voice didn't fail her once during the brush off.

Reece yawned and looked at his phone. I think he knew Blaze was torn about staying or running… I mean coming with me to the shore. He made the decision easy for her because *he* made it for her.

"Well, ladies, I think I better get some rest. It's after 2. Blaze, why don't you go back to the shore with Jade. It's much too late for her to be heading back alone. We can talk tomorrow after all of us have had a good night's rest," he stated diplomatically.

Blaze nodded. She didn't let on, but I knew she was relieved.

Reece reached out to her and she complied. "We'll talk in the morning, baby," Reece whispered, which prompted Blaze to lean in and kiss him softly on his mouth.

Baby? I could vomit.

Breaking from their kiss, yet still holding Blaze's hand, Reece addressed me. "Jade, I appreciate the trip you took here tonight and for calling my son at my somewhat forward request. We'll talk more during the week," he said as if he wasn't quite done with me yet.

I nodded. "I can't wait." I turned and rolled my eyes as I said goodbye to Reece and waited outside of the room for Blaze.

Just as we were about to leave, the nurse came to us and stated that Reece's tests confirmed a very mild heart attack, which was what the doctor had originally suspected and with cardiac rehab and at-home instructions over the next few months, he would make a complete recovery.

She also stated they would be moving him to a private room on the cardiology floor. That explained all of the screaming and dramatics on Reece's part when I first arrived. He was so self-entitled—when he found out he had to stay, he decided to request, no, demand a private room. I agreed with his prognosis. From the look of things and his actions, Reece Montgomery would walk away from this better than ever. I wondered if Blaze would have the same outcome.

Hopefully, after a good night's rest, things would seem brighter in the morning.

chapter *four*

Jade

MY MORNING JOLT was not caused by the buzz of my alarm clock, nor the wail of the fishing boats on the water. No, the sound that interrupted my rest was the obnoxious purr of my best friend in the next room.

Both Blaze and I left Reece to sleep; at least someone was sleeping… and we drove back to LBI by 4:30 am. The clock on my nightstand now said 8:00 am.

"Okay. I might as well get up," I said, whining loudly, hoping I'd wake her.

Not a chance of that happening; Blaze just continued to snore blissfully. I looked out in the direction of the guest room with slight disdain, not that she cared. First off, she was comatose, and secondly, she and Reece each got what they wanted.

I walked downstairs, shaking my head and smiling. It was good to be home, finally.

Reaching the kitchen, I grabbed a cup of coffee and the mail Viv collected for me while I was away, before sinking into one of the chairs on the deck off the living room. My staff members agreed to cover the morning shift for me. Viv had said she would check in with them to see if they needed additional help.

I had called her last night, even though it was late, so I could explain what had happened with Blaze and Reece. I left out the part about knowing the house was rented and that she helped my father do it right under my nose. I figured I'd save that conversation for this afternoon when my head was a bit clearer and my body was sated with caffeine.

She wasn't at all moved by the Blaze and Reece connection. She had the uncanny ability to read people fairly well. There weren't many situations that got to her, scared her, or surprised her. Maybe it was because she had been married to a former Marine turned detective? Viv had to deal with so much being a cop's wife. It shaped her into who she was. Yet, as tough as she appeared, she was also warm and loving. Perhaps it was because she knew how precious life was and how easily it could change, as if in an instant. She saw it with her husband, Robert, who died in the line of duty during a huge undercover investigation some years back, and she saw it with my brother, Jimmy, whose death was sadly self-inflicted, but no less devastating for any of us, especially me and Viv.

I avoided the thought of Jimmy's tragic accident, and let the morning rays soak into my skin. My eyes closed automatically as I sat back, allowing the sounds of the powerful waves on the beach to soothe my stress levels. The seawater's slow rhythmic motion lulled me into the day ahead, but for a brief moment I drifted off. That was…before my morning peace was violently taken away by the startling hum of a power tool in the next yard.

What the hell?

I jumped up and leaned over the banister to see what all of the noise was about. I looked to the left, nothing. I looked to the right, although I knew it wouldn't have come from my bro…my parents' old house. Kim mentioned that Viv had rented it to some hot guy, but he didn't own the place, so he couldn't possibly be stupid enough to change anything in or on the property. Perhaps, it was our landscaper? Although he wasn't due to come until sometime next week for the springtime clean-up, I hadn't even confirmed with him yet.

My eyes grew wide and wild with anger. The landscape company must have misunderstood me and sent out one of his crew members to clean up today. He was just about to cut down the rose vine my brother gave me years ago.

"No! What the hell do you think you're doing?" I screamed as I ran down the side stairs of my deck to reach the landscaper before he could do any more damage than he had already done.

The noise stopped immediately and he looked around for the person screaming loud enough to wake the dead.

In fact, I did.

Out of the corner of my eye, I got a glimpse of Blaze standing on the second-floor deck watching from the doorway of the guest room. Her make-up was smeared and her long red hair looked like a matted bird's nest. She was wrapped in a robe, which was more than I could say for me. With all of the commotion, I had forgotten that I wasn't dressed. I came to realize I was barefoot and wearing the T-shirt I slept in and a pair of black bikini underwear. My attire wouldn't have been an issue if I had stayed put on my deck and screamed from there, but as I stood in front of this perfect stranger, I felt almost naked.

He finally faced my direction with his electric hedge cutter in hand to greet the crazy lady whose shrills abruptly stopped his morning activity. Temporarily blinded by the morning light, I moved to the right to get a better look at his face before I addressed him properly.

"Hi, I'm Ja—" I stopped mid-introduction. It was him. The guy from the dance floor, the guy from The Palm…last night…my mystery man.

His smile was a bit devilish when he saw it was me and noticed I was barely wearing anything.

"Hi…I didn't think I would see you so soon after our date last night."

I hated to admit it, but he looked even better in the sunshine. I hadn't noticed in the darkness of the club, but I'd had a feeling his body would be amazing, and it was. He was built with an incredible display of artwork inked into his tanned skin. If his tattoos were any evidence of his interests, then I would have to say that he was a surfer. I imagined how he must look in a pair of board shorts, all wet and…

"Oh, is that what they're calling what we did last night these days, a date?" I sounded haughty.

He froze, taken back by how I responded to him.

"I'm sorry for my rudeness. I haven't had much sleep in the last two days. Let's start over. Hi, I'm Jade. Good to meet you." I smiled and held out my hand.

He reached for my hand, but then paused before he took it.

"Hi Jade, I'm Tommy. Wait… Jade? You mean Jade Stanton?" He was hesitant. I wondered why.

"Yes, I'm Jade Stanton." Leave it to Viv to already talk to the new tenant about me, and …speak of the devil.

"Good morning, I see you two met without any help from me."

No help? Give me a break. She had to be joking, right?

Viv's interruption was positively perfect. Her exuberant self was in rare form as she floated toward us wearing a yellow and white sundress and oversized straw hat.

"How can anyone be that happy and that well-dressed in the morning?"

Tommy chuckled at my observation.

Viv kissed both of us on the cheek before continuing her salutations.

Her smile was too wide and filled with guilt. "I didn't want to get into this with you last night or while you were away at your conference, but I rented your brother's old house to Tommy, with your parents' approval, of course. Isn't it wonderful?"

Meeting her elated explanation with a flat expression, I methodically turned on my heels and waited for Tommy to speak.

"I assumed Viv had told you by now."

"No, she didn't tell me, and she knew that I wanted to be part of the process." I didn't recognize my own irritated tone. I withheld the fact I had known the house was rented thanks to Kim, but what I hadn't counted on was Tommy being one-in-the-same person…the renter and the guy from the dance floor last night.

"Listen. I'm sorry, but I needed a place and the conditions were worth it."

"Conditions? What conditions?" I asked. I was unaware of any conditions that my parents had decided to impose on the would-be renters or buyers for that matter.

"I told Tommy that the house was in need of repair, so one of the stipulations in renting with an option to buy was that he had to help with the updates to the home. If your parents decided not to sell, then he would be reimbursed for the labor and materials that he put into it. Yet, if everyone agreed Tommy could buy it at the end of his lease, *including you*, then your parents wouldn't raise the price because Tommy did all the work. I thought that it was a more than fair offer, and he agreed and moved in the other day."

I couldn't believe what I was hearing. I was in the city for less than a week and in that time Viv worked out a deal with Tommy and my parents. Yet no one had the decency to call me to let me know.

"I see. Can I ask you how long you're leasing it for?"

"Sure, I signed for one year. That should give me plenty of time to get the house in shape, should your parents agree to let me buy it, and if not, it gives me time to see what other properties are available here on the island at the end of my lease."

"Can I ask a favor of you?" I said.

"Jade!" Viv snapped as she was sure I would say something to stop this rental.

"It's okay, Viv," Tommy said. "Sure…What do you need?"

"Could I ask you to not cut the rose vines down? Well, at least until you know for sure that you'll be the new owner? Those plants hold a huge sentimental value for me." I explained, without revealing the true reason behind the plants.

"Of course, but to tell you the truth I have a very close friend that has roses similar to these. When we were growing up, the one thing her mom always did in the spring was cut them back, so that they would have huge blooms in the fall. That's exactly what I was trying to do. I guess I got carried away," he chuckled.

His smile was contagious. I giggled at him. "Well, maybe you would be better off with some manual sheers instead."

"They're in the storage closet in the garage. I'll get them for you." Viv added.

We laughed and agreed we'd talk later. I had to get to the shoppe and then while there, I decided to have a little talk with my aunt in private.

"Thank you again, Tommy." Walking away, I sneaked a look back to see him one more time. Viv stayed behind.

"Viv, are you coming?"

"I have to talk to Tommy about something, but you go on ahead, and I'll meet you there."

He stood next toViv with a smile on his face, his hand raised to say goodbye. My aunt mimicked his gesture.

"Bye, sweetie"

Bye sweetie, my ass; she was up to something.

I returned to my house and walked directly up the stairs into my best friend's care-free and inquisitive smile.

"Wipe that smile off your face," I said, walking past her without a glance back, as I headed to my room. Of course, Blaze was not far behind.

"What was that all about?" She asked with humorous amazement.

"None of your business," I replied, flatly.

"C'mon, Jade, who was that guy with you and Viv? And why do I get the feeling that this was not the first time you two met?" She teased.

"I don't have time for your inquisition right now. I have to get to the shoppe."

"Okay, don't tell me, but I'll be here all day. Right next door to Mr. Tattooed and Sexy. I'll just have to bring him a big, tall glass of cold lemonade and ask him how you both know one another."

"You wouldn't dare?" I pivoted back around, to stare her down.

"Sweetie, you know I would. Save yourself the trouble of having to explain all of this to me later, and spill it now." She grinned. She knew she had me right where she wanted me.

Bitch.

"Let's have it." Blaze was never one to beat around the bush and she expected others to be just like her.

We sat on the edge of my bed, while I explained my evening with Tommy.

"Please don't be like Viv," I looked her straight in the eyes to make sure she heard me.

She looked straight back at me. "I'm not. I just don't get why you're no longer open to the possibility of love."

I closed my eyes to collect my thoughts and address her statement.

"You know I believe in love and happily ever after, but both of those things aren't for me, not anymore, not now anyway."

"It's been almost three years. Don't you think it's about time you get back out there again? You have so much to offer, sweetie." She pressed me further for a reason without actually asking the need-to-know questions.

I grinned. "I'm out there. I just told you I danced with a perfect stranger last night before I even knew his name."

"Big deal! I don't consider jumping around on a dance floor an intimate moment." She was annoyed.

"It is a big deal when your bodies are rubbing against each other and your lips are so close they touch a person in areas they never felt before or at the very least haven't felt in a long time."

"You did that...with him?" Blaze's eyes widened, as her mouth hung open from my vivid description of my brief dance with Tommy.

I stood up to get dressed. I needed to leave. Blaze didn't try to stop me this time.

"Yes, I did that with him." Finally, I was off the hook.

"Wow," was all she could say when I walked back to Blaze to go in for the kill.

"Yeah, and for your information, if it wasn't for your untimely phone call, our lips would have been doing a lot more than teasing each other." I gave her some food for thought.

Hmm...that should keep her quiet for a while.

chapter
five

Tommy

HERE WITH VIV, we looked on as Jade disappeared into her home with some redhead. I would never have guessed in a million years the beautiful woman I met last night on the dance floor would have materialized this morning on my patio. Well, more like ferociously confronted me this morning in my yard.

I had to admit when she ran down the stairs in just a T-shirt and black lace panties I was taken back, but when I recognized her, I was pleasantly surprised. Jade was even more beautiful in the daylight. Her cheeks were sun-kissed, which matched the subtle fire she exuded as she demanded my gardening cease and desist.

Being my neighbor, I would definitely make it a point to get to know her better and be more...*neighborly*. Speaking of neighbors, I addressed... "So, do you want to explain to me why Jade thinks I'm renting?"

Appearing aloof yet whimsical, Viv turned her attention up and into the air before addressing me.

"Not really. So, would you like tell me why no one knows you're here, except for Daniel, that is?" She quickly rattled off her rebuttal.

I shook my head.

"Well, then, I guess we're even. See you at 8." Except for a satisfied smile, Viv said nothing more as she waltzed out, whimsically, the same way she came in.

Just then, my cell phone vibrated on the glass table by the deck that was located at the beach level patio of the house. It had to be Daniel. I told him I would call him last night after I had dinner, but I hadn't gotten around to it. Someone more beautiful had stolen my attention.

I ran back toward the house and answered it. Looking at the screen confirmed I was right; it was Daniel.

"Hey! Good morning," I stated, almost excited to hear from him.

"Wow. Dude, you sound great. You're not even down the shore a full week yet, and it seems to have already affected you." Daniel said, surprised.

"Yeah, I gotta admit more and more this was the best decision I made for myself in a very long time," I agreed with unequivocal sureness. One reason was the house on the beach. Another was the plan of meeting someone new. Both of which seemed to have materialized almost immediately.

"I'm really happy for you, Tommy. So how did it go yesterday? I didn't hear from you, so I assumed you were exhausted and crashed early."

"Not exactly," I said, alluding to the fact that I had been doing more than unpacking necessities all day and night.

"Oh man, that statement has a woman written all over it," he said, amused.

"You're right, it does," I chuckled.

"So, who is she and more importantly, does she have any friends for me?" Daniel lightheartedly asked.

"She's Viv's niece. I'm not sure if she has someone for you, but from what I can tell she has a girlfriend, a good looking redhead that appears to be staying with her for the weekend."

"Let me get this straight. You're there, what, less than a week? And you've already been out with Viv's niece, and you know her well enough already that you're aware of the comings and goings of her and her friends?"

I laughed out loud. "It sounds like that doesn't it?"

"Yeah, from this end, it certainly does. By the way, just for your information, the redhead that's staying with Jade is her best friend Blaze," Daniel added.

"Blaze, huh? Well, her name definitely suits her."

"It certainly does and not just in her appearance. From what I can remember, Blaze does everything full throttle. She's fiery in more ways than one," Daniel remarked with a bit of whimsy.

I chuckled. "Listen, do you have some time? There's a lot I want to fill you in on."

"I have all the time in the world. The center is closed for classes today." Daniel was referring to the Center for Addiction and Disabilities near Philly.

He was employed there as an art therapist and counselor. He himself had been treated there for many years due to issues with his immobility. He had spinal cord issues that made movement from his legs difficult. He has sensation in his lower body, but his inability to walk comes from his muscles, not his nerves. Unfortunately, his condition doesn't allow him to be fully mobile.

"Great! Here's what happened," I paused. I had a better idea.

"Is something wrong?" He asked.

"I have a thought. Is the center closed for the entire weekend?"

"Yeah, actually it's closed through Tuesday. Why?"

"How about I ditch all this work for the weekend and I pick you up, so we can hang out down here? Unless you made other plans, of course."

"No, actually my plans fell through and I wasn't up for going into the city this weekend."

"Problems with your family?" I asked.

"No, not at all, but they've come down here every holiday, so this holiday I had a date with a hot nurse I met at the hospital when I went for my physical therapy. She bailed on me and I didn't want to call my folks to come down and babysit their forty-year-old son. They had already made plans to go away for the weekend with my brother and his family," Daniel added.

Daniel's sister-in-law, Rain, and I grew up together. If she knew Daniel would be alone for the weekend, she would have insisted he stay with them, whether he wanted to or not.

"What do you say?" I asked with the hope that Daniel would agree to stay for the weekend.

"I'm in, but you said that your new place has quite a few stairs. I wouldn't want that to be a problem for you."

"That's not a problem at all. There's a bedroom on the main floor, as well as a bathroom with a walk-in shower, so that should make it easier for you. Plus, you'll be right near the living room and the kitchen. There's also a deck that runs around the parameter of the house. You'll be able to take in all the views."

"Are you sure it's not any trouble for you?" He seemed awkward.

"Well, we all know that you can be trouble, but not the trouble that you're referring to." I needed to lighten the conversation up a bit.

"Thanks, Tommy, I'm definitely up for a weekend at the shore," he agreed.

"Great! Then it's all set. I'll just shower and get to you as soon as I can."

"Shit! You're going to hit major traffic."

"No big deal. My story will make the car ride back more interesting."

"Okay. I'll see you when you get here." Daniel was just about to hang up when I realized something.

"Wait. Did I ever tell you Jade's name before?"

"I guess it's a possibility, but I've known Viv and Jade for years."

"Oh, that's right, Viv had a family member at the Center with you."

"Yeah, Jimmy Stanton, he was Viv's nephew and Jade's older brother."

"Was?" I wondered what Daniel meant by that.

"You didn't hear this from me, but Jimmy died almost three years ago."

"Oh, I'm sorry to hear that."

"Yeah, and the worst part about it was that he was way too young to die. He was an incredible surfer and a very talented artist. Although the whole thing was unfortunate and what was worse was that it was also preventable."

"I don't follow." I was confused by what Daniel just stated. It sounded more than ominous.

"He didn't have to die. He took his own life. It was so devastating for the family, but Jade was hurt the most. From what Viv told my parents, Jimmy's death nearly destroyed Jade in the process. I don't know if she ever moved on from it. You don't ever get over that, but you find a way to live. Hopefully, with the time that has passed, Jade has done that," Daniel said.

"I don't know what to say. I knew there was more to the story about this house than Viv was letting on, but I had no idea about any of this."

"Now, I'm the one who doesn't follow you."

"I'll explain once I get down to the Center and we're on our way back."

Daniel agreed the ride back could be long, and that we could talk more then, to fill the time. After we hung up, I showered and headed to Philly. I put the top down on the Camaro. It was too beautiful of a day for air conditioning. With Daniel coming to hang out for the weekend, it was going to be better than I had originally planned.

chapter

six

Jade

AFTER I FINISHED cleaning up, getting dressed, and giving Blaze strict instructions to steer clear of my new neighbor, I headed to Summertime Sweets to start my day. A day I was no longer looking forward to. Apprehensive nausea bubbled to the surface at the thought of the long talk I was going to have with Viv about Tommy and the beach house. My reluctance gnawed at me for leaving Blaze to deal with Reece today. She knew he was demanding and I knew although she could handle herself better than most, her guilt for sending him into a heart attack during sex would have her feeling like she either owed him in some way or would have her running from him to parts unknown.

I opted to take my bike to the shoppe to clear my head in the sunshine and sea air. Hopefully to prepare myself for what I was about to say to my Aunt Viv. The roads on the island were filled with locals and tourists, so pedaling to work was the more practical option. When I wanted to get around the island effortlessly, it was my favorite mode of transportation.

I arrived to find the shoppe was packed. People were placing their pre-orders for the weekend, picking up their favorite treats for tonight, or they had just discovered the place because they were vacationing here on LBI for the first time and happened to stumble upon it. I was happy no matter why they chose Summertime Sweets to satisfy their sweet tooth. Aunt Viv was at one end of the shoppe with some locals, while a few of my summer staff were in the kitchen and the others waited on the customers at the counter who were ready to pay for their orders.

When Viv noticed me walk in, she finished up with her customers, then she politely excused herself to greet me. Once everything quieted down, I kissed her on the cheek and took her hand to lead her to my office where we could talk in private.

"Why did you keep it a secret that Jimmy's house was rented out?"

"A secret? It was more like a surprise. Besides, I would think after learning about Reece and Blaze last night, anything I surprised you with would pale in comparison," Viv said with a smirk on her face. I tried to hide my amusement, but it was always hard when it came to Viv. She had the uncanny ability to settle me.

"Yeah, I have to admit, I wasn't shocked that Blaze slept with her client. The events of the day pointed in that direction, but when I saw it was Reece in that hospital bed and he had a mild heart attack from his game of sheet tag with Blaze, well, that took my evening over the top." I tried to contain my laughter.

"All kidding aside, I hope you'll be okay with everything…with Tommy I mean."

"That depends."

"On what?" Popping up on her seat…preparing herself, as if my response was not what she had expected.

"It depends on why you kept Tommy a secret in the first place. Did you think I'd come unglued at the fact that the house was rented out to him?"

I paced, I couldn't sit. I knew if I sat and looked at her, it was over. I would lose what little composure I was still holding onto. Viv calmly rose from her seat and moved in front of me to take hold of my shoulders and firmly stopped me in my tracks.

"Aren't you? Look at you at how you're acting, Jade. It's a house!" Her voice raised slightly before it softened. "It's a house, a building, not a memory. My sweet girl, those memories of Jimmy are in here." She gently tapped my chest above my heart. "That house can't hold them or make them. Only the people who lived there, are the ones who created them. You and your brother made that house a home, not the other way around."

My eyes stung and my nose burned. Tears prickled with the realization of what she was trying to drill into me—as she tried her best to set me straight, yet again. The problem was that the beach house felt like the only tangible thing I had left of my brother. It was true, I had his surfboards and his bracelets and his old car, which was still stored in one of the two garages below the house, but that house held the intangible. It was the framed box that contained our laughter and our tears. It held food fights and late-night movies. It held long talks…well, it mainly held conversations of me talking while Jimmy listened and gave me sage, big-brother advice. It held what I could no longer touch within its walls…it held all that Jimmy was.

"I was going to tell you last night when you had gotten in. Yet, when you called in the middle of the night, I definitely didn't feel that was the appropriate time to discuss the house," she said to assure me. I know she never intended to deceive me.

"I just wish you had told me that you had been speaking with someone and not have me find out as he was cutting down the rose bushes Jimmy and I planted years ago." I turned away to walk over to my desk. I quietly propped myself against the edge of it, crossing my arms and legs as I waited for her response.

"I didn't mean for you to find out the way you did. I mean, I'm glad you met him. If for no other reason, it'll make dinner this evening less awkward. Now, at least we won't have to go through all of the formal introductions and traditional small talk."

"Wait. Let me get this straight. Tommy is the friend you invited for dinner this evening?" I asked.

"Yes, Tommy is who I was talking about when I told you about the dinner. My plans were to tell you about the rental and then have both of you meet for dinner so that you could get to know each other in a less tense atmosphere," she confessed.

"So, this dinner wasn't one of your infamous matchmaking schemes?"

"No, but if you would like it to be, then say the word, and I will do my best to make that happen, too." She seemed way too enthusiastic to kill two birds with one stone during this dinner.

I put up my hand to stop her in her tracks with ideas of arranging prospective dates for me.

"Viv, stop…I can find a man on my own without anyone's help, especially yours." I insisted.

In fact, I found Tommy last night, all by myself. Well, I fell into him.

"Okay, but you must admit, Tommy could be the perfect match for you."

The woman was relentless.

"How is that?" I asked with a small huff.

"Well, he's attractive."

"So are serial killers," I retorted.

She said nothing but gave me the famous single raised eyebrow of annoyance.

"Okay, go on. Tell me why Tommy would be good for me, because I know you're going to tell me whether I like it or not, so you might as well get it out of your system, Viv," I stated, as I surrendered to my aunt's will and also to save my withering sanity.

"As I was saying, he's attractive, with a great personality. He loves the shore. He surfs, and the best part of all, he's unattached."

Attractive, no…he was hot. Great personality…that remains to be seen. Small talk never revealed enough. He surfs…now that was certainly a plus.

Jade get a grip, you're not in the market for a man, remember?

"I would think to be single would be the number one factor here, but that's just me." I tried to be witty and gave her a quirky grin.

Viv grinned back, yet shook her head at my statement.

Just as I was about to pry more information out of her about Tommy, there was a knock at my door. It was one of my staff members letting me know there was a customer on the phone who wanted to place a special order for the 4th of July. A day of celebration for most…for me, it was just another day now.

Viv immediately stated she would let me get to work. She kissed my cheek and said to be at her house at 8. I believed it was her way of making a quick getaway, so she didn't have to answer any more of my questions.

I answered the phone and was tied up for quite some time. I secured an order of breakfast foods and scones as well as dessert for 150 people for their event and promised to have it all delivered very early that holiday morning.

Once I finished going over everything with the client on the phone, I proceeded to the kitchen to prepare the treats for tomorrow's crowd. I prepped breakfast bread and treats with the help of three staff members. We placed the raw products on baking trays and then slid the trays on the shelves which we rolled into the walk-in freezer until morning when I would bake them up fresh for the early morning rush. With everything completed and the last customer gone, we finished at 2 o'clock that afternoon. My staff member locked up as usual, while I stayed behind to do some paperwork and set up a schedule for the next few weeks.

My landlord was gracious enough to let me stay here and keep this location open until I moved down the road.

Sure, it was to his advantage to have a solid renter, but real estate in this area, especially beach real estate, was quite easy to rent during the summer season. Luckily my landlord had someone ready to take my place at the end of the season when I moved on.

With all of my work completed, I filled two of the pastry boxes on my way out the door. One box was for tonight's dessert at Viv's house; I chose petite French-creme filled pastries and individual shortbread cookies, mini fruit and custard tarts, Viv's favorite and I anticipated that Aunt Viv was making her famous London broil on the grill, so with such a heavy meal, the smaller desserts would be perfect.

The second box was for Tommy. I didn't know what he would enjoy, so I put together a variety of bite-size cheesecake squares, chocolate covered strawberries, and some mini scones, which I thought would be perfect for someone who lived alone. I assumed since he just moved in, and since I knew that the kitchen in the old beach house needed renovating, perhaps cooking might not be an option this week. Plus, after the way I acted this morning, I decided that the treats could be a peace offering of sorts.

Even though he was the perfect gentleman earlier, and he didn't seem at all upset by my sudden invasion of his privacy and my abrupt request to leave the rose vines that my brother had given me alone for the time being, I felt it necessary to start over with him. I had a terrible feeling about our confrontation today. I hoped another apology and some sweets would make amends. I was packed up by 4 pm and carried the boxes out to my bike, secured the stack to the small rack on the back, and placed some French baguettes in the basket on the front.

Once home, I checked for Blaze. She couldn't have gone too far; my car was still in the driveway. I called out to her. She was on the deck off the living room seated on one of the chaise lounge chairs. She had made a pitcher of Sangria, which was at the ready and very much a welcomed surprise.

"You look rested," I said as I poured myself a glass of Sangria.

"I may look rested, but I don't feel rested." She tensed as she spoke.

"Oh no, what's wrong?" My eyes involuntarily rolled, as I quickly asked what went on while I was at work.

"Everything," Her voice cracked with frustration, as she hinted about her day.

I took the pitcher and my glass over to Blaze and sat down next to her, refilling her glass.

"Okay, what gives? When we left Reece last night he stated he would talk to you over the weekend. He seemed perfectly fine at the hospital and was more than satisfied that you would be down here with me for the holiday."

"Yeah, I felt the same way about the situation when we left," she said but hinted at the fact that something more happened that I was unaware of.

"I take it something else went on since I left for work?" I prepared myself for the next shoe to drop.

"Well, you would be right. I spoke with Reece in the morning after you left. He said he was going to take it easy, but texted me all day long about *us*. I didn't answer any of them, because to tell you the truth I was tired and went back to bed after you left. Then the phone calls started to ring in. He was incessant." Blaze was exasperated by Reece. I was exasperated by her response. She knew how he was. Reece's behavior should have come as no big surprise to her.

"Really? You know how he can be. You've seen it first hand with Damien. It's always about what Reece wants. Granted, he did just have a heart attack, but by the sound of it, nothing is keeping that man down. For God's sake, you saw how he was last night with me. Do you honestly think that you don't fall into the same category as the rest of us in Reece's life?" I couldn't believe that I had to explain this to her, of all people. She had been with him for six months, intimately for six months, not to mention she grew up around him. She had to know his idiosyncrasies by now.

"I know how he can be, but these calls and texts today were not remotely close to how he's acted since we started our relationship. I'm not saying things can't change with time, but we both agreed at the very beginning that we had a mutual sexual attraction for each other. We enjoyed doing things together and we were happy to spend time in each other's company, but that was it. Any other emotions that remotely resembled commitment were off the table. Now he wants more and I don't. I'm not ready for this shit, Jade. You know how I get when *they* get too close for comfort. This will not end well." Her head shook, as well as her body, as she started to become dramatically unglued.

The term "they" in her statement meant the men she had relationships with in the past. It was true. When they got too close, Blaze bailed on them. It wasn't that Blaze was opposed to love; she loved being in love. She loved the idea of love, but she felt it had been a short-lived experience for her in the past and resigned herself to avoid it at all costs in the future. Besides the fact that Blaze set the bar very high when it came to the ideal man.

She always wanted someone powerful and sexy like Reece. Someone in control, but also someone closer to her own age. Yet many of the men she met were not accomplished like Reece was. That being said, Reece was almost sixty and had had much more time to cultivate his empire.

The one thing Blaze never looked for was financial support. She was completely able to support herself and her lifestyle. She didn't need a man in her life for that, but what she did expect was a partner that had a vision of what he wanted to be and have enough drive to go after it. Basically, she wanted herself as a man.

"You have to talk with him once he's discharged from the hospital and is cleared by his doctors. You can't let this go on. Look at yourself. You're completely stressed out and Reece isn't even here yet," I explained.

"You're right. I am stressed. Do you see what he does to me? I can't even think straight." She was being overly dramatic. No, she was just being Blaze.

I laughed and poured myself more Sangria.

"Oh great, I'm so glad that my life is a joke to you." She acted insulted, but I saw it as ridiculous.

"I wasn't laughing at your life. I was laughing at the way you're reacting to your life. You know very well that Reece Montgomery was probably not the right choice to sleep with. Sure, he is, well was, noncommittal, so that made you both the perfect match, but if what you say is true and he wants more, then you have to talk it out with him. You can't run from this like you have done in the past." I reminded her of her actions when she broke up with her last suitor. She would take off to parts unknown until the storm was over.

"And why can't I? I mean, just leave that is?" She questioned.

"Reece would find you. He is one very rich and capable man. A capable man with many resources at his disposal. You wouldn't be able to hide from him like you had with the others."

"Shit! You're right. So, what do I do?" Blaze looked to me for answers.

"You need to talk it out with him. Or maybe you misunderstood him. Maybe he just misses you and wants to see you after all that happened this past week." I tried to be practical, but I knew Reece and if Reece wanted a commitment, then Reece would get a commitment.

"Sure, that's why he said that once he's home we needed to tell Damien about our relationship. That doesn't mean he's missing me; that has commitment written all over it," she snapped.

"Okay. So, before he plans a walk down the aisle with you, you're just going to have to go to him and stop this. Unless..." I stopped for a moment, because I thought there may be a slim chance Blaze was happy about this and that she possibly enjoyed the cat and mouse banter in this situation with Reece, but might really want the more he was proposing.

"Unless what?" She asked.

"Unless you like all of the attention Reece is showering on you," I speculated.

"Have you lost your mind? You couldn't possibly think that I would enjoy the idea of Reece and I in a serious relationship? I told you this was supposed to be fun, not permanent."

"Some women might say a permanent relationship with Reece Montgomery could have been fun."

"Reece is fun and exciting. I'll grant you that, but a commitment with him would be an absolute nightmare." She was adamant.

"Because he's controlling?" I asked but already knew the answer.

"Of course! He's controlling and manipulative and possessive... and stop me anytime now." Blaze was being sarcastic, but on point with her description of her current bed buddy.

"Then here's my hot button question to you. Why get involved? If you knew exactly how he was, why did you sleep with him and continue a relationship that you, yourself, didn't want to go anywhere?" I asked as I stood up, leaned against the deck railing and faced her.

Blaze looked down and shook her head, while she ran her index finger along the rim of her Sangria glass.

"You know me, Jade. I work hard, long hours, weekends, sometimes even holidays. My career is not always convenient, nor traditional, but I love it. In my past relationships, there always came the dreaded time where my partner wanted to change that about me, and when I wouldn't budge or at least budge enough for their liking, then it ultimately caused the destruction of the relationship. With Reece, I never had to worry about those issues. He was just as busy and committed to his career, as

I am to mine. It was never a problem nor up for debate, but now all bets are off. You know, if he wants a commitment, then he'll go to great lengths to change me. I can't accept that."

"It's still not up for debate, even with Reece. I'm not telling you to commit or not to commit to Reece Montgomery. I'm just stating a fact. You have to lay it on the line with him. Whether you want to stay with him and commit to a mutual understanding of how it will be for each of you, or you tell him that you want to continue the status quo, or you say that you're done and over it because it's getting all too serious, and that wasn't what either of you wanted. What you decide will determine whether you have to work it out or not work it out with Reece."

She shook her head once more, as she surrendered to the idea that a talk with Reece was the only way.

I knew that Reece would want Damien by his side, but I thought they would stay in New York, not come down to Long Beach Island. Well, at least the Montgomery house was on the opposite end of the island. I wouldn't have to see Damien or Courtney while they were here.

Blaze had at least a week or so before she had to deal with Reece, so, for now, it was time to relax and enjoy the weekend ahead. We didn't have to walk over to Viv's just yet, either. We had time for another drink before we showered and got ready for the dinner ahead.

chapter
seven

Tommy

MY DESTINATION WAS about two hours one way if traffic was good. The one good thing was I had plenty of time to fill Daniel in on what had gone on the last few days. I did have a funny feeling, though that I might just learn more from Daniel about Jade and her family than he would learn from me.

Daniel was outside on the porch of the main education building when I arrived. He was seated in his wheelchair, but he had his walker by his side. Daniel had been trying some alternative methods to stimulate his muscles so that perhaps he could strengthen them enough to walk on his own someday. He'd probably still need some sort of assistance like a cane, but the new walker by his side signified he must have made some improvement.

He waved as I pulled near the ramp. Daniel was about to reach for his bags when I stopped him.

"Leave them, I'll get them."

"Thanks. Good to see you, man." Daniel had a welcoming smile for me, as I reached the landing to shake his hand.

"Thanks for accepting my invite."

"Be serious. Do you honestly think I would turn down a weekend at the shore with all of those beautiful women running around with bikini-clad bodies, over staying home and doing nothing?" He smirked.

"Well, since you put it that way, I see your point. Nice to see you too, bro." I grinned, as I helped Daniel into the car and then retrieved his bags to place in the trunk.

Once we were settled, I headed back out onto the highway towards home. Daniel broke the silence first.

"Enlighten me on the whole 'Jade Thing.' What exactly has been going on with you for the last week?" Daniel was always straightforward and to the point. He never pulled any punches and he wasn't about to start now.

I looked at the road ahead and smiled. Then I filled my friend in on my life as of late.

"Well, as you know I bought the house and moved in at the beginning of the week. Viv met me there and I spent much of the week taking photos and writing out plans on how I wanted to update the place."

"Great! You're settling in nicely, but what's with Jade?"

"Always right to the matter at hand," I observed.

"Dude, there is no other way for me to be. Now get on with it," he pressed.

"When I bought the house, Viv had one strict condition, which I honored. She asked me not to tell Jade about the purchase of the home just yet. I was asked to say that I was renting it for the next year. I happily agreed, because the moment I saw it, I knew I could start my new life here. Plus, I asked her not to tell anyone I bought it either," I explained.

"Yeah, I get why you don't want anyone on your end to know that you purchased the house, but I'm not sure why Viv placed such a condition on the deal."

"I had hoped you'd be the one to know. You've known her for quite some time. Are you sure you don't have any ideas?" I asked.

"Man, I would have thought that the memories of that house would only remind them of what happened to Jimmy, so they would be glad to sell it, but now that you've explained that Viv doesn't want Jade to know yet, it makes me think."

"Think of what?"

"Maybe the reason they wanted to sell it, is the same reason they want to hide it from Jade," he stated.

"And that reason would be…?" I asked, pushing him further for an explanation. I wanted to get a better handle on Jade and who she was.

"Like I told you earlier, Jade's brother died several years ago. What I didn't tell you was Jimmy had broken his back in a surfing accident. The accident left him with severe spinal problems, which kept him from ever being able to surf again," Daniel said solemnly.

"I'm sorry for having pressed you for an explanation. It's just that I had a feeling Viv wasn't giving me the full story."

"Yeah, Viv is extremely private and very protective of her family, especially Jade. You see, after Jimmy was injured, Jade stuck to him like glue. She and her brother were about five years apart, but unbelievably close. She truly idolized Jimmy. Then when he moved to the Center, she visited constantly. Every chance she got, she would be with him. It even caused serious issues between her and her then-boyfriend, Damien Montgomery."

"Damien Montgomery? Reece Montgomery's son?" I inquired.

"Yes, how did you know?" Daniel seemed perplexed by my questions.

"I didn't know about him and Jade, but I knew of them from doing marketing shots for their wine companies in Napa and Europe a few years back. I never saw Jade with Damien back then," I admitted.

"No, you wouldn't have. You see, Jade grew up at the beach. Yet, Damien wasn't down here full-time, just summers and holiday breaks. Eventually, though, they started to date, and when it became serious, they got engaged, but Jimmy's accident consumed Jade. She did everything she could to help her brother," Daniel added.

"I don't follow…What's wrong with a sister helping her brother? Especially with the situation you just described," I questioned.

"There's nothing wrong with it, but Damien felt left out and he turned his attention to other things." Daniel stopped there for the moment.

"Other things?" I was so intrigued by Jade, I needed to know more. I urged Daniel forward with his explanation.

Daniel hesitated, but explain further. "Viv said during the time Jade was helping her brother and even after he died, Damien appeared preoccupied. Jade hadn't noticed, but Viv did. She told my mom about it, and my mom suggested that Viv go to Damien. She did and he dismissed it. Viv was grieving herself and she was taking care of Jade, so I think she cautiously accepted what Damien had explained to her."

"I have a feeling you haven't told me the end of the story, yet." I presumed there was more and when Daniel didn't answer me, I quickly took my eyes off the road to see his expression.

He nodded.

"Before you go on, let me tell you why I'm so curious."

"I was hoping you had a reason for all of this." He sounded relieved.

"I met Jade for the first time on Thursday night at The Palm. I danced with her. All I can say was that she was incredible. I can't tell you why. I honestly don't know why. I just know that I want to get to know her better. I'd like to ask her out on a real date."

"I get it. It's soon, but I get it." That was all Daniel said, but when I glanced at him, I noticed he had a sly grin to go along with his statement.

I grinned back. Then I put my mind back on the road. The traffic started to break up and I knew we would be back on LBI soon, but I needed to hear the rest of the story.

"Where was I? Yeah, after Jimmy's death, Damien and Jade were still together, but from what Viv told my mom, he was not himself. He was short with Jade and distracted. One night, Jade had been out with a girlfriend and when they returned to Jade's beach house, there were Damien and Courtney, another friend of Jade's, in the bed that he shared with Jade." Daniel was embarrassed to have to disclose this information, but he knew it wouldn't go any further than this conversation.

"What the hell was he thinking? Jade was his fiancée. He should have been there for her," I remarked, as I became tense and shook my head without taking my eyes off the road ahead. I barely knew her, but I was ready to tear this guy Damien apart for hurting Jade. Yet who was I to talk? I had my own problems with my brother Mike and his fiancée.

"I know. Jade is a beautiful woman, inside and out. Damien was a fool. That night, after Jade and her friend let them both have it. Damien stayed behind to talk with Jade, but ultimately, he left. They never worked it out and Damien moved in with Courtney, much to the dismay of everyone…except for Jade. From what I understand she was quiet about the news and never discussed her feelings about it. My parents said she was a real class act. She never said anything negative about Damien either. Jade left him to his own devices and she moved on." Daniel was candid.

"Did he at any point try to get her back?" I asked.

"I don't know. If he did, then Viv never mentioned it," Daniel added.

"You said she moved on. Did she meet someone new?" Again, my need to know more about Jade crept into the conversation.

"Not that I know of. I know she left the company she worked for as a chef to open her own business. From what my parents said, Jade moved on alone, but kept herself busy with her career, not a new man." Daniel's statement was good news for me. I wasn't sure if Jade and I would go out again, but I was relieved to know that she was unattached.

Just then I took the exit to the Causeway that led me back to LBI. We arrived at the house around 4:30 in the afternoon. I explained to Daniel that I was invited to have dinner with Viv this evening and that I had called her before I left to ask for a raincheck. Daniel said I should go and that he would order something in for himself while I was out. Viv nor I would hear of it. I told him when I tried to cancel she said no and was insistent that he come to dinner as well. She said she and Jade would love to see him after all these years. Daniel seemed pleased and agreed that he would join us.

Thinking about the evening ahead, especially with Daniel there, made it feel like everything was falling into place. It'd been a long time since I felt good…it felt right. I pulled up to the driveway and parked the car so that I could retrieve Daniel's things from the trunk. Daniel asked that I get the walker, so he could use it on the stairs. He joked that it would be a slow go for him and that he should head up first while I unpacked the rest of his stuff from the car.

Once we reached the landing to the deck, Daniel said he needed his wheelchair. Daniel was very strong in his upper body, but he still tired from the steps. He sat down and composed himself and then wheeled himself forward along the deck at the side of the house until he reached the open area of the deck that faced the Atlantic Ocean. He sat there and took it all in. I placed his bags near the sliding glass doors and joined him.

Leaning on the railing to face him, I smiled when I saw his peaceful expression.

"I'm happy for you, bro." He stated with a wide smile, as he nodded with the clear intent that he agreed I made the best decision in buying this house.

I smiled and asked if he would like a beer. He said he would love one. So I went into the house with Daniel's bags and placed his stuff in the bedroom on the first floor.

I then grabbed two cold bottles from the fridge and heard laughter, so I went to see who was here. I looked out the sliding glass door in the living room to see Jade on the deck smiling as she and Daniel got re-acquainted after several years of not seeing each other.

I watched the two of them for a moment. Daniel spoke softly to Jade. I couldn't hear what he said, but whatever it was, it meant a great deal to her, because she reached for his hand, leaned down, and kissed his cheek as her eyes filled with tears.

She then knelt down in front of Daniel and continued to speak to him with her hand in his. She was comfortable with him. She seemed grateful and at ease. Whatever he had conveyed to her made Jade's demeanor brighten once again. I watched as her angelic face glimmered with the warm, golden hues of the late day sun. Her smile radiated a tenderness that could be felt by everyone who was around her. I knew she had to be one special lady. At that moment, I pledged silently to definitely get to know her better.

In the few brief times we had been in each other's company, Jade awakened me to feelings I had buried so deep inside that I didn't even realize I missed them until now. Feelings that bubbled to the surface and made me feel alive again. I had my neighbor, who I barely knew, to thank for that.

From the first night I saw her, danced with her and touched her, she had gotten under my skin. No woman had ever done that to me, not the way Jade did. I didn't know who she was, but I wanted to see her again. I needed to find out if these feelings were due to the atmosphere at the club that evening, or was it the excitement and expectations for the new life I had planned to start at the shore or was it just— her? Was Jade the woman that I had waited subconsciously for all this time? The one that I decided to look for as part of my plan when I moved here? Or was all of this fate?

I wasn't sure, but I intended to find out.

chapter

Jade

OUR DISCUSSION CAME to a halt as Blaze and I heard my neighbor's car pull into the driveway. Tommy had a friend with him. His friend was not only attractive, he was someone to my surprise I recognized. It was Daniel Rosso. It had been several years, almost three to be exact, since I had seen Daniel. Seeing him now reminded me of how kind he had been to our family when my brother passed away. He felt our grief, but more importantly, he understood what haunted Jimmy.

His knowledge and understanding comforted me and helped me to move forward. I don't know if I had ever really healed from Jimmy's death, but Daniel helped me to place it somewhere in my heart, where it was protected. A place that allowed me to continue to live.

"Is that Daniel from the Center with your neighbor? You never mentioned that Tommy knew Daniel?" Blaze asked.

As I watched Tommy carefully assist Daniel from the car, my heart melted. That moment between Tommy and Daniel made me see that Tommy might just be the perfect person to care for and buy my parent's old beach house.

"Jade, were you even listening to me?" Blaze questioned with a hint of persistence in her tone.

"Yes, I heard you the first time. And to answer your questions, yes, that's Daniel from the Center and no, I didn't know they were friends."

"Well, at least you know how Aunt Viv was able to get the house rented without you knowing about it until now," Blaze said.

I smirked. "Yeah, one less thing to talk with her about before dinner."

Our conversation was interrupted by the buzz of Blaze's phone. That meant Reece needed her. She answered with a sigh of frustration as she excused herself to appease her lover. I noticed that Daniel was sitting alone on the deck next door. He didn't see me when they drove up and he hadn't noticed me now, so I decided to go to him and say hello. It had been awhile since we saw each other, and after Jimmy's funeral we had lost touch. I always liked Daniel and I felt bad that we didn't stay connected; now I would see if that could be fixed. I walked up the stairs to the deck that Daniel was on. He turned his wheelchair slightly to see who was behind him.

He smiled warmly at me. "Jade, good to see you."

"Hi Daniel, it's so nice to see you too," I stated, as I walked over and leaned down to hug him.

His arms embraced me firmly. All of those memories flooded my body and my tears escaped me.

"Hey, what's with the tears? You're going to ruin my reputation. I never make the ladies cry."

I stood up, wiped my eyes, and chuckled at his response to my emotions. "I don't know why I'm crying. I'm happy to see you I guess."

"Well, as long as they're happy tears." He grinned.

I nodded. "Yes, they're happy tears. How are you?"

"I'm good. How are you? Are you still making those delicious desserts?"

"Wow, you remembered?"

"Of course, how could I forget?"

When I took them to Jimmy, I took them to everyone.

"Yeah, he always did share them with you, didn't he?"

"Yes, he certainly did."

"Since you brought it up, I'm now the proud owner of Summertime Sweets right here on LBI, and soon to be the owner of a newer, larger building." I boasted teasingly to Daniel. He always loved the pastries I brought to him and Jimmy. I think sometimes he ate more than Jimmy did. That small memory made me smile.

"That's fantastic! I'm so glad you followed through with your plans. I remember you had talked about it when you came to visit Jimmy at the Center. It's nice to see that your dreams have come true."

"Thank you. Are you staying for a while? You'll have to come and see the place in person while you're here," I said. I was excited to see Daniel. It felt great to talk with him again. For some odd reason, it made me feel like Jimmy was close by.

"I'd love to. I'll ask Tommy to bring me by sometime this weekend."

"I'll make sure to have a care package ready to take home with you. Are you still at the Center or have you moved?" I was curious if Daniel left the Center.

"No, I haven't moved. I'm teaching art therapy there now. I have my own condo on the compound," Daniel explained.

Daniel's statement reminded me of the fact that I wasn't a very considerate person. Daniel was still at the Center and I had only seen him two times since Jimmy's death. Today would make three. I can't even remember why we lost touch. He and Jimmy had become great friends while Jimmy was there. Why hadn't I kept in contact with Daniel? He was always so kind to me. I decided that today gave me a chance to apologize and get reacquainted with him. I hoped he would forgive me.

I looked down to collect my thoughts and get up enough nerve to give a proper apology that was a long time overdue.

"Daniel, that's great that you're teaching and living on your own." I hesitated and turned to get strength from the surf.

Chicken.

Daniel, sensing my hesitation said, "Jade, please don't feel bad."

I couldn't face him. It really hit me that I essentially moved on without a word to Daniel when Jimmy died.

"Jade, please look at me. You didn't do anything wrong."

That got my attention.

I turned to face Daniel slowly, baffled and surprised that he knew what I was thinking.

"How did you know?" That was all I could assemble.

He smiled a knowing smile. "After Jimmy died, I had a feeling that I wouldn't hear from you. Viv told me that you, naturally, took it very hard, but she said that there was tension between you and your parents, and Damien, too. I knew you had a great deal on your plate. I called Viv to get updates on you. She told me you opened the dessert shoppe, but I must confess I haven't talked to her for a while. In the last year, a lot has changed in my life as well, so I was busy dealing with that."

I knelt in front of him and took his hands. I stared at him with a heart filled with thankfulness. He was so gracious to understand and to not hold it against me. Not everyone in my life was that understanding, except for Viv and Blaze.

My parents were the least understanding, and they said that I needed to move on. They continuously chanted that Jimmy wouldn't want me to live the way I was living. I wasn't living any differently than I had when he was alive. I was completely productive. I left my job as pastry chef at one of Reece's places in the city and took my savings and the money Jimmy left for me and opened up Summertime Sweets. I bought the house that was available next to my parent's beach home and slowly made it my own. I had also been in the process of planning my wedding with Damien. He was the one person that came to mind who I thought would have understood the most, but he was even less understanding than my parents. After a year of mourning and changing my career, I guess he had enough of my so-called defiance. When things didn't go Damien's way, he fucked one of my close friends.

Hmmm... he was more like Reece than I realized.

My negatives thoughts were washed away by the squeeze and jiggle of my hands. I looked at Daniel as he gave me a playful wink. He knew what I was thinking about. I knew that I would never let Daniel's friendship drift away from me again.

"I am sorry I wasn't a very good friend to you, but I promise right here and now that I will never let our friendship slip away again." I smiled warmly with the hope that he believed me.

Daniel smiled back and leaned forward. "I'm going to hold you to it."

We both laughed and turned toward the house, as the sliding door opened to display Tommy with a tray of drinks. I stood up immediately, excited to greet him.

Jade, you are far too old to be a school girl. Get a grip.

I surprised myself that my emotions heightened each time I saw Tommy. I definitely had to get them under control. I didn't want him to get the wrong idea or think I was available. I mean although I was single, I wasn't looking for a long-term, complicated relationship with any man. I just wanted to be free to have fun. Jimmy would have been proud of me, no strings.

"Can I help you with anything?" I asked as I saw him struggle with the door and the tray. He couldn't close the door as easily as he opened it. The truth was that door always jammed. It was nearly impossible to close it without this certain trick to loosen it up.

"Could you take this?"

I nodded and took the tray with the drinks and placed them on the patio table. I turned to see Tommy as he pulled on the door with sheer frustration. I giggled as I watched him struggle the way Jimmy had every time he closed that door. Tommy stopped what he was doing when he heard me laugh. He turned towards me and grinned before he walked over to me and leaned in close.

"Okay, smartypants, what's so funny?" He teased.

"You."

"Me?…Me?" he asked once and then again, but this time he directed it to Daniel, who had his hand over his mouth. Probably to screen the chuckle that was trying to escape.

"If you know so much, then you fix it." Although Tommy seemed amused, he challenged me to fix the door.

This was one challenge I knew I would win.

I looked at both Tommy and Daniel. Daniel's smile was playful but curious. Tommy's grin was more of presumed satisfaction that I wouldn't be able to release the door from its current state of damage. Boy, was he in for a surprise. I walked over and stood in the doorway, my feet straddled the threshold so that I could get a firm grip on the door as I jarred it out of its current position. I lifted it up slightly from the handle and yanked hard. There was a loud crack and then the door slid forward. I moved outside and closed it slowly with the tips of my fingers gently on the handle and pushed it shut. I turned and lifted my chin, as I walked back to my new neighbor and my old friend with a delighted, satisfied look on my face. I was completely pleased by how my tiny maneuver made the door respond.

"I guess she showed you," Daniel said just to hassle Tommy, all in good fun, of course.

Tommy turned to Daniel, who appeared to be holding back his laughter. I laughed because of Daniel. When Tommy caught a glimpse of me from the corner of his eye and saw that I was amused, he turned his full attention to me.

"So are you going to tell us how you did that?" he asked.

"I'll think about it."

"Fine, don't tell me. I'll just knock on your door anytime I have trouble with it in the future," he said, as he stood in front of me and waited to hear my response.

"You know where I live."

Just as Tommy was about to respond, Blaze came racing up the stairs as if she was on fire. This couldn't be good. Blaze ignored everyone and pulled me to her.

"He's here." She was out of breath and out of sorts.

"Here, as in his house, here?" I asked, but I had a feeling that is not at all what Blaze meant.

"No, here, as in your front doorstep, and here, as in Viv's house for dinner." She panicked as she spoke about Reece.

"Wait, you're telling me he's at Viv's?" I began to panic right along with Blaze.

She nodded frantically with a cryptic smile on her face.

"Shit!" It was all I could say.

"Shit is right. What do we do, now?" She looked to me for some sort of epiphany, which wasn't about to happen, because I didn't have a clue on how to handle Reece Montgomery. I knew what he was like, and when he set his sights on something. In this case, that something being Blaze. He wouldn't let anyone or anything, not even his health, stand in his way.

"If he's at Viv's, then does that mean Damien is there too?" I raised my voice slightly and looked away from Blaze to Tommy and Daniel. They didn't say anything and tried to appear nonchalant, as not to show that they were listening. Not that they could help it, Blaze vividly exposed the situation when she made her grand entrance onto Tommy's deck. I didn't give Blaze a chance to answer. I felt I owed Tommy and Daniel, an apology for our behavior, and I felt it would be a good time to introduce Blaze to the both of them. I was almost positive that Blaze had met Daniel before, though.

"Tommy, Daniel, I apologize for all of this craziness. Some of us shouldn't have brought their problems here." I cleared my throat and cocked my head to indicate to Blaze it was her cue to apologize for her abrupt entrance and that it would be a good time for her to introduce herself.

She stopped in her tracks, paused, then recovered. She stiffly raised her hand and awkwardly said hello. "Hi, I'm Blaze, sorry for my obnoxious intrusion."

Tommy immediately came forward to welcome her. He took her hand, which for some strange reason made me uneasy. He was being kind and I was being ridiculous. He was a single man and I was a single woman with no expectations because I didn't want anything serious. There was no reason for me to feel this way. I just met him. This was insane. I chalked it up to being overtired and overstressed from the past week, with all the drama created by Reece and Blaze, not to mention my surprise about my parent's house being rented out without Viv advising me on it beforehand.

"Blaze, I'm Tommy Conte. Good to meet you. I assume you know Daniel already," Tommy said as he turned in Daniel's direction.

"Yes, hi Daniel, it's been awhile. How are you?" Blaze said with a smile that could make the sun melt.

"I'm good, Blaze. I'd ask you how you are, but by the sound of things I think I already have my answer." Daniel remembered Blaze.

"Yeah, again, I'm sorry about all of this," She said as she waved her hands aimlessly in the air. She was about to explain further, but Tommy's introduction finally hit her.

"Wait..." She reached for Tommy's upper arm in a flirtatious move. I would have reached for her throat if I could.

What the hell was wrong with me! No expectations, Jade, remember?

With her hand still curled around Tommy's bicep, she questioned him further. "You said, Tommy Conte?"

Tommy nodded with a quirky smile on his face. Where was she going with this? I think everyone was intrigued.

"The photographer?" she continued.

Tommy nodded again in response to her question.

"I love your work. My company has used your services several times to acquire photographs for staging many of our properties in New York City." She explained her presumptive action to his introduction.

"Thank you, I really appreciate the compliment." Tommy was sincere. I had no idea he was a photographer. I wondered what else I would learn about Tommy as Blaze continued to grill him.

"What a small world; I assume by the work that needs to be done on Jade's childhood home, you aren't currently taking on any photography work?"

"You're right. I'm taking a leave of absence for the time being, but my parents and my business partner have it all handled. My partner took a break for a while after having her children, so now it's my turn." Tommy's business partner was a woman? Why should this surprise me?

"And you know Daniel. The world has gotten even smaller." Now Blaze was fishing. I needed to put a stop to this and fast, yet I hesitated. I didn't want Tommy nor Daniel to be put off by her questions, yet I learned a great deal in the past few minutes.

"Yes, Daniel's brother is married to my childhood friend and business partner," Tommy said, and I was surprised by that, too. Daniel never mentioned he had a brother in all the time I'd known him.

"I thought you were an only child?" Now, I was the one being nosy.

Both Daniel and Tommy grinned at each other as if they had some secret that only the two of them knew about.

"No, I'm not an only child, but I hadn't gotten to know my brother until recently, so it was something I've never talked about."

"I want to apologize on behalf of Blaze and myself," I said to Daniel. "We should have never pried."

He laughed and Tommy smiled, while Blaze sulked. She obviously felt like I was being ridiculous for my apology, but his personal life was not our business, especially since I hadn't kept in close contact with him for the past few years.

"Believe me, Jade, it's okay, but it's a long story and not one that I can really talk about without going into enormous detail, and also one we don't have time for right now, but I'd love to tell you about it, so why don't we all have dinner one night soon and I'll explain everything." He grinned.

"We're having dinner tonight," Blaze interrupted.

"Blaze," I snapped, and she closed her mouth tight.

Daniel let out a huge laugh. "I don't think tonight would be a good idea. Let's take one drama at a time, shall we?" He was referring to Blaze and her issues with Reece.

"So, while we are on the subject, and if you don't mind me asking, what is all the drama you ladies are dealing with at the moment?" Tommy jumped in.

"Blaze is having boyfriend problems."

"Thanks for making it sound so juvenile," Blaze said, directing to me.

"That's because it is." I justifiably smirked, but I looked at Tommy; he was already staring at me. I looked down. Strangely, my shyness when I was around him hadn't dissipated after our original introduction.

Just as Blaze was about to explain what had happened in the last few days, a familiar voice called out her name from my garden. It was Reece. He'd probably tried the bell and when neither of us answered, he decided to walk around back and intrude. Or maybe, knowing Reece, he just barged in and didn't ring my bell at all. Anyhow, there he was, fully recuperated by his standards and calling out for Blaze.

Blaze made her apologies and headed down the stairs of Tommy's deck to cross over onto my patio. It was only a matter of time for Reece to come and look for Blaze. He probably got an earful from Aunt Viv and decided that he would make an excuse to go find her. Tommy, Daniel, and I approached the side of the deck to watch as Blaze went to Reece. He had a huge bouquet of red roses and a bottle of champagne. She jumped into his awaiting arms.

"Oh no…clearly, she doesn't want a serious relationship with him, not at all," I stated, snidely. Both men turned their heads and looked at me, but said nothing. They knew exactly what I meant.

I decided to head back to my house to get the desserts for later. I told Tommy and Daniel that I would meet them over there in about an hour. I was initially relieved to see that Reece was alone. I thought that meant he took it upon himself to get a ride down here with his driver or a car service, but when I cleared Tommy's stairs and headed to mine I could see that Damien was in the car. He must have surmised that it would not be the best idea to wait inside of my house.

Unfortunately, Damien saw me too and awkwardly waved. I stood still for a moment. I didn't know whether I should pretend he didn't exist or if I should address him. I decided I had better deal with him now while he was alone. I imagined that if he was back here on the East Coast, Courtney wasn't too far behind. I walked over to the convertible that I had assumed he'd rented. I didn't know of Reece or Damien owning one. Reece rarely drove his car. He had a full-time driver and Damien always drove a four-wheel drive vehicle, like me, so that he could get easily on and off the beach.

As soon as he saw that I would talk with him, he got out of the car to meet me half way. He came close, to kiss my cheek. I was surprised that my skin didn't crawl like it had in the past when I met him. Now was not the time to negatively reminisce. Now was the time to find out how long he planned to be here, and what he was doing about keeping his father on a short leash.

"Thank you for calling me the other night," he said after his hello kiss.

"It's fine. Actually, your dad made me call you. He said you wouldn't have answered if it was him."

Damien chuckled. "Yeah, he's right. We only talk when there's a concern with the business."

"I'm sorry to hear that." Although I had no reason to feel bad for Damien, I knew that Reece was his only family and family was very important to me. Regardless of the ill feelings between us, I hated to see that he and his dad were still not repairing their relationship.

"You know how he is. He won't stop with his demands on how my life should be."

"You mean who should be in your life," I remarked.

"Yeah, he just won't let us go," Damien said with an exhausted sigh. Reece never liked Courtney, and he certainly didn't approve of how his son and Courtney became a couple. He voiced his opinion on the subject every chance he got. That was the main reason why Damien moved to Napa Valley. That, and the fact that with everything that happened between us, he felt it necessary to distance himself. Although he still helped run his dad's business out there. I was glad when he left. It made a very complicated and heartbreaking situation slightly easier for me.

I smirked. "He pulled that same garbage with me at the hospital."

"How did you get him to stop?" he asked.

"I threatened not to call you." I smiled.

Damien laughed. "You always had a way with him."

"Well, I don't know about that," I said, modestly.

"Trust me… you do," he whispered.

I had to admit that when I saw Damien just now, I thought I would have had a flood of emotions, from hate to sadness, even maybe some small attraction. Yet, it wasn't like that at all. I didn't feel anything, good or bad. I wondered if I was still numb. Whatever it was that I was feeling, I hoped it held up until Damien left. My thoughts were broken when Reece decided to join the conversation.

"Well, well, well, I knew I would find you two together," the voice of doom echoed, as he came up from behind us.

"It's not what your mind thinks it is," I said, turning to acknowledge his error in judgment.

"Then what is it, Jade? Do enlighten me. You two belong together, and once you both realize it, life as we know it will finally get back to normal."

"Why don't you worry about your own love life, old man, instead of sticking your nose in where it doesn't belong," Damien injected with some visible resentment.

"Ignore him, Jade. You and Damien will be back together sooner rather than later, if I have anything to say about it," Reece persisted.

"I'm going to tell you this for the last time. Damien and I will never be together again.   And for your information, you don't have a say in this matter. This is my life, and no one gets to have a say in it, but me. Who I decide to be with in the future is my business and mine alone. Do I make myself clear?"

Reece didn't answer me. He addressed his son.

"I can't believe you gave Jade up so easily for that bitch you are warming your sheets with."

Our anger erupted, causing footsteps to pound the stairs and stop short in front of us.

"What the hell happened? I can hear you guys from upstairs," Blaze asked, breathlessly.

"Your boyfriend is what happened."

Oops!

"Boyfriend? What the hell are you talking about?" They hadn't talked to Damien yet. I thought they had because Damien drove Reece all the way down here, and yet, instead of going to their home, they were at mine. I assumed he knew, but I guess my assumption was wrong.

Both Blaze and Reece fell silent. I guess if I was the one who opened my big mouth, then I should be the one to elaborate on the situation.

"Damien, your dad and Blaze are sleeping together. They have been for months." There, I said it. I didn't want to be the one to tell him, but he had to be told. Now it was up to Reece to put it all into perspective for Damien.

Damien stepped in front of me to confront both Blaze and Reece.

"When were you both going to tell me?" Damien was eerily calm.

"We hadn't said anything to you before, because we weren't sure where all of this was headed." Reece approached Damien with caution.

"Do both of you know where this relationship is headed now?" he asked.

"Don't be condescending." Reece seriously advised his son to back off.

Blaze cut in before Damien could respond. "Maybe now, outside in front of Jade's neighbors, isn't really a good time or place to have this discussion. Not to mention the fact that Reece, you are supposed to be recovering from a heart attack, or did you forget?"

"No darling, I didn't forget. I just want my son to understand that I don't appreciate his tone." Reece's words became tight as he spoke to Blaze, yet his statement wasn't directed at Blaze. It was directed at his son.

"You're telling me that you don't appreciate the way I speak to you? You must be joking. What about the way you have spoken to me for the last few years?" His son asked, but that wasn't truly a question. They were more like comparisons. In some ways, Damien and Reece were mirror images of each other and, in other ways, they were complete opposites.

"I want what's best for you, Damien. Even if you can't see that. I've been trying to show you what a mistake it was for you to leave Jade..."

I needed to stop this now.

"Reece, that's enough!" I yelled to the point that I not only had complete silence but their undivided attention, as well.

I softly spoke to him with the hope that he would understand what I was about to tell him.

"Listen to me. For once, Reece, just listen to me. What happened between me and Damien was years ago, but now it's over. We had so much good and then it all went bad. It wasn't completely Damien's fault. I was to blame as well. I let Jimmy's death consume me back then. It took me away from Damien more and more every day. And when that happened, he looked elsewhere for his happiness. And because of that, I'm sorry to say I can never trust Damien again. I don't blame him anymore for what happened, but I'm not now, nor will I ever be, in a place in my life where I want to revisit the past with him again. I know you hoped we would be together, but that will never happen. For the last time, please understand and respect my feelings."

I went to let go, but Reece pulled me forward to him. He let go of my hands and placed his arms around me. Then he held me at arm's length to assess me further.

"Okay, you both have my word, no more meddling in your future. Jade, I'm sorry. I just want what's best for you and Damien."

Although Reece sounded sincere enough, I decided to reserve my judgment until he proved that he would not involve himself in my life, or even Damien's life, as he has in the past. If he proved that he was done playing matchmaker, then maybe I would believe him completely.

All of us at once realized it was getting late and that it was time for Blaze, Reece, and myself to head over to Aunt Viv's for dinner. Damien explained that Viv extended the dinner invitation to him. He said he would cancel if it were to be too uncomfortable for me, but I told him that it was fine. Blaze thought I lost my mind, and Reece showed a small hint of enjoyment when he found out that Damien was going to join us. I had a strange feeling that Reece was not at all finished with his plan to get me and Damien back together, but unfortunately for him, I had a plan of my own.

I went upstairs to get the desserts, leaving Tommy's box home for now. Perhaps once dinner ended, I could walk out with Tommy to let him know that I had some sweets from the shoppe for him.

chapter
nine

Jade

WHEN I ARRIVED at Viv's with Blaze, Reece, and Damien in tow, Tommy and Daniel were already there. Tommy noticed me first, yet his veil of a smile faded when his focus went to Damien and then back to me again. His blank expression ignited my curiosity as to what he was thinking and why such a reaction from a man I barely knew.

I walked over to my aunt, who was seated with Daniel. Kissing her cheek, I handed her the pastries that we would serve later for dessert as I whispered in her ear.

"This is not the dinner party I expected to be with tonight." My tone was tight.

She leaned away and with a haughty smirk she said, "My darling girl, you'll get through it, I promise. Besides, I think my new bartender is more than eager to help you with that this evening." Viv placed down the box and lifted her martini glass in the direction of Tommy, who returned the gesture.

She just doesn't quit.

I closed my eyes, bit my tongue, and then straightened my body like a stick, as I rotated on my heels and turned to say hello again to Daniel.

I kissed him as I turned my back towards my aunt, or as she is affectionately known, 'the matchmaker.' I must admit Viv looked delighted to see Daniel again, as they appeared to be catching up before I interrupted them.

The small conversation between Viv, Daniel, and myself was short lived. I could feel Tommy's gaze on me again. A cold drink was my excuse to leave and join the hot bartender at the other end of the deck and put wider distance between me and Reece, Damien, and Blaze, as they made their way over to thank Viv for having them stay for dinner. I wished my aunt was less hospitable in situations like these, but she didn't want to be rude.

The bar where Tommy was standing was in a small alcove of the expansive porch. My body was ready to enjoy a glass of wine with my new neighbor— to wash away the stress of the past few days and perhaps lighten up my mood enough to get on with the evening ahead.

"Can I get you something?" he asked, as I took a seat. *God, his voice...Jade, STOP!*

"Hi, I see Viv made you the official bartender for the evening." I teased.

"It looks like she has, doesn't it? She wouldn't let me bring anything, so it's the least I can do." His smile returned as he warmly answered me.

"Well, in that case, can you pour me a glass of wine, sir?"

He grinned and played along, as he snatched a chilled bottle of Pinot Grigio and displayed it before me.

"Will this do, Miss Stanton? I have it on good authority that it was a fine year. Yes, a very fine year. Besides, I have a feeling by the looks of things you could use this right about now," Tommy commented, meaning the situation at hand as he poured me a glass.

"What was your first clue?"

He shook his head. "I didn't need a clue. Your Aunt Viv said she invited some additional guests and one of them was your ex. I took that as a not so good thing."

"Yeah, Damien flew in from Napa to stay with his dad, Reece, who is recovering from a slight heart attack. Damien was very close with Viv…" I hesitated for a moment, "…when we were together, and he continued to keep in touch with her even after our split."

"Doesn't that make it hard for you? I mean… him being here."

"Not anymore, but in the beginning it was awkward, to say the least."

"I can imagine. I don't mean to intrude, but do you think the reason he kept in touch with your aunt was to indirectly be closer to you?" Tommy suggested that it wasn't over for Damien. Little did Tommy know, but Damien was the one who left, not me.

I found it interesting that he was curious about Damien.

"I guess at the beginning that could have been possible, but it's been over for quite some time and he moved on long before our relationship had officially ended," I explained.

"I see, and I don't mean to pry, but will you be okay eating dinner with him tonight?" Tommy seemed truly concerned for someone who barely knew me.

"Damien is the least of my worries. His dad is the one I have issues with," I said, as I rolled my eyes at the thought of Reece Montgomery and his unrelenting need to interfere in my personal life.

Tommy nearly choked on his drink.

"Why would your ex-boyfriend's father be a problem?" Tommy questioned.

"Because Reese Montgomery refuses to learn the word no."

"I thought that was him," Tommy said, to my surprise.

"You know him?" I inquired and wondered how they could possibly know each other and yet, I had never met Tommy until the other night.

Tommy shook his head. "Not personally, by reputation, and my company did some shots for a marketing campaign he requested in Italy. My parents run the office, so they deal with all the boring stuff, like the paperwork."

"I take it you did the photos for Reece?"

"No, actually my partner, Rain, did. Her family owns a home in Capri, so while she was out there for an extended visit, she had received the call from our office in New York that a client in Rome needed some pictures for his vineyard and restaurant opening. Rain happened to be available, so she did the shoot for Reece's company."

I was just about to comment, but my aunt called us over for dinner.

I told Tommy to take any seat. Then I went inside to bring out the salad that Viv had prepared earlier. When I came back out, Tommy was by the door. He took the salad from me and placed it on the table. I closed the patio door before I returned to the table with him.

Such a small gesture.

At that point, everyone had taken their places at the table. One end of the table was occupied by Aunt Viv, and of course, the other by Reece. I took my place between Daniel and Tommy. Across from us sat Damien, who was closest to Aunt Viv and Blaze, who was naturally closest to Reece.

We began to pass the food and wine around. There were small conversations that occurred as we ate. Aunt Viv was speaking with Damien and Tommy. Daniel and I were talking. Reece and Blaze appeared to be involved in some sort of deep discussion, and by the look on Blaze's face, the conversation wasn't in her favor.

As each individual discussion subsided, Reece decided he needed to know more about Tommy. This brought us to the inevitable inquisition. "Viv tells me you own a photography studio in Manhattan."

"Yes, I do. Actually, my company did some work for your restaurant and vineyard in Italy a few years back."

"Really? I don't get out there often, but I never forget a face, and you don't look familiar to me," Reece responded like the bastard I always knew he could be.

Tommy grinned. "Well, my partner was the one who took your contract. She happened to be staying in Capri at the time."

Reece cocked his head to one side. His partner being a "her" had gotten Reece's attention.

"Who's your partner?" Reece inquired.

"Rain Medici," Tommy stated.

"Ah, yes, Rain… if I remember correctly, she was an exceptionally beautiful woman and she had quite an eye. She shot photos of things at the vineyard I never thought would be appealing to the readers for my magazine article, but it was a tremendous hit. Tell her hello from me when you see her," Reece said, as he raised his glass to Tommy.

"I certainly will," Tommy said, as he reciprocated the gesture and raised his glass to Reece, but didn't elaborate further.

Reece continued to direct the conversation. As usual, he liked to be in control of the stage he seemed to think he was standing on. His fifteen minutes of fame was over a long time ago, but it seems he didn't read the memo. Or he ignored it, which was unequivocally Reece's style. This time his targets of interest were Damien and me. I knew his promise to lay off was too good to be true.

"So, Viv, now that I have my son home, how about you and I work as a team to get Jade and Damien back together?"

Damien and I both groaned in sync with each other as our silver fell to our plates. That man had no filter. He just said anything he wanted, when he wanted, and in front of anyone he felt would hear him. He cared about no one else's feelings, just his own. I knew his promise was too good to be true.

My skin burned with fury, but my aunt stepped in.

"Reece, unlike you, I don't tell my niece who to date or who not to date. I suggest you stay out of Jade's business, seeing as this is none of your concern in the first place."

"You know I don't mean any disrespect, but can't a father want only the best for his son? It's a parent's job to step in when they see their child headed in the wrong direction."

My aunt didn't have a chance to respond. Damien stood up and addressed his dad, but not before he looked across the table to see if I was okay. It was the first time in over two years that we actually agreed on something. I nodded because after being with Damien for so long, I knew exactly what he was thinking. Damien nodded back and placed all of his attention and anger onto Reece.

"You just couldn't let it alone could you? Viv invited you here as a guest and as such you need to respect your host and the other people she invited. You know no boundaries. You need to stop this, I'm with someone else no..."

The patio chair's harsh rumble made everyone look up at me, as I had abruptly stood up to make my announcement. I quickly interrupted Damien to prevent this argument between him and his dad from continuing. I was flying by the seat of my pants at that moment and no one knew what I was about to do or say, especially me, but I went for it anyway.

"...And I'm with someone too." I said emphatically, as everyone at the table continued to stare at me in shock...everyone except Tommy, which was odd being that he knew me the least.

He seemed to be waiting for the punchline, because he knew I wasn't in a relationship, not after that dance we had Thursday night at the club—strangers don't dance like that. Well, I never had anyway. It was hot and I wanted more—more of Tommy's body against mine, more of his strength wrapped around me, more of his mouth on my lips and everywhere else that my clothes covered. I knew this was wrong. I was physically attracted to him, but I also knew I wouldn't be able to commit to any sort of real relationship. Then again, I was overthinking it; what happened didn't make for a marriage proposal. Yeah, I was overthinking it and needed to put it out of my mind and return to the problem in front of me…Reece Montgomery.

"Really? And why haven't we heard of this someone until now?" Reece pushed.

"Because I haven't had the chance to introduce you to him until now."

"Introduce us to who, Jade?" Reece persisted.

I had to think fast and not panic. My plan didn't include an actual man. I thought, if I told Reece at some point I was with someone and faked the name, he would take me at my word, but now it was put up or shut up. I couldn't let Reece know the truth. I would never hear the end of it and he'd continually try to push Damien and me together again, so I did the only thing I could do; I introduced my boyfriend to the dinner party.

"Tommy and I are dating." I blurted out, yet paused for a moment to look around the dinner table for the reactions from the guests. Blaze looked dumbfounded, Damien sized up Tommy, Aunt Viv and Daniel appeared amused, Reece seemed unmoved by my announcement, but when my eyes settled on the most important person in this equation, Tommy, I didn't know what to expect. He didn't hold a clear expression.

Oh boy, I may have just blown it.

Then a slow, sly grin crossed Tommy's face which showed me that he was a willing participant who decided to play along. For this stunt, I knew that I owed Tommy an explanation and a huge favor, but for now, we just had to convince Reece Montgomery of our new relationship.

"Don't worry, Jade. Your little secret is safe with me," Tommy whispered in my ear, as he stood behind me and placed his hands on my shoulders.

God…his strong hands felt so good. Focus, Jade, focus.

Reece assessed each of us with smugness and disbelief. "Let me get this straight. You expect us to believe that you and *you* just met, and you're already dating?"

"I truly don't give a shit what you believe, Reece. You have no idea how long we've known each other, and as I said, Tommy and I are dating, and that's all you need to know. Believe or not, it's your choice." To my surprise and relief, Tommy made it even more convincing, moving his hands from my shoulders as his arms came around me from behind.

Blaze grinned with a delicious twinkle in her eyes. I knew she liked the idea that I might possibly be interested in someone again. Blaze was a true romantic at heart.

"I know what you're doing, Jade. Don't worry, I won't spoil this for you. I'm more than happy to play my part and get this prick off your back, baby." Tommy's reassuring voice whispered in my ear and had sex written all over it. I was immediately and secretly turned on.

Baby.

"You may not give a shit, as you put it, but Jade you know as well as I do, you're not the type of girl to haphazardly jump into anything without thinking it through. You've always had a good head on your shoulders. You have always been smart and sensible and, yet this is anything but." Reece stated as he put his hand out to me and Tommy as if we were on display.

He acted like it was absurd to think that I could fall for Tommy. He was convinced the only man for me was his son, Damien. Maybe he needed a bit more from me to convince him otherwise?

"You've made it quite apparent you aren't happy to hear I've met someone who makes me happy. I think we can all agree you proved that by saying you have your doubts that I'm even telling the truth."

Reece looked down at his plate, his lips strongly perched in contemplation. He took a deep breath in and wiped the corners of his mouth with a slow, precise diligence. He then methodically folded his napkin before he placed it on his plate in front of him and stood up to address the dinner party, but his eyes were on Tommy and me.

"I will not discuss this with you here, Jade, but we will talk privately and very soon." The tone of his voice was balanced. He didn't raise it, but his tone was insistent.

I had just about enough. I pulled away from Tommy and stormed toward him so that we were eye to eye.

"You listen to me. I will not discuss my personal life with you. I am sick and tired of your continuous and intrusive behavior. Damien and I are over. That will never change. Get used to it. Do you understand me?" My voice was tight and stressed, but I didn't flinch or waiver. Yet neither did Reece.

Reece turned and placed his hands on my shoulders, as he regarded me at arm's length. Yet, he had no regard for my feelings or anyone else's here tonight for that matter. He just completely pushed the issue and me.

"You know that I only have your best interests at heart." He spoke to me like I was a small child and that was the last straw that finally set me off.

I grabbed his hands and abruptly brushed them off and shoved them away from me. It may have been the only time I'd ever seen Reece Montgomery wide-eyed. Then, except for Daniel, everyone stood up immediately, as Tommy came to my side and placed a supportive hand on my shoulder before he intervened.

"You didn't listen to what Jade said, so now you're going to listen to me." I didn't know Tommy very well, but as he spoke I could tell he was not someone you wanted to mess with.

Reece and Tommy stared each other down. Thick tension began to build in the atmosphere around us, and just as I was about to put an end to their confrontation of wills, Blaze nervously tried to break the tension between the two men.

"Listen, I think we all need to calm down."

Reece snapped around and addressed her. "If I want your opinion, I'll ask for it."

Blaze closed her eyes, lowered her head, and stepped back somewhat embarrassed. I had never seen my friend like that. Blaze was always a happy soul. She never hurt anyone and never let anyone hurt her, but this time she allowed Reece to walk all over her. I wasn't the only one pissed at this. Damien went to Blaze and placed a supportive arm around her shoulder. It was a kind gesture because although Damien didn't approve of Blaze and Reece's relationship, he knew exactly how his dad could be. He saw it first hand with his mom and from what Viv told me, he shouldered the brunt of it with Reece's continued attempts at manipulation into Damien's personal life with Courtney.

"Don't you dare speak to her that way," Damien warned.

"She isn't with you. She's with me, and I'll speak to her the way I see fit." He was rude and unapologetic. This was when I lost it.

"Get out!" I screamed as Reece stood, stoic, unaffected.

"You heard Jade. You need to leave." Viv addressed him.

Reece let out a deep sigh. Annoyed, he resigned himself to the fact he was no longer wanted here. He walked to the end of the patio and turned back to address his son.

"Damien," was all he said.

Damien looked at Blaze who weakly smiled and nodded that she was okay. Without saying anything he knew Blaze would not be joining them. Damien nodded in return. He couldn't blame her for remaining here after the way Reece had acted. He then addressed my aunt and me.

He stepped forward and took Viv's hand and kissed her cheek. Then he let out an exhausted sigh of his own.

"Viv, Jade, I'm really sorry. If I had known the evening would have turned out like this, I would have never agreed for us to join you and your guests for dinner."

Aunt Viv touched his face.

"It's not your fault. You better take him home. I suspect you are going to have your hands full with him this evening." She added, giving him a small comforting smile.

He grimaced, at the thought of the night ahead of him with his dad.

"Not if he knows what's good for him," Damien stated as he left to take Reece home.   As they were about to leave, Reece turned and called out to Blaze.

"Blaze, you'll hear from me tomorrow," he confirmed, but the look on Blaze's face was no longer bright and whimsical. He took that from her when he treated her like trash just moments ago. She had the look I knew so well, the look of regret. Blaze may finally be done with Mr. Montgomery once and for all.

…And she wasn't the only one.

chapter
Ten

Tommy

THE EVENING TURNED out much different from what I'd expected. It should have been a quiet dinner overlooking the Atlantic Ocean from Viv's patio, though it ended up being a battle of wills between Jade and her ex-boyfriend's dad, as well as Blaze and his son.

Once Reece and Damien Montgomery left, we all sat down to discuss what had just happened. Viv decided to question Jade and me on our new relationship.

"Feel free to tell us what's going on with the two of you." Viv resolved herself to the fact this was going to be a long story, so she pulled up a chair and was fully ready to listen.

"I'm sorry. None of this was Tommy's idea. He just played along." Jade admitted, and then apologetically looked in my direction. I smiled agreeably, letting Viv know there was no harm done.

"I gathered that this was your idea, Jade, but why?"

"Ever since Damien and I broke up, Reece would hint in one way or another that he wanted to help me get Damien back."

"It's my understanding that you and Damien have been apart for several years now. Why has Reece suddenly turned up the heat to get you both back together? Why didn't he try to do that when you both first broke up?" Daniel spoke up.

"He did, but when he saw it wasn't going anywhere he let it go. At least, that's what I thought."

"What happened now to make him start this all up again?" I asked Jade to see if I could get more of a clear picture of Reece's motives.

"I can tell you why I think Reece is doing this," Blaze said.

"Why?" Both Jade and I looked at each other when we realized we both asked the same question at the same time.

Blaze's uncomfortable smile confirmed she discovered something about Reece's motivations.

"Go on. I can tell I'm not going to like this," Jade prompted.

"He had said he thought Damien was going to propose to Courtney. He wasn't positive, but he said he couldn't let that happen."

"Courtney is Damien's girlfriend," Jade explained, directly to me. I nodded as to acknowledge the information. Although, thanks to Daniel having explained everything to me when I brought him back here this afternoon, I already knew who Courtney was, yet I couldn't let Jade know I was aware of the story. I didn't want to cause any discord between her and Daniel.

"Do you think that Reece is trying to get Damien and Jade back together again on the slim chance that their old feelings will come back?" I asked.

"Yes, and I think he has convinced himself that if he can do that before Damien asks Courtney, then there is no chance that Courtney and his son will stay together. You have to understand, Tommy, when Jade and Damien were engaged Reece was thrilled. He loves Jade. I know that his little display tonight makes it tough to believe, but he truly does care about Jade and he loves his son more than anything."

"That man has a terrible way of showing it," Viv added.

"You know as well as I do, Reece was livid when he found out what Damien did to Jade, but I guess now that so much time has passed he feels the old wounds have healed and perhaps they could start over," Blaze said to Viv.

"You know better than anyone I will never get back together with Damien. He cheated, that's it, it's over," Jade was emphatic.

My immediate attraction to Jade was crushed by her words, without her knowing. Getting to know her better could end up being unattainable once she found out why I moved to LBI and what I left behind. She might never be able to get close enough to me to form more than a friendship, and even being friends was debatable. I knew my past indiscretions would drive any woman away; I wasn't delusional, but to hear Jade's words bite, gave me a more vivid picture.

"Well, that explains Reece's excuse, but it doesn't explain yours." Viv scolded and was adamant to get Jade's reason behind stating that I was her new boyfriend.

"Reece started to turn up the pressure when I went back to the city Thursday night." Jade's explanation made me realize why she left me on the dance floor at The Palm. Did she always run to Reece when he called for her? Maybe that was half the problem?

"You've lost me," Viv said.

"I was at The Palm when my phone rang. It was Blaze. She sounded distraught and said she was at Mt. Sinai, so I assumed she was hurt and I headed back to the city, but as you know it turned out it was Reece in the ER. He had a mild heart attack when he was with Blaze, so she got him to the hospital," Jade continued to explain, more for me and Daniel and less for Viv.

Hmmm...glad to see Jade isn't at Reece Montgomery's beck and call, after all.

"I understand that. Yet, you're still not telling me why you cooked up this scheme with Tommy. He just moved here and this is a horrendous way to become friends and neighbors," Viv said.

"I was getting to that. At the hospital, Reece insisted I called Damien to get him to come back home. That was when I knew he was up to something. I mean he was physically able to call his son, but he pressed for me to do it. I wondered why he didn't ask Blaze, but then I came to find out they've been sleeping together for the past six months and…"

"Wait, you've been with Reece Montgomery for six months" Viv burst into laughter.

"It's not that funny, Viv" Blaze tried to justify herself, while Viv, Jade, and even Daniel were amused. It was contagious. Blaze and I started to laugh as well. When we calmed down, Jade continued.

"Anyway, I could tell Reece wasn't going to let up, so I decided to get a fake boyfriend. I never in a million years thought that he would call me out on it so soon. I had planned to tell him I was seeing someone, but I wasn't prepared to elaborate on who it was. I thought telling him that I was in a relationship would make him back off."

"So you pulled Tommy into this. Jade, you know better. You know Reece is the type of man who will go to great lengths to find out if you are telling the truth or not, especially when the outcome involves his son." Viv's tone showed her disappointment in Jade.

"Yes, I pulled Tommy into it. I apologize. I wasn't thinking. I panicked," Jade's voice dimmed, somewhat ashamed.

"Don't apologize to me. Apologize to Tommy," Viv directed with a stern tone, pointing her finger in my direction.

Jade turned to me with those beautiful doe eyes. I couldn't possibly be angry with her. Reece Montgomery was nothing but a rich, self-absorbed asshole. I was happy to help.

"I'm sorry, Tommy. I didn't mean for any of this to happen the way it did and in your first week here. I hope we can still be friends." Jade was sincere.

I chuckled. "Sure, I was glad to help. He was being a real jerk. Hopefully, after what happened tonight, you won't have to deal with him again."

"Let's hope not," Jade agreed, but didn't seem convinced of it.

We sat and talked for a while longer. I explained about the house and the repairs that I had decided to work on first. Viv seemed visibly relieved that I didn't let on that I already owned the property. Jade appeared thrilled with my proposed changes. She explained that she was also dealing with a renovation of sorts. Her pastry shoppe would be moving at the end of August, down the street from the location she was at now, to a permanent building that she recently purchased. She was going to be neighbors with the club where we met. I understood her excitement. It was much like the way I felt when I purchased the beach house.

We called it a night at around eleven. Jade kissed her aunt and then said goodnight to me and Daniel before she left with Blaze. Daniel and I both thanked Viv before leaving to head home.

Home…it had a nice ring to it.

Once inside, Daniel expressed how tired he was and decided to head to bed. I grabbed a beer and went out onto the deck to settle down before I turned in. I couldn't sleep. The excitement of the events of the day had me on edge.

I heard footsteps on the stairs and then along the deck on the side of the house that led to me. I looked over my shoulder to see Jade with a large bakery box in her hands. She was just about to knock on the sliding door near the side of my living room when she stopped herself and came to place the box she was holding on my patio table where I was standing. This was my opportunity to talk with her alone. I'd wanted to do that all night, now I had my chance.

"Hey, I thought I was the only one who couldn't sleep."

She looked up at me and smiled. The brightness that shone over the shore this evening illuminated Jade's features and long dark hair.

"Hi, I thought I'd leave these here." She tilted her head in the direction of the box.

"Would you like to come in for a nightcap?" I asked, as I came toward her and peeked in the box to briefly see what she brought to me.

"I don't want to bother you. I just wanted to leave you and Daniel some desserts and breakfast treats for the holiday weekend. With everything that went on today, I forgot to give them to you," she awkwardly explained.

"You're definitely not bothering me. So, why don't you come in and share a drink and some dessert with me? Since it was kind of your fault that I didn't get to have any at your aunt's house tonight." I grinned playfully at Jade, hoping she would take me up on my offer.

She looked down at the drink in my hand and bit her lip. Shit! I wanted to kiss that mouth. Then she looked back at me and said, "Okay, one drink, being I owe you."

I smiled and stepped to one side to let her in. I went to close the door and realized the box was still on the patio table. I went back and retrieved it, placing it on the center island, near where Jade was standing.

"Let's take a closer look at what you've brought us," I teased, as I reopened the box.

She appeared overly excited to see me open the box that contained mini desserts and scones of every variety. I placed it aside and smiled.

"I know what we need…Champagne. I have a bottle on ice," I revealed, as I eagerly retrieved a bottle and two glasses. While I set everything down on the island, Jade grabbed a plate from one of the old cabinets to place the chocolate strawberries on, reminding me how at home she must have felt here.

I popped the cork and poured our drinks. "Let's sit on the couch; it's more comfortable in there." She nodded and took the strawberries as she followed me into the living room where we toasted.

"Cheers," she said.

"Here's to new friends and neighbors," I added, as our glasses and eyes met.

"Yes, to new friends, and less dramatic new neighbors" She was being funny, but continued to glimpse at the floor or look the other way. I quickly placed my glass down on the coffee table and sat closer to her.

"Hey, what's wrong? Did I do something to make you feel uncomfortable?"

"No, no, it's not you. I truly feel bad about tonight and what I involved you in. Aunt Viv was right. I should have never used you like that. It was childish and I shouldn't be playing games. It was inexcusable. I'm sorry." Jade was extremely remorseful for her actions earlier this evening. She was being way too hard on herself.

"There are no apologies necessary, Jade. Like I said, Reece was being an asshole. You had to do what you had to do. I was glad that I was there to help." I reassured her that what happened was no big deal.

She forced a smile and still didn't seem convinced by what I said to her. Even though less than two days had passed since we met, something made me want to get through to Jade—to make her feel at ease. Maybe it was my feelings of guilt, which made me unable to tell her the truth about the house she grew up in and clearly loved so much, or maybe it was because for the first time in a long time I was intensely attracted to someone I wanted to get to know better, or maybe it was a combination of the two? I was drawn to her and felt wrong for having lied to her about the house. I really did understand how she felt about deceiving Reece. Whether he deserved it or not, Jade wasn't at all comfortable with the recent decisions she had made concerning him, and I got that.

"You don't seem convinced." I gently pressed her for more.

She closed her eyes tightly and let out the breath she had been holding. She appeared to be conflicted about what to say to me. She got up with her drink in hand. She took a sip and leaned on the door jamb as she stared out at the surf. Her body briefly shuddered, as if she remembered some negative from the past, as she turned to face me.

"It's not that. I thought everything that went on with me and Damien was over a long time ago."

Fuck me. I always meet women who are unavailable, emotionally and otherwise.

"So, what you're saying is that Reece is right? You miss his son and want to get back with Damien, but perhaps pride wouldn't let you admit to it?"

"Hell, no. I don't want Damien. That's been over forever. I don't want any man for that matter." Jade was adamant.

"So if you don't want Damien and you aren't involved with anyone else, then you lost me."

"It's a very long story. How much time do you have?" A small nervous, suppressed laugh escaped from Jade's lips, as she asked in an amused sort of way.

I was playful in my response, as I stretched my arms out across the back of the couch.

She smiled at my awkwardness, walked over, and settled next to me. She didn't get too close, but she appeared more relaxed, more at home again.

"Are you sure you want to hear it?"

I refilled her glass and mine and got comfortable in my seat. I was ready for whatever she had to throw at me.

"Okay, I'm ready. Let's have it." I grinned. My actions got me a tension-free laugh, as Jade began her story.

"Damien and I knew each other since we were kids. At the time, he only stayed down here when school was out. You know, weekends, holidays, summer vacations.

That sort of thing. I admit I had a crush on him and was always excited when I found out he was here."

I nodded, and Jade continued.

"I, on the other hand, lived down here my whole life." She stopped and looked around the room. A soft smile formed on her face, which suggested to me that another childhood memory invaded her thoughts.

"It's funny," she said. She stood and looked around the living room at the all of the boxes that still needed to be unpacked before her focus turned back to me.

"What is?" I wondered what she thought.

"This room seemed so much bigger when I was growing up."

"You were smaller then."

"I guess so. Yet it reminds me of when you get a craving for a chocolate bar or a cupcake that you loved when you were a kid, but haven't had in a while, so you go buy it, only to find out it shrunk. You're probably right, though. I was smaller, so it seemed so large in my tiny hands back then. Maybe that's how this room is now. I was smaller, care-free."

"Or maybe your memories are larger than the room?" I grinned. Jade agreed with a slow nod.

"Perhaps you're right. Anyway, let me get back to my story so you can get to bed."

"I can't sleep, remember?" I whispered, and she blushed.

"Give it some time, my story may just do the trick," she joked. Jade seemed more visibly relaxed with each passing moment. She took a sip of her drink and placed the glass on the table in front of us. Then she curled comfortably in her corner and continued with the story.

"You know, I forgot how much fun we had here. Even my parents were different when we lived here." Jade stared intently into the room, taking in the invisible visions of her past. Her thoughts drifted again, but she quickly recovered to continue her tale.

"Anyway, in the beginning, we were just young kids having fun and taking in all that the island had to offer, paddle boarding, waterskiing, bike rides, and surfing."

"You both surfed?" I asked.

"Yeah, but I was better at it than Damien." A pleasing smirk covered Jade's face.

I raised my eyebrows and laughed at her comment.

"No, seriously, I'm not being conceited. My brother Jimmy was an incredible surfer, so he taught me all his techniques. Besides, living down here year-round afforded me the opportunity to surf every day, even in the winter months. Damien didn't have the same type of exposure to water as I did."

"Your aunt mentioned that you surfed. She said you would be able to show me some of the best spots on the island." I had hoped that maybe Jade would go with me at some point.

"I figured as much from your tattoos."

"Yeah. I'm not a professional by any stretch."

"What spots have you surfed?" Jade asked enthusiastically.

"I learned while growing up in Capri, at Licola Beach on Italy's West Coast."

"You grew up in Italy, yet you don't have an accent. Why is that?" She wasn't the first person to ask me that question.

"I thought tonight was about you?" I said, answering her question with a question.

Jade's expression flattened.

That wasn't the response I was going for.

"I'm joking; I'm joking." I quickly replied, so that I could get the conversation back on track. She giggled. Good, my panic may have saved me.

"I was born here and grew up there with my friend Rain and her family, but came back and forth to the States and eventually moved back here permanently over ten years ago."

"Your business partner?" she asked.

"Yes, I think I mentioned her before…we were childhood friends long before we were business partners."

"I think that's great," She said in awe.

"What is?"

"That you have a friend like that for all these years. One that you can trust enough to be business partners with," she added.

I didn't want to get into my friendship with Rain. To many, our story was strange at best and extremely complicated. For now, I decided not to elaborate on it, but Jade had a different idea.

"Is she excited that you moved down here?"

"Umm…" I didn't know how to respond. Rain and her family were very close to me, but they didn't know that I bought the beach house or even where I was at the moment.

"Did I say something wrong?" Jade appeared conflicted.

I reached over and took her hand to reassure her that her questions were fine. I realized how comfortable I was with her and yet couldn't believe it.

"No, No, not at all. She doesn't know I moved down here, or what I'm doing. She thinks I'm traveling abroad right now."

"But why?"

"Truth?" I asked.

"Always," she definitively replied.

"In the last couple of years, my life hadn't been going the way I thought it should," I confessed.

"Join the club," Jade blurted out.

I smiled and continued. "Some recent circumstances made me realize I needed to turn my life around. It was like I was waiting for happiness to find me, instead of going out to grab it. I had told Daniel what I was going through and he suggested a change. That's when I met Viv. She had told Daniel's parents your family was thinking of selling this place. I had become interested and the rest is history." I stopped there because I feared I might slip up and reveal that I already owned the house.

"You're telling me no one except Daniel and his parents know where you are?"

"No, just Daniel knows," I said, adding to the confusion.

"You just said..." She stopped as if she missed something.

"I told Daniel's parents the house was too much for me to take on, and I also swore Viv to secrecy. I knew if everyone found out I was here, they would want to help and that's not what I needed right now."

"So your plan is to fix up this place and possibly buy it and then what?" Jade pressed forward.

"Sort of."

"Sort of? I'm not understanding," she stated.

"You have most of it right. I intend to fix it up and hopefully buy it and also raise a family here." I knew that statement in and of itself could scare any woman away. I just met Jade and my gut was gnawing at me to get to know her better, but if she knew my plans before knowing me, this whole thing might not end well.

"I can tell you from experience there is no better place for a kid to grow up." She sounded more alive, happy when she described the island.

"I can see that."

"Sorry, I got off track. Now, where was I? Oh yes. After years of hanging out as friends, Damien had come down to stay for the summer after his college graduation. His parents were going through a divorce, and he was out of control. My brother Jimmy noticed it immediately, and he basically called Damien out on it. To make a long story short, they had become closer than they had ever been, and Damien decided to make amends with his parents and go to work for his dad in New York. I had finished school about a year after him and I was looking for a job as a pastry chef. Damien spoke with Reece because they needed a pastry chef for a restaurant Reece was going to open the following year. I was immediately hired."

"Wow, they must have really had confidence in you. I mean, you were a new chef, straight out of school with little experience and they gave you a job."

"Well, Reece did. Reece knew I was a good chef. I had catered private parties for him when I was home during the summer."

"And Damien?"

"He just wanted to get me into his bed."

Her honesty made me spit my drink out all over the place. My surprise reaction got me a huge belly laugh from Jade. "Thanks, thanks a lot."

"You asked."

"Okay, but you were engaged to him?" I inquired further because Jade definitely didn't seem like the type the of girl to sleep with a man to thank him for a favor of a new job.

"After several years of trying to openly pursue me, I finally took pity on him, and we went out on a date. To my surprise, he was nothing like his dad, or so I thought at the time. We began to date, and everything was amazing between us. Or at least it seemed that way, so we decided we wanted to get married. Damien proposed, and I accepted. Everything was going great, but then the call came that Jimmy was injured in a devastating surfing accident out at The Mavericks. That was the beginning of the end," Jade's soft voice drifted away and changed into something eerily ominous.

"The Mavericks? That's one of the most dangerous spots in Cali to surf." I was in shock. As much as I loved to surf, I had never imagined I would want to take that on. If the massive waves didn't kill you, the rocks nearby would saw you in half. I wondered what would make Jimmy attempt such a feat.

"My brother had become quite a skillful surfer. His dream was to surf The Mavericks, so he decided while he was out there on business for my dad, he would take a diversion and go to Northern California to check it out. We had no idea he would actually attempt it at that point. Then the authorities called the house to say he was badly injured and was rushed to Stanford Medical Center. My mom called my dad, who at the time was in New York with me. We met her at the airport and we all flew out there together."

"How badly was he hurt?" I already knew the answer, but Jade didn't know that, so the obvious thing to do was ask.

"His back was broken, but that wasn't all of it. If it had just been his back, then more than likely he would have recovered. He had a spinal cord injury, which left him paralyzed from the waist down."

"Jade, I'm so sorry."

"Thank you." Two small words that spoke volumes.

"That's how you know Daniel?"

"Yes, Jimmy had months and months of therapy in California before he could be moved back here to Jersey. Once home, my dad found the Center just outside of Philly that made amazing strides in helping adults with spinal cord injuries. Jimmy was moved there. I can tell you at first he hated it. He was almost impossible to deal with. In fact, the head of the center wanted him discharged and moved elsewhere, but Daniel stood up for him and he was able to remain there until..." She stopped.

"Until?"

She took in a shallow, shaky breath, "Until his death almost three years ago on his 37th birthday." Jade turned solemn. Darkness cloaked her. She'd obviously never recovered from the loss of her brother. I moved closer to her; I didn't think about the pushback of touching—there wasn't any.

"Come here." I took her arm and gently pulled her into my lap. She didn't resist. "No more. It was never my intention for you to tell me a story that would do this to you. You barely know me, but I want you to know I never meant to bring up so much hurt in you. This is not how I wanted our friendship to start." I felt her pain. Pain that may not have originated here, but a pain I stirred up. My thumb gently wiped away the sadness of the single tear that trickled down the warm skin of her face. She looked into my eyes searching for the comfort she needed. Or was it something else?

"It's not your fault. I haven't really talked about Jimmy's accident since Damien and I broke up. Actually, no one ever likes to mention it around me. The truth is, they think I'll break or something. I guess tonight I proved them right." She seemed annoyed with herself for letting her bad memories of her brother get to her.

"Your secret is safe with me," I said to reassure her that no one had to know what happened here tonight.

"Thank you, again." She whispered, as she yawned and rested her head against my chest. She was weary and needed a safe place at the moment. This evening I was that for her. Holding her close to protect her from the intensity of what just happened between us and the awkward stillness in the room, coupled with the sound of Jade's soft breaths, caused my eyes to become heavy. I knew I would be unable to fight it, so I laid Jade back and placed a blanket over her. Knowing she was resting, I watched her until sleep found her and went off to bed.

chapter
eleven

Jade

COMFORTABLE AND WARM, I didn't want to wake from my rest even though I heard Blaze as she pounded on the glass door. Had I locked her out? Or had she left in secrecy to go to Reece in the middle of the night and forgotten her key? I was halfway between sleep and time to get up modes when I also heard Daniel. I vaguely wondered why Blaze was still knocking on the door and why Daniel was in my house ready to let her back in. My subconscious questions were answered as I felt warm lips kiss my cheek and whisper in my ear.

"Good morning, Jade, how did you sleep?" My heart stopped and my breath hitched in one brief second. That voice was Tommy's.

Oh no, I slept with him? I didn't think I drank all that much last night. Wait a minute. Waking further, I knew no matter how much I drank, if I slept with Tommy I would absolutely remember it. Tommy had the body a woman wouldn't easily forget. I peeled my eyes open carefully, one at a time, and looked down. There was a huge Native American Indian blanket that covered me. I realized then, I must have fallen asleep during our talk last night and Tommy had covered me.

GOD...this could have been embarrassing.

It did get pretty emotional for me when I spoke about my brother Jimmy. I remembered I had begun to cry when Tommy wiped my tears and pulled me to him. He was tender, and he made me feel comfortable. I was completely at ease with him; I must have become totally relaxed and fell asleep.

Blaze halted her assault on Tommy's door when Daniel let her in. They both approached Tommy and me on his couch. Daniel grinned and Blaze was somewhat awestruck.

"I can't believe it. You slept with him…already? That's so not like you." Blaze wrongly observed with wide-eyes.

"I guess you're right, it appears I have," I toyed with her.

"You could have at least called me to let me know you were okay."

"Blaze, have you lost your mind? I was right next door. What trouble could I have possibly gotten into from my deck to Tommy's?"

She crossed her arms and cocked her eyebrow, as she gave me a bit of a judgmental look. She had to be kidding? She was going to disapprove of my actions last night when she was sleeping with not only an older man but one that she had been sneaking around with for six months and kept her relationship with him a secret from me the entire time they had been together.

"I suggest whatever that look is on your face, you get rid of it and quick," I said, as I untangled myself from the blanket and stood up to face my friends.

"What look?" She was being coy.

"Exactly," I said and turned my attention to Daniel.

"Good Morning, Daniel, I hope my intrusion last night didn't disturb you?"

"No, not at all, I haven't slept this good in months," Daniel replied.

"It must be the ocean air," I added.

I looked around and picked up my phone from the coffee table. It was 6am. Wow, 6am and Blaze was awake. She really must have been worried. I had to be at the shoppe for 8, so I needed to get a shower and some coffee. I was about to say goodbye when Tommy pulled me close.

"Stay and have coffee with me." His bright eyes searched for my response, as the morning light hit them. His hands holding my upper arms, gently, as he waited for my decision.

When I turned to look at Blaze and Daniel, they both tried to hide their amusement. Oh, sure, now she's okay with this. I turned back to Tommy, but before I could ask for a raincheck, he was asking Blaze to stay, as well. She eagerly agreed and made herself at home on one of the stools at the island in the kitchen. Daniel followed her but settled at the kitchen table.

"I guess we're staying," I said to Tommy.

"Good, you get the breakfast treats and I'll make the coffee." Then he kissed the tip of my nose and walked into the kitchen to join our friends. His actions made me smile, which surprised me. I didn't want to be with any man and I still don't, but Tommy's carefree attitude was making my decision more difficult, especially since I struggled with the fact I just met him.

Before retrieving the breakfast, I called the shoppe to let them know that, yet again, I was going to be late. I couldn't continue to make a habit of this. I only worked about six months out of the year to begin with, and I had a business to run. I was certainly not setting a good example for my staff, especially being late two days in a row *and* on the first weekend of the new season. I ended the call and joined Tommy, Daniel, and Blaze seconds later with the breakfast I had brought over last night, which got me into this situation in the first place. Once everything was on the table, we sat down together to talk. Blaze, of course, needed to know everything, so she started the conversation.

"So now will you tell me what happened? What had you sleeping on Tommy's couch in the first twenty-four hours you know him?" She was insistent and finally realized sleeping on my neighbor's couch didn't mean sleeping with my neighbor.

"Tommy had asked me about my relationship with Damien and how we met, so I started to tell him the story."

"Okay, but that still doesn't explain why you fell asleep here."

"I was okay until I got to the part about Jimmy."

"Oh," Blaze said, but that was all she said. My statement explained everything. She knew how hard it still was for me.

"Yeah, oh," I flatly repeated.

"So, Tommy knows everything now?" Daniel asked and as I took a sip of my delicious brew, Tommy answered his friend.

"No, we were getting to that point, but when I saw our talk was upsetting Jade, I cut it short."

"So he doesn't know all of it?" Blaze addressed me.

I shook my head.

"What… don't I know?" Tommy was confused.

"Are you going to tell him, or should I?"

"I'll tell him."

"Would you like Blaze and me to give you and Tommy some privacy?" Daniel asked. He was always so considerate. He knew much of the story and felt that maybe it was something I needed to discuss alone with Tommy. Probably because it could become even more emotionally charged than last night.

"No, Daniel, both you and Blaze should stay. You both know what went on. There are no secrets here." I really think I asked them to stay more for moral support. I was afraid to get close to Tommy. I was extremely attracted to him, but I had promised myself not to get deeply involved with any man since Damien. I knew if our friends stayed here, there would be less of a chance for intimacy between Tommy and myself. What happened between Tommy and me last night was one thing, but I couldn't lead him on. I had basically abused his kindness when I told Reece that Tommy and I were in a relationship. I wouldn't take any further advantage of him.

"Okay, but just say the word and Blaze and I will get lost," he said, as he gave me his sweet smile.

Tommy placed his hand over mine. "You don't have to do this."

I placed my free hand on his and took a moment before I finished what I had started last night; looking at him wasn't an option.

"It's okay, Tommy. Thank you, but I'm fine now." I paused to collect my thoughts and myself. "Let's see. I told you about The Mavericks and Jimmy going to the Center where he met Daniel." I rehashed part of last night's conversation.

"Yeah, you had said Jimmy passed away," Tommy's low hesitant tone proved it was a tough statement for him to make.

I took a deep breath, his grip tightened further. His support helped me to continue and helped me to look up at him.

"I remember when your brother and I first met. He was one angry son of a bitch. Yet, later on, after many arguments and long late-night discussions, we became really close. Damn, I miss him." Daniel became teary-eyed. Using my free hand, I reached out to Daniel, nodding in agreement with his assessment of my brother.

Daniel knew exactly how Jimmy felt. Yet, Daniel would always say that someone who is born with his condition has somewhat of an easier time psychologically in dealing with it, because they only know that one way of life. Whereas, Jimmy's life changed in an instant from one bad decision…a decision he himself made. It was a hard thing for any person in Jimmy's position to live with, because he had to live with himself knowing it was his choice that put him in the condition he was in at that time.

"Eventually, Jimmy did settle in and became one of the art directors at the Center. He loved to draw and take photographs. He also became a counselor like Daniel. Life started to improve for him. Even his relationship with my dad had gotten better."

"Jade, I don't mean to interrupt, but I'm kind of confused. Yesterday you said Jimmy passed away on his 37th birthday. Did his health take a turn for the worse or were there complications no one was aware of?" Tommy struggled with my explanation, but his confusion was justified. I couldn't blame him. He didn't know what to expect after last night and being that I hadn't elaborated on how my brother died, now I had no choice but to tell Tommy the complete story.

"Yes, his emotional health did suffer greatly and in many ways silently. I mean to say we knew he was distraught. No one needed an explanation about that, but there was a great deal of pain that my brother was feeling, which we weren't fully aware of. Pain that he kept inside and pain that in the end, destroyed him." I had to let what I said sink in and in doing so, Blaze took over.

"Yeah, and through no fault of his own," Blaze added. I loved my friend. She supported me through all of this. She knew as well as I did what sent my brother over the edge. I mean who sent him over the edge...Courtney.

I smiled supportively at Blaze. She understood and got up to kiss the top of my head and squeeze my shoulder before she walked over to the counter to retrieve more coffee.

"What Blaze means is that my brother had been in a long-term relationship with someone, but after his accident, her demeanor towards him began to change."

"I see," Tommy said with a bit of sadness and a hint of disgust.

"You don't know the half of it." Blaze chimed in once more.

"Huh?" Tommy remarked.

A sympathetic smile crossed my lips. Tommy was confused, so I continued. Even though I knew up until now wasn't the toughest part I had to reveal to Tommy, and I knew it would hurt me even further, but for some strange reason I needed for him to hear all of it. I don't know why I felt I needed to be this forthcoming to a man I hardly knew, but a man I wanted to know better, even if it was just to become good friends.

"You see before Jimmy went out to The Mavericks, he had proposed to his girlfriend and she had agreed wholeheartedly to marry him. Then, after the accident, she was understandably scared and confused. In the beginning, Jimmy was very bitter. Sometimes even cruel. He would kick her out of his hospital room. He would look for any excuse to have an argument with her. I believe he did it to make her break up with him, but she never did."

"No, she did a hell of a lot worse in my opinion. That bitch drove him to his death," Blaze lost it and her temper.

We all stared at her.

"I'm sorry, Jade, but it had to be said," Blaze stated, and then quietly retreated in her chair, as she stared outside; her grimace reflected the swirl of emotions Blaze was dealing with inside. Her emotions were in a fight with each other as she spoke of Jimmy.

"Go on, Jade," Tommy mildly prompted me to continue.

"I'm sorry to say the way it turned out proved Blaze wasn't wrong about Jimmy's girlfriend. What she said to him on the day before his birthday is what killed him. I mean…it's what made him kill himself." It was still hard to say it after all this time, but in some strange way telling Tommy was cathartic.

"You can stop now if you need to." Tommy was being sensitive, but Blaze halted that in its tracks.

"Oh, please don't stop her now. Everyone in her family stops her from speaking about it. Let her speak. You need to hear the rest." Blaze's anger was palpable and for good reason.

"Tommy, I'm fine. I know this may be hard for you to believe, but this has been somewhat liberating for me." My heart began to race. I needed to get it out…all of it. It was liberating, but not without heartbreak.

Tommy nodded. I wasn't sure if he fully understood, but he was respectful throughout my entire story. I needed to end this once and for all, especially for my own sanity.

"We had gotten the call at 10 am. It was the 4th of July, ironically my brother's birthday was on Independence Day. They wouldn't say over the phone what had happened, just that we needed to get there. My parents were down here with Viv, and I was with Blaze in the city. Damien was in LA with his dad on business. When we got there, the doctors at the Center had explained that Jimmy somehow managed to get up to the balcony on the third floor which over-looked the fountains in the gardens at the Center. He was then able to lift his body up just enough to topple over it. My brother fell to his death." The darkness, the image I created in my head of Jimmy going over the railing shook in my voice.

I looked at the coffee in my cup as the all too familiar lump of clay formed in my throat and those tears I remembered so well burned my eyes. The silence in the room drowned out the waves of the ocean that roared only steps away from us. Yet, a part of me was liberated when telling the story to Tommy. The other part endured the pain… my brother was gone. In a split second my life changed. I knew Jimmy had been unhappy, yet he seemed to have adjusted very well. He was the one person who never took life for granted. Because of that, I never thought his sadness would be the sum of all his fears and those fears would have forced my fearless Jimmy took to end his own life.

"Let's shut this down. No more, I don't need to hear any more. I understand." Tommy whispered, but Blaze wouldn't let it go. She wanted me to tell him all of it because she was right, the story wasn't done yet. It needed its not so happy ending to make it complete.

"Tommy, let her finish it." Blaze pushed.

"Maybe Tommy's right. Why rehash it?" Daniel said, trying to reason with Blaze.

Blaze was about to speak, but I beat her to it.

"It's okay. I'm almost done, and I'd like for Tommy to know the truth… all of it. You'll understand why I did what I did yesterday. Why I came downstairs in my underwear and yelled about the rose vines. Why I did what I did at the party…once I'm finished, you'll understand all of it."

"Okay, it's your story to tell. Go on," Tommy said.

"After Jimmy died, I was beside myself with grief. I wouldn't go to work. I barely ate. I just wasn't me anymore. Part of me died with Jimmy. Damien tried his best to make things somewhat normal, but it finally took its toll on him. He was spending more time away from me and the shore and more time in New York. He traveled more. Our relationship began to unravel. Finally, I knew I had to do something, so I quit my job at the restaurant and moved down here to my parents' house on the other end of LBI. I had been going back and forth from here to the city, but when my parents offered to sell me the land next door to my childhood home, I had decided to build a place of my own and open Summertime Sweets. I felt better and for a while, my relationship with Damien seemed to be improving. Then one weekend I had told Damien I'd be going into the city to stay with Blaze. He was away on business and said he'd be back from France on Monday. Blaze's meeting fell through, so we agreed that we would come down here instead and relax before Damien returned. It was late when we drove back from the city on Saturday evening. I had noticed that Damien's car was in the driveway and the first-floor lights were on. We went inside, but there was no one around, yet we heard something upstairs, so I assumed it was Damien. I went upstairs to surprise him, but the surprise was on me."

"Go on, Jade," Blaze coaxed.

I sighed and blurted it out. "I found Damien having sex with Courtney."

"I assume you booted him out on his ass," Tommy snapped, but not at me.

"No, I just stood there… and laughed," I said it and just like back then, a small laugh escaped my lips.

"What?" Tommy said as if he couldn't understand my reaction.

"It was a strange way to behave; I'll give you that. Perhaps the norm would have been to scream and throw things, but it was my house. Why should I have wrecked my place for him? Blaze, on the other hand, lost it. She started to yell at them both. She even went so far as throwing their clothes over the deck onto the sand. It forced them to leave naked. As I think back on it now, that was the best part of the night. Well, that and the fact that Blaze and I dragged the mattress out of the house and burned it on that beach that very evening." Blaze and I both grinned with sheer satisfaction.

"Yeah, that was one hell of a bonfire, sweetie," Blaze added with a satisfied grin.

"After everything, I had been through that year or so before, Damien sleeping with Courtney seemed so…I don't know, laughable. It really did. I lost my brother and now the girl who broke his heart was fucking my fiancé, in my bed of all places."

"Wait, Courtney was Jimmy's girlfriend?" Tommy stopped me.

I nodded. "Yeah. Obviously, she had been sleeping with Damien before my brother had died and before our relationship troubles began."

"Did you speak to either one of them again?" Tommy asked.

"I saw Damien shortly after the incident. He came to pick up his stuff. He said they had started to sleep together after my brother died, but I never totally believed him. I haven't seen Courtney since that evening and hopefully, I won't ever have to see her again."

"So let me get this straight. Even though Damien was a total shit to you, his dad still wants you both to start over again?"

"Yeah. He has always disliked Courtney. I'm not really sure why he has such a disdain for her, but he always has, even before Jimmy died. He had no use for her and he had even tried to keep Jimmy from becoming involved with her."

"I know you don't like her and for good reason, but I wonder why Reece doesn't like her, so much as to tell Jade's brother not to get involved with her?" Tommy questioned Blaze.

"Because Courtney is a know-it-all. She's pushy, and she likes to one-up the people around her every chance she gets. And when she doesn't get her way, she whines. Reece doesn't tolerate women like her very well." Blaze explained.

"So that's why he was so determined to get Damien back with Jade. Some of the things you've said about Courtney are very superficial things for a man like Reece to bother with. Are you sure there isn't anything else going on?"

"Reece loves Jade and has always loved her. He would love for his son to wake up and realize what he's missing. I believe Courtney is just a means to an end for Reece so he can get what he wants. He is not one to lose." Blaze continued.

"It doesn't matter what Damien is missing out on or that Reece doesn't like to lose, Damien and I are done. We've been over for a long time. I'll never go back to that. Frankly, that's why I decided not to get into a serious relationship with anyone anymore."

"Forever?" Tommy seemed stunned and weirdly disappointed.

"Umm…I don't know about forever, but what I do know is life can't always be about forever. It has to be about the here and the now, something I took for granted. I do know I wasted so much time on Damien, time that could have been spent enjoying life. That's what I intend to do, have fun and enjoy what's in front of me, not what's possibly down the road." Just then I looked down at my phone and realized it was almost 8 o'clock; I jumped up to rush out.

"Not so fast, baby. Don't I even get a kiss goodbye? I mean I was your boyfriend last night and you did fall asleep in my arms, *and* I was a perfect gentleman. Don't you think my acts of valor deserve a reward?" Tommy teased as he grinned from ear to ear.

He was too sexy not to take him up on his offer, and I was all about having fun. I wrapped my arms around his shoulders, my fingertips grazed the back of his neck, then I kissed his cheek, letting my lips linger there before I whispered in his ear.

"I can't thank you enough for such a perfect evening. Maybe we can do it again sometime?" My voice was soft and breathy. I wondered if I turned him on like he unknowingly had done to me that night at the club.

When I pulled away his mouth hung open slightly. His stare was blank, and he was speechless.

Yeah, I did...Good.

chapter

Tommy

JADE RAN OFF abruptly, but not before she left me with the most sensual memory of her silky lips on my skin. Last night continued to confirm I wanted to get to know her better. She was outwardly beautiful. No one could deny that. Yet, my desire to spend more time with her came from a more intimate place—an inner beauty that peeked out through her words and mannerisms.

From what Jade had said about her brother, the way she sounded when she spoke of him, told me she and Jimmy had an amazing relationship, prior to the accident. She beamed when she mentioned his name. I truly believed she loved Jimmy more than anyone else in her life, but I had felt that Jade used her love for him as a security blanket of sorts. It was an invisible shield that protected her every day. If she kept things positive, then the hurt and the memory from the loss of her brother wouldn't be able to swallow her up whole and quite possibly destroy her, as well.

Perhaps all of these assumptions about a girl I just met were allowing me to get way ahead of myself where Jade was concerned. The very little I observed, combined with what she explained to me, made me create these illusions, maybe delusions in my head. I needed to stop this and take a step back.

Jade wanted time to stand still, right in this moment…where she could create a safe haven of happiness that didn't include a man. Yet, I wanted time to move forward. Maybe not with the speed of light, but just fast enough to be with someone I could spend the rest of my life with, or at least to start spending the rest of my life with. I had wasted so much time already.

I had to hand it to Jade, though. She kept herself busy by putting all her efforts into her business. Not only was Summertime Sweets successful at its present location from what her Aunt Viv had explained to me, but it was getting a complete makeover in a much larger space just down the street from where her shoppe was now. I needed to put that same attention into this beach house and get my mind off my new neighbor. That would be easier said than done.

Jade had left only a few minutes ago and I wanted to already see her again. Even though last night and this morning, proved to be eye-opening about her past, it really only skimmed the surface. I knew there was more.

Maybe I could pay a neighborly visit to her shoppe later in the day. A bake shoppe would have a huge morning rush, so I believed it wouldn't be a good idea to interrupt her so soon after she had just left my place. Plus, I didn't want to appear too eager and scare her off.

With my mind preoccupied with thoughts of her dancing in my head, I almost forgot I had guests in the kitchen. I walked back to the table to find Blaze and Daniel huddled together in what appeared to be a conspiracy of sorts.

"Cozy…so from the looks of things I'd say you two are up to something." It was a statement, but it was also a question that they needed to answer.

"We're not up to anything. How can you say that? We were just reminiscing about old times. I haven't seen Daniel in years," Blaze answered first and too quickly I might add, which proved she and Daniel were up to no good.

"I can say that because the both of you have the look of guilt on your faces. Now, which one of you is going to tell me what this little meeting of the minds is all about?"

"I guess I'll tell you," Daniel chuckled and looked at Blaze who shrugged and offered no opinion at that point.

"Finally! A voice of reason. Let's have it," I said, as I threw both my hands up in the air in exhilaration for what I was about to hear.

"Don't be angry, but I told Blaze about your plan for moving down here."

"Why the hell did you do that?" I snapped. I was confused why Daniel would reveal my secret to Blaze of all people.

"Hear me out." He firmly stated, gesturing his hand up to quell my current state of anger.

"Go on."

"Listen, I'm your friend, and as such, I feel it's my duty to stop you before you hit that proverbial brick wall."

"For God sake, what are you talking about?" He wasn't making any sense. He knew better than anyone, except for myself, what my plans were when I decided to leave my past life behind, lie to my family and friends and move down here to start over. Now he thought that I had made a mistake? In the beginning, he was all for it. I wondered what had changed his mind.

"When you first told me about your plan to buy the beach house, I absolutely thought it was going to be the best thing for you, but now after seeing you with Jade, I'm not so sure it is."

"Why? What's changed?" I became worried.

"You have." Two words…that was all he had for me?

"That's it? I've changed? How have I changed? I've been down here for what…a week? And you think I've changed? I'm still me. I'm still fixing the house and hopefully in the next six months or so, I'll have someone to share it with."

"That's just it, Tommy…when you started this whole thing and said you were going to buy the house, fix it your way, and find a wife, I was cautiously happy for you. But now that the woman you seem to set your sights on, and so soon, is Jade, I've gotta tell ya, bro, I don't think that's a good idea."

"Don't listen to him, Tommy. He's overthinking it. I, for one, think it's absolutely fantastic that you and Jade have found each other. It may be soon for you, but Jade has closed herself off for far too long. Plus, I know she believes she won't give into Reece's pleas, but I'm not sure about that." Blaze was beyond excited, she was almost exuberant.

"I don't know if you'd call it finding each other. It's only been forty-eight hours since I met Jade, but I also don't get why you're so dead set against it, Daniel. Especially since you were my biggest fan of the idea in the beginning." I addressed both of them, but only Daniel responded.

"I was your only fan in the beginning because you refused to tell anyone else about this. Now don't get me wrong, I still think it's a great idea to change what's not working for you in your life, but I just wish Jade wasn't part of the equation. She's a beautiful person and under normal circumstances, I think that the two of you would be the perfect couple, but you're looking for a family and a future. Yet, from what Jade has only briefly mentioned to me in the past couple of days, she's not, and she's looking for something very different and totally opposite to what you want."

"I heard what she said, Daniel, but that's because Damien hurt her and because Reece is trying to pressure her to go back with his son. Who wouldn't want to run in the opposite direction? Besides, I just want to get to know her better. It's not a marriage proposal or a long-term commitment. I just want to see where this goes. I want to see if the attraction that I have for her is mutual, that's all." I tried to convince Daniel of my intentions where Jade was concerned, but maybe I needed to convince myself of it as well. I did plan on being with the woman of my dreams within six months and Jade had clearly stated she didn't want to be anyone's woman, not now or in six months.

"Can I give you my opinion being Jade's my best friend and all?" Blaze asked.

"Sure."

"She is not as tough as she appears, but she can't let anyone see what both Courtney and Damien did to her was so devastating it nearly wrecked her. She was already fragile when she found them together, but…"

"Because of Jimmy's death?" I cut her off.

"Yes, because of Jimmy's death, but in my opinion, there was an underlying cause. Jimmy would have committed suicide regardless of Courtney. She was the means, the excuse if you will, to his demise, but that wasn't the whole story."

"I'm not sure I understand what you're saying." I was thrown off by Blaze's statement, so she attempted to clear it up for me.

"You had to know Jimmy to know that there was more to Jade's decision about staying single and avoiding a commitment with someone new than just her breakup with Damien. So let me give you some background on him and the entire situation that I believe is guiding Jade now."

I nodded and looked at Daniel. He was quiet but reluctantly nodded in agreement. I needed to listen to Blaze before I could move forward with my desire to get to know Jade more intimately.

"You see, Jimmy was filled with this lust for life for a long time. His energy was always positive. He barely said a negative thing about anyone. Everything he did turned to gold, yet he was never conceited. He had it all. He was good-looking, a natural athlete, and he had an incredible head for business. He was comfortable whether he was on a surfboard or in a boardroom. He could command a room just by his presence. People gravitated to him. They loved when he was around. Jade, on the other hand, was not as aggressive as her brother. She, by all means wasn't meek, but because she at times lived in the shadow of Jimmy's limelight, she tended to be more reserved and took fewer risks."

"That must have been awful for her." It hurt to think that Jade hid in the background of her brother's popularity. That was one thing I never had to deal with when it came to my brother and me. Michael and I always had gotten along, until recently. We were the best of friends most of our adult lives.

Damn, I miss him.

"Please don't misunderstand me. She and Jimmy had a great relationship. He never made her feel like she was second best. Neither did Mr. or Mrs. Stanton. In fact, they were extremely proud of Jade and continue to be very supportive of her success. It was Jade's own insecurities that made her think that she could never measure up to her brother's accomplishments, but it was also those same insecurities that made her start Summertime Sweets."

"Now, you've really lost me. If she was so insecure, then how did she build up such a successful pastry shoppe? I'm not sure how Jade could be so shy, yet so determined, as you say."

"Easy...her feelings of insecurity made her accomplish more. She was determined to be in control of all that she did so nothing would be a surprise to her any longer." The more Blaze revealed about Jade, the more conflicted I became.

"Well, not the best way to live."

"For Jade to move forward, it was the only way. She has always loved Long Beach Island. Unlike the rest of us who have either grown up here and left to work in the big city or like Damien, who only spent summers and holidays here, Jade knows the shore as her home. Even when she worked in New York, she made sure to commute home regularly. She hated being in the city. She did it for Damien, but ask Jade and even she'll tell you that she would rather take the surf over success any day."

"Sounds like my kind of girl," I added, and all of us smiled.

Blaze nodded and continued.

"Like I had said before, Jimmy was an over-achiever, but not the type that had to work hard at it. It came naturally for him. Yet, once he had the surfing accident in California that all changed. He had to answer to others. His time was managed by the people at the Center. Daniel can attest to the fact that you live on a schedule that is customized to your own needs, but you don't have the freedom you would have if you weren't a resident there," She stopped and Daniel continued.

"It's true. When you become a patient at the Center, you need help with your daily rituals. You're monitored constantly. It may seem overwhelming, but that is the job of the medical staff there. You have no choice but to follow their rules."

"Daniel, you seem to have adapted well. You live on your own and teach. It doesn't appear that you're being run by the Center."

"You're right, I'm not. You have to remember I've lived there my entire life. It's what I know, and I have adapted well, but I must agree with Blaze, I don't think Jimmy ever did."

"Before, you hinted at the fact that you believed he would have killed himself regardless of Courtney. Does Jade believe that as well?" I directed my question to Blaze.

"It's hard to say, but I don't think Jade would allow herself to accept the fact that Jimmy would have died that day no matter what."

"Why?"

"Because it's easier to blame Courtney for Jimmy's death than it is to accept the fact that her perfect brother had demons. Believe me, I do think Courtney was partially to blame, but at the end, Jimmy wasn't a fraction of the man he was before the accident. That's why she's built the life she has here on the island."

"She's playing it safe."

Blaze nodded.

"Yeah, well, she has been playing it safe since she and Damien broke it off, but since you've moved in next door, I've seen a side of Jade in the last two days that I hadn't seen in a very long time."

"Which is?" I asked.

"She smiles when she's around you. She was completely spontaneous when she told Reece that you were her boyfriend, and that kiss this morning…Jade would never have done something so playful, so easily with someone she just met." What Blaze now revealed made me feel good to know that Jade was comfortable with me, but what it also revealed was that I had to proceed with caution if I wanted to get to know her better.

Blaze realized she needed to leave and check up on Reece…more like deal with him. As she walked to the door, she stopped short of walking out. Her hand smacked the doorframe and she stalled there for a moment, before turning around to release a confession of sorts.

"Tommy, I hope you and Daniel both understand that I love Jade with everything I hold dear to me. It may have seemed like I just betrayed her confidence, but I'm worried about her and when I see her act the way she has around you in such a short time as I stated before, it gives me hope that the person Jade was before Jimmy's death and before the incident with Damien and Courtney, will come back to us again."

Walking over to Blaze, I wanted to give her a sense of relief that what she told me would stay between the three of us.

"Listen…you don't know me and honestly, you don't owe me an explanation. I could tell from your story of what happened to her that you care very deeply for her and want her to be okay. So, I'm here to tell you that I won't cause any further stress on her. Since we're being honest…I, myself, am drawn to Jade, but I realize we just met and whether it be a friendship or more than that, all of it takes time. I promise you and Daniel, I won't do anything to hurt her. Even if that means backing away and just being the friendly neighbor.”

“Okay…” She stopped and then turned to say one more thing. “Oh, and you're welcome by the way. I’m the one that got the papers processed for you to buy the house.” She laughed revealing her part in this.

“Wait… you were the one?”

She nodded.

“Viv told me it was through a friend she got the sale through without Jade knowing. I just thought it was friends of her parents, but it was you?”

“Guilty…so let's keep this between us because if Jade finds out the truth just yet, we’ll all be out on the street.”

Blaze disappeared out my door. I hated lying to Jade about the house, now knowing Blaze was directly involved in the sale didn’t ease my worry in any way. Yet, I appreciated she took me into her confidence about the house and Jade and gave me her opinions on what affected Jade’s decisions for her future, namely her love life.

Daniel and I talked some more. I hoped I allayed some of his concerns about my interest to pursue Jade. It seemed by the end of the conversation that I had.

At that point, we both agreed that we had stayed in this house for far too long. Daniel and I got our suits on so that we could head over to the end of the island where I could surf, and Daniel could take in the sun to work on his tan.

The conversation decidedly postponed my visit to Jade’s shoppe. I realized after talking with Blaze and Daniel, I needed to not run headfirst into the proverbial brick wall, as Daniel put it. I’d slow down and not appear too pushy, but I had to admit, I was completely drawn to her and I wasn’t sure how long I could keep my promise to steer clear. For now, and for the sake of everyone involved, I knew I had to do my best to strictly remain friends with her and nothing more.

chapter

Tommy

AS PROMISED, I avoided Jade for most of the weekend. Daniel and I went to the surfing beach each day, this morning included. On Saturday and Sunday night, Daniel and I tried two of the restaurants Viv had suggested. They both had great seafood. One had a deck that overlooked the bay, and the other one had a huge patio with a built-in pool on the oceanfront.

The place on the bay was very mellow. The music playing was typical of lounge music and old standards, such as Frank Sinatra and Tony Bennett. I had to admit, Daniel was a complete chick magnet. They were all over him and he loved every minute of it.

"I don't know how you do it," I said on the ride back to the house.

"Do what?" Daniel asked as he seemed intrigued by my statement.

"Attract so many beautiful women in such a short period of time."

"It's the wheelchair," he grinned.

"Stop joking." I smirked, but truthfully Daniel was completely comfortable with who he was and how he dealt with his condition. He never seemed awkward and because of that, people were drawn to him.

"Who's joking? Let's face it, it's a conversation starter."

We both laughed as I drove down the boulevard, heading home for the evening.

Once I helped Daniel up the stairs, he headed inside to his room to change into sweats. He agreed he would meet me on the deck shortly to enjoy a few cold beers.

As I waited for Daniel and enjoyed my first drink, I could hear what sounded like voices coming from the alley between my house and Jade's. The voices faded, so I assumed it could have been the ocean breeze carrying a conversation from one of the other homes nearby.

Within seconds, I was proven wrong, as the voices seemed closer and elevated.

"You just can't leave it alone and respect my wishes, can you?" Jade snapped.

"Jade, I do respect your wishes, but I also know you have your pride…and even if you wanted to try again with my son, that pride would stop you. Look at it this way, I'm giving you a way to get back with Damien and come home, where you belong."

"Reece, what are you talking about? I am home. This is my home and I couldn't be happier." Jade said, irritated, as two sets of footsteps ascended the stairs on her deck. The first pair was her's and the second was that of Reece Montgomery.

"What I mean by that is this…you and I both know you are not in a relationship with that photographer Tommy Conte. It was all a facade to hide the fact that you're bothered by Damien and Courtney being back here on the island while I recuperate."

A loud quick, sharp laugh escaped her lips.

"You are completely delusional. I'm dating Tommy and we are starting a new relationship together whether you like it or not." I had to grin when she said we were dating. Although it was a complete lie, it rolled off Jade's tongue as the truth and it was for a good cause, especially if it kept Reece Montgomery out of Jade's life.

"Well, I don't. He's not good enough for you."

Fumbling with the lock, Jade opened her door and stepped in just far enough to block Reece from going any further.

"How dare you tell me what's good for me and what's not. How would you know anyway? Your son was supposed to be good enough for me and we see how he turned out."

"Jade, he made a terrible mistake."

"No, Reece…he made a permanent one. Now, if you'll excuse me, I'm done listening to your bullshit."

"Please listen to reason."

"I won't listen to anything else you have to say on this subject. And why did you come here anyway? Blaze headed back to the city to meet with clients. There's no reason for you to be on my doorstep. Now go!" Jade bellowed, but Reece stood his ground.

That guy was a real prick. My decision to sit here and stay out of it ended. I couldn't let him malign Jade, or me, for that matter. I left my beer on the table, headed down my stairs, and up Jade's. As I came around the corner to the front deck where both she and Reece were standing, their heads were already turned in my direction from the sound of my footsteps.

Without thinking, I pushed between Reece and Jade, placing my hand on the side of her face and drawing her lips to mine. Insult and anger that Reece incited drove my actions. Thinking clearly wasn't part of the equation.

Fuck him! I am good enough for Jade.

"Hey, baby, how was your day?" I asked, as I broke our kiss with a closed-lipped smile and a wink, which was unobserved by Reece.

She surprised me completely with an almost identical gesture. Touching my face, her eyes went from my focus to my lips, as she slowly leaned forward to reciprocate my kiss to her. Her plump mouth pressed gently to mine, pausing there briefly before speaking. She pulled back, but not too far. She mouthed the words 'thank you' as not to let Reece hear her, but then she spoke up loud and clear. "It's much better now that you're here." She disclosed as she stepped back outside and into my arms and we turned in unison to face Reece.

"I guess this conversation is over, isn't it Reece?" Jade waited for a response from her unwelcome guest.

"For now, yes, we're done here." Reece turned to walk away but turned back to add one more thing.

"I almost forgot. I did want to extend an invite to you and Mr. Conte."

"An invite for what, Reece?" Jade's patience was all but diminished.

"I'm having a celebration of sorts. Let's call it my new lease on life party."

"You have to be joking?" Jade moved forward with crossed arms.

"No…no joke, my dear," Reece said dramatically and with solid grace, he walked around the deck as if it was an imaginary stage, performing his solo act, confessing he now realized how precious life was and he wanted to share his newfound happiness with Blaze and his new lease on life with the ones he loved.

I chuckled in disgust, amused by this man's gall. Jade slowly shook her head, not believing what she was hearing. She clapped her hands at his one-time performance.

"Give me a break, but I will hand it to you, your acting abilities never cease to amaze me, and it sure does come in handy for crap like this, huh?"

Swiftly, Reece turned back to explain.

"I'm not acting. It's all sincere and true. After my almost near-death experience, I've concluded that I've been taking life for granted and decided to throw a party here at my home to celebrate my renewed health and my new relationship with Blaze."

I stood silently as Jade stepped forward onto the deck to confront Reece. Her facial expression said it all. It appeared as though she smelled something so horrible she was about to vomit. The truth was, she smelled bullshit in the air.

"Who the hell are you kidding?" Jade quipped as she laughed in Reece's face.

"Excuse me?" Insulted and taken off guard, Reece walked toward her, but not fast enough.

I swiftly moved in front of her, stretching my hand out against his chest.

"How dare you put your hand on me? I'm Jade's family. Something you will never be, as long as I'm around."

"You listen to me, you self-entitled son of a bitch. You may have been close to becoming Jade's father-in-law, but your son's indiscretions changed all that. As far as being Jade's family, you're right I'm not, not yet anyway, but like hell I'm going to stand here and let you manipulate her any further. Your guilt trip is finished. Now, you can either leave here under your own volition, or you can leave here under mine. The choice is yours." I finished, with a quick push back against the chest of a man I clearly had no respect or use for.

Reece straightened his suit jacket before he addressed Jade, who had stood silently through the entire confrontation. I couldn't tell if that was a good thing or a bad one, but I knew one thing for certain…once Reece left, I was sure Jade would tell me how she felt about my interference in her personal life without her permission.

"Jade, I apologize. You know I always want what's in your best interest. With your father away, and Jimmy…"

Jade stepped closer. Her blank red face now in Reece's personal space…a lethal frustration emanating from her body.

"Don't…don't you dare use Jimmy as an excuse for your behavior," she said in a low, hard-edged tone.

"I didn't mean anything…" Again, Jade stopped him.

"No, Reece, you never mean anything by what you say or do. No, you're always the good guy in any given situation. The trouble is, I know better. Your words are an invisible veil of bullshit. I've always been grateful to you for giving me the opportunity to learn my craft. I cared about you and your son, but my love ended for him when he chose to fuck someone else in the bed we shared together, and my love for you ends now that you chose to steal my brother's memory in an attempt to bring me to your side, and because you chose to insult Tommy."

As Jade's words ended, an unusual silence drowned out the surf crashing on the shoreline. She walked to the edge of her deck, hypnotized by those very same waves, gripping her hands on the railing, she squeezed the wood like a vice. Maybe it was to prevent her from saying more? Or maybe it was the only solid object that was physically and emotionally holding her up at that moment. She continued to look away. Her long dark strands billowing slightly in the evening breeze, masking her face and her emotions.

"Please leave. I can't stand the sight of you anymore tonight." She didn't turn back. She just kept standing there.

Reece did the right thing this time and left without another word to either of us.

Minutes seemed like a lifetime before she turned to face me.

"I'm sorry, Tommy. I'm so sorry." Tears filled her eyes, as Jade lowered herself down on the deck, her back supported by one of the posts behind her. Her head was down in defeated exhaustion.

I walked over and stood in front of her in the hopes that she would look up at me.

She didn't.

I wasn't sure what to do, because I wasn't sure what had actually transpired between Jade and Reece prior to the confrontation here this evening. Although what happened just now was enough to tire anyone.

Several minutes passed, or at least it seemed like they had, when I determined Jade was more than likely too embarrassed to look at me. So I did the only thing I could do. I knelt down in front of her and found her eyes.

"Jade, please look at me. Let me know you're going to be okay." I took my thumb and my index finger, and lightly pinching Jade's chin, I tilted her head up, so I could see her beautiful face. A face that was now smeared with black makeup and tears, while her lips delicately quivered.

"I'm fine." Her voice gutted me. She squeaked, as she spoke.

Touching her… she stilled and didn't push me away. I knew there was something building between us…I felt it. Then, as quickly as it came, it faded…like the sunset.

"Tommy, I can't."

"Jade, you're not giving this…us, a *real* chance."

"What's the point? Anytime something good happens, it always ends in heartbreak."

"Baby, anything that's good enough to break your heart, is worth taking a chance on."

I waited for her to speak, but her words never came—yet, more tears did.

"Come here," I said and wrapped my arms around her.

Jade relaxed her body forward and fell completely into my embrace. I could feel her tremble as she placed her arms firmly around my shoulders and buried her head in my chest. I tried to soothe her as she tried desperately to silently hold back her cries.

"Hey, c'mon now. I'm here. That asshole can't hurt you anymore."

"It's not that." She sounded frustrated.

"Then what is it?"

"I'm just no good at this, this pretending. I don't like lying to anyone. I particularly don't like the fact that I've used you and pulled you into something that wasn't your problem. Not to mention, we just met."

I couldn't believe my ears.

She wasn't concerned about Reece and what just happened at her home. She was worried she didn't know how to be good at pretending we had a relationship. She couldn't be serious? Wasn't I clear in what I just said? I didn't want to pretend with her. I wanted to take a chance, but she wasn't ready, and the situation, as it were, had her even more conflicted. I needed to change that and lighten the mood.

"Is that why you're crying?" I lightly chuckled.

"Stop laughing at me. Of course, that's why I'm crying." She let out a small whiny snicker, so I knew she was okay and we were good.

"I'm not laughing at you. I swear." I leaned back and put my hands up to show my defeat.

"I know it doesn't seem like a big deal to you. I'm pretty sure you've never had to deal with a Reece Montgomery in your life." What she said wasn't entirely the case.

I had to deal with Rain's husband on more than one occasion. Dominick Kane, Daniel's brother, was just as bad as Reece Montgomery when it came to getting what he wanted.

"You'd be surprised." That was all I said in hopes that Jade would be curious and perhaps continue this conversation over dinner with me tomorrow night.

"I don't believe you. You're just saying that because you're a nice guy and you feel sorry for me." She was cute when she argued. Tilting her head to one side, she examined my expression.

"Oh, baby, trust me, you may think you have me all figured out, but what you're thinking couldn't be further from the truth. Although you're right that I am a nice guy."

Her smile came through.

"Let me prove it to you," I challenged her.

She took both her hands and covered her face. Then she wiped her tears to the side, as she let out a long and cleansing exhale.

"Okay, go ahead, enlighten me." She voiced, with a bit more confidence.

"No."

"No?" She questioned.

"Not now but over dinner tomorrow night. What do you say?" I waited for her response and hoped it would be a yes.

"Why do I have the feeling you're stalling?" She said, but still had a smile on her face, so I was pretty sure her answer was a yes.

"Probably because I am." I wasn't holding out on her to come up with a good story. I just wanted more time with Jade. I was breaking my promise. Tonight, proved to me, I wanted her. I couldn't back away, but I was a patient man and would move at a pace her heart could handle if that's what she needed, and it appeared by all accounts, she did.

"Ah-ha! I knew it," She said, as she acted as if she has discovered something spectacular.

"Ah-ha! Nothing. I don't think right here, right now is a good place to talk about me and my personal life," I explained.

Her voice became soft and serious as she shook her head and looked around at how her world was right now.

"I guess you're right."

"So is that a yes?"

"Yeah, it's a yes, but let me cook. My brother's old kitchen hasn't seen a decent meal in years." Jade suggested and wasn't wrong.

The kitchen at the beach house was in need of a serious facelift. I guess I should tackle the new appliances before I offered to cook anyone a meal in there, especially Jade.

"How about I cook here at your place and you make dessert?" I countered her offer.

"Sure, but you do know how to cook, don't you?" Jade seemed unsure of my culinary skills.

"I know how to boil water," I admitted but was only half joking at the same time. I could throw a frozen pizza in the oven as good as the next person.

"That's what I thought. I've changed my mind."

"What?"

"I'll have dinner with you, but on one condition."

"Okay, state your demands."

"That I cook and bring a dessert from the shoppe, and you bring the wine."

"Deal, and because you're cooking for me, I'll clean up." I put out my hand so we could shake on it.

"Even better deal." She took my hand and we agreed for me to be back here around 7 tomorrow night.

As she went to pull her hand back, I held it more firmly in mine and pulled Jade up off the floor of the deck, so we were facing each other. She looked down and then back at me inquisitively.

"I just want to make sure you're okay now." My hand cradled her cheek.

"I'm fine. Thank you, Tommy," she said and placed a quick peck on my cheek.

I got ready to leave, but turned back to look at her one more time. I placed my hand around her upper arm, as my mouth found hers. Her lips were soft and receptive, but before I let things go too far, I broke our connection and walked to the stairs.

"We'll talk more tomorrow."

She nodded, her smile bashful, as her fingertips partially covered her lips.

I wasn't sure if that was a good or bad thing. I guess tomorrow would reveal more for each of us.

chapter *fourteen*

Jade

DISTRACTED, MY FINGERS trembled as they traced the remnants of Tommy's goodnight kiss over my lips. I wondered if he noticed the sexual charge between us or how he truly felt about it. Without warning, that similar energy manifested itself every time we were together. Yet, I was determined not to think about it.

I could have easily fallen for his genuinely sweet personality. The kissing on the cheek and whispering in his ear to do more than just appease his questions, were far too playful and inappropriate for someone I just met *and* needed to stop, because of the promise to myself—a promise I intended to keep. I was sure once we had dinner, I'd convince him being friends was best for both of us.

He's going to hate me. Who am I kidding? I'd hate me too.

Frustrated, I dragged myself upstairs to wash my makeup riddled face and turn in for the evening. The cool water soothed my tired tear-stained eyes. Grabbing a towel to pat my face dry, I looked at myself in the mirror. I realized how stupid I had acted this evening, as second thoughts of Tommy crept back into my mind.

Again, I lied and allowed Tommy to come to my rescue with Reece. I was too afraid to tell Reece the truth; I hated it. Tommy was kind enough be my knight in shining armor because the evil king wouldn't lay off when it came to his son Damien, no prince in my book. I should have told Reece from the beginning I wanted to avoid any serious relationships in my life. I wasn't going to date. I wanted to see where the future took me, but Reece knew as well as I did, my idea to love em' and leave em' without the structure of a relationship was a good concept, but one I couldn't go through with.

A jackhammer pounded inside my skull and violently hummed inside of me, while my body hurt to move. Running the water in the tub, I decided a long bath before bed was what my body and mind needed to wash away the humiliating events of the day. In the bath, my muscles slowly relaxed, as my body steeped in the warm water. I ran the sponge across my bare skin and let it settle between my legs. My thoughts drifted back to the one man I tried to put out of my mind…Tommy. I could hear his voice, feel his body, and I remembered the way he smelled and how he looked in his sweats when he came to check on me earlier.

The memory of him made me lightly rub my clit with the outer edge of the bath sponge. My head dropped back as the delicious feeling of my arousal began to build. My hips curled forward, the sponge circled my core. With my other hand, I firmly grasped my left nipple, moaning at the pleasure I gave to myself from the combination of the gentle wisps of the sponge on my hardened nub to the intense movement of my fingers caressing my breast. I knew I needed to come and wanted Tommy to be my fantasy that brought me there.

My thoughts of him intensified…his strong jawline, dark eyes, carefree dark hair, oh and his lips…his soft lips against my skin when he called me baby. The memory of his voice made me abandon the sponge for my fingers. Touching myself between my legs proved even the water couldn't wash away how slick my pussy had become at the idea of him inside of me.

Vivid thoughts of Tommy's body blanketing mine, his mouth taking my lips, my neck, my breasts…licking my swollen nipples, taking each of them fully…taking me fully, his hands affected every inch of me as he slowly pushed himself inside me, his tone commanding me to let go, to fall further and further in this imaginary world. A place I didn't want to leave, where my desire for Tommy could be fulfilled…realized through my overactive imagination.

I slipped further down into the warm fragrant bath to surrender in the sexual thoughts of my new neighbor, thoughts which took over my body completely…where I couldn't decipher between what was real and what was fantasy. I wanted to come, but I had to admit I didn't want the intensity of this self-gratifying, secret moment, nor my longing for Tommy to end just yet. *Shit!* I couldn't believe how much I needed this or wanted him. Every girl was entitled to some sexy make-believe me-time now and then… besides, he'd never find out.

As the sensual assault on my breast was reduced to a delicate yet playful massage, the illicit attention I gave to my sex increased with each press of my fingertips. My heartbeat pounded, my breaths…shallow, almost non-existent. The throbbing between my legs grew more evident as my strokes became more deliberate. My entire body shook with this salacious feeling as my arousal peaked, I found my release through a strained declaration of Tommy's name.

I continued, but with apprehension coaxed myself back to the present. Slowly, my breathing returned to normal, my heartbeat softened, and the constant ache that had once existed between my legs quelled and was replaced with total satisfaction. I stayed in the tub for a short time before the water cooled enough to provide me with the hint I needed to turn in for the night.

I finally climbed into my bed exhausted, but completely sated. My body was heavy, as were my eyes. I didn't fight it, because I knew the sooner I slept, the sooner tomorrow would come, and that meant the sooner I would share an evening with the man that I had just secretly fantasized about.

I would hold on to this feeling through my dreams until tomorrow came, but in reality, the attraction for Tommy couldn't move beyond the confines of these walls. My secret allurement of my new neighbor would remain just that…my little secret.

The sun rose over the eastern side of the island like it did every day. I felt the warm glow on my cheeks as I woke from a completely restful night's sleep. I was snug and contented. I stayed in bed for a while longer before I started my day.

Tuesday was my usual day off. I followed my normal routine of having my morning coffee out on the deck off my bedroom. While still in my nightshirt, I placed my mug on the table in between the two chaises. As I stretched out on the oversized lounge to enjoy this beautiful summer morning, my thoughts drifted back to last night. I squirmed as I remembered how turned on I was, and how exactly I worked off all of that built up sexual tension.

When I looked down from my chair, through the railing, I caught a glimpse of Tommy and Daniel on the oceanfront deck of my family's old house. He still had on the sweats I saw him in last night, but now he was shirtless. I became wet almost immediately with the familiar pulse between my legs again.

What the hell was he doing to me? And how do I make it stop!

Feelings of apprehension and second thoughts ran through my head. I couldn't do this. I couldn't explain my reactions, but I also couldn't keep leading him on, or myself for that matter. I told myself after Jimmy died, loving someone so deeply would only end in disaster. I was proven right when Damien broke our relationship in two and slept with Courtney. I decided back then I would not put myself or anyone else through the hurt I lived with every single day. I could deal with being alone, but I couldn't lead someone as nice as Tommy on and hurt him because I wasn't ready to love again.

Face it, Jade, you'll never be ready.

Between my frustrated thoughts and my frustrated body, lying there any longer was futile, so I jumped up and changed into my wetsuit, headed down the stairs, grabbed my board, and drove out to the end of the island to catch some waves before the rest of the beachgoers hit the sand.

When I pulled up and walked to the edge of the lot and onto the sand, the beach was practically empty. Other than myself, there was a man walking his two dogs along the surf. The waves were strong and the water choppy. The weatherman had forecasted rain for later tonight, so the turbulence made perfect sense with an impending summer storm on its way.

I pulled my board out from the back of my car and headed for the shoreline. When waxing it was completed, I began my stretching ritual, as not to injure myself. I secured the leash to my right leg and headed out into the water. I paddled well beyond the breaks in the waves and finally reached my desired position. I waited and waited and waited until I caught my perfect one. I began to paddle, and at the precise moment, popped-up to ride it in.

Although I was far from a beginner, I continued to stay with my beloved longboard. After I took a few waves, I headed back to the sand and stretched out on the beach for a bit. At my towel, I removed the leash from leg and laid the board down on the sand next to me. Reclining back, I took in the warmth of the day.

I must have been more tired than I thought, or perhaps this morning's surf run put my body over the edge, because when I woke up, the beach had become crowded. Looking at my phone showed it was noon already. I needed to get back home for a shower and to address so many things before dinner.

The market was somewhat crowded, as I picked up the food for this evening's meal. I didn't have any fresh treats in the house, so I decided to swing by my shoppe on the way back to retrieve something sweet and chocolaty. It was more for me than for Tommy. Although it did appear he liked chocolate as well, when I surprised him with the covered strawberries the other night.

I returned home by four in the afternoon. I cleaned the house and showered again before I dressed for the evening. I called Blaze to see if she was coming down from the city this weekend, but her phone went directly to voicemail, so I left her a message to give me a call when she came in.

Looking at my recent calls, I don't know how I missed it, but there was a voicemail from Daniel, which stated Tommy took him back to the center this morning and he was sorry he didn't get to see me before he left, but he would be back for the 4th of July holiday and that he would see me then. I made a mental note to call him sometime tomorrow. I didn't want to wait until the Fourth before we spoke again. Now that Daniel and I reconnected, I didn't want to lose our friendship, as we had before.

Next on the call chain to-do list was Aunt Viv but she wasn't home either. She had been out a great deal lately. Oh well, she must have been working with her garden club or at the animal shelter in town or one of her other pet projects that she tended to join when the springtime began.

It was getting late, so I prepared dinner and put it in the oven before I went upstairs to my closet to decide on what to wear. We were having a relaxed evening at my home so something comfortable would suffice. I chose a pair of white jeans, a red low cut, v-neck tee and a pair of white thong Ralph Lauren sandals.

Slate grey clouds began to roll in, confirming an impending storm. I finished setting the table in the dining room near the sliders off the first-floor deck, making it easier to be close to the kitchen while the food cooked, and without fear of becoming saturated from the rain if we ate outside. I put a CD in the player, filling the house with the soft sounds of some jazz music. A few candles on the table in the living room needed to be lit, but not too many. I wanted the atmosphere to reflect a relaxed and casual mood, not a romantic one.

Tonight, I resolved myself to the fact I needed to ignore the undeniable attraction I had for him because last night clearly proved I wasn't ready to be with anyone. My emotions were raw and all over the place. It was my hope Tommy would get used the idea of us being friends and just friends…loud and clear; and this dinner tonight would set straight some of the ridiculous things I involved him in since we first met.

The DVD player displayed 6:45. He'd be here soon. Out of nowhere, I became nervous at the thought of him spending the evening with me tonight.

Jade, you were the one who accepted his invitation. No turning back now. You have to go through with it. It's not a date or anything. He said so, himself.

I shook off my unwanted and unwarranted nerves. It was dinner, that's all. It wasn't like he would be staying the night. Just as I was about to continue to overanalyze it, there was a knock at my door. I looked up to find Tommy there with his arms full. I smiled and hurried to let him in.

"Thanks. It looks like the rain is going to start at any moment," he said, as he walked in.

"They said storms for tonight. Can I take any of that from you?" I asked because he hadn't attempted to hand me what was in his arms or place anything down on the table in front of him.

"Yeah, sorry… these are for you." Tommy handed me a beautiful bouquet of sunflowers. Then he showed me the two bottles of wine he brought to dinner. One was the Champagne we had the other night and the other was a Pinot Noir from Italy.

"Hmm…Pinot Noir, it'll be perfect with the Beef and Mushroom Risotto I have in the oven." I took the bottles, opened both, and poured the Champagne, which had been previously chilled. The Noir I left on the counter to breathe before dinner. I found a vase that would be a good size to accommodate the sunflowers.

"Dinner sounds and smells delicious," he remarked, as he took his glass, looked around, and took a seat on the couch. He was comfortable, not the type of man who needed to stand up and command a room, but one who was at ease with himself. One who, unconsciously, was in command.

"Thank you for the flowers. They're my favorite," I said, as I put the vase with the sunflowers on my coffee table.

"I know. I called Viv to ask her what you liked." He grinned with an audacious sense of pride in his voice.

I'm smiled at him. "I'll need to have a talk with my aunt about revealing my secrets," I joked, but was kind of honored he went out of his way to find out what I loved.

The timer buzzed on the oven. Excusing myself to set up for dinner, I was about to bring the hot serving dish out to the dining table when the house reverberated from a powerful electrical boom sounding outside. Along with that sound came the roar of the thunder, the violence of the rain, as the loss of electrical power ceased, and the room went dark.

"Great…that's just great," I said and gazed up at the ceiling as if I would find the answers to my power issues floating somewhere above my head.

Tommy looked out the window to check on the storm. His silhouette was illuminated by the light of the candles nearby. His physique, accented by the tight-knit t-shirt he wore tonight, was incredible.

"Boy, it's coming down out there. Don't worry, I'm sure it will let up soon. These types of storms usually pass quickly."

"I'm not worried. I just don't think dinner will work out quite as well in the dark."

"Would you like to have a raincheck? We can do this another time." He misunderstood. I didn't want him to go, so I had to think fast.

"No, I'd like you to stay. We can eat in the living room around the coffee table. I think it will be easier than trying to maneuver with no light in the dining room."

He walked closer to me. "I'm glad you want me to stay," he said, as his fingertips lightly grazed my cheek.

Goosebumps covered my skin from his touch.

Maybe it wasn't a good idea to have dinner with him, after all.

He turned around to survey the room, clapped his hands once, and rubbed them together as if we needed to get down to business. "Do you have any flashlights?"

"Oh yeah, I almost forgot. I have two under the kitchen sink. Let me get them."

I fumbled a bit in the dark but eventually retrieved the flashlights. Yet, when I returned, Tommy had already lit additional candles in the living room. My house glowed with hues of gold, white, and cream.

I handed Tommy a flashlight, but the living room was now bright enough, so we didn't need them.

He placed his on the coffee table. He was quiet, but then reached out for me to take his hand. "Come and have a drink with me before dinner."

I placed my hand in his, as he pulled me to the couch. We raised our glasses and toasted to an enjoyable evening with great company.

We both took a sip. It was cool and delicious, as bubbles lightly tickled my face. Up until now, we made some small talk, which worried me. Even though we had just met, there never seemed to be a problem when it came to a conversation with him. Tommy's awkwardness was explained once we were comfortable and he asked the burning question that must have weighed heavily on his mind. He put down his glass and took my hand again. This time he entwined his fingers with mine and gave them a supportive squeeze. He stared at them for a minute before looking up at me.

"Were you okay today?" He spoke softly and with a great deal of concern.

"Oh, is that what this is all about?" I deduced.

"I'm not sure I understand?" He appeared confused by my question.

"Well, you haven't said very much since you walked in, but I get it now."

"You didn't answer my question." He voice was sexy and attentive.

"I told you last night I was fine. Slightly humiliated, but no worse for wear," I admitted, as I looked down at our hands.

Tommy jiggled them briefly so he could get my attention.

"You have no reason to feel humiliation. You didn't do anything wrong."

"I allowed Reece to get to me, and I lied about us…again."

"So?" He said bluntly.

"So, I guess he felt it was his job to insult you last night. Tommy, if it wasn't for me pulling you into this nightmare, you wouldn't be dealing with Reece on a day to day basis," I explained.

"I'm a big boy, trust me. I told you before I've dealt with a few Reece Montgomery types over the years."

I nodded.

"Hey, I mean it. Reece Montgomery is not worth my time."

"Yes, but he asked me if he could walk me to my door after we had an uneventful and almost normal dinner. Maybe I should have known he was up to his old tricks when dinner was too good to be true."

"So?"

"So…" I stopped there and stared at Tommy. I didn't want to talk about Reece Montgomery or Damien anymore this evening.

"C'mon Jade, you can't believe because you agreed to let him walk you to your door, it was okay for him to think he could manipulate you?" He asked as if my view of last night's situation was ridiculous.

"No. But I haven't dated anyone since Damien, and I'm starting to think this is all my fault. If I had kept my mouth shut, he wouldn't be trying to trip us up at every turn when he sees us together."

"It doesn't matter. Reece will keep trying to get you and his son back together, regardless of *us*. Like I said, I know his type. He doesn't have boundaries." Tommy's voice became strained, as his hand tightened further around my fingers to the point I could physically feel his anger.

"I guess then I should be grateful you were home to rescue me, again." I smiled, and his grip loosened.

"From the look of things on my end, you didn't need much rescuing. You handled him pretty well, and appropriately I might add."

"I've had a great deal of practice where Reece is concerned. I was pretty good, wasn't I?" I teased.

"Yeah, you were pretty good." He warmly agreed and looked at me with a new intensity I hadn't seen from him before. I didn't know what to make of it or how to handle it, so I changed the subject quickly.

"Are you hungry?" I asked quickly.

He grinned because he knew what I was doing. Yet, he didn't let on.

"Starving."

"Okay. I'll get the food. You get the plates. I set the table in the dining area. You can just grab them from there, and we can set it up over here." I pointed to the large wooden coffee table in the living room.

My living space on the first level of my house had an open floor plan, similar to Tommy's, except my living room and dining room were in one large great room up front, and my spare bedroom was toward the back of the house or should I say the front, near the main door and the foyer I rarely used, on the street side, away from the ocean. To most people that *would* be the front of the house, but to me the front was the beach, where my living area was.

Tommy's place, on the other hand, had a more narrow layout for the living room, dining room, and kitchen. The living space was open, but parallel to those rooms was a huge master bedroom that ran the opposite length of the house, divided by a main wall. It wasn't always that way, but my parents had changed it when Jimmy and I were growing up so they could have a bedroom suite on the main floor. While Jimmy had the original master bedroom on the second floor, I occupied the smaller room adjacent to his.

I brought the dish to the table where Tommy had set out our plates and wine glasses. I placed the dish down and went back to retrieve the Pinot Noir I had opened earlier. Tommy placed some of the large throw pillows he took from the couch onto the floor around the coffee table so we could eat comfortably. He also brought some of the candles from my sideboard by the dining room window over to the table, giving us some extra light while we ate.

Tommy filled our glasses and proposed a toast.

"To lasting friendships" I mimicked his sentiment.

"This looks delicious." He said, viewing his dish.

"Hold off on your judgment until you actually taste it."

"Don't be so negative."

"Oh, I'm not. I must warn you, I'm not the greatest cook."

"Huh? How can you say that? You're a chef." He appeared perplexed.

I laughed at his confusion.

"I'm a pastry chef, big difference. Some people are amazing chefs when it comes to savory foods, and some chefs have the art for sweets. Sweets are my specialty, savory not so much." I explained.

"So… if I recall, you had my culinary skills in question last night, and that's why we agreed you would cook for me tonight. Now you're telling me this food may be inedible?" He looked down at the plate before him in disappointed awe.

I smirked playfully at him.

"No, I'm just saying if you were expecting culinary genius, think again."

With that, Tommy took a large spoonful of the risotto to give me his honest opinion. He was savoring every bite, but he gave nothing away. I couldn't tell if he liked it or not.

"Well?" I coaxed.

He wiped his mouth and placed his napkin next to his plate.

"Well, what?" He continued to be vague.

"Stop joking. How is it?" I pressed him for an answer.

"Oh, you want to know how the risotto is?"

"Grrr… yes! I do. Do you like it or not?"

"Not," he said.

"Oh no, it's that bad isn't?" With a grimace, I felt defeated. Give me an order for Creme Brûlée and I'd nail it, but give me a simple dinner and it's usually burnt or raw. Yet, I was surprised about the risotto. I thought after all these years of practice I finally perfected it.

He laughed out loud.

"What's so funny?"

"You."

"Me?" I was confused.

"You can't tell I'm joking with you. It's amazing, Jade."

"Amazing, really?"

"Yeah, amazing, just like you." His expression changed into something I hadn't seen on Tommy's face before. It was dark and intense…not scary. It was hot and sensual.

I squirmed in my seat at the thought of Tommy and that statement, but I prayed with our close proximity he hadn't noticed. I looked down. I didn't know how to respond. I couldn't believe how self-conscious I felt around him. It wasn't something he did; it was me. I never had this problem around Damien. Or maybe I reacted differently back then, when Damien's opinion of me didn't matter as much as I once thought.

"Hey, don't look down. I'm sorry if I embarrassed you." He lifted my chin and stroked my jawline, making certain I heard what he said.

I surprised myself when I placed my hand on his.

"No, it's not that."

"Then what is it, Jade?"

"It's not easy for me to take a compliment. I never know how to act," I admitted. "Although my desserts are complimented on a regular basis at the shoppe. The personal compliments feel unnatural to me."

"Unnatural? How can someone as beautiful as you not be used to men complimenting them all the time?" He was taken back by the fact I wasn't used to being the center of attention by any man.

I wanted to change the subject, yet I knew this could be the perfect time to set the record straight, and if he wanted to get to know me *more,* friendship and being neighbors was our only option.

Removing my hand and placing it on the table, he followed my action but gave no reaction when he looked to me for an explanation. Swallowing hard, I began what I thought would be a convincing declaration of why we should only be friends.

"Maybe unnatural is not a good definition? Maybe the word I'm looking for is insincere?"

"I think I liked unnatural better," he teased, trying to break the tension that I caused.

"What I mean by that…and this is not directed at you in any way…" I clarified.

"Duly noted."

"After Damien and I broke up, I had plenty of time to think and I realized, even when we weren't getting along, or I should say we weren't being intimate, he would still compliment me and put on a show. You know, act like everything was good in public, but what came out of his mouth was forced. I hadn't noticed it at the time."

"That's because you were dealing with something so devastating...real life."

"Perhaps, but like I said, I've had time to get over it and I'm happy where I ended up." Hopefully, Tommy would take the bait.

"Where is that?" He questioned.

Good...now for the hook, "Here on the island, building up my business and not having to answer to anyone but myself."

"And to the occasionally nosy ex-father-in-law to-be." Tommy justifiably smirked.

"I'll give you that. Reece is nosy and stubborn and adamant and controlling, but unfortunately for him and fortunately for me, he will never get his way."

"Are you sure?"

"Yeah, positive, because I know I can never be with Damien again. Besides, I don't want to be with anyone else either."

More bait...

"Why is that?"

Letting out of the breath I was holding, I explained.

"Because as heartbroken as I was to see our relationship crumble, I was far more broken without Jimmy."

The elephant in the room was the silence that loomed between Tommy and me, brought on by the mention of my dead brother. Tommy studied his glass of wine, took a drink to ease the gravity of the situation, and then sat back and studied me.

"So what you're telling me is that your brother's death has changed how you feel about being in a relationship...about falling in love?"

"Yes, Jimmy's death and Courtney and Damien's betrayal have changed the way I feel about being in love. I don't want it. I don't want to think about it. I just want to have fun. No ties, no commitments." As the words left my lips, it was as if I didn't even know who the girl was making that statement anymore.

I knew it's what I said I wanted, but as I tried to justify my reasoning to Tommy it sounded more and more wrong, and it certainly didn't sound like me. Nevertheless, I put it out there, and there it would remain. I couldn't change my mind now.

"Can I ask you something?"

Not the reaction I expected.

"What's your plan?"

"Plan? I don't have any plan."

Where was he going with this?

"Well, you said yourself that Reece is nosy and if you don't want to be in a relationship with someone else, then how are you going to keep him from continually badgering you about his son? It's not like you can avoid him."

"Why not?"

"For one, he's staying on the island and two, he's dating your best friend. You're bound to run into each other. Besides, wasn't it you who had dinner with him yesterday?"

"You're right, but our dinner was more about Blaze than Damien. That is until we'd gotten home last night. Yet, it's true, I haven't really thought that far ahead. Reece has been on me about Damien ever since we broke up, but much of the time he was in Europe or in the city. I'll have to see how it plays out. I can't be concerned about Reece Montgomery. I'm far too busy with my business to worry about him."

"Yet, you were very concerned the night of your Aunt Viv's dinner. Enough so, that you professed you were in a relationship with me." Feelings of hurt emanated from Tommy's statement. I couldn't blame him. Everything I did up until now in relation to Tommy and Reece was to protect myself. How could I be so selfish?

Jade, you're a rotten person.

Embarrassed by my actions from the time Tommy and I officially met, I stared at my food as I tried to come up with the words to mend fences with him.

"Tommy, I'm sorry. And I know all I've done is apologize since we've met, but I *am* truly sorry. The next time I speak with Reece, I'll tell him the truth. I expected the truth from his son and yet all I've done is use you to avoid dealing with Reece's wish to get Damien and me back together. I hope you can forgive me and we can start over, as friends." I was leery of his response, but when I looked up and saw Tommy's expression, relief blanketed me.

He laughed. "That was the nicest brush off a guy could ask for."

"Oh no, it wasn't meant to sound like a brush off. Now I feel worse."

He laughed some more.

"Listen, since we're being honest, I'll admit that I would have liked to get to know you better…and by that I mean more than just friends, but I can see you're not ready to do that with me or anyone else, so why don't we settle for building a new friendship and becoming better aquatinted as new neighbors? Okay?"

"I'd like that."

"Me too, Jade." Tommy left the awkwardness of the conversation there, and we continued our dinner.

Once *he* cleaned up as promised, I brought out the dessert…chocolate cheesecake in a cup.

"This looks delicious," he remarked, as he raised his cup above his head to examine the contents and then to toast the end of our interesting evening together.

"Here's to…" he started.

"To new friends and new summertime memories…" I finished.

He smiled and nodded and started to eat.

Sound…other than the clinking of our spoons scooping out our nighttime treat from the dessert cups…sound was nonexistent. The music had long since ceased, and Tommy hadn't uttered a comment. I couldn't just sit there and eat, so now it was my turn to get to know him better.

"Can I ask you something?"

"Sure."

"What made LBI your destination of choice for your new beach house? I know from what little you've told me, you've lived and surfed in some of the most exotic locations around the world. Why settle down here at the Jersey Shore?"

Looking into his cup, at the last remnants of his dessert, he carefully placed his spoon in the cup, sat back against the couch, ran his fingers through his dark locks, and turned toward me with his answer.

"I've always loved this place, and to be honest, all the traveling I've done in the past, whether it be for business or pleasure, never ended quite like I had imagined."

"How's that?"

"I don't know, Jade. I guess I thought my lifestyle would have found me someone special to spend the rest of my life with. Yet, all it's done for the past year or so is show me how far away I've gotten from what I wanted for my future."

"Which is? No…wait you don't have to answer that. Here I am going on and on about me, and then prying into your personal business, how rude."

"Not at all. Actually, I don't mind discussing it with you. Up until now, only Daniel knew of my plans. It would be kind of nice to get a woman's perspective."

"Perspective? On what?"

"On why I moved here and my plan to move forward with my personal life."

All this time I thought he just wanted to live at the beach, but his statement held hints of something far more serious…or someone.

"If you're comfortable with sharing something so personal with an almost perfect stranger, I'd be glad to give you my opinion."

"Baby, you're far from being a stranger at this point, and truthfully I'd love to hear what someone outside of my family has to say."

Baby... I've got to get over him calling me that.

A bit of shyness came over me from his last statement, but I quickly brushed it off by straightening up, crossing my arms, and resting them firmly on the coffee table as I waited for him to explain his life's journey.

"For years I spent my time looking after others. Mainly, Rain..."

I stopped him for clarification, "Your business partner?"

"Yes, as I had said before, we grew up together, and I grew up protecting her. She was sick when she was young, and her parents, mainly her mother, effectively kept her sheltered, hidden if you will, from the rest of the world and a normal life."

"That's horrible, but at least she had you as her prince charming."

"No, no prince. It wasn't a romantic story in the least. Like I said, friends but very close friends. I'd never let anything happen to her, but then almost two years ago she met her husband, Daniel's brother, and her life took a new direction. One that, in the beginning, I had a hard time dealing with, but in the end, I envied."

"Envied? Why?"

Tommy leaned forward, then back again. He looked up for answers or possibly approval from the heavens to confess what he seemed to be struggling with for quite some time.

"She was free. Free from her past, free to move forward and to move on. She was happy...truly happy. And I was lost...I had spent so much time protecting her that I lost me—my one true self. Don't get me wrong, I love Rain and I always will, but I'm so angry with myself that I allowed me to get lost in the process. That's when I decided to stop all of the reflection in self-pity and move here."

"To rebuild your life?"

"Yeah, ironically while rebuilding a beach house." He smiled, possibly to push away the awkwardness he felt while admitting his story to me.

"So far, I don't see the problem. You're here building a new life and fixing up the house that in a year or so could be your new home. What's wrong with that?"

"You're only half right."

"Then give me the other half."

"I set out to do this with a specific plan in mind. I want to fix up the house, that's true, and while doing so, meet the person I'd like to spend the rest of my life with."

"Okay, I'm still not seeing the problem."

"I have a timeline. I want to wrap it up all within six months."

"I see, you want the house to be completed before the lease is up and want to see if my family will sell it to you earlier than agreed upon. I'm sure—" This time he interrupted me.

"No, no, no… I wanted to fix the house and find the woman I want to be with by summer's end and start a family in six months." He was matter of fact and to the point. It was almost clinical and as if his life depended on it.

"You realize although it's not impossible, finding someone and making a life together shouldn't be contingent on a timeline. Love should grow naturally."

With his eyes closed and a flat-lipped expression, Tommy's demeanor changed as he shook his head in almost slow motion. "I knew it. I shouldn't have said anything to you. I knew you wouldn't understand." Standing, he whipped his napkin onto the table and headed for the door.

Before he could leave, I reached for him and placed my hand on his arm. He stilled but didn't turn to face me.

He turned his upper body partially to face me. Looking at my hand, he gently took it to his mouth and kissed my fingertips. It took everything I had to keep my body from outwardly reacting to what was happening inside of me. My outer-self was fighting my inner-self. I wanted to comfort him more but held back.

Tommy's jaw tightened, he further turned and faced me head on. His hands framed my cheeks. Our bodies quaked and our mouths came close enough to touch. We looked to each other for guidance…for an answer. Our breathing grew intensely shaky, and our breaths heated the small space between us. The seconds that passed heightened our emotions that had been building since we first met each other on the dance floor that fateful night.

The rain outside my door cooled off everything, everything except what was happening between us, right here…right now. I couldn't speak or swallow or move. All I could do was watch as Tommy changed course. He pressed his lips to my forehead…hard, and said, "I can't do this. I can't drag you into something I know is wrong for you, something you're not ready for. Thank you for an amazing evening, Jade." With that he let go of me, vigorously pushed the sliding door open, and without closing it, he rushed out into one storm…leaving the other brewing between us, behind.

The space in the room was filled with a numbness I hadn't felt since Jimmy died. I quickly grabbed my bearings because my heart told me to go after him, yet my common sense, still fighting me, told me to let him be.

Unfortunately…my common sense prevailed.

chapter
fifteen

Jade

TOMMY WALKED OUT of my house over two weeks ago and other than the occasional wave and false pleasantries from across our decks, there was nothing between us until the awkward moment I had the not so great pleasure of walking in on, in the alley between our houses yesterday afternoon.

At first, I assumed he was embarrassed about what transpired between us at dinner two weeks back, then I thought he wanted to keep our relationship tenant and owner driven and he was consumed with the house, as it did need a great deal of updating.

It's not like I laughed at his plan. I said it wouldn't be easy, and apparently, my response hit a nerve. It hit my nerve too. If he didn't like what I had to say, then why even ask at all for my opinion? Part of me wanted to tell him to grow up and make him understand that just because someone, namely me, doesn't necessarily agree with what he's doing, he shouldn't have walked out on our night the way he did. Then there was the other part of me who had wanted on numerous occasions to walk over to his house, knock on the door, and apologize for not believing in his choices. Of course, the reality was his personal life wasn't any of my business, so I felt it best to leave it alone and let him cool down.

Then I thought, maybe he was starting to put his plan in motion to meet his future bride? And if he was doing that in the last two weeks, why was it bothering me? He was single, and he could do anything he wanted, without any interference from me.

Today proved, in some bizarre way, he was doing exactly that. Today, I had gone to work like any other day, but it was slow, so I phoned Blaze, and said I'd be back early. If she was down here with Reece, and she was free for the afternoon, we could go paddle boarding in the bay. She said she was up for it, so I locked up the shoppe and headed home.

By the time I sped into my driveway and crossed over to the alley...there they stood looking at me. The banter between what sounded like Tommy and a woman could be heard clear to the street.

Why me? Why now?

I didn't want to pass by them to get to my stairs, but it was too late.

Holy Shit! Jade, remain calm, smile, and run for the door!

As I walked through, between our houses, this woman, who wasn't any older than me but appeared to be because of her business attire, far too much makeup for daytime wear, and her strict slick bun, charged past me...then stopped, silently remembered something, and turned back in my direction.

"Are you his neighbor?" She said in a fluster, pointing up toward the beach house.

"Uh, yeah...I am."

"Well, let me just say you'd better watch out for yourself." She huffed in a hushed and serious tone.

"Excuse me?"

"Honey, were you listening? I'm trying to give you some womanly advice...move!"

"Move?"

"Yes, move! He's not normal!" Her voice elevated.

I peered around her, trying not grin, only to see Tommy pinching his lips together trying to keep himself from laughing.

"Okay…I know I'm going to regret this, but why?" I asked as Blaze walked up.

"What's going on? Who's this?" Blaze cut in.

"I think she's Tommy's date." I leaned into my friend without looking away from the hysterical woman in front of me.

"Yes, I am…was…he's…."

"I know, not normal. I heard you the first time. Do you want to explain why?"

"I was getting to that."

Blaze and I both crossed our arms, cocked our heads, and leaned in for what was going to be the biggest waste of time. Straightening her business jacket and her collar, she continued. "Well, if you must know, I thought we were going out for a good time, but then he tells me he's basically looking to get married. Can you imagine?"

Not moving, Blaze and I looked sideways at each other before I spoke.

"Really… marriage? You don't say?"

"Yes, I do say. What normal guy wants to jump into marriage?" Then she leaned in closer and whispered to us. "I mean look at him…that body, that face…I thought he wanted to have some fun, then he gets all weird and serious on me; that's not normal."

"Yeah, I get it," I said, now truly annoyed at this foolish woman who had no idea what a great guy Tommy was and that she was ruining my day of paddle boarding on the bay, on such a beautiful afternoon.

Blaze went a bit further.

"So sweetie, I take it he didn't sleep with you?"

Appalled, Miss "Three-piece-suit" stormed off, stating she tried to warn us. Her presence left the alley and turned the corner. That's when Blaze and I'd turned back to each other and laughed.

Our amusement came to a halt with Tommy joining in.

"Ladies."

"Sorry, Tommy, but I don't think that one will be back." Blaze hardly contained her laughter. She kissed his cheek and headed upstairs to change for our afternoon on the water. The minute she was out of sight, the alley shrunk. No scents of the ocean or summer, only awkwardness between us.

"Jade, listen…I," he said, stepping in closer…too close.

My hand touched his chest, over his racing heart, to stop him.

"There's nothing to explain."

"Damn it, Jade, will you please just…" he said— his frustration calling out to me, as I ran up the stairs like a chicken.

I didn't think there was a need for apologies from him, or an I told you so from me, and being alone again with him after these two weeks away, made me want him more. The pain inside me cut deep, leaving him behind, the expression on his face—but I had to. I had to keep my clear thinking intact…and it was only clear when I wasn't staring into his eyes.

I peeked out of my window, to check the alleyway. It was empty. The coast was clear, so Blaze and I took our boards and headed to the bay area beach to paddle board for the rest of the afternoon.

Once on the water, tranquility turned to tension as Blaze felt it necessary to point out every reason why I should give Tommy a chance. We spent more time quibbling and splashing water at each other than paddling. Finally, each of us gave up, agreed to disagree, and went off on our separate ways.

The rest of day and the rest of the week, I spent my time avoiding Tommy, altogether. I'd scoot out of my house early every morning and work until late in the evening. He didn't try to call or knock on my door. No matter, much of the time, I worked at the shoppe, scheduling special events, including the annual fundraiser for our local animal shelter and meeting with the contractors to go over the final designs for the new building. I did call Daniel to see if Tommy was doing okay, and he said he was out of town until the weekend. I was curious if he met someone, made up with that hideous woman, or went away on business. I didn't ask, and Daniel didn't divulge Tommy's whereabouts.

The week finally came to a close. It was Friday, not my usual day off, but because one of my staff needed Tuesday off, I traded with him and now I got to relax and surf with my favorite ladies.

Blaze arrived last night, Kim would be here shortly, and Aunt Viv said she would stop by before she left for her weekend in Philly. I should say her third weekend in Philly. If I didn't know any better, I would wonder if she had a special man out there in the "City of Brotherly Love."

Checking the clock and seeing it was almost 11, made me succumb to the fact that I had to reluctantly slide out of bed and get my day started. I loved being lazy on my day off, but I wanted to set up the food and drinks for our first get together of the summer.

Looking from the deck off my bedroom I noticed Blaze had started the party without me. Scents of coconut and tropical fruits filled the air, while the sounds of the waves in the distance were muffled by playful beachgoers nearby and Blaze's choice of 60's surf music.

Our boards, leaning on the side railing of the lower deck, were waxed and ready. The old rectangular, turquoise cooler on wheels, marred by its faded paint and surfing stickers, was filled with an assortment of drinks embedded in the mounds of store-bought ice cubes. The grill cover was off and stored, while the grill itself was yet untouched, but ready to go. Surfing came first and the food came later.

My eyes welled up in unison with my heart as the sights and sounds of my childhood days flooded my present moment. The memories that followed were a bit painful, yet in a strange way comforting. Reconfirming this would be my home…for always.

Breaking free from my thoughts, and once downstairs with snack tray in hand, I headed outside to join Blaze and the land of the living.

"Well, I wondered when you were getting up?" She stated, looking up at me with arms outwardly stretched wide with a Bloody Mary in each hand. I smiled, shook my head, and rolled my eyes at her over the top greeting.

She popped the glass with alcohol infused tomato juice and a tall stalk of celery into my hand, while she grabbed a chip with some guacamole on it and settled on one of the six lounge chairs that faced the magnificent ocean view. I took my cue from Blaze and joined her, as we both stretched out under the midday sun.

"Hmmm…this was a great idea, Jade," Blaze purred, as she shimmied her string-bikini clad body into just the right position for optimal comfort and just erect enough to gawk at several hot guys playing volleyball on the sand not far from the edge of my property.

"Wow, you're in a good mood. What did you do, break up with Reece?"

Blaze's head turned. Her chin dropped like a heavy weight in my direction, as she slid her glasses down to show her disapproval of the witty jab I took at her current lover's expense.

"Funny—no, I didn't break up with Reece. For your information, I'm just happy we're doing this…you, me, and Kim. It's been a long time since the three of us surfed together. Can't we just enjoy ourselves and leave Reece out of it?"

"I'm sorry. Of course, we can. I'm happy we get to spend the entire day together, too."

"I bet you are." Blaze could give as good as she got.

"What's that supposed to mean?"

"I would say by the looks of things you need this break as much as I do. You know, from the man in your life?"

Instantly pissed and now sitting up to face her, I asked the burning questions. "What the hell do you mean, 'by the looks of things,' and what man in my life? I don't have a man in my life."

"Listen, since you came down those stairs, you and Tommy have not even once acknowledged one another. He's almost within earshot and you haven't even said hello—neither of you. Plus, for you to declare a make-believe relationship for Reece's benefit and for Tommy, who you knew like, what, two minutes, to play along, and now he's not speaking to you either, except for that little incident in the alleyway on Tuesday, then something's wrong. So, what's going on, Jade?" Her long-winded analysis ended with her usual loving concern for me.

Touching my lips, remembering how close we came to kissing, made my explanation all the more painful. I looked off at the beautiful blue waters of the Atlantic and told Blaze about the dinner I had with Tommy.

"We had dinner two weeks back and everything was going relatively smooth. Well, maybe a few bumps here and there, but basically good and then he told me about why he moved here."

"And?"

"He said he wanted to find a wife and start a family?"

"So?"

"So…are you going to keep up with your one-word inquisition?"

"It's just that I'm not seeing anything that would cause the both of you to stop being neighborly toward one another. If you get what I'm saying?"

"Trust me, I know exactly what you're saying."

"Meaning?"

I paused. I hated when she did that.

"Sorry, Jade, go on."

"Like I said, he wants to fix the house, eventually buy it, and have an *at the ready wife* to move in with him and then start a family."

"Jealous?" She asked, in a sing-song tone.

"Get serious. I have no expectations in that area of my life."

"I am serious. Why would you stop talking with a guy as sexy as Tommy and avoid an opportunity to talk with him the other day unless you're upset about his plan?"

"Blaze, he walked out on me that night."

"What?"

Sure, now she's dumbfounded.

"I'll tell you what I told him. I said that I didn't think it was an impossibility, but that placing a stringent timeline to meet a girl and wine and dine her into marriage is basically unnatural."

"So is deciding to become a spinster at thirty-five."

"You know full well I'm not becoming a spinster."

"What makes you think I was talking about you?"

"Bitch."

I wasn't afraid to be alone, nor was I ready to share my life with someone again and risk having my heart broken. I could do 'alone' all day long, but that feeling of being crushed was not something I wanted to entertain at this point, and I was just about to remind my friend of that when Kim arrived.

"Hey, ladies," was all she said when Blaze and I got up to greet her with excited schoolgirl screams and hugs all the way around.

Holding up not one, but two very large bottles of wine, "Ready for a night of laughter and libations?"

There were Cheshire cat grins and nods of agreement all the way around as we settled into our chairs and began to catch up with each other. We agreed with all this alcohol, we needed to head out soon or surfing would be completely out of the question today.

Blaze immediately started in. "So…have you heard from him?" Curious to know about Kim's one and only love.

Kim took our friend's assertiveness in stride. "You ask me that question every time we're together, and my answer never changes."

"So that answer is a big fat *NO*... once again. Right, Kim?"

"BLAZE! What the hell is wrong with you?"

"With me? She's the one waiting around for …"

"Hey, hey…why are you two yelling?"

"Viv…we didn't see you standing there?" Blaze admitted.

"No, of course, you didn't, Blaze. You were too interested in giving your advice where it's not needed than to see anything else that's happening around you. Good to see you, Kim."

"Nice to see you too, Viv." Kim smiled, as she walked over to my aunt to kiss her cheek.

Blaze and I both walked over to properly greet Viv, as well.

"Glad you stopped by Aunt Viv. Can I get you a drink?" I asked while kissing my aunt on the cheek.

"I'd love a glass of iced tea, thanks."

"Coming up." I walked upstairs to the get the tea as I briefly heard Blaze apologize for her behavior that Viv witnessed. Blaze always hated if Viv was disappointed in her. Even as kids, she admired Viv, as did many of my friends, but Blaze in particular.

I never truly figured it out, but my guess was because Blaze didn't have the greatest relationship with her own mom growing up, and Viv had taken her under her wing when we were kids, and in doing so she helped guide Blaze during her impressionable years. Support was part of what Blaze needed to fill a piece of her life that was missing. With support, came the necessary times when Viv put Blaze in her place. Viv did that with all of us, but it was only because she cared and always felt the straight truth was best. Viv was never one for coloring anything for our benefit or because we were too young. She did it then, and she did it now.

"Viv, I'm sorry."

"Damn it, Blaze, don't apologize to me; apologize to Kim," she said, pointing to our other friend, who appeared amused by the banter that ensued between my aunt and our fiery redheaded friend.

Like an awkward child caught with her hand in the cookie jar, Blaze turned toward Kim…and with a child-like pout she held out her arms and acquiesced to Viv's request and apologized to her.

Kim knew that Blaze's comments came from a good place no matter how bad they sounded. Blaze, like the rest of us, just wished that Kim would realize that the man she loved all this time wasn't coming back and that waiting for him was futile.

Viv was of the opinion that Kim was a grown woman, and it was her choice, no matter how agonizing it was. It was Kim's decision and we needed to respect it. For the most part, we did.

When I returned, Kim and Blaze were hugging one another. All was well with them, so they turned their attention on me as it was time for the trio to pick on me and my love life.

Great, just what I needed…a tag team.

Handing Viv her tea, I shared the lounge chair with Kim, while Viv and Blaze sat on one of the others directly across from us. Viv's questioning came fast and hard, not giving me a chance to breathe.

"Sweetie, what exactly is going on between you and Tommy?"

"Ugh…Viv, why does something need to be going on with us? We're new neighbors… that's it."

"That's it? That's not it, and you know it. You used that man the very first day you met him to hide from Reece's attempts to have you cozy back up with Damien, and now all you have to say for yourself is that you're new neighbors? If that's the case, then why aren't you acting like neighbors?"

"What are you talking about?"

"Don't play coy with me. I live right near both of you, and from what I've been seeing, the two of you have now stopped talking to each other."

I looked to Kim and Blaze for help, but it was clear they wouldn't dare touch this conversation.

"Well, he asked for my opinion about something and when I didn't agree, he walked out in a huff."

"I see…well, after I leave here for the weekend, I'm going into Philly for a few days with some friends. I hope should Tommy have any issues with the house, you'll be available to help him in my absence. Do I make myself clear?"

"Viv, really? I'm not a child."

She had to be kidding.

"I'm not joking. I need to be able to count on you without worrying about some sort of discourse between the two of you!"

"Of course, whatever he needs, I'll be glad to step in."

"Good, I'll see you in a few days." Viv stood abruptly with pinky pointed, as she delicately placed the glass with her unfinished tea in my hand, said goodbye to the girls, and left for her trip into Philly.

"That was short…" Kim noted.

"…And sweet," Blazed added.

"Yeah, and strange?" I questioned.

"What do you mean?" Kim asked.

"Why come over to say you're going to spend the afternoon with us, have one drink, barely finish it, and leave? Oh, and not before discussing our new neighbor and my lack of goodwill toward him."

"Maybe she just wanted to make sure that whatever the reason was for the both of you to be ignoring each other this soon, it wouldn't interfere with him renting the house," Kim surmised.

Lying back while taking a sip of her drink, Blaze added, "Yeah, or maybe Viv was worried you would kick Tommy out while she was away. I mean, she did rent the house out to him while you were gone and without your input." Following Blaze's lead, both Kim and I reclined back in our chairs respectively.

Not opening my eyes, I said, "You know I wouldn't kick him out."

When both women didn't respond I looked around to see what they were doing. Both were staring in the direction of my childhood home, as they ogled Tommy and watched him remove his shirt to expose his myriad of ink and flexed muscle.

"Sweet Jesus, you sure you don't want to date him, Jade?"

"I told you for the millionth time. NO! I don't want to start a serious relationship with anyone right now."

"I have to agree with Blaze."

"Not you too, Kim?" I directed my question to her, but Blaze naturally answered.

"You have to admit he'd be fun." Blaze tilted down her chin and raised her glasses as well as her brows ever so slightly to get a better view of him.

"Yeah, even if it was only for the summer. Blaze is right, Jade. Why not have some fun?"

Kim added while she examined Tommy even further, as well.

"Stop that! Stop staring at him. You're both going to get his attention and I don't want him to know he's the topic of our conversation," I said, teasingly slapping Blaze's hand to put her sunglasses back where they belonged, on her face, while throwing a beach towel at Kim.

As my friends and I looked at each other, passing around playful smirks between us, we busted out in laughter like high-school teens, because we knew that although we were too old to be schoolgirls, that didn't stop us on this beautiful summer beach day.

With an incredible view of the ocean, spending this perfect day with my friends came with a price. Darkness hadn't fallen over the island. It was early, yet darkness didn't fall from the sky. Well, unless the sky dropped Reece Montgomery on the deck outside my kitchen.

"I knew it. This day was too good to be true. Don't you have anywhere else to be? Perhaps a session of cardiac rehab or something?" My mood was squashed further when Reece made a not so surprising appearance.

"Ladies... I'm not here to disturb this little get together of yours."

"Too late... you are disturbing us, so what do you want?" My tone proved no explanation was needed in the way I felt about him at the moment.

"I'm just here to see when Blaze will have finished with her girls' day with the both of you, so she can be ready for an evening with me."

"Wow, Reece, has your cardiologist given you the green light to get back into the saddle again, so to speak?" Some not so hidden smirks appeared on the girl's faces as they were amused by my observation.

Reece had the gall to constantly slither and worm his way into anything and everything that was none of his concern. It was early, and we just got started. Yet, he wanted Blaze with him. I would not allow him to cut our day short.

"You're making me feel like I'm not wanted."

I spun in his direction, but stopped and held onto the table. "That's because you're not. This was supposed to be our girls' day. 'Girls' being the key word here, Reece."

Walking over to Blaze and winding his fingers through her long red hair, he held her still while he surveyed her face, and then he turned back to me and said, "Can you blame me for not wanting to be away from this beautiful woman for too long? Besides, what's he doing here if it's a girls' day?"

With all the commotion that Reece brings with him, I hadn't realized that Tommy was behind us.

"I just stopped in to see if Jade needed anything; I'm heading to the store," Tommy answered for me, as he casually walked toward me, touching a strand of hair and kissing my forehead.

Nicely played.

Although, I wasn't sure why Tommy was here. Seeing him made my heart race like a high-octane engine. Why was he here? He had me curious. Curious and in a trance to the point I hadn't noticed Blaze's reaction to Reece showing up here unannounced. She was fuming.

Blaze stood stiff and frustrated, not knowing what to do about the man in her life and his need to know everything that was going on in her world. She, therefore, used what appealed to him and appeased him with a sexy pout and a bit of extra attention in hopes he would be satisfied enough to leave.

Let's hope it worked.

"Reece, baby, you know I'll miss you all day, but the girls and I rarely have the time to get together like this. You understand, don't you, sweetie?" Sugar never tasted so fake, but I had to hand it to Blaze, Reece was eating right out of the palm of her hand.

"Okay, my love…I'll bend to your will, because you asked me so nicely. You could learn from Blaze, Jade." Reece spoke with his usual bit of smugness in his response.

Reece and his son were examples of why I don't want another man in my life.

At least he was leaving, or so I thought…just as he turned to go, he turned back.

"Oh, and one more thing…I'm having that party I mentioned to you the other day on the Saturday of the July 4th weekend. I hope you and Tommy can make it? You're invited as well, Kim."

"Thank you, Reece, but the club will be far too busy that weekend for me to get away, even for one of your parties."

"Maybe next the time, then? So, Jade, can I count on you and Tommy to grace us with your presence?"

"We'd love to come," Tommy responded.

"We would?" I whispered. That question got me another kiss. This time on the side of my neck… with a heated, breathy response in my ear.

"Yes, baby, we would," he whispered back, as he held my hand firm, pulling me against his chest, realizing that his response sent me off balance and caught me just in time…like our first night on the dance floor.

"Perfect…I will see you both at my house at 8 pm that evening. Oh, and I have one more request."

"This ought to be good," I said, as Tommy chuckled, and I grinned.

"I'm creating a theme for the party, so everything will be done in white and silver and gold. I'm requesting that my guests wear white and adhere to this dress code. I hope this won't be too much trouble?" We both shook our heads at Reece's request for proper attire. It didn't seem that unreasonable being summer and all.

"Good, I'll see you then, and you my gorgeous girl, I will see *you* tonight." Reece kissed Blaze on the mouth and after feeling satisfied, he slowly took carefree strides to mark his exit. Blaze and Kim followed Reece's lead and instead of heading down the stairs, they headed inside to give us some privacy.

"Tommy, I need to say something. I'm sorry about the dinner we had. I was worried you were never going to speak to me again after the way it ended."

"Listen, about that. I owe you an apology. I would never have gotten up like that and left. You didn't do anything wrong. I was the one concerned that you would never speak to me again."

"Me?"

"Yeah, you… I can't expect everyone to understand why I'm doing what I'm doing, but you did, and I left because of …I don't know…I wanted you to tell me it was the right thing to do and when you said that you felt that a relationship shouldn't occur on a timeline, I got pissed off and that's why I walked out."

"And now how do you feel?"

"Like a fool, especially after what transpired in the alley the other day."

I tried to hide my amusement until he lifted my chin to see my full reaction.

"By the looks of things, you agree with me."

"All kidding aside, I don't think you're a fool. I just think you're far more optimistic than most people. Although if your optimism sends more women like the one in the alley your way, then I think I would be saying I told you so."

"Fair enough…so does this mean you forgive my abrupt departure from our dinner date, and you'll go with me to Reece's party now?"

"Uh…yeah…about that, why would you agree to go to the party when you know full well this is all a pretense between us that I created from the very beginning *and* you clearly don't like Reece in the least?"

"It's the only way I can get you to go out with me? So are we on, baby?"

"Tommy…" My mouth hung open, literally, because I couldn't form the words to respond to his admission.

"Jade! Let's go, already," Blaze exclaimed like a two-year-old, as she wanted to hit the waves before Reece possibly returned with some outlandish excuse to whisk her away from here.

We looked to Blaze and then back to us.

"You didn't answer my question."

"I'll meet you at the party."

"So we're still pretending?"

Hesitant, I answered him. "I'm afraid so. It's just that…"

His fingers touched my lips sending a vibration clear through to my toes. "Shhhh…I get it. You've sworn off men and after what I told about me, you just want to be friends. Right?"

Actually, I was hoping you'd replace those fingers with those lips of yours, but I can't tell you that.

He smiled. "It doesn't have to be a real date unless you want it to. If that's what you're worried about? Let's just go to the party. Make some summer memories and have a good time. What do you say?"

"C'mon, Jade. Would you answer him already, so we can surf...today?" Blaze summoned.

We laughed, and I tried to ignore her and give Tommy my answer.

"When we had dinner, and you walked out, I felt horrible. I still do."

"There's nothing to feel bad about. I told you I should never have walked out. It was stupid on my part. Can we agree to disagree where my love life is concerned? *And will you still meet me at Reece's party?*"

Tommy made my heart melt.

Damn it! I didn't want us to disagree on his love life, but I wasn't ready to explore the possibility of Tommy and me being part of that equation in the next six months. Then, there was the other side of me, who wanted to explore it. Perhaps it was the selfish part of me who was afraid he would find someone else as he was intent on this timeline of his. For some reason, I wasn't sure how I felt about that. My emotions were tying me into knots, but I knew I couldn't have it both ways. Regardless...now was not the time to approach this conversation, especially with Blaze and Kim within earshot.

"You have yourself a deal. I'll meet you there as promised, and we can agree to disagree that placing a timeline restriction on falling love is a recipe for disaster."

"Jade!" Blaze blasted off one more time.

"I'm coming!" Blasting back at her, then turning back to him. "Sorry, I promised them a girls' day."

"It's okay. We can talk tomorrow. The party is still some weeks away. A lot can change by then." His devilish grin distracted and attracted me as he plucked an apple off the table, took a bite, and headed down the stairs.

"Nice to see you, Tommy." Both ladies said simultaneously and watched him leave as we carried the boards over our heads, and in single file patted down the stairs to the alleyway between my house and Tommy's, and onto the sand-filled path to the crowded shoreline.

Standing before the raging ocean, whose tide was influenced by the storm that passed the night Tommy and I had dinner and the storm predicted for this weekend. Today it presented a rougher surf than normal. Perfect for us ladies and several of the local surfers already out on the waves carving out their rides.

With our boards tucked under our respective arms, we moved forward shoulder to shoulder simply and simultaneously. We stopped. Looking to the left, then to the right, then at each other, then back to her...our magnificent lady...the Atlantic...We silently made our move.

After several duck-dives, we made it into the lineup. The current momentarily stilled, so we waited, with Blaze acting her usual impatient and chatty self. Since we were kids, Blaze hated this part of surfing. Then again, she despised anything or anyone who made her wait. Her solution was to distract Kim and me with chatter.

"I never understood your logic, Blaze."

"With what?"

"With this?" I asked. My extended arms presenting her with an unforgettable view of the shore before us...blues skies, a northeast wind, children building sandcastles, surfers nearby waiting as we are for the next best wave, the strength of the sun burning overhead as streaks of light from its center flashed between the houses barricading the beach from the rest of the town.

Blaze responded with a "Huh?"

"What Jade means is that you constantly pay attention to everything, except what's surrounding us ."

Blaze practically turned her head completely around to see what she had missed.

"Blaze...the waves, the waves!" Kim quipped.

"That is not true! It's just that we have the time, so why not talk about Jade's new neighbor. Who right now, I might add, is watching you from his deck. I'm telling you, Jade, he's got it bad for you."

Before I could respond…it was time.

Kim was up first, then Blaze, then me.

This was it. This was what you paddled your ass off for… What we wanted and remained still for as we floated…waiting to connect. To glide on its liquid surface. To magically fly free across nature's massive ever-churning machine …to fight against it, to work with it…to honor it… never wanting the ride to end.

And when it did…

We paddled right back out beyond the break, again and again,…holding onto the rush of adrenaline coursing through our veins, pumping our blood…heightening our senses.

And then again…back into the lineup…we waited.

Blaze was silent; we all were this time. Reveling in the experience, until an aggressive surfer came into the fold. Stupidity and the sea didn't mix. Several of the locals who I recognized from surfing with Jimmy noticed his antics and quickly intervened. Yet, this jerk wouldn't listen.

My eyes caught the attention of my friends as we nodded in agreement that we would make this our final ride of the day. Our time cut short due to a rude and unsafe intrusion.

It was time…but not only for catching a great wave. Before I knew it, my body was being slammed by one much larger than mine and the board attached to it. The impact sent me reeling, the current sucking me into and under the surf. My arms and legs flailing through the cyclone of water toward inevitable impact.

Then the cycle stopped and a different one began.

Crushing pain took over as the left side of my face throbbed after hitting bottom and being bounced off the ocean's floor. As if in slow motion, I was naturally being raised amidst the bubbles and stirred up sand to the water's surface, where complete nothingness turned into shrills from Blaze screaming my name, while Kim, along with the other surfers nearby, fervently barked out commands to get me to shore.

A chill spread over my exposed skin as I was lifted out of the water and placed on the sun-heated beach. As my rescuer released me, a hint of a tender kiss was placed at my temple.

Tommy

My insides jumbled just moments ago, sunk down deeper within my core and settled with my rubbery limbs into the warm familiar softness of the sand.

I could make out a mixture of voices…questions, concerns, arguments, and especially my name being called…

"Jade…"

"Jade, wake up…"

"Jade…can you hear me? It's me Blaze!"

"Jade!"

chapter
sixteen

Tommy

J ADE!
Jade!
"Blaze! Calm down! You're not doing her or the professionals tending to her any good." I shook her shoulders before her panic worsened the situation for Jade.

"Let her be and let the paramedics do their job, sweetie." Kim agreed.

Not long before I carried Jade's listless body to shore, I was on my deck contemplating if I should join her and her friends in the water. It wasn't like the surf was off limits just because Jade was out there. I walked toward the shoreline with my board in hand, but as I watched the situation on the water unravel, I could see there was some guy on a longboard to Jade's left who clearly didn't know a thing about surfing. It was surprising by his actions now that he was able to balance or paddle his way out as far as he did.

As the waves surged, Jade, her friends, and the other surfers around her paddled forward and popped up, but this guy stayed in a kneeling position. White knuckling his board, he was terrified to move and as such, was slammed in the precise place propelling him and the board into Jade's side…snapping back her head, then her body, while kicking her completely off balance and sending her under the whitewash. I scrambled…ripping off my leash, I abandoned my board behind me. Panic consumed me as I headed in for her. Jade's board rocketed out of the water, spun in the air, and returned from where it came, eventually floating on the surface without its rider.

My world stopped. I could no longer hear the screams from Blaze, the siren coming from beach patrol, or the onlooker's gasps. Nor could I hear the water from the Atlantic Ocean that stole Jade away in its ever-swirling wall of saltwater. Whatever I was feeling, all the questions I had, didn't matter now. What mattered was getting Jade out of a dangerous situation, and what we'd talked about, what we couldn't come together on, and all the rest could be sorted out later or never, as long as she was safe.

Stomping ahead of the rescuers through the shallow surf to scoop her up even with the waves crashing at my back as I hurried her in, I knew I couldn't falter. Jade consumed too much water and met with one hard blow too many. I wouldn't allow the ocean to rush my body and overtake me while I was carrying her. Once on the beach, I laid her down, so that the lifeguards and EMS workers could examine her.

Although the water wasn't as deep out where I lifted Jade from further harm, and clearly wasn't as deep as other locations I've surfed, I was reprimanded by the lifeguard on duty for getting involved, more like getting in the way. I wasn't insulted or even angry; I knew it wasn't the job of bystanders, no matter how experienced, to jump in. Yet many of us did. I've seen it before and it's saved many a life, but I knew going in, it could also be a distraction for the actual lifeguards who do this for a living…even so, my concern for Jade out measured my concern for my own safety at this point. I apologized to the officer and returned my attention to Jade, who appeared to be coming out of it slowly.

"Jade! Honey, please, please say you're okay," Blaze rambled and cried.

"Miss, you need to give her some space, or I'll have to remove you." One officer addressed Blaze for her manic hovering over her friend.

His command stopped all that, as she turned to address him.

"Remove me! Me…me? I'll have you know she's my best friend. Instead of badgering me, why don't you stop wasting time and arrest that fool for hurting her!" Blaze pointed in the direction of the water where a weathered, but no worse for wear surfer sulked onto the beach.

The crowd of onlookers that weren't tending to Jade, followed Blaze's extended arm and index finger to the wannabe surfer who'd hit Jade.

"That's right…arrest him! He was the one screwing around out there. You can ask any one of the boys. They warned him, but no, he had to be an asshole! Now, look what he's done… because he had to show-off!" Blaze stormed forward to confront him, but Kim held her back.

"Not now…Jade needs us. The beach patrol will take care of him."

Blaze…water soaked, weary, and with bloodshot eyes stared at Kim. There were unspoken words only they could hear—a silent meaning only the two of them understood. Each snapped a quick nod of agreement and went back to their friend, who was now leaning up on her elbows taking a sip of cool water from a bottle being held by one of the emergency workers.

Blaze and Kim dropped to their knees to check on Jade as I stood behind them. Blood was trailing down the left side of her face along her hairline. I swiped a clean cloth from an EMS bag nearby and placed it at her temple.

"Man, listen…you have to step back so we can examine her now that she's alert." One of the lifeguards addressed my gesture.

"I understand," I did but was reluctant to leave Jade, even if that meant I was only a few feet from her. The decision to listen was hard, but thankfully and surprisingly it was no longer my decision to make.

"It's okay. I want him to stay." In her weakened tone and with a tired smile, Jade stopped me from moving by placing her hand over my hand holding the cloth.

"Are you sure, miss?"

"Positive, I'm fine. I just had the wind knocked out of me, that's all," she explained, as she extended her hand for me to take and help her up.

Jade leaned into my shoulder as my arm came around hers to brace her, while still putting pressure on her head wound with my other hand.

"Miss, the ambulance will be here shortly to get you to…" Jade stopped him.

"No hospital!" She was adamant.

"Jade, sweetie, it's important that they check you out," Kim pushed, yet comforted Jade at the same time.

"You need to be checked out." Blaze pressed.

"I said no, I'm fine."

"No, you obviously have some damage in that thick skull of yours if you think we're just going to stand here and have something happen to you later." Blaze insensitively said, but for good reason.

Jade was hit by a man twice her size, holding a surfboard while being moved by rushing water. She needed to be checked out.

"Baby, listen to me," I said, softly patting the side of her head with the cloth while searching her face. Examining her as if I could read into her thoughts, I cautiously broached the subject of having her checked out, but she stopped me, as well.

"Don't you start in on me too! I'm fine. I'm not going to say it again." Her chin lowered, her eyes hooded, so as not to expose the pools of water fighting to remain unseen.

I pulled her into my chest to keep her and her secret pain safe with me…let me take it from her and physically absorb it. A pain that wasn't caused by today, a pain not brought about by the clown on a surfboard. No, a pain that ran deeper than Jade's superficial wounds from the mishap on the water. This pain came from a memory. Today's incident was a reminder of her past. Today, reinforced Jade's ever-present gut-wrenching hurt for Jimmy. Her brother's death was something she couldn't come to terms with. The accident proved that. Yet, I felt the need to try and persuade her to go, and that I would come with her.

"Jade, please listen to me. I'm not telling you what to do, but you sustained a blow to the head. You need to get checked out. Please." One of the lifeguards stepped in, who appeared to know Jade. Not that it was odd for them to know each other. Jade lived on the island year-round for most of her life and Jimmy, her brother, seemed to be a legend to the local surf crowd.

Her chest fell, as her eyes closed. It appeared he won this fight. "Okay, I'll go … on one condition." Even with the seriousness of the situation, that pout on her face was priceless and amusing.

"What's that?"

"No ambulance."

"But Jade…" Blaze intruded, only to add to Jade's apprehension.

"I'm tired, and I'm definitely not in the mood to argue with you, but I will if you nag me about this."

"I'd be happy to take you over to there so you can get checked out," Kim added, but I wish she hadn't.

I didn't want Jade to forgo treatment, but my gut instincts told me Jade's emotions were more in need of repair than her physical cuts and bruises. I could be all wrong with this, but I felt she might open up to me more than her friends. I may have been imaging it, but in the short time I'd been here and got to see Jade with the people close to her, I barely saw her discuss or speak of Jimmy at length around them, other than that night we had dinner at Viv's and Jade explained some of it to me when she stopped by afterward.

Again, a gut instinct told me she was holding back. It was as if she wanted to scream, but couldn't. As if she wanted to let go, and let it all out, but wouldn't. Perhaps I was giving myself too much credit in thinking I could coax the hurt out of her and help her put it in the past or at least in a place she felt more comfortable…more at peace.

"Kim, thank you. I'd liked to go home first. I really need a shower, and I'd like to change before I spend the rest of the day and possibly the night in an emergency room."

"You can't be serious?" Was all Blaze said, and that was all it took for Jade to leave my arms to confront her friend.

The two women faced off, but Jade wrapped her arms around Blaze and kissed her cheek.

"I love you, Blaze, and yes, I'm serious. I don't feel sick or dizzy or anything out of the ordinary, so I'd like to shower and change first. I promise I'll let you and Kim take me after that."

The lifeguard who knew Jade interceded.

"Jade sweetie, please listen to me. I've seen this before. You'll feel fine. On top of the world even, but when the adrenaline swirling around inside of you crashes, it's not going to be good. I want you to go to the hospital, and if you don't want the ambulance, so be it. The boys and I will take you."

She looked everywhere around her to find the answer that would help her to decide what to do. She wanted to avoid that hospital at all costs, but what her lifeguard friend said next made all the difference in the world.

"Jade, please do as I ask. What kind of friend would I be to you or Jimmy, for that matter, if I didn't keep my promise?"

"What promise?" Exhaustion and annoyance echoed through Jade's tone.

The guard paused as if he realized he was leading into shaky territory with Jade. "Jimmy asked me to always look out for you when he wasn't around. So let me ask you again, what kind of friend would I be to Jimmy if I broke a promise to him now? Not a very good one. Now, what do you say? Will you let me take you?"

Answering his own question, he asked Jade again, but this time she looked to me.

"I think you should do what he says and if you'd like, I can take you."

Jade then took my hand as she guided me out of hearing distance of her friends.

"I want to thank you for what you did, but I don't want to impose on you any further." Her voice a weakened whisper, as her focus went from our entwined fingers to my eyes and straight through to my heart.

I shook my head as I answered her. "No thanks necessary. For your information, you're not imposing at all, I'm just glad you're doing okay."

"Thanks to you." Her shyness and slight amusement in her smile confirmed she was going to be fine.

Less than panicked, but deeply concerned, I asked Jade if she wasn't telling me something. Now probably wasn't the right time to pry it out of her, but it didn't appear she made up her mind yet, for the mode of transportation she would be using.

"If you don't have a family doctor, I have a friend on the island who's a doctor. I can ask him to meet us at the hospital if you'd like?" Thinking my proposal would make her decision easier. It did, but it didn't go as I had planned.

"Thank you. That's okay, I have a family doctor who could see me, but I hate to admit it, Blaze is right, I need to go now and get checked out. My brother's friends will take me. I've taken advantage of your good nature…far too much."

"It's only an imposition if the person you're asking doesn't want to do it. I offered, and I'm happy to help."

The smile she gave me, as she let her fingertips touch my shoulder was the nicest brush off a guy could ask for.

"Thank you, but maybe it's best I go with them. If it's true that I'm not imposing as you say, could I ask you to let Viv know what happened if she should call? I know how hospital emergency rooms can be, and I'm pretty sure they are going to make me get a scan or some sort of X-ray. I don't want to miss her call and I certainly don't want Blaze or Kim explaining this to her, so if I leave you my cell phone would you handle it for me?"

I said yes for two reasons. One, because Jade was right. Cooler heads needed to prevail and although Kim was fine, Blaze wasn't, and I knew Kim would have her hands full with Blaze while they waited for Jade at the ER.

And two, because having her phone would allow me to see her when she returned. These feelings whirling inside of me for Jade were understandable given her personality and the many things we had in common, but more than just attraction at first sight and my need to be with her since that time was hard for me to comprehend.

"Sure, I'd be happy to help."

"Great, I'll text you from Blaze's phone or Kim's with updates."

"Okay, and I'll text Blaze should Viv call. I assume her phone number is on your list."

"Sounds good." She nodded and walked away, but turned back briefly when I remembered something and called out to her.

"Wait! What's your password to get into the phone?"

She laughed, which was an odd reaction to me until she told me the word.

"It's wipeout," She laughed some more as she joined her friends and disappear over the dunes that lead to the street.

I chuckled as the irony wasn't lost on me.

Back at the beach house and not even two minutes after Jade left for the hospital I was checking the phone for…a text, a call, an update. Being patient didn't seem to be my strong suit when it came to her. From the moment we danced that first night, I felt drawn to her. Yet, I couldn't have predicted that the beautiful body wrapped around me on that dance floor would be the same body to show up barely dressed, livid, and yelling on my doorstep the next morning…or be the same woman connected to my beach house's past.

If my pacing continued, I was guaranteed my new floors would be aged before their time. I had to do something.

Calling Daniel seemed like the logical choice, but me not being logical or rational at the moment, I called Rain instead.

"Tommy!" She picked up and her voice took the edge off but didn't calm me as I thought it would.

"Hey, baby…how's everything?"

"I'm good, but maybe I should be asking *you* that question?" With Rain's inquisitive emphasis on the word you…pertaining to me, couldn't possibly mean she knew I lied. Could it?

"What do you mean?" I tried being as nonchalant as possible…more like playing stupid.

"What I mean is, you must be having a great time. I haven't heard from you in almost three weeks. So, tell me…who is she?" I could hear Rain's inquisitive, playful grin forming on this side of the phone.

I should have known calling Rain and trying to put anything passed her was a mistake. She always knew what was going on with me, even if I never said a word. This time, I had to try my best to avoid this line of questioning. I wasn't ready to discuss Jade and what I was feeling for her with my best friend just yet, so I lied.

"Rain, if there was a she, believe me, you'd be the first to know. So tell me, how are the twins and Kane?"

"Nice try, but you're up to something, and you know I'll find out eventually, and if you've been keeping things from me…" That was the Rain I knew and loved all these years. The fiery, take no prisoners attitude.

I laughed as she knew her idle threats didn't work on me.

"You'll what? You know you can't pull that shit with me. Listen, baby, you knew I had to get away, and I'm doing that. It's not all it's cracked up to be…finding myself, that is. But, Rain, I have to do this for me. Please understand."

"Damn it, Tommy, I know. I know you had to do this. I get it. Probably more than anyone, but I don't like to think of you as hurting. That wasn't what this trip of self-realization should be about. Now, promise me something."

"Okay, I promise." I didn't even have to think about my answer when it came to Rain. That's how it always had been with us.

"Promise me that whatever is going on with you, if it becomes too much, or if you just need a break from the reality you're searching for, you'll come home."

"You don't need me to promise that, Rain. You know I will. Just like I would if you said you needed me. That's how fast I'd get there."

"I love you, Tommy." She comforted and cut me at the same time. I shouldn't have called in the state of mind I was in, yet it brought me clarity.

"I love you. I'll call you tomorrow."

"Yeah, please call me tomorrow. I have to talk to you about a call I received from a client the other day. I need your input."

As Rain and I ended our call, I dismissed any business we needed to take on for another time, and decided to head over to the hospital, even though I said I would wait for Jade's call at home…a promise I couldn't keep.

I arrived at the medical center and searched for parking near the emergency room, but it was packed. That worried me further. What if Jade didn't get seen quickly enough and the injury she sustained was worse than we originally thought? I needed to see her. A renewed surge of energy hit me. I slammed the car into reverse to find a place to park—I needed to get to her. I finally found a spot on the other side of the building and furiously ran around to where I had just come from, barely skimming through the opening of the electric doors which presented a flood of people, confirming it was a busy night.

Peering over and around the crowd in the waiting room proved fruitless. Jade and her friends didn't appear to be in sight. Hoping this meant she was already taken in to be examined, I inquired at the nurse's station.

"Excuse me, nurse?"

"Yes, sir. How can I help you?"

"I'm looking for a friend that came in tonight."

"I'm sorry, sir. We aren't allowed to give out information of that nature…HIPPA regulations."

"I'm not asking you to give out information on her condition. I just want to know she's here and that I can be with her," I persisted.

"And how are you related to the patient?"

I had to think fast. "I'm her fiancé." Desperate measures, I know, but I said it anyway. I wasn't leaving here without seeing her.

"Let me check to see if she's here, and if she is I can get someone to clear it with her or another family member, then I'll bring you in."

"Thank you. I appreciate it"

"Don't thank me yet. We're overwhelmed and understaffed tonight— this could take some time."

"I understand."

"What's your girlfriend's name?"

"Jade Stanton."

"What was she brought in for?"

"She was hit in the head while surfing."

"I see. Was she brought in by a family member or by ambulance?"

"She was brought here by some close friends."

"Okay, let me put this request in the system and as soon as I know anything, either way, I'll page you overhead."

"Thank you, again."

"Don't mention it. Have a seat over there until you hear from me."

I did as she instructed and took a seat at the back of the waiting room where there were fewer people milling around. She wasn't kidding when she said it would be awhile. More like three hours. During which I checked the phone numerous times with no response from Jade, Blaze, or Kim… and no page overhead with my name attached it.

I saw familiar faces emerge from the swinging doors connected to the ER triage section. They were smiling and even laughing when I realized that the last one out and in a wheelchair, was Jade. The minute the wheels hit the public waiting room she shot out of the chair like a bullet.

I was about to walk over when a dark shadow bypassed me and approached the crowd.

It was Montgomery and Damien. I should've known that bastard would take every opportunity to bring his son closer to Jade. The problem was I had no say in the matter. I wasn't really Jade's fiancé or boyfriend. I wasn't even family. I was a guy that knew her a mere week…that was it. I was nothing. All I could do was watch as Damien approached her…skimming his thumb across her cheek, getting close enough to kiss her, as his snake of a father looked on with sheer satisfaction and pride.

My fingers cut across my scalp as a reminder of what little sanity I had left after watching someone else touch her. I wanted her. I knew this. Who was I kidding? I wanted her from the beginning. I wasn't playing along with her masquerade. I wasn't acting. I was hoping somewhere deep inside that she'd notice… she'd want it too.

Now, I was done playing games. I was done with the charade. It was time to tell her the truth. Stop the bullshit and be real. She had hints of it from earlier today, but I was skirting around it. That was never me and it never would be. It was time to tell her that I wanted to get to know her better and be more than friends and neighbors. Fuck the plan. To hell with it. I didn't care if it took six months, six years, or six lifetimes. I wanted Jade to be mine. Fuck trying to change. I said I didn't want to pick up the pieces of anyone else's life, yet I would do it forever if she'd just notice me…I would do it forever for her. I needed to do it now, with this anger toward Montgomery inside me. I needed to get Jade and bring her home.

I made my move, weaving my way through a confusion of nurses, doctors, hospital staff, and loved ones until a hand gripped my shoulder from behind.

"Tommy, I thought that was you. Are you all right? What are you doing here?" A familiar face in a white lab coat greeted me.

"Hey, Dr. Roth, how are you?"

"I'm good, Tommy, but you didn't answer my question. Is everything okay?"

"Yes, yes, I'm fine, just here visiting a friend who was brought in tonight," I explained, as I torqued my neck to see if Jade and her group were still there.

They were. Blaze was explaining everything to Reece and Damien. Kim and Jade's lifeguard friend were talking, and Jade was seated at the desk observing them. Come to think of it, she appeared almost lost. As if she had walked into a party, but was the only one in the room. I saw Jade tonight as if I was seeing her for the first time—seeing inside of her for the first time. Putting on a good front, while sadness peeked through giving little inklings of isolation. The funny thing was that no one around her seemed to realize what was going on. They were either in their own worlds or too busy trying to insinuate themselves into hers with their own agendas. Telling her it was time to move on, but never listening to what she wanted. Blaze, for the most part, wanted her to move forward, but she was too busy trying to reign Montgomery in than to see what Jade was going through. All she saw was that Jade was being released and tomorrow, normalcy would begin again. Yet, Jade's life was anything but normal. Viv was the only one around her who understood what she had gone through and the only one to notice, but she was away for the weekend.

Tonight, I noticed.

"Tommy? Have you heard a word I said?"

Unfortunately, all I could do was watch Jade. Everything else was muted.

"Doc, I'm sorry. I've got a lot on my mind. You were saying?"

"I said, is there anything I can do for your friend while I'm here?"

I was about to explain when my name was being called over the speaker. I excused myself, telling Dr. Roth that it was great seeing him once again. Then I quickly went to the front desk, but instinct must have served him well, as Dr. Roth went with me.

The nurse explained she located my fiancé and her file, but I wasn't on the list of close relatives, so if I wanted to know about her condition I needed to contact them.

"Tommy, I just spoke with Rain and Dominick the other day, and neither one of them mentioned you were engaged. Congratulations!"

He held out his hand, but pulled it back stiffly, when he noticed I didn't extend mine, or it could have been when he saw the tight-lipped grimace of frustration combined with embarrassment on my face.

"Now, for someone to look like you do, tells me there's more to this story than meets the eye. Let's go to my office."

I nodded and reluctantly followed him, not wanting to leave Jade, but I knew with the Montgomery men there, I didn't stand a chance of getting close to her without causing undue stress.

"Tell me what's going on, Tommy."

Frustration growled through an elongated release of air I wasn't aware I was holding.

Sitting back in the chair, another wave of forced air emanated out from my tense body.

"Doc, it's a long story."

He smirked, as he looked at his watch. "You're in luck. I'm off the clock as of now and my patients tell me I'm a great listener."

Able to give him a crooked smile, I stood and paced and explained everything. He listened, just as he had said.

"For some time, I haven't been myself. Since Rain and Dominick married…no, no, since they had gotten together, I started to question myself, my life, and everything around me. I decided to stop the internal whining and do something about it. That's when I had the idea of moving down here, buying a house, and starting a family. So, for the next six months, I was going to do exactly that. My family and friends, except for Daniel, think I'm traveling—finding myself. I bought the house and the pieces started to fall into place."

"Until?"

"Until I met Jade."

"But."

"But, she's not looking for a relationship." I couldn't bring myself to elaborate. The thought of not being with her or explaining why gutted me.

"Well, Tommy that was some story but it seems to me you know what you want, and you know what you're dealing with. I remember Jade's brother from the local papers some years back. Surfing hero, all-star athlete, great head for business, good-looking guy who had it all, but I also remember when he died the local paper didn't portray his death a suicide."

"But Doc…"

He stopped me and continued.

"I know exactly what you're going to say. They twisted it just enough to call it a surfing accident. You have to understand the family lived here full-time for a very long time. This is their home, but this island is small. People talk. To keep the chatter down, I'm sure Jade's father, Jim and Viv, as well as Reece Montgomery, had enough pull to prevent Jimmy Stanton's death from becoming a scandal. Don't get me wrong, people knew the truth back then and many still talked, but it was easier than if it had become front page news, and with time it faded away."

"Life goes on."

"Yes, Tommy, it does."

"Thanks, Doc."

"But I didn't do anything."

"You did more than you think. Can I ask you for a favor?"

"Sure."

"Can you direct me out of here without passing through the ER? I need to get home before Jade does."

He smiled and nodded. "Right this way."

I returned home to see that Jade had beat me there. I looked at the phone. The one she had given to me earlier…nothing. Climbing the stairs, muffled voices from Jade's home became louder but still unrecognizable. At this point, I knew she was with her friends, and she was safe, so I let her be. Tomorrow, I would drop by to check in on her and give her back the phone.

Tonight, I decided a hot shower would help to wash off the remnants of the anger, frustration, and confusion of the day that remained trapped between my muscles. Morning would be here soon enough.

chapter
seventeen

Jade

SUMMER ON LBI was supposed to manifest feelings of paradise…long walks along the shoreline, parties with friends, lying under a seasonally planted King Palm, or basking, not burning, in orange, lemon and tangerine hues. Then real life sets in and snaps you out of your fantasy when you're slammed in the head with a longboard because some drunk novice thought he owned the surf.

Maybe I needed to get knocked in the head to finally wake up? To make myself realize playing it safe in life wasn't worth everything I was missing out on…Yet, I was having trouble focusing on me at the moment, because the worst part of my day wasn't walking away with a minor concussion and the traditional headache that followed. The pain from the blow to my head would be annoying, but I'd live.

Unfortunately, the blow to my privacy every time Blaze decided to inform that man she was sleeping with of her whereabouts, was far more painful. I couldn't believe her. This woman, who has been my best friend forever, who I thought I knew as well as I knew myself, was now bending over backward for that Neanderthal of a man, Reece Montgomery.

Not only did he make an annoying appearance back at the house earlier today when he undoubtedly knew he wasn't invited, but he's here with Damien, causing my head to throb from his constant verbal assaults on my personal life. He doesn't have to do or say anything. His breathing alone annoyed the shit out of me.

His presence caused me to go into a tailspin, but couple that with the fact that his son was fawning all over me as if I'd had a near-death experience, was completely laughable, especially when he couldn't care less where I was or what I was doing, when he fucked another girl in our bed.

"Jade, Blaze called and said you were hurt?" His hand framed my face, as his thumb slithered across my skin.

I tilted away from his attention, and silently chastised Blaze for the call.

"Sorry," Blaze cringed.

"Well, as long as you're okay, that's all that matters," Damien said.

"Of course, she's okay. You must be, especially since that inconsiderate man you're sleeping with isn't here to support you. You must be perfectly fine, with him missing at a time like this, where he should be here, caring for you." Reece raised his voice and surveyed the walls, the ceiling, and the room like the stage actor he was.

"Jade has been through enough for one day. Could you please let it lie?" Blaze tried as she might to thwart the encounter and the fight that was about to ensue between Reece and me.

To her dismay, she failed, but I wouldn't.

"Listen to me, you piece of shit. I asked Tommy to stay behind and make sure if Viv called or came home from her trip early, he could inform her of the mishap out on the water, and let her know I was fine and not to worry. Now, I suggest you back off with your snide and unwanted observations."

"Dad, let's go. Blaze is right; Jade's been through enough today. Your personal remarks aren't helping."

"You see, Damien, that's where you're wrong. You can't read Jade the way I can. You couldn't when you dated her, and that's precisely why you lost her. I, on the other hand, can read her. She needs our help. She's involved with a man who's not in her league. An insignificant matter of infatuation, but one that is standing in the way of your happiness with Jade and vice versa. One I intend to rectify before Jade is hurt any further."

"Listen, old man, I came here with you to make sure Jade wasn't hurt. Now that we know it's a concussion and the girls are with her, we need to go," Damien snarled as he walked away from his father; his impatience and anger grew with each passing minute.

Of course, it didn't stop Reece from continuing his banter.

"Damien, please tell me where you think you're going? Back to my house? To that waste of time you're bedding down?"

I was sore, and although there was very little left emotionally between Damien and me, it was time to shut Reece up, not in the hopes of protecting his son, but to protect my wavering mental health. I was about to confront him when fate stepped in.

Arguments unleashed themselves, insults were strewn across the ER waiting area in every direction from all parties involved—all except me. No one could hear me; no one would listen. I needed to escape the madness and leave them to their own devices.

The real truth was I wanted to leave to see Tommy. He was all I thought about the entire time I was being poked and prodded. I decided while my menagerie of friends were fighting amongst themselves, I'd get the ball rolling and sign the papers to leave.

As I turned, to my surprise, he was here. Tommy came to rescue me a second time that day, but disappointment very quickly set in when I saw the hurt on his face, as he stared at me and everyone around me. He turned to speak with some guy I'd never seen before, a doctor I think. Both men nodded and exited the other side of the waiting room through doors that led into the main area of the hospital. I was far too weak to go after him on my own, so I enlisted the help of my brother's friend, who was an innocent bystander watching this shit show along with me.

He directed me toward the doors to leave. On our way out, I finally caught the attention of Blaze and blew her a kiss. She winked and gestured she'd call me tomorrow. With a brief nod, I concurred.

My brother's old friend quickly whisked me off to my home and made sure I was settled before leaving.

Although, I knew Tommy was back at the hospital, not seeing his car in the driveway when we pulled up had my stomach falling, as an eerie numbness enveloped my body and my mind.

Who was that guy Tommy was with? Was he a friend? Tommy looked heartbroken. Why didn't he come over? Why did he leave with that guy without a word? Maybe he wasn't going to rent the house after all.

Getting ahold of my emotions and the questions my mind was forging, felt like an impossible task. I needed answers from Tommy, but he wasn't there. He had to come home eventually, and if I was still awake, I'd face him then, but until that time came I came to the conclusion that stewing over my thoughts under a hot shower would be far better than sitting and brooding.

My shower went from practical...I was clean, to futile...I was soaked...drowning in thoughts...thoughts of him. That was it, I needed to dry off, throw on some sweats and tell him how I felt, there and then—before I chickened out.

Wait! What if he wasn't home, yet? This was silly. He had to back by now.

Then again, it was early evening and like me, I'm sure he hadn't eaten. I took a deep breath in, got up my nerve, swiped my keys from the counter, and headed next door. Once down the stairs in the alley, I saw Tommy's car was back in its normal parking spot. Relief washed over me, as I scaled his stairs quickly and knocked at his door.

I knocked several times, but no answer. His car was there. He had to be home. I then did what any irrational girl on a rational mission would do…I let myself in.

Slowly, I slid the screen shut behind me, careful not to allow it to jam. I called out to Tommy again, but still, there was nothing. Walking in further, I noticed the pictures and sketches Tommy had of his proposed renovations splattered across the massive island Jimmy had made to order years ago. Like second nature, I smoothed my hand over the aged and brittle surface of the driftwood, trying to reconnect with my past.

Remembering a moment Jimmy and I shared, what seemed like a lifetime ago…

"Babygirl, just don't stand there doing nothing. Help me get the boxes in from the deck before the storm hits." Jimmy struggled, lifting three boxes at once as he slammed into the screen door, taking it off its tracks and him off his balance.

All I could do was giggle.

"Nice, Jade… Are you going to help me or not?"

I rolled my eyes as I sat down on the floor, picking up his surfing magazines that were released from their cardboard confines as the boxes dropped open during his little mishap.

"I'm helping; I'm helping. You wouldn't need my help if you just took one box at a time, Jimmy."

"Unlike you, Jade, I don't have time to chase away the sun while I follow the moon."

"Huh?"

Frustrated with my confusion, he plopped down to where I was kneeling, dumped the one box he remained holding to the side of him and ran his fingers through his long curly locks.

Grabbing my wrist and pulling me over, next to where he was seated, he wrapped his arms around me, kissed my forehead, and explained his definition of me chasing away the sun while following the moon.

"Jade, I love you more than...surfing." His broad smile appeared as he tried to keep from laughing.

Shaking my head, I couldn't keep from laughing either.

Smiling, my thoughts returned to the present...the laughter and voices faded like ghosts into the background. Jimmy was right... that statement—the definition of me never really hit home until this moment.

My eyes welled up and a familiar edginess came over me. I decided after the walk down memory lane, now was probably not a good time for me to talk with Tommy. I was about to leave when I heard a thud in the room above my head. Looking at the ceiling I waited for more.

Nothing.

I turned to go, then hesitated before turning back and heading up the stairs to the room where the noise came from. As I reached the second-floor landing, the hiss of steam became clearer. The sound I heard was more than likely him closing the old hollow door to the bathroom. Another item on the endless list of things neglected since the house was left to be sold.

Jade, stop stalling. Do what you came here to do.

The closer I inched my way to the door, the more apparent my apprehension became; I was at war with my attraction for this man, but I couldn't turn away. I kept seeing Tommy's face at the hospital. His hurt, his avoidance of me, probably due to the people around me. None of them were here now. I could do this. I could make this about him and me with no interruptions.

I took a deep breath, entered the bathroom, and softly padded across the cool tile until the shower door with Tommy behind it was close enough to touch. His blurred image barely moved. His arms outstretched against the inner walls as the water fell over his head and down his neck and back...confined in thoughts he hoped would wash away.

The thumping in my ears grew increasingly loud, reminding me, pushing me toward something I never expected to happen…to feel for someone so deeply who I barely knew, yet seemed like I'd known forever. With trembling breaths, I weakly knock on the door's tin frame, startling the body behind it out of his trance. Multiple jiggling and jumbling occurred inside. A menacing crack echoed as it stiffly opened part way for him to peer out with my fist in mid-knock.

Retreating slightly, Tommy couldn't believe what he was seeing. It was written all over his face.

"Jade, wha-what are you doing here?"

I tried to think of something profound, something that would make sense.

Jade, the truth would be nice. Tell him the truth.

If only I knew the truth—I knew why I was standing here, but with everything I told myself now going out the window, I wasn't sure how to explain my change of heart. Maybe I just needed to stop this, walk out and lock myself in my home…not answer the door should he follow me. I didn't want this to exist, but I couldn't stop how I felt every time I was near him. He was a magnet and I was the used scrap metal being pulled in—automatically attaching myself to him.

"Jade, is something wrong? Are you sick? Do you need me to call someone?" True to form, he was kind and always willing to help.

He continued speaking, but for some reason, I couldn't understand what he was saying. The water pounded the walls; my thoughts were racing with questions. Maybe I didn't think this through? Again, did I turn and run and explain later the concussion caused my confusion, or did I do something for me and only for me for once in my damn fucked up life? It wasn't something to make Viv proud of me, or to keep my parents satisfied, it wasn't for Blaze or Reece or Kim or even Damien, but for me.

My throat tightened, dried up, and swelled. It was almost impossible to speak. Swallowing was a chore, words to give him seemed unattainable, but then, out of nowhere what gutted me spilled out along with my tears.

"I don't know," I barely squeaked through a whisper, not looking his way.

"Jade?"

His voice called to me. Swiftly, my eyes looked up as my tears rolled down with my simple world crashing around me. The world where I didn't need nor want a man in my life. Now, three years after Damien, three years after Jimmy's death, Tommy barely walked into a small part of that world...the beach house my brother called home. Where old memories and new emotions were unleashed. Ones I wanted to deny, ones I didn't want to feel. I could be on my own, an already successful businesswoman enjoying the sandy universe around me without the complication of a relationship. Yet, this man by his presence, his gestures...his unexplainable ability to do nothing, and still draw me to him was making me rethink everything I wanted or thought I wanted.

"I don't know, Tommy. I don't know why. Does there always have to be a fucking reason? A typical answer? Does there? I had to see you...that's all!" I paused to steady myself, which was virtually impossible. "Shit... that's not all. I know I'm not making sense... and no, it's not this damn concussion." I stopped.

"Hand me that towel next to you." He directed from behind the blurred door.

Looking around to the left and right of me, I found the large beach towel he was referring to and gave it to him. After a second or two, the water stopped and a bit of fumbling with the door and the towel occurred before he appeared in front of me. His dark locks randomly falling on his face. His chest still covered in droplets of water that trailed down to where the towel settled low on his hips covering the intimate parts of him he modestly kept hidden.

Our bodies close, yet not touching until he touched me. His hands cradled my face, his thumbs skimmed my cheeks, his eyes studying me, pondering and examining me as he tried to read what was inside without asking, without pushing. Holding his questions back, his powerful jawline visibly tightened, making my heart race. Together, our breaths were a measurable force between us, a force present from the beginning whether we recognized it or not, engulfing the room with an energy, a passion that neither one of us could deny.

After what seemed like a long calculated breath, Tommy spoke softly and held out his hand.

"Come with me."

chapter
eighteen

Tommy

THE LAST THING I expected to find was Jade at my door, let alone—my shower door. Barely dressed, wondering what was going on, and concerned with her demeanor tonight, I did the only thing I could do…

I took her to bed.

Not where I normally slept as I remembered Viv explaining the upstairs bedrooms were once occupied by Jade and her brother as children and eventually Jimmy as an adult. I didn't think to spend the night with her in a room where her brother slept before his accident was a good idea, so with a firm grip of her hand, I guided her back downstairs to the master turned guest room on the first floor.

We reached the kitchen island when Jade pulled back, dug in her heels, and demanded an explanation.

"Wait. Where are you taking me?"

With a coy grin, I simply told her, "To bed." Without giving her a chance to speak, I turned away and pulled her along once more until we reached the main floor bedroom. Still holding onto her, I lifted the comforter with my free hand and tipped my head to motion her in. More than a bit of annoyance and confusion played on her face. Her hand slipped out of mine, as she did what she was told.

"Now…how's your headache?" Asking with arms crossed trying to look as controlled as one could when wearing only a towel.

"What?" She leaned forward, her lips parted, not believing any of this.

"I said, how's your headache?"

"It hurts, but it's not something I can't handle."

"If it worsens…"

"I know; I know. Don't worry, I'll follow doctor's orders," She whined, cutting me off and avoiding the question she really wanted to ask, but I answered without her prompting.

"You're probably wondering what we're doing here in this room and what you just said is exactly why. You have a concussion and you're supposed to be resting through the weekend, but instead…" She finished my sentence.

"…I'm here with you." Her sweetness softened me.

"Yeah."

"Okay, now I have a question."

"Which is?"

"How did you know I had a concussion? I mean I just got home. Who told you?"

"I have my ways," I stated proudly.

"Which are?"

"I told the charge nurse at the desk I was your fiancé," I reluctantly confessed.

A giggle with a gasp escaped Jade's lips as she sat back studying me.

"What? Why is that so funny?"

"You told the nurse we were engaged? Don't you think that's a bit over the top? I mean all you had to do was ask me once I got back from the hospital."

"No more over the top than announcing to your friends at dinner that we were dating, especially since we had only met the night before," I stated, as to justify my behavior.

"Fair enough, but neither of us knew who the other one was on that dance floor."

"That's true, but the next morning you knew who I was and you still proceeded to tell everyone we were a couple that night at the dinner table," I teased, and she became miffed.

"I didn't see you complaining." She plopped back on the pillow, arms crossed, justifying her actions, yet a bit sullen…defeated.

"Jade, listen, I want you to stay here for the night. I'm not talking about sleeping with me. I'm talking about me making sure your concussion stays a minor one. It wasn't my intention to upset you. I hope you understand that?" Jade's face fell slightly.

Did I miss something? Did she want us to sleep together?

Compelled to figure her out, know her and get closer to her, I subtly sat next to her and placed my hand over hers. Jade stayed, no flinching or jumping or pulling away. It told me she was at least willing to listen and hopefully willing to stay the night after what I was about to say.

Staring at our connection and squeezing firmly, I began.

"I want you to know I've heard everything you've said from the very beginning. I know you're not looking to get seriously involved at the moment and that you're not sure if you ever will, but I'd be lying if I said I wasn't attracted to you. I think you've figured that out by now. I enjoy being around you and if that means friends, then so be it, but as a friend, I'm not going to stand by and not make certain you're okay after the incident you had on the water today. I can't, so don't ask me to."

I wondered if she'd thought I was overly intrusive. After all, we didn't know each other very long. I couldn't explain it, but I felt connected to her from the beginning, and with her being hurt I wanted her here, where I could watch her…care for her, even if that meant no strings attached…I could be okay with that. At least I thought I could.

I stared at our hands. Hell, I looked everywhere but at Jade herself. She must have thought I was a fool. First, my plan to move here and now tonight out of nowhere basically dragging her into the bedroom and ordering her into bed like a child.

What was I thinking?

I was about to apologize for my behavior when Jade did the unimaginable. She let go of my hand, climbed forward, placed a kiss on my cheek, and sat by my side on the edge of the bed.

"You're sweet, Tommy." She smiled, but it was slightly forced.

"What do you say? Will you stay tonight? You shouldn't be alone with a concussion."

She continued to smile and nodded.

"Can I get you anything? I'm sure you haven't eaten."

"I'm not really hungry, but I'd love a cup of tea. If it's not too much trouble."

"It's no trouble at all. I'll be right back."

"Tommy, wait… I'd rather stay out on the couch, if that's okay with you?"

I was perplexed, but whatever she wanted was fine. I put the water on and excused myself to trade my beach towel for a decent pair of sweats and a T-shirt.

When I returned, Jade had made herself at home by curling into one corner of the sectional and taking the large throw from the back of the sofa and placing it over her. She settled in and perused the lack of progress I made on the living room/dining room area.

"I know…go on say it."

"Say what?"

"How unfinished this room is."

"Why would I say that?"

"Because it's true?"

"You can't be serious? You haven't lived here long enough to complete a tenth of what needs to be done. Remember, I know what shape or lack thereof this place was in."

"I appreciate that. It means a lot coming from you. Thanks." Her words and my relief brought a smile to my face.

"You don't have to thank me. I understand."

I wanted to kiss her, but instead, I made small talk.

"Would you like to see some of the plans and changes I'm thinking of making? I'd love your opinion."

Jade nodded, as I handed her the tea and went to retrieve some of the photographs I took and magazine clippings I saved to give her an idea of where I was going with the renovations. After gathering the items I needed, I returned to find Jade asleep where I left her. It was a long day for both of us. I kissed Jade's forehead, making sure not to wake her. For me, I settled in the guest room downstairs; in case any issues arose in the middle of the night.

It wasn't long before I heard what I thought was a small whimper. I listened further, my head cloudy and in sleep mode; I dismissed it. What came next I couldn't dismiss.

"No, no, no, Jimmy…why…no…no!" Jade's anguish echoed through the house and engulfed me. Frantically running to her, she was up, awake, sweating, and holding her head.

"Jade, Jade…what's wrong?" Fear's ugliness crept through my body, questions swirled in my head as I sat down to take her close.

Had I caused this? I should have let her be.

Jade's breathing rattled, her body trembling…physically and emotionally she was weakening before my eyes. I had to do something. I *did* cause this by insisting she stay.

"Let me take you to the hospital?" I declared, lifting her body in my arms.

Pain shot through my shoulders. Her fingers dug deep.

"No, Tommy, no, I'm not going back to the hospital. Please…put me down." Sobbing, yet completely adamant she wouldn't allow me to help.

Fixing this wasn't going to be an easy task. She needed medical attention. Viv wasn't here. This was more than a memory or a nightmare. I was lost on how to help. I could call Blaze, but that would only set-off Montgomery, and she didn't need him or his help. Daniel hadn't seen Jade after Jimmy died, so I wasn't sure if calling him would make things better or set her further down a darker path.

Think ...

"You definitely need medical attention. Let me call my doctor friend. It's late, but he lives here on LBI and I'm sure he'd be happy to help."

The pounding of her breath was reduced to a muffled murmur, but still present. Jade nervously nodded in agreement, so without hesitation, I continued to hold her in my arms and called the doctor.

He arrived shortly thereafter.

Letting him in, he immediately honed in on Jade's weakened state on the couch across the room. He looked to me, but I said nothing. What could I say? I wanted him to do something, anything to make her well.

"Jade, I'm Dr. Roth. It's good to meet you." He extended his hand and Jade gingerly took it. Holding her focus at the connection of their hands at first, but then with shallow breaths and teary eyes, she acknowledged him.

"Thank you for coming. I'm so sorry you have to be here at such a late hour."

"No problem at all. Can you tell me what happened? I'm aware of the concussion. I was making rounds when you came into the emergency room this evening, and although I wasn't assigned to you I did see your chart."

Looking to both of us, a slanted smile played on Jade's face.

"You mean Tommy filled you in."

Cautiously, he sat next to her with me behind him like a hovering but concerned idiot.

"Yes, that too…now can you tell me what's going on? Have you had nightmares before? Or is this the first time?"

Jade stalled.

"I can leave and give the two of you some privacy," I said, walking towards the stairs.

"No, Tommy, please don't go." Desperation rose from Jade's voice instantly. She climbed over Dr. Roth and off the couch to stop me.

My arms folded around her, nuzzling her. "Okay, baby."

She turned to him, still holding me…her anchor, my strength lending her strength to explain what happened less than an hour ago.

Shaking her head, letting out a blunt sigh, Jade explained more than I anticipated.

"No, it wasn't the first time and although it's been awhile, I'm sure it won't be the last."

"What makes you say that?"

"Well, Dr. Roth…" Jade released me and positioned herself back on the couch to explain.

"…Tommy told me you're from LBI and you're a doctor, so you're obviously aware of my brother's sui…death. It was in all the local papers. You couldn't miss it, besides, you know how people talk." Her weakness was replaced with an arrogant resentment.

"Yes, well…living in a tighter community and the fact that your brother was somewhat of a local legend, I understand, but that doesn't completely explain tonight's situation. You have a concussion, and by all accounts, that alone can cause confusion and some temporary neurological effects post-trauma, but your nightmare doesn't appear to be a symptom of that alone."

"I wish it were."

"Why is that?"

"If this was an isolated incident then it more than likely wouldn't happen again or at least once my concussion healed, but…"

"But it's happened before." Dr. Roth didn't ask. He inquisitively stated.

"Yeah, for the most part. In the beginning, it happened all the time."

"The beginning? You're referring to the period after your brother's death?"

"Yes, you see, I was living in the city working for Reece Montgomery at one of his restaurants while Jimmy was living at the center in Philly after the accident. This house was unoccupied, so I'd come down and stay here versus my parents' place." Jade stood and ambled around the room explaining more.

"My parents had been consumed with the 'what if's or what could have been' and I couldn't deal with it. I was dealing with my own shit as a result of Jimmy's accident. Then when he died, I got it. I caught it like something contagious…what if Jimmy had told us about The Mavericks? What if I had only tried harder to stop him? It went on and on and on…and so did the nightmares."

"Did you speak to someone?"

"In the beginning I did. The counselors at the center where Jimmy had been were great and for a brief period afterward, I did speak with them, either in person or by phone, but eventually, I stopped."

"Why?"

"I felt better. Maybe better's not the right word. I felt like the situation was livable. My parents restricted me from staying at the house. They eventually started to rent it out and I had one built next door. I could finally do the day to day living. Eventually, the bouts of hysterical crying ended. Life was easier again. I could do this life all day long. The nightmares lessened almost completely."

"But…" Dr. Roth knew there was more.

Jade sat back down and faced us. Running her fingers through her long strands, feeling more comfortable, she continued.

"But my then fiancé decided I wasn't enough for his palate, so he screwed my brother's ex in a bed we shared in my new house. That's when, although less frequent, the nightmares started up again…not a lot, just here and there."

"You learned to live with them?"

"Yeah, in fact, until recently they were almost nonexistent."

"Shit! I caused this! I'm so sorry!" My outburst interrupted their conversation, but I couldn't just stand there and not own up to the past few weeks. My delicate hints to Jade for us to become more than neighbors. Pushing to take care of her tonight. Going along with and helping her fabricate a fake boyfriend. It all added to her stress and to her emotional state.

Jade looked at Dr. Roth and then to me, partially grinning.

"It's not your fault. The house has always been here, whether you lived in it or not. Jimmy existed. Damien still exists, just not in my life. No one can change that, nor would I want to. Tommy, things happen. The nightmares, the sadness, the anxiety happened before. They went away and now they've happened again, but I'm pretty sure they'll disappear as quickly as they came." Jade was calm, almost practical, which told Dr. Roth she was better for the most part and this episode was over, but I had gotten the feeling he was not completely convinced.

He tried to give her a prescription to help her sleep and explained she should couldn't start it for at least seventy-two hours, even so, she wouldn't take it. She said she had never relied on medications in the past and wasn't going to start now. We both thanked him for coming out and Jade promised to make an appointment to see him in a week.

I walked him out.

"Do you think she'll be okay?"

"For tonight, yes, Tommy, I'm a medical doctor and no expert, but I do believe Jade hasn't resolved the hurt that went along with her brother's passing. I'm not talking about the initial shock and grief. I'm talking about the here and now. The way she's living."

"I don't follow."

"You heard her. She was very practical, and it appears that she's come to terms with it. Perhaps the issues she had with her ex, yes, but her brother's death seems to be as prevalent as it was when it happened. Like I said, I'm not an expert, but I do think she needs to speak to someone…a psychologist or a counselor."

"Doc, I'm in no position to suggest that."

"I'm not saying you are, but you know her friends and relatives. You should explain to them what happened and have them speak with her, and of course, I'll discuss it with her when she comes in for her follow-up."

"Thanks, Doc."

"No worries. Say hello to Rain and Dominick for me when you speak with them."

"I will. Thanks, again."

Once Dr. Roth disappeared down the steps, I went back in to check on Jade.

The inquisition began the minute I stepped foot in the door.

"So he wants me to see someone I presume?"

"Were you listening?"

"No, but thanks for the heads up." A sly smile formed on Jade's face.

"Great, I couldn't even do that right." Running my fingers through my hair, I slumped next to Jade on the couch.

She reached for my shoulder. "Please don't worry. It doesn't take a genius to figure out that Dr. Roth would want to refer me on to a specialist, but I've been through all of that, and I'm not going to be analyzed any further."

"Maybe it would be good for you to talk with someone and get the past off your chest."

"The problem isn't with the past. The past is the good and ugly blended into one memory. It's there because it happened. It's not something to be denied by me, that's impossible, or picked over like a vulture, as some therapists would like to do. The problem is with moving on." She stood and abruptly turned back, contemplating how to put all of this in perspective…for me, not her.

"Like I told Dr. Roth, I could do this life here on the island all day long…on autopilot. It's when I think about how different it could have been…I don't know." Shaking her head, she paused. "I don't know how to explain it, Tommy. Jimmy was always better at coloring things than me. I guess I wish I could get the 'what could've been' out of my head and stop rethinking it after all these years. Believe me, I'm not in denial. I know what happened. People make it look easy, but it's harder than you could ever imagine. I lived it and now I live with it and for the most part, I've made peace with it in my own way. That's all anyone has to understand and respect my feelings about it. That's all I ask."

"In some weird way, I know what you're going through. It's true I haven't had a devastating loss, and please don't misunderstand me, I'm not minimizing your pain in any way, but my brother and I had a bad falling out months ago and we've been barely speaking to one another. I miss our relationship because prior to what caused our situation now, we weren't only brothers, we were the best of friends…were being the present tense."

"You have to make amends. No matter what happened between you and your brother, you have to work it out. Nothing is ever that bad and even if it is, it's not more important than the two of you or your relationship. I mean it. I get it and, yet I can't get what you could have…back. It's gone forever. You're both alive, and life is far too short for bullshit." She came to me and kneeled in front of me, placing her hands on my thighs. Searching my eyes. Desperate for me to agree with her—agree I would try. She wasn't hysterical. Her words weren't frantic. Jade was determined and nothing in her would allow a bendable plausible excuse.

"Promise me you'll try?"

I didn't respond. Instead, I ran my hands back and forth over hers, nervously. This night, this girl, this conversation placed me on edge. I missed Mike. I missed my life. The life I left. It wasn't perfect, but it was mine. Fuck! I could have done all of this that I'm doing right now and still shared it with my family instead of lying about it, keeping them in the dark.

Get serious! You couldn't have told them. They would have stopped you or gave you that same old advice that you weren't interested in. Wasn't your move the point of this renovating your life and not just a beach house?

What she said had my mind racing. Was I wrong? What now? The more I thought, the more I struggled with my decision in a way I hadn't before. I kept my connection to her. Feeling her skin kept me sane. It kept me in the present, shielding me from the past. Jade witnessed my distress and stopped it. Halted it completely by allowing her fingers to intertwine with mine, making our connection deeper.

Now it was just us…unveiling our weaknesses for only Jade and me to see. Her struggle to live a life without her brother. For me, it was to live a life away from mine because of the mistakes I had made. Mistakes that ripped me and Mike apart. Jade wanted me to make amends. Leaving, for me, was doing that. Giving him the space to not have to look at me, know me, or even deal with me…moving away allowed him to move on.

Jade saw through me. She saw the hurt—the hurt I never talked about. Hurt that stemmed from a reason and a situation she didn't know about, and one that tonight, didn't matter. To her,

I mattered, and she did for me. Nothing else did, not our families, or friends, or the world beyond the roaring ocean outside these weathered walls…only us in this moment.

Not a word was uttered between us. In an instant, everything changed from her to me. I was caring for her and now she was doing the same in return. Her concern, our attachment, prompted her to stand and climb into my lap, not allowing our hands to break the link. Jade's long mane fell forward, creating a veil of intimacy around us. She closed the gap, her chest against mine. Her breathing rapid, her nipples peaked through the thin swath of cotton she was wearing. My cock hardened, her body squirmed in response as it had on our first night together on the dance floor. I couldn't think. I wanted her and for tonight she wanted me. Could this be all we would have? Would I be satisfied with only a single night with her? Do I stop this now and regret it? Or make her mine for the moment and deal with the aftermath when it came?

Her lips brushed my mouth, as her pussy rocked my cock. I was crazy to think I could end it. I wanted her. I wanted inside of her. Our fingers pulled free with her arms draping across my shoulders and around my neck. My hands cradled her head and our lips pressed together, pushing, opening for our tongues to explore. To more than kiss, to free fall…exit our bodies that betrayed us with loss and hurt and guilt. Using what tortured us separately, to bring us together.

Our senses heightened…alive. Our mouths grasped for more…the more we needed to stop the hurt, heal the loss, and banish the guilt. The more—we could only find in each other. The more that I wanted to continue. I knew I was being foolish, but I needed to be sure she wanted me the way I wanted her. The day's events were complicated enough without me adding to them…I had to know.

Breaking our kiss…"Baby, do you want this?"

Her breaths shortened…shallow, and her eyes closed, she uttered nothing.

"Jade."

Looking up, her lips parted as she nodded, but didn't stop there.

"Take away the nightmares, Tommy. Replace them with you." Her kiss was brief but telling. She lifted her top over her head exposing her breasts.

Trailing my hands down, supporting her back, I kissed her mouth, her chin, her neck, her chest, reaching her nipple and covering it while allowing my tongue to trace my desire over the hardened bud. Her whimper muted, her skin washed in goosebumps.

Continuing, I teased, nipped, and licked, as I turned to lie her back against the cushions and settle between her legs. My fingers dedicatedly grazed across her throat, my head followed down between her breasts, making her body arch up in response. Her heart's center was inches from me, within earshot; it aroused me further. Its beats created a frantic rhythm describing her inner wants, which mimicked my own.

My fingertips gently skimmed the top of her sweats. With each deliberate brush along the material's edge, I lowered them slowly.

Jade's back bowed further. Her moans characterized her needs. Her tone subtle at the start, strengthening in the present with each kiss I placed on her skin. My lips followed the deliberate trail of my hand below her waist. My mouth reached the line of material that needed to be crossed. Jade's fingers weaved through my hair, pulling at first, then applying tender pressure to direct my mouth where she wanted it to go.

"Tommy, please," her voice strained, requesting more of what I wanted to give.

"I know, baby." My words were there to soothe, but also there to keep my actions above a snail's pace, yet deliberately staying back enough to make our night together last.

Jade's delicious pleas emboldened me. My mouth kissed her lower belly, my hands gripped the plush waistline of her bottoms, yanking them down, as her long limbs assisted in kicking them off.

I looked to her for permission, her eyes glazed over—she nodded. My eyes went to her closed off center. Gently, I pressed her thighs open. The scent of her sex invited me in; I stalled by touching—massaging her clit. Her body shuddered at the connection, as I pressed forward with my thumb, rubbing hard against her swollen nub. I continued to stroke her core, and my tongue followed. Her pussy was slick, needy, and fully engaged by my actions. She was running away from the past—escaping, focusing on what my hand and mouth were doing to her. Tasting her took away her pain, stroking her soothed her sorrow, but for me, it raised the emotional stakes. I knew having her now, made me want to take her further. Would there be more when our night was over? Apprehension battled my desires at every turn. I couldn't let it win. I would make her mine, give myself to her fully. My physical body reinforced what I felt for her; I wasn't like Damien...I didn't want or need anyone else.

Without knowing, Jade pulled me in the first time we met—there was no turning back for me. From that night on the dance floor, I felt it and I knew she felt it, too. I needed to bring that connection here fully...now. To take her to that moment, to the point where everything that was hurting her would be destroyed, and the only thing left would be us.

My wait was over. Her body arched back, completely giving in—strengthening our intimate bond, before she settled into the pillows, letting her shoulders relax down as her fingertips lightly feathered through my hair—her delicate touch coaxed my body up, while her hands took hold of my shoulders.

Her voice ached, calling my name. "Tommy, please don't stop."

With her plea, my mouth kissed hers briefly as I obliged and slid my body over her until I settled between her legs. My mouth on her mouth, we shared the taste of her arousal, as she slid my pants down, over my hips and away. She freed me, allowing her hand to take hold of my shaft as she guided me inside her.

I stilled. My head exploded with thoughts of us racing through my mind. Her pussy firmly pressed forward and pulled back, softly—hesitant to break our connection. Finding our rhythm, we buried our pain in the sex—for her, a love that was lost. For me, a love I never thought I'd find.

Her voice trembled, the way she begged—moved me. Being inside of her, making love to her, wasn't real. It seemed an impossibility, but together...there we were, where I wanted to remain.

I hesitated, again. She'd been injured by her past. I wouldn't hurt her—the possibility, the guilt... held me back. Skin to skin, I was careful...cautious. Somehow she knew...

"Tommy, I'll be okay." Her voice soothed me.

"I know."

She met my gentle, yet deliberate thrusts. Our breathing accelerated, her cheeks flushed as my eyes flashed to her beautiful face. This was our time...together...entirely us, in the present. To let go, to release everything we held inside, our hurt, our desires, our wants, our secrets...our fears...the good and the ugly. No kissing, just watching, two imperfect people perfectly coming together. Her body quivered, tightening around me...holding on, yet still holding back.

I wanted my cock to stay in her body. I painfully held back, knowing once we reached that point ... our first, it would never happen again. Hell, my mind ran with the thoughts of it being our one and only time together. My mind crushing me, tormenting me, keeping me steps back from my desires, holding off while savoring each and every second—searing them into my brain.

Please, I don't want this to end.

But the end came as did I, my release…spinning my mind and body out control, completely lost inside of her while hanging on for dear life.

There we were…our breathing balanced, but not yet tempered. Lying down carefully next to her, I buried my head in her neck. Her pulse against my lips kept me there with her, telling me she was real, but could this last or would this be over before it started?

I didn't want to think about it. I didn't want to think at all. It was the same for Jade. She didn't speak, she simply turned her body to mine, and we drifted off to find sleep together.

chapter
nineteen

Jade

DAYLIGHT HEATED MY cheeks. The warmth of the morning's sun mixed with a coastal breeze carried with it the alluring scent of coconut and briny saltwater, and the sounds of early beachgoer's muted breakfast conversations on the sand, gently coaxed me to wake.

That wasn't the only warmth I felt that morning. The coziness of Tommy's body around mine, and the heavy blanket he'd covered us with compelled me to stay put. It was a long time since I had been with a man, and yet never in that time, had I responded the way I had with him.

Secretly, I didn't want our night to end, and now I didn't want our morning to begin. I wanted to keep the closeness, the intimacy that we'd shared for a bit longer. Before the world woke up and the mindless bullshit of the day came crashing in. I wanted it to be just us, hidden away from all outside interferences.

"Hey," Tommy murmured, then kissed my temple as he pulled me closer to him. Raising my chin, I kissed the edge of his jawline.

"Morning," I said as I buried my head against his chest, pulling the covers higher, not wanting to move.

He didn't protest. Instead, he deepened his embrace, letting out a sated sigh and letting me in on a little secret. It wasn't morning. With yesterday's disruptions from Reece in the midst of my girls' day with Kim and Blaze, the surfer who thought he knew the deep blue sea, the accident that followed…the hospital, the beautiful memory of Jimmy, then the not so good nightmare, Dr. Roth's evaluation of me, and ending the night with the incredible sex I had with this man next to me, my body slept past noon.

What I thought were the sights and sounds of morning were actually midday.

See what being in bed with Tommy does to you?

"Noon…huh?" Thank goodness for my staff. After the accident, I came home and called each of them to explain what occurred, knowing I would be out of commission for a few days, but told them they should call me if any problems should arise while I was recuperating.

"Baby, your body needed it. That reminds me. How's your headache?" He asked, lightly massaging my temple in the spot where the longboard hit.

"Gone. The sex cured it." I playfully smiled.

He returned the smile. "It did, did it? Did the sex also cure your lack of appetite? As I remember, you haven't eaten anything since this time yesterday."

"Now that you mention it. Yeah, I am."

"Good. What should we order?"

"Order? You mean you're not going to cook me lunch?" I teased.

"I would if I could, but that kitchen in there seems to be closer to a fire hazard than I originally thought."

I laughed because Tommy's description wasn't far from the truth.

"Eggs, French Toast?"

"Breakfast it is." With a quick peck on my mouth, a push back, and then another more intense kiss, Tommy left to place the order.

After he left the room, I swiped my clothes from the floor and dressed. He returned to the living room in a pair of old jeans and a loose-fitting tee, carrying the plates, napkins, and utensils for when the food arrived. Once it did and we were eating, silence emanated throughout the room, which proved we were both starving. Finally getting through a few bites satisfied us for the moment, our conversation began.

"I'm glad you stayed with me," Tommy said, not smiling and sounding unsure of himself.

"So am I." Three words that relaxed him visibly. The night with Tommy was more than natural. All things considered, it was perfect. I hoped perfection would continue now that we were fully awake and talking. Though by the looks of things, I doubted it.

"I'm happy to hear that." Tommy's somber appearance as he stared at his plate told me he had something on his mind. I think I knew what he was thinking.

"You are? You don't look happy."

Throwing his napkin down, he explained, but I knew what was coming.

"Shit! Jade, I don't want last night to be…the last night." He stood and walked around the room and began to pace. "I want to start fresh. I wish I never told you about…"

"Your plan?"

"Yeah, my bright idea to change my life on a schedule."

"Why have you been so insistent on a timeline?"

Tommy stood in the doorway leading to the patio. Leaning on the doorjamb, rubbing his chin, I saw my question took him back, possibly to a time or to feelings he may not have wanted to revisit, but did for me.

"I never asked to go to Italy and stay with my friend Rain and her family. I was a little boy when we moved there. Cella, Rain's mom, seemed to have a way of manipulating situations and everyone around her. My parents were traveling with their business and much of their time was spent in Europe for long stretches. Back and forth to the States was grueling, but my mom didn't want to leave us with others during those trips, so we went with them. As we grew closer to school age, Cella suggested that we live on the compound her and her husband owned in Capri. This way, my parents could commute by boat or plane and, except for a few instances, be home in time for dinner. It worked out well for the adults in the room, but I was thrown into something I didn't know how to handle as a child, yet I adapted; I had Rain right there with me. She and I were inseparable, and the closeness had grown stronger as the years went on. It wasn't sexual; it was so easy to be with her and to not have any expectations placed on me or on her, for that matter. As grownups, we dated other people. We came to each other if there were problems…when there were problems. Then one day, Rain's world changed, and from that day on, she needed me less and less."

"Why? Did she meet someone?" I asked.

"Yes, she did." Tommy turned away from the view to focus on me while he continued his story which led to his explanation.

"She met the love of her life. A man who was her polar opposite. He was as controlling as her parents were, but couldn't control her because Rain was older and stronger and wouldn't allow it. She became his weakness and him, her strength. I know I said she was stronger, but in some ways, it was a facade. He broke that down. I hated every minute of it. I hated what it did to her at times, but in the end…Rain won. She got a love she wasn't looking for but found in him. I watched them over that year; how they fought to stay together when everything around them was tearing them apart. I wanted that. I wanted that kind of love for me."

"So, you set out on a journey that led you here?"

"Not here originally, but then it made sense. I loved the ocean. LBI was far enough away from the city where I lived, but still familiar and close enough to the ones I loved. Like I said, it made sense."

"I see." I thought he was done, but I was wrong, he continued.

"What didn't make sense was you."

"Me?"

"Yeah, I mean my immediate feelings for you didn't make sense. I never had that with anyone before. I wanted to explore it. I wanted to make sure I wasn't reading something into what happened between us…that wasn't truly there. Do you realize no matter what I'm doing in this house, it always comes back to you? Whether you'll like it or if it's in keeping with what your brother would have done for the place? It always comes back…to you."

"Why?"

"Why? Because I was worried I blew my chance to keep the house."

I chuckled, not laughing at him, but because I found his statement bizarre.

"Jade, c'mon…Put yourself in my shoes. I just started these renovations, hoping in a year I would get to keep the house and start a family," Tommy said, returning to share our lunch together.

"Like I said, it's not out of the realm of possibility, but you're right. After last night, I'd say you need to revisit and revise."

"Does this mean…?" Eager to know what I was thinking, Tommy stiffened and braced himself for what he assumed would be my change of heart.

"Tommy, like I told you before, I'm not ready for a serious or permanent type of relationship, but after last night, I know I'd like to spend more time with you and get to know you better. I just don't want it to feel planned. I'm not sure I'm ready for that."

"I can be spontaneous. Spontaneity is my middle name."

"Yeah, that's very true. I mean you did jump right in while I lied to Reece about us dating, and you played along on numerous other occasions, none of which were planned."

He thought about it, smiled while he chewed a mouthful of food. He seemed satisfied with my description of him, but then Mr. Spontaneous turned the tables on me.

"I guess you're right, but what about you?"

"Me…what about me?"

"Well, think about it. You started this. I just played along. I would say you are far more spontaneous than I am, baby."

"What are you getting at?" I smirked. I had a feeling he was leading into something to prove his point.

"As we established, you are just as spontaneous as me, possibly even more so, then why hadn't you been out there dating?"

I opened my mouth to speak, but he stopped me.

"And before you go off on me, I mean why have you sworn off men if you have such a carefree attitude?"

"I haven't sworn off men. I think last night proved that. I've sworn off serious relationships."

"I see."

"It's true. I date, but that's just it. I date, and I don't have to deal with commitment or expectation or …"

"Or the complications?" He added.

"Exactly…I can be myself, and if we click, great, and if not, so be it…no harm done."

"How's that working for you?"

"Before last night, it was nothing special or surprising, except…"

"Except what?" He smirked.

"Well, except for you and me pretending we were in a relationship. Oh, and the guy I went out with last month."

"I'm afraid to ask." He sat up straight knowing this would be interesting.

"Don't be."

"Okay, I'm asking."

"Well, after he asked me what I did for a living, and I told him, he said I was lazy."

"Come again?"

"I explained that I lived here on the island, and that I owned a specialty food shoppe and I worked about six months out of the year, and he said it was because I was lazy and not motivated to move ahead in life."

Tommy went to speak, but I interrupted him.

"Oh, yeah, and then he said he couldn't possibly be within someone like me because I lacked drive and initiative."

"Holy shit. What an asshole."

"You think?"

"So what did you say to him?" Tommy was smiling. I guessed partially because he was curious, and also because he had the feeling there was a punchline, and there was.

"I told him since he believed I had no drive in life, I would prove to him that evening that I had lots of drive. I had the car and I drove us to the restaurant, so I drove out of there leaving him to find his own way home. There's drive for ya."

A quick arch of my right brow and a smug purse to my lips ended my story but gave Tommy a huge belly laugh as he tilted back and clapped his hands in approval.

His smile faded, his laughing stopped, and his face darkened as he noticed the nausea from my stomach had cast a green hue on my face.

He moved closer.

"Are you going to be sick?"

My hands held his forearms, steadying myself, reminding me of our first night together on the dance floor, and the way I held him last night when I opened for him.

Deep, slow breaths in and out lessened the sickening feeling enough to respond to him.

"I'm fine. I think everything has finally caught up with me."

"Can I get you anything? Do you want to lie down in the bedroom?"

We stood up together, Tommy holding my arms gently to make sure I didn't fall.

"Maybe it would be a good idea."

I looked to find him watching me, regarding me. Something came over me…something I felt inside when I first met him…a security, a safe feeling…a trust. That's when I did the spontaneous.

I leaned in, kissed his cheek, and said, "Thank you, for everything. Thank you for us… last night." I couldn't leave him there for some reason. I couldn't move away. I wanted the closeness now.

The tips of his fingers traced through the edge of my hair, as he studied me intently, "My pleasure."

My insides deliciously twisted, "Tommy, did you mean it when you said you'd like us to be more than just pretend?"

"Yeah, I meant it. You know all of this. But I know that after what you went through last night…the nightmare I mean, I'm willing to slow this down. I never want to be the reason for…"

"Shhh…" I placed my fingertips over his lips to quiet his unfounded thoughts.

His smile carried a hypnotic power over me, making me feel a pull for this man that I hadn't felt for anyone in my entire life. One I had been trying hard to fight off. To keep the promise I had made to myself …to avoid getting hurt by not getting serious. Considering the attraction that started between us instantaneously, the almost immediate attachments we formed toward one another.

It looked as though I was in the toughest fight of my life…my love life. With Tommy I wanted to break the self-inflicted promise I imposed three years ago.

And the fight…was one I wanted to lose, slowly.

chapter twenty

Tommy

JADE APPEARED PREOCCUPIED following the hospital's orders to rest while healing from her concussion. Work for her was out of the question for a few days, but she wanted to check on her shoppe and drive over to the new location to see how the renovations were progressing. I agreed to take her. The day was clear and warm, a slight breeze still holding steady since the morning.

We pulled up in front of the building. "It looks like it's closed."

"That's because it is. On the weekends, the locals and vacationers swarm the place in the morning and they're finished picking up their orders by noontime. I'm the only one who hangs around to get the week's paperwork completed." She explained as she was managing to unlock the door for us to go inside.

"Wow, your former date was right?"

Jade turned back with a smirk and looked at me.

"You are lazy, closing at noon," I joked, which got me an eye roll and a laugh.

"Very funny, are you coming?"

"Right behind you, baby."

Once we finished picking up some paperwork Jade wanted to complete while resting at home, we headed to the new location not too far down that same street. When we pulled up, the workers were calling it quits for the day.

"Hi, guys. How is everything coming along?" Jade addressed the group of men as we approached.

"Wonderful, Miss Stanton, we're waiting on a few permits for the next phase of the project. They should be in by next week."

"First of all, call me Jade and secondly, did you guys get the boxes of treats to bring home to your families?" Jade looked in the windows and around the outside perimeter as if the delivery of food never arrived.

"Yeah, Miss…Jade, we put them in our coolers when they arrived about an hour ago. Thank you for doing that. Our kids look forward to your cupcakes, and I'm on my wife's good side when I surprise her with your chocolate covered strawberries."

Jade smiled proudly.

"I'm glad. It's the least I can do for all of your hard work to get this place ready."

The men nodded and smiled back, and filled her in on a few last-minute changes that were necessary for the reconstruction of the building. Other than that, Jade seemed pleased and sent them off wishing them a nice weekend. We couldn't go inside the building, but we peered in the two large windows and spied through the closed large double door in the center of the facade.

"It's really coming along." Jade acknowledged with her nose to the glass like a kid at a candy store.

I followed Jade's cue.

"Hmmm, it looks great! What color are you going to paint the walls?"

She backed away to face me. "I'm not sure. That's the toughest part of this project. Well, for me anyway. The equipment…ovens, freezers, and mixers are being brought over from the other location, but the decor is harder to decide on than I originally thought."

"Why so difficult?"

"Well, I want to change the decor. I don't want it to be the same as my current place."

"That's understandable being a new place and all."

"Exactly, and the truth is when I originally launched Summertime Sweets, I was with Damien and he helped in directing his opinion on anything and everything. Now, I have the chance for a clean slate, so I want it to be perfect."

"I understand."

"I know you do." She was referring to the beach house—my clean slate.

"I have an idea. What do you say we head home, and I'll bring over the paint cards and color books I received from the interior design store in Manhattan? They came in the mail last week and I really haven't looked at them. We could order in later, and perhaps go over them after dinner?"

She was about to say something but stopped.

"Fuck! I said we'd take this slow and I've done the opposite."

"Stop…that isn't it."

"Then what is it?"

She pulled on my arm bringing me closer.

"This is what it is." Jade placed her mouth on mine.

Taking hold of the back of her neck, I pushed my tongue into her mouth and allowed her words to carry my feelings deeper into our kiss. Jade moaned slightly, tightening her grip on my arm, telling me she was aroused, as was I.

Each time Jade kissed me, my inner reaction was the same—disbelief. It couldn't be happening, but it was. There was only one problem. I was falling fast and hard for this girl. With my descent came worry. The worry of when the time would be right to tell her what caused the rift between me and my brother. *And* what my reason behind what destroyed our family was, which in turn could cause Jade to walk away from me forever. What would I do then? How could a life after her be worth living?

I internally shook it off. We were here. We were now. That's all I should have been focusing on, and I did my best to do that.

"Let's go home."

She nodded, climbing into the car.

We pulled up to our respective homes and noticed a small familiar crowd which included Blaze, Reece, Kim, and Viv were standing in front of the alleyway between my house and Jade's. Blaze rushed the car first, barely allowing me to stop and effectively blocking Jade in the car.

"Where the hell have you two been?" Frantic, windblown, and taking no prisoners, Blaze demanded answers, but Jade was having none of it.

"Let go of the door."

Jade opened the passenger door of my car, slid out, and closed it discreetly. Pausing towards my direction to prepare herself for the onslaught of her nosy, albeit concerned friends and family.

"Okay, now would you like to explain where you've been since yesterday?"

"What are you talking about?"

"I even called the police, but they wouldn't do a search until you were missing at least 24 hours."

"Would you please give me a break? That's a bit dramatic, even for you."

"Blaze was thoroughly worried. I don't understand why you didn't pick up the phone and call one of us." Reece intruded as usual.

"If any of you had called me, I would have called you back."

"We did." Their voices blared in unison.

"I didn't get any messages." Jade stopped, thought about it, and realized I had her phone.

"How could you forget something like that? Blaze was worried about you," Reece scolded her further.

"For your information, I'm a grown woman and when Blaze is off with you as she has been for the last six months, she wasn't at all worried about my well-being then."

Viv and Kim smirked as I went to join them.

Blaze went to respond, but Jade cut her off.

"Furthermore, being a grown woman, I was otherwise occupied for the past 16 hours and finally…as you can see, I'm completely fine." She winked in my direction.

Blaze shakily pulled Jade down the driveway out of earshot of the rest of us. After what seemed like an hour, but was only several minutes, Blaze pecked her cheek, summoned Reece, and they sped away toward the other side of the island.

Viv, Kim, and I came forward to meet Jade.

"Everything good between the two of you?" Viv inquired.

Jade kissed her aunt's cheek. "It will be when Blaze learns to not poke her nose where it doesn't belong. Hi, Kim, sorry you had to be pulled out here at this hour. The Palm must be mobbed."

"It is, so if you'll excuse me, I'm going to head back to the club. Are you sure you're well?"

"I'm in good hands, Kim." Both ladies smiled and promised they'd talk tomorrow.

Last but not least was Jade's Aunt Viv. She was owed an explanation.

"Aunt Viv, I'm so sorry you were dragged back here for nothing."

"Yes, Viv, I'm sorry too…I forgot all about Jade's phone." Explaining to soften the situation the best I could.

"No apologies necessary, Blaze has an issue when it comes to self-control. I knew there had to be a logical explanation for what happened, but her hysteria prompted me to return home not because I was worried about Jade, but I was worried about Blaze's reaction to the situation, and Reece playing into her hands to help further his own personal agenda."

"Aunt Viv, you look tired. Let's go inside, and I'll make us all a cup of tea."

"Jade, how about we go inside and I make you ladies some tea instead," I suggested, as she was supposed to be resting and so far, she had done anything but rest.

They nodded in agreement.

"I'd definitely love a cup of tea with the two of you and an explanation of how your relationship appears to have changed from yesterday morning." Viv's flat-lined smile was humorous, yet she seemed rather elated with the idea of her niece and I being together.

After tea and a revealing conversation about Jade's accident and our new-found relationship, omitting the part about the sex, of course, I went home and pulled out the brochures and samples for the old kitchen cabinets. The cabinets would be coming out in the next week or so to make room for the new ones, which wouldn't be here until after the 4th of July weekend, next month.

I returned back with the samples, to find Jade in bed, fast asleep. Quietly, I went downstairs and placed the brochures on the kitchen island, and took this opportunity to call Blaze and Kim. I wanted to set their minds at ease after what transpired in the alleyway earlier today. Finally, by 9 pm, I realized Jade wasn't getting up, so I checked one last time before heading back downstairs and crashing on her couch.

Sunday morning, or I should say early Sunday afternoon, I woke, still in yesterday's clothes. I washed up and went upstairs to check on Jade. I knocked on her door, but no one answered. Perhaps Dr. Roth was mistaken; perhaps the tests weren't clear and Jade's blow to the head was worse than first thought. Yet, she seemed to be improving. I knocked harder this time…still no response.

"Jade!" I called out and again… no answer.

Stepping back, then moving forward, I apprehensively opened Jade's bedroom door and entered the room. The bathroom was empty. I looked around and noticed the patio doors to her bedroom deck were open. As the breeze swelled, her curtains billowed outward. I called her again, checked the deck…there was nothing.

Looking off into the distance, I saw the image of her walking along the shoreline away from our homes. Wondering why she hadn't come over to wake me, I rushed down to catch up with her and find out what was going on.

In the past, I was usually the one to keep a cool head when things were in chaos, but with Jade, things were different. In mere moments, worry consumed me, and I feared the worst. Why didn't I crawl into bed next to her instead of opting for the couch? I should have checked on her more, but I thought I was doing the right thing by giving her some space and letting her rest. I thought we agreed to take it slow, but maybe I was being too cautious, I see now it was a mistake. Maybe taking her to bed was a mistake? Then, forgetting about everyone in Jade's world, but us, may have caused her more hidden distress.

Jade was different from any woman I had ever met. At first, I thought she held together pretty well, not letting the broken pieces of her past control her todays or her tomorrows…at least that's what she wanted everyone to believe.

Until yesterday, I believed it myself, but after her nightmare, I knew she was fighting something deep inside of her. Something she wanted to deny, because denying it made it less real…less confrontational and therefore something she could live with.

In my opinion, Jade wasn't living. She was not unlike me. She was existing. Conceivably, she might not have realized it. She quite possibly didn't know how to move on from her brother's death, not that anyone in that situation ever moves on, but perhaps they learn to survive and live differently.

On the surface, she was doing that. She admitted to it the other night, but how long before living like that no longer works; it's been several years already. Could she feasibly go on like this forever or would something change? From the people around her appeasing her, or you could say monitoring her, distracting her, it quite possibly could go on forever. Maybe that's why it's gone on this long.

They loved her and meant well, but they weren't helping. By all accounts, they were enabling her. I wanted to change that, and I secretly hoped if our relationship progressed, the dark clouds that followed Jade from a distance would eventually evaporate.

As I continued at a steady clip along the shoreline, Jade's form became clearer. Her walk turned into a light jog, and if I didn't pick up the pace, she would disappear from view.

That woman never listens. She's supposed to be taking it easy.

The closer I got, the more I could tell she'd been crying. Maybe she had another nightmare, and I didn't hear her this time? Slowly, I approached her. Her cheeks were wind-bitten, her eyes somber. She didn't turn. She just stood there.

Aimlessly, but securely holding the smooth white water stone Jade stared off into the distance at two older gentlemen fishing out on the jetty early this morning. I wondered if she knew I was there with her. Her silence tortured me.

Her head turned slightly, her chin delicately laid across her shoulder. Her eyes closed briefly, as a tear trailed down her cheek and a false smile formed on her lips.

"I'm so tired. Tired of trying to be everything to everybody."

I caught a wild strand of her hair, billowing in the wind, and gently secured it behind her ear.

"Jade, you know it's not your job to be everything to everybody."

"I know." She whispered, then nodded…her stiff body pivoting completely to face mine.

"I know, Tommy, but for once…just once…I'd like to be everything to somebody."

Letting out a deep breath, I went to her. She didn't pull away. Instead, she searched my face for a response to her statement…I complied.

"Baby, I'll do whatever you ask me to, but I've got to tell you after the other night, after tasting you, touching you, holding you, I don't want us to take it slow. I want you, Jade. I want you now. Not tomorrow, not a week or six months from now, but now; what do you say?" I kissed her mouth, brushed my lips against hers, and left them to linger there briefly as I waited for her to answer.

More tears came, as Jade wept in relief. Her arms wrapped tightly around me.

"Yes, Tommy, yes…I thought I could wait, but what am I waiting for?"

I smiled against her cheek and kissed the tears that continued to come.

"What made you change your mind?" I asked without letting go.

"Last night." Two words…I heard them but didn't get it. This time I pulled back to understand her completely.

She nodded and wiped her face before she explained.

"I woke up in the middle of the night and realized you never came to bed. I sat there watching you sleep, overthinking everything, this past weekend—when we first met, the night on the dance floor at The Palm. Even the last three years."

"What did you decide?"

She walked toward the water and tossed the stone she had been holding out onto the waves.

"I came to the conclusion I was lying to myself. I told myself I was happy. I was a good daughter, a good niece, a good friend, and three years ago a good sister and a good fiancé. Everybody in my life moved on after Jimmy died, including him. Yet, I was living for everyone else, but me. The shoppe and the home I had built were the only two places I had been truly happy. Come to think of it, I'm not even sure if happy is how I would describe it. I was safe. My life was predictable, I did what I wanted to do when I went to work and came home, but it was mundane…boring."

I smiled knowingly, "Safe."

"Yes…safe."

"I know exactly what you mean…to live a life of predictability you know exactly what you're getting out of it and exactly what you expect to put into it, nothing more nothing less. There are no bumps in the road to contend with." We started to walk hand in hand down the coast and talked more.

"I guess that's why you moved here and created the life that you did for yourself, as well?"

"Yeah, I guess you're right. I thought I was being spontaneous, but the more I look at it the more I wanted to direct my situation, be in control."

"We both did."

I pulled her back into my arms and kissed her. Without guilt or apprehension or pause, I kissed Jade long and hard, letting her know I wasn't going anywhere and that she was stuck with me, for as long as she would have me.

chapter
twenty-one

Jade

EACH TIME TOMMY looked at me, kissed me—touched me, my insides confirmed I did the right thing. I stopped denying him. I stopped pretending that getting serious soon after we met was a bad thing, *and* I started breathing again. The life I created had me holding my breath for three years… three long years. Finally, I exhaled.

"Tell me what you want to do today, baby." Tommy's shadowy tone, caressing touch woke me slowly.

"Hmmm…I'd love to stay in bed with you and do everything we did last night and more, but it's back to work for me," I giggled, as I kissed his mouth and rolled away, taking the sheet with me; allowing my naked backside to be the last thing Tommy pictured as I headed into the bathroom for a shower.

"Hey, get your beautiful ass back in bed."

I peeked out of the doorway. "Oh, I see how it is. You love me for my ass." Grinning, I went back to turn the water on.

Jade…love you is too soon.

Tommy thought nothing of it and played along. "True…I love you for your ass, but I thought Dr. Roth said you couldn't head back to work until tomorrow?"

Peeking out again, I responded.

"He did, but I called him yesterday and explained I was doing much better thanks to my hot and sexy caregiver, then I begged him to let me go back to work today."

"I think I should be insulted. First, I'm sexy, and then you're begging the doctor to go back to work to get away from me."

Climbing back into bed and into Tommy's lap, I explained between kisses, "It's not like that. I have a great deal of work to finish for the new place to open on time. But, speaking of time, I guess I'm going to be late." Then, I showed him vividly just how not insulted he should be.

After the best morning sex a girl could ask for…in the bed, against the wall and in the shower. I dressed and left for the shoppe, leaving Tommy to deconstruct the beach house while I was gone.

The beginning of my day went off without a hitch. There were little glitches here and there, as usual, but when I reached the construction site, black clouds formed in the sky, not over the entire island, only over my future. The permits the workers were counting on this week were going to be delayed, and not for a day or two, but delayed until after the 4th of July holiday.

The foreman asked me not to worry; easy for him to say, but he assured me this wasn't the first time a building he was working on had gotten pushed back on the schedule. It happened, and he would work around it to get Summertime Sweets up and running for its opening date.

I was worried, but for some reason, I didn't let it get to me. The situation would work its way out. The construction woes seemed less important than they usually did.

It wasn't some odd reason…it was Tommy. I had him in my life—and I was grateful. Things were normal…easier.

The hours flew by, so I closed up for the day and headed home for the evening.

I reached my stairs. It was then I heard the sounds of hammering, silence, swearing, and then…

"I give up!"

And what came next, were the sounds of wood, glass, and metal crashing down.

I grimaced and shook my head.

That can't be good.

I ran the stairs to Tommy's place, to find him standing in a cloud of white dust, as it rose in slow motion around him, while he stared at the remnants of the ceiling debris on the floor.

Carefully, I crept forward, stopping short of entering the house, by remaining in the doorway.

"Are you okay?"

Just his head turned in my direction, no smile formed on his face. He allowed the crowbar he was holding to slip from his grasp, joining the rest of the mess on the floor.

"No, I'm not okay."

"You wanna tell me what happened?"

"Took on more than I could handle, obviously. I set out to do the impossible…and lost," Tommy sulked, sarcastically.

"Not exactly defeated, though. *And* in less than six months," I said, with arms crossed, leaning on the doorframe.

"What do mean?"

"Well, you did get the girl," I said, with a wiggle to my raised eyebrows, and satisfaction in my smile.

His head dropped forward like a dead weight. He knew I was right. He proved that when he couldn't hide the happiness in his smile.

He brushed the soot from his hair and walked over to me. Leaning in close, he placed a chaste kiss on my mouth, and pushed back, regarding me, tenderly.

"You're right. I got my girl," he said, and kissed me hard.

My girl.

The rest of our evening was spent at my house, going over color samples for the shoppe and the beach house as Tommy explained the mishap over dinner.

"I ripped out the floor and moved onto the kitchen cabinets. I was on the last one when it took part of the ceiling with it."

"The house is old, I guess things like that are bound to happen."

"You're probably right. Besides, there's no use in complaining about it. I knew there was a great deal of work to do."

"Just add it to your list."

He nodded and smirked.

"Enough about my day. How was yours?"

"Good, well, sort of, then, not so good."

"What happened?"

"Let's just say the beach house isn't the only renovation that's going to take longer than expected."

Tommy put down his fork, quickly wiped his mouth, and anxiously dragged his chair closer to mine.

Grabbing my hand, "Jade, what do you say to a few days in Capri…away from all of this? Away from work, the beach house…away from people."

Not the reaction I was expecting, but one that was tempting. Yet, one I couldn't possibly agree to.

"I can't," I said and felt worse when I saw the excited look on Tommy's face drop away.

"Listen, I'd love to go away with you, but it's impossible right now. Even with construction at a standstill, I have my business to consider. I've taken off far too many days, already. It wouldn't be fair to my staff or my customers, to go on a vacation of sorts, when we just reopened for the season."

He nodded and appeared to understand.

"How about this…once the new building is completed and the business is up and running for a few weeks, I'll go away with you then. What do you say?" I asked, excited at the thought of being with Tommy in such a beautifully romantic part of the world.

His mouth kissed my lips and touched my heart.

"I guess that's a yes."

"Yeah… It's a yes, baby."

chapter
twenty-two

Jade

THE WEEKS FLEW by with the renovations at the new Summertime Sweets and the beach house. Our days were filled with the work, but our nights and free time were filled with us. Life was peaceful. What added to that peace was not only Damien and Courtney returning to California, but Blaze and Reece returning to New York, as both of them needed to go back to their respective careers.

Blaze called to say they'd be back for the party on the weekend of the Fourth, which was next week. It was never a good time for me because of Jimmy. Tommy knew this and gave me my space, but texted me every so often throughout the day to let me know he was thinking of me.

The Saturday of the party arrived. I left early for work, leaving Tommy with Daniel, who we picked up yesterday. I had some last-minute things to do for the animal rescue event tomorrow and I wanted to double and triple check the desserts Reece had ordered, to make sure they were up to his specifications. Reece could be a true asshole when it came to food, but in all honesty that was his business, and he took anything pertaining to food and wine seriously.

I was just about to head over to the new shoppe location when my phone rang. It was Blaze.

"Hey, sweetie, what's up?"

"Jade, listen, I'm sorry to do this to you on such short notice, but the party needs to be postponed." Her voice was tight.

"Oh boy, what happened?"

"I'm not sure, but I can't believe he has me doing this. I don't understand why he didn't have his secretary call everyone? You know, I would have called you regardless, but he asked me to do it for a personal touch…it was his damn party, he should be apologizing for this fiasco, not me."

"Blaze, slow down."

"I'm sorry. I just don't get how a man like him could forget a business trip and then proceed to catch a plane to Europe and text me his instructions, or should I say order me to call the entire guest list!" Now she was screaming.

"Do you need any help?"

"Could you let Viv know? Oh, and Tommy and Daniel, of course."

"Sure… Oh shit!"

"What now?" Blaze's annoyance was heard loud and clear.

"What about the desserts? I made enough for over 100 people."

"I forgot about those. Wait! Isn't the rescue event tomorrow?"

"Yeah."

"I'm donating them on Reece's behalf. If he says one word about it, I'll handle him. No reason for all of those delicious treats to go to waste."

"Thanks, Blaze."

"Don't thank me. It was Reece's pleasure."

We both laughed harder than we had in months. Much of the tension between us was due to her current love interest, but Blaze was, and always would be, my best friend for life. Before hanging up, she explained the party would be rescheduled for the last Saturday of the last weekend in August. She knew my grand opening for the new Summertime Sweets location was happening on Labor Day weekend, and she said Reece didn't want his party to interfere with the success of the new place. I knew better. He didn't want to be in direct competition with it. He always had to own the spotlight and for good reason, he paid high dollar for it.

After hanging up, I felt some relief knowing I could avoid Reece until the end of the summer. I quickly called Tommy to let him know not to head to Reece's home for the party, due to the cancellation. He didn't answer. His phone went straight to voicemail. I left him a message to call me back.

I then called Daniel to inform him of the change, and he thanked me and said Tommy had some errands to run before tonight, so he would let him know when he got back. He also said he would relay the message to Kim, but I told him I had that covered already.

Since the party was canceled, I now had an extra hundred or so desserts on ice. I boxed a few to bring home with me. I called Kim and told her of the change. She said she spoke to Blaze and had already left Daniel a message suggesting they could have dinner together at the club and invited me and Tommy to join them.

Interesting...Kim and Daniel were still possibly going to meet up.

I thanked her, but I explained that I made plans of my own for Tommy and me this evening.

I ended my call with Kim, went over the checklist for tomorrow, and headed out the door to pick up Tommy for an evening that would top Reece's summer party any day.

I pulled into my driveway as Kim was pulling out of Tommy's with Daniel. I smiled, while she rolled her eyes and Daniel grinned. Out of the car, I noticed Tommy's vehicle wasn't there.

Good...this would give me time for a shower and to pack up the car for tonight. Once dressed in my swimsuit, shorts, a loose-fitting tee, and my flip flops, I ran down to the kitchen to set up the picnic basket and then load the car with blankets and the boards. Closing the trunk which was filled with everything except the food, I heard Tommy's car making its way up the street. I turned to see Tommy with the top down. His Camaro was filled with every seasonal plant imaginable.

He pulled in slowly, careful not to bang into anything.

"Hey, baby, I just got your message. What happened?" He said when he'd parked and climbed out with a bouquet of sunflowers in hand.

Tommy kissed me without touching me, his tongue did the talking and I reciprocated the gesture, but couldn't stop myself from wrapping my arms around him while deepening our connection. Everything in his kiss gave me pause to rethink going out tonight. His mouth was warm, his tongue commanding. The more it danced with mine, the more I wanted it to lick other places on my body…places that were craving him…places that needed to be soothed.

He kept up his assault on me, as I softly voiced my demands. "If you keep this up, I going to need that tongue elsewhere." We kissed more, consuming one another, our breathing escalating, our moans more prominent.

"If you want it, I'll make it happen." His smile was devilish, his voice promising.

"That's very tempting, but since we have the entire evening to ourselves, I made plans for us tonight."

"A plan that better include this, and more of this later," he said, lightly nipping my lips.

"Without question," I confirmed and kissed him again, then stopped, because the truth was, if we didn't stop, the only place we were going for the evening was bed. Although enticing, I had something special to share with Tommy and what it was couldn't be shared in bed. Well, part of it anyway.

Tommy's eyes gleamed. His personality was carefree, his growing contentment since we've been together proved he felt at home…this was his life now and he wasn't going anywhere.

For me, it was another exhale.

I took my flowers and headed up the stairs to put them in water and grab the food.

Tommy stopped at the bottom of the stairs. "Jade, did you want to tell me where we're going?"

I turned back from the top of the landing. "It's a secret."

"Sure, that's all well and good, but am I dressed for it?"

Tommy had jeans and a t-shirt on. Hot…yes, but hardly appropriate for what I had planned.

I descended the stairs but remained two to three steps away as not to get charmed by more of this man's mouth.

Leaning forward, I said, "Put on your board shorts." Then quickly ascended the stairs, leaving him guessing.

With my flowers in water and the picnic basket in hand, I returned to the car to meet Tommy.

"Get in. I'm driving," I demanded.

"Can't you give a poor guy a hint?"

"I could, but I won't."

I placed the basket and the sweatshirts in the trunk, and upon closing it, I was cornered. Hanging his head down between his arms, which tactfully fenced me in, as not to allow for an escape, he expelled the breath he had been holding. His body shuddered as his head shook slowly from left to right. He stood firm and didn't move. He looked at me with purpose. Irritated no, but posed close enough to me physically to cause my heartbeats to pulse out of my chest.

"Okay, do you want to explain to me what this secret is all about?"

It was killing him not knowing what was going on.

Oh! This was going to be fun.

"Not really?"

"What?" His response was sharply dumbfounded.

"What I mean to say is that I want to take you somewhere, which I've already explained is a surprise, so if you agree to get in the car, I'll give you more of a hint on the way."

"Okay, I'll play this your way, but what you have to tell me better be good." His whisper left a hint of sexual play fueled by his growing annoyance in the space around us.

Pressing away, he walked backward, and then over to the passenger door.

"I mean it, Miss Stanton. It better be good." No smile, no smirk, no nothing…

Don't worry, Tommy…it will be. Breathe, Jade, breathe.

Seated, Tommy turned only his head to face me.

"Okay, one hint. Let's go make a memory."

That little hint earned me a warm and satisfied smile.

"Is this really yours? I mean I can't believe you drive a 181?" Shocked wasn't a good description, looking at Tommy's face…baffled came to mind.

Leaning on the door, I answered. "Ah…That's right, you've only seen me on my bike. Yeah, it's mine. It's vintage and it's very practical for when I need to make large deliveries for the shoppe and for carrying my board. Besides, we're going to need it where we're going tonight." My goofy, justified smile got me a slinky one from him in return, as Tommy turned to make certain our boards were secured in the backseat.

The trip from Beach Haven Crest down the island's Boulevard to the town of Holgate was a short one. Yet, for me, and especially because Monday the Fourth was not so far away, the ride stirred a fight with my emotions; part of me was melancholy for the past, and part of me felt trepidation and excitement for the future. The combination placed my senses on high alert…the scent of the breeze off the ocean, the smell of sugary snow cones and funnel cakes drifted through the air. The sounds of small children's joyful screams on the rides nearby and of the Beach Boy's music playing in the distance. Palm trees decorated with white Christmas lights, the lines to get stamped-in for the local clubs, the traffic on the boulevard, couples kissing, and the people on their porches after a day at the beach reminded me why I missed Jimmy, and why I loved this place and wanted to share a piece of that love with Tommy tonight.

The lights faded, the people and the traffic lessened, the noise and the music drifted away as we approached the far end of the island.

"Jade, where are we going? It's desolate down here," Tommy voiced concern.

There was nothing to worry about, and once I parked the car on the beach and we climbed over the dunes in front of us, he would understand. Tommy grabbed the boards, the bag with the towels and change of clothes, and I took the picnic basket. As we both reached the top of the sand, Tommy looked to me. His eyes filled with gratitude and something more.

"Thank you for this, baby." He stated when he discovered the surprise.

I took Tommy here to join a few of the local surfers who'd hung out with my brother. It was a tradition for them every year since his death to honor him by doing a few of his favorite things. One was night surfing, and two was watching Endless Summer on the beach, a classic surfing movie. I found it hard in years past to come, but this year was different.

Tommy found a spot for us on the sand and helped me with the blankets and the food. One of the guys who met him the night of my accident came over to talk with him. I sat myself down and relaxed. I was slightly chilled and decided tonight should be for Tommy. I would sit this one out and watch as he surfed with the guys in memory of my brother. The money raised each year for this event, which goes on each night surrounding the 4th of July holiday, is donated to the center where Daniel works.

The boys, including Tommy, headed out on the water. The lights from the boards or from the apparel they were wearing, glowed. The ocean took on a magic all its own. I sat wrapped in a blanket mesmerized by how beautiful the waves looked in the dark.

Some surfers continued to stay out on the water, while others, including Tommy, ran in to be with their dates. Tommy reached the blanket, shook out his hair, and grabbed a towel from the overnight bag to dry off. Once done, he wrapped the towel around his waist, removed his shorts from underneath, and replace them with the sweatpants I brought for him.

"That was incredible! Thank you for this." Leaning down, he gave my lips a quick peck.

Completely dressed, he sat down next to me, immediately pulling me into his lap, as I wrapped the large blanket around me, now, around us. The movie Endless Summer started on the screen set up on the beach, while Tommy and I kissed, holding each other close.

Neither of us said a word for quite some time. We were content to just be in each other's arms, here on the sand, taking in the movie, enjoying some delicious wine and dessert foods, snuggling and not worrying about the universe around us.

Once all of the surfers had left the ocean and sat down to watch the movie, I thought this was a good chance to give Tommy his gift.

"Tommy, this is for you," Kissing the side of his face and placing the small teak box in his hands.

Tommy looked at the box and then to me and back again.

"Open it. I hope you like it."

He carefully opened the lid and removed the leather rope bracelet with 3 beads dangling on the knotted tail.

"I don't know what to say. I love it. Thank you." He wrapped his arms around me, then he loosened our embrace to hold the gift between us, running his thumb over each bead. Maybe he was contemplating the meaning, or maybe he wanted to admire it more.

I felt at this point I should explain.

"I noticed you wear several of them already."

"Yeah, I started buying them years back on some surfing excursions. You know, to take a piece of paradise with me. I noticed you wear them too, plus, a sailor's knot."

"Everyone at the Jersey Shore has worn one at one time or another," I said, deflecting away from my bracelet's true meaning; I made light of wearing it.

"Maybe they have, but you don't display yours as a souvenir." Tommy looked down at the rope at my wrist, caressing it briefly as he looked up for me to confirm what he was thinking.

Resting my head on his shoulder, I explained.

"Well, I definitely don't wear it for the purpose of wiping my brow in the heat as many sailors did. I've had it such a long time. Jimmy and I bought them together. Perhaps at first, I bought it for what it was intended to represent…good times and good fortune. But now…"

"It's not?"

Thinking some more, I realized, or Tommy did, that it still represented those things, even more so tonight.

Looking at this beautiful man—a man I had denied my feelings for, yet felt them from the start, a man with each passing day and experience I've come to trust, a man…I'm falling in love with, I answered his question.

"You know, it's funny. I thought I'd say it was a memorial to my brother, and as siblings, that's true, but it's not exactly how I see it anymore. It's the fun of summers past. It's truly good times, not so much great fortunes, but fortunate to have had the opportunity to live here, around an amazing backdrop with best friends and family and to be able to get up each morning and work here *and* enjoy what I do…" I stopped, although there was one more thing it represented.

"And…"

"Even though you didn't give me the bracelet, it's a symbol to remember the person you're with even if they're far away."

He smiled because he understood. He knew the sailor's story. It meant leaving the shore and their loved ones behind, but not forgetting them while they were gone. For us, it wasn't the physical separation. The bracelet represented the emotional. It symbolized the strength we have around us. The support of others when the darkness becomes too much to bear.

"Now… are you going to tell me about the beads you chose for my gift?" He asked.

Sitting up on my knees and taking the tail end of the bracelet, I explained the meaning of each one. I knew he would understand why I picked these specific beads for him.

"This one, the Coco-wood bead, represents finding one's inner treasure. You came here in search of more than just a girl and a beach house; this bead honors that. This one, the green one with the etchings, is the emblem of the Green Sea Turtle. This turtle is one of the oldest creatures on earth. This bead symbolizes a long life and the guardian spirit "Aumakua." If you're ever lost, it will guide you home. The last one with the orange wash of color and the blue waves is for the future…kind of. This bead represents Banana Beach and Cape St.Francis, from the movie. It's a place I've never surfed and don't be mad, but I asked Daniel if you surfed in South Africa and he said you never mentioned it, so I took a chance on this bead. This bead is for our tomorrows."

Tommy's hand covered mind. He was still, reflective, and intense as the Atlantic was right now. He took my face and guided my mouth to his. His kiss was slow, savoring…loving, and when it broke, he stood up and held out his hand for me to take, pulling me to him.

Still not saying a word, we packed up and left for home. Leaving everything in the trunk and the backseat to remove tomorrow, Tommy took my hand again, still not speaking, but leading me into the house, through the first floor, up the stairs, and to my room. With the bedroom dark, the surfaces were bathed in the outside glow of muted light, casting long exaggerated shadows on the walls.

"Our tomorrows…that's what you said, right?" His question confirming, almost demanding.

I nodded.

Tommy's tone was serious. His lip-line flat, his jaw engaged, his eyes intense—studying on me, he seared into my body what he craved—he wanted to make me his.

"Well, Jade, it looks like our tomorrows start now."

Without a word, I reached my hand up, holding the side of his face, and placed a delicate kiss on his lips. Pulling away slowly—my mouth first and then my hand, I stepped back for him to see me…for me to bare all completely—to be with him fully, with no more reservations.

The darkness in the room gave me courage, as he regarded me intensely.

I slipped out of my bottoms, allowing them to drop to my ankles. I stepped away from the material, as I reached for the strings of my top and released them, allowing it too, to fall away. Exposed, but not unsure, I stepped forward into Tommy's waiting arms…wrapping mine around his shoulders, I kissed him deeply—more deeply than I had before. I pressed against his body, while my hands dropped from his neck to his waistline.

Unhurried, I wanted to savor every second with him. I removed his pants, sliding them down, as I lower myself onto my knees, to his arousal. His breathing escalated. Through a strained groan—his desires were revealed. Taking him into my mouth made me wet and emboldened. My fingers gripped his thighs; his hands pulled back my hair, so he could watch.

I rocked back and forth, my mouth taking every inch of his hardened flesh. My warm tongue slid across his erection, causing his thrusts to be more deliberate. To slow him down and make our connection last, I pushed away, ever so slightly, releasing him, and then taking him in my mouth once again.

Tommy moaned, and in a split second my body was being lifted over his shoulder and dropped playfully onto the bed.

Close enough to kiss, but just far enough away to see his sexual grin... "Baby, now it's my turn," he said, lowering his head down to my stomach, as my legs dropped open exposing my most intimate parts.

His jaw grazed along my midsection, causing my body to squirm. I wanted him to take my sex—to own it, to soothe it...to have me. I forcefully curled forward— my arousal meeting the harsh licks of his tongue. My skin flushed, my breathing quickened.

"You have no idea how beautiful you look right now." Tommy's eyes pierced mine, before taking me in his mouth, again.

I gasped at the assault his tongue performed on my clit. I wasn't sure how much longer I could hold on. I tried, but it was no use. My legs tightened and trembled, sending shockwaves throughout my body, spinning me out of control. I fell deeper and deeper under Tommy's spell. My hands gripped the bedsheets as I pushed hard through my climax, screaming out his name, screaming through my orgasm.

The tingling pleasure between my legs slowly waned, but only briefly...

"I'm not done with you, yet, baby," he said, covering my body with his, as his cock took over for his mouth.

Tommy's eyes darkened, his thrusts demanding, his mouth covered mine—making me taste the remnants of my sex. Our kiss breathy, our mouths wanton, our tongues more deliberate as our arousals grew. My hands went from the sheets to his shoulders. I met each of his thrusts, with my pussy clenching around his erection.

"Tommy..." I whimpered.

"You have no idea what you're doing to me, Jade." He exhaled powerfully.

Taking my nipple between his teeth, he lightly bit and teased the hardened nub, while moving his hand to my hipbone—holding me there, not allowing my body to move as his body rocked between my legs.

Our breaths escalated, proving we both needed to come. We were at the edge. One step closer—both of us, ready to fall, together. *And,* as we did, he took me in his arms, holding me there, holding tight…this man, my shelter from the storm.

***

The sound of smoke alarms and the smell of burnt 'something' drifted up the stairs and into my bedroom. It wasn't the ideal way to wake up after a night of intense sex with the man who wanted to buy my brother's house. But he was the man who quite possibly in this short time changed my mind about learning to love again.

Click, crack, squeak, and swoosh were the sounds of Tommy jumbling with a breakfast tray, crashing into the door, and entering the room to greet me that morning. I sat up, modestly wrapping the cool cotton bedsheet over the front of my body, as Tommy nearly fell over when he came to an abrupt halt in the center of my bedroom.

"Don't be alarmed," He said ominously, as he held a tray with items resembling food and coffee on it.

I giggled at his expense and pointed in the air.

"As opposed to listening to it." I was starting to get a headache from the howl of warning bells that were not only sounding near the kitchen but outside my bedroom door, because the smoke tagged along with Tommy up the stairs.

"Here, it's edible. I'll be right back." He awkwardly and almost hesitantly placed the tray at my feet and scurried out of the room to shut down the noise.

Leaning forward in slow motion and examining the tray more closely before taking a bite, I conceded the toast was edible and the coffee was actually quite good. I turned with toast in one hand and a cup in the other to await my sexy chef's return.

It wouldn't be long now…peace and quiet replaced the siren's blare.

Right on cue.

"See I told you it was edible."

"It's more than edible," I said, gingerly placing the cup and the unfinished piece of toast back on the tray.

"Then why aren't you eating it?"

"Because breakfast in bed should be enjoyed by both of us." I lifted the sheet so he could join me. "Get in."

Climbing in next to me, I wrapped my arms around his neck and kissed him deeply.

"Mmmm…I like the way you think."

After settling back against the pillows, our bodies wrapped around each other and our free hands intertwined, we talked about the evening spent together.

"Do you really like it,Tommy?" I asked fiddling with the beads on the bracelet I gave him.

"I love it, baby. No one has ever given me something so thoughtful or so planned out." A comforting smile formed his expression and peace settled in his eyes.

I fidgeted with his fingers, what I was about to say was uncomfortable for me.

"Thank you for last night…I mean thank for taking care of me and sharing the evening making memories with me."

"I love that you asked me to." Tommy brought my hand to his lips, as he stilled and looked into my eyes."You never have to thank me, Jade. It was easy for me to care for you. I was crushed to see you hurt. If I can steal your hurt, I always will."

"Always?" It was a question, but a definitive tone of confusion in my question needed to be clarified.

"Yeah, always."

"How do you know?"

"How do I know what?"

"How do you know that all of this…" I repeated the same gesture as Tommy, pointing back and forth between us, "isn't just because you set a challenge for yourself to meet someone new?"

"The same way you knew to put our tomorrows at the end of this bracelet."

Checking the time, I knew I needed to get up, so I stretched and asked if he'd like to join me for a tradition that Viv and I started after Jimmy died.

"I have a commitment that I keep every year at this time and wondered if you'd like to join me?"

"Sure, what is it?"

"You're agreeing before you even know what it is?"

"Yup, now what are we doing today?"

"I volunteer at the local animal shelter and today starts their summer adoption event. It tends to be the biggest one of the season, so would you like to join me to help these precious babies find homes?"

"I don't know how much help I'll be, but I'd love to join in any way I can."

"Good, so let's shower and head over to my shoppe to bring the desserts I made for the volunteers and the selling table. I have more now because Blaze graciously donated the ones I prepared for Reece's party last night."

Tommy smiled, nodded, and off we went. First, we stopped at Summertime Sweets and then we doubled back to pick up Viv to head over to the event, which was being held on the bay.

We arrived just as the event was in full swing. Many of the volunteers were manning the tables, while others were holding the adoptable animals on their leashes. While a few more were tending to the crated cats and bunnies in the adoption bus.

Viv kissed each of us before she walked away to help with the refreshment table. Tommy decided his talents would be best used to help with the larger dogs that needed walking and to photograph the families with the pets they adopted.

He not only volunteered his time, he donated the film and the development of the photographs from the event that would be mailed to the families at a later date. My heart was full as I watched him from the food tables. His tender touch as he spoke to each animal, who at times appeared frightened by all of the commotion an event like this could bring, and from a past that betrayed them, brought tears to my eyes. He wasn't doing this to score points with me. He truly cared and enjoyed the day as much as I and the many volunteers who came here did.

As programs came to a close, we cleaned up. Tommy asked if we could head back to the house and pick up Daniel for dinner. He felt bad that he had left Daniel at the beach house while he was gone all day, but Daniel understood as he was spending the day with Kim and catching up on some paperwork he needed to complete before heading back to the center next week after the 4th of July celebrations.

I agreed, and we asked Aunt Viv to come along as well, and this time, she happily accepted.

My vehicle was larger than Tommy's, so we took it to get to a restaurant on the end of the island, off the beaten path. The place was crowded but evoked a much more relaxed and tranquil atmosphere.

Once home, Viv said goodnight and turned in. Daniel and Tommy decided to sit out on the deck and enjoy the view, while I mimicked Viv and went to bed. Later, Tommy crawled into bed and settled next to me, nestling his body close and holding me tight. Exactly what I needed now that something painful and special needed to be done tomorrow, as always.

***

Like every 4th of July, I barely and reluctantly crawled out of bed to start my day. The holiday hadn't been a holiday since Jimmy left. Three years without him, not hearing his voice, feeling his strength, enjoying his laughter…

Three years ago to the day, my brother made a decision that would destroy me…a decision that he could never take back.

I left the house heading for the rocks at Jimmy's favorite surf spot on the island to leave him the only gift I could give him now…my heart and my tears…

"Happy Birthday, Jimmy…I love you."

Reaching into the small bag I was carrying, I lifted out two cupcakes decorated in the colors of freedom. I placed both on the rocks in front of me and lit three candles, placing them in Jimmy's cake. Closing my eyes, I made a wish and placed a prayer for him in the morning air.

I sat there as I always had for the last three years, watching as the early morning surfers arrived to start their day. Each of them were from here and knew my tradition. A mere nod, a small wave, and a shortened hello I received from most, as they allowed me my privacy. If that was even possible in such a public place.

I sat there for a few hours, this time telling Jimmy about Tommy and how I was falling in love with him. Telling him he could rest, knowing that I was happy. I was no longer chasing the sun to follow the moon as he put it.

As the tide rolled in, the cupcakes were consumed by the waves. Perhaps this year I'd be arrested for littering, but I doubted it. Besides, as the cakes floated away, the usual flock of seagulls circled and made a morning feast out of them.

I smiled and chuckled at the fight between the two large birds, promising that next year I would bring a tray for all to enjoy.

Leaving the beach, I pedaled over to the Summertime Sweets construction site. No one would be at the building today, but I just wanted to take a look in before heading to work. Progress had been made, up until recently. Now that the delayed permits were in, the renovations would begin to ramp up again, and hopefully, we would be right on time for Labor Day weekend.

I was just about to leave when I received a text from Tommy, saying he had a surprise for me tonight. That was odd. He knew I wasn't in the mood for any surprises today of all days. Hopefully, this wasn't going to turn into our first argument. With a busy day at the shoppe ahead of me, I didn't have time to or want to think about any surprises even if they were coming from my neighbor turned boyfriend.

I arrived at Summertime Sweets current location to open up and get the orders lined up for the hectic customer pick up. Other members of my staff we preparing the coffee for our regulars, while others were constructing boxes for the last-minute cookie and pastry orders which came in every year.

The day was done and I went into the office to clean up some paperwork before heading home. Looking at my phone, I had a missed call and voicemail from Tommy.

"Jade, I hope you're done soon. I think I bit off more than I can chew at the beach house. Can you come straight here after work?"

Sitting there, I listened to the message again and again and again. Was I a fool? He wanted me to go there so we could talk? He bit off more than he could chew? None of this made sense. A nauseating lump formed in my throat and a hollowness in the pit of my stomach. Everything seemed fine. Then I started to think, everything seemed fine with Damien at one point too, and he screwed me over royally.

I scrambled to get home quickly to see what this bullshit was all about.

I parked my bike and headed up the beach house stairs. Tommy was yelling inside.

"Shit! Shit! Shit! How are we going to explain this to Jade?"

"Tommy?"

"Jade, baby, can you help me?"

Baby…I guess everything is not what I thought.

I rushed up the rest of the stairs and opened the door to Tommy's place. Once inside, I saw the surprise and started to laugh.

"There's nothing funny about this, Jade. Look at this place. Look at the new floors. I can't fix this. Don't just stand there, help me!"

Don't just stand there…

I smiled…that's what Jimmy said the night we were moving him in. I closed the sliding door behind me and for once, it closed with ease. There in the corner, with white paint already on her white paws, was a dog from the shelter event. As I recall, Tommy had been talking to her and walking her most of the day yesterday. Though, I had no idea he wanted to adopt her.

"Come here, sweetie," I cooed as I knelt down and held out my hand to the precious mostly tan Pit Bull with blue eyes and white paws covered in paint. Cautiously, she came to me with her tail wagging.

Once she realized she was safe with me, she basically plopped down onto my lap. Tommy joined us on the floor as we created a closeness to help this baby know everything was okay; her still wagging tail was a small sign she trusted us.

"This was your surprise?" I said, petting his newest member of the family.

"Yeah, I fell in love with her. I couldn't watch them cage her. I knew I had to do something, so while you were out I called the number for the shelter on the slim chance one of the staff would be in to feed the dogs. I caught one of the volunteers on her way out to an emergency. She told me the shelter supervisor was expected back shortly. She called me about an hour later and I went down to fill out the papers and took Lucky home."

"Lucky?"

"Yeah"

Tommy didn't explain the name or elaborate on Lucky's past. I knew from volunteering at the shelter, many of these animals dealt with the harsh reality that not all humans were good, but instead of dwelling on it, I chose to help him make the beach house dog-friendly.

"So…will you help me?" A cringed expression formed on his face, knowing he took on more than he expected.

I looked at Lucky. Her goofy smile hit me as her head flopped backward to meet my acknowledgment of her. When I smiled back and carefully kissed her, the tapping on the floorboards from her tail started to increase.

"How could I not help you?"

"Where should we start?"

Standing, I walked Lucky over to the large beanbag Tommy had bought for her. She happily climbed in to rest. From there, I went to check the damage. I walked to over the area where the new black floor was splattered with paint, which gave me an idea.

"It's pretty bad, baby." Tommy's hands rested on my shoulders as he nuzzled my neck. I smiled, warmth surged through my body…life was perfect.

"Nothing a little acetone can't fix." I ran back to my place since Tommy didn't have any. When I returned I saw Tommy on the floor with Lucky, speaking to her sweetly and kissing the top of her head.

Tommy left Lucky with a bone while we cleaned the floors.

"Jade, you missed a spot," Tommy said, looking at the trail of several dried paw prints on the floor. Tommy was dumbfounded.

"No, I didn't," I smirked as I put my idea into motion.

I poured some of the left-over paint that hadn't spilled from the accident, into a paint tray. Placing the tray on the floor, I swiped a beach towel from the kitchen counter and directed Tommy to take a chair and sit.

He smiled and obliged.

"Put your foot in the paint. Only let the bottom touch."

"What are you doing?"

"You'll see," I said, strategically taking his foot and placing it on the floor next to the paw prints. First the left, then the right, before cleaning up both his feet and moving on to the next phase of my project.

"Do you have a small paintbrush?"

Tommy nodded and brought me one. I took the brush and dipped it into the same paint can, meticulously making sure I had just enough paint on the bristles. Purposefully, I painted a starfish at the very top center where the feet and paw prints were. To the area, I added some whimsical lines to frame out the impressions on the floor. I searched the kitchen for plastic wrap and paint tape, leaving the paint to dry and Tommy to stand guard, so the active puppy in the house didn't barrel through and smear my design. Once dry, I taped the clear plastic wrap over the design. Tommy and I moved the dining room table over the area for now.

"There, once it's completely dry you can spray a clear coat over it and have it forever."

"This means you have to be pretty confident I'm not leaving at the end of my lease?"

Tommy turned me to him, studying my reaction to his question. He didn't wait for me to answer. He simply lowered his mouth over mine and allowed our kiss to speak for him.

chapter
twenty-three

Tommy

THE PROGRESS ON the house was coming along nicely, not as planned, but nicely. I wouldn't be done within my six-month timeframe, but it didn't matter anymore. Jade and I were together and getting closer.

Finding her without looking, feeling for her without trying, was the biggest surprise to me. The summer was flying by. Besides the renovations on the beach house, another project was now complete. Jade's new location was ready for its Labor Day weekend grand opening. It was odd to me that she would open it at the end of the summer as opposed to the beginning, but Jade explained she had her regulars, so nothing was really changing except the newer, larger space. She revealed she was thinking about staying open year round for catering services for weddings and special parties but hadn't finalized the plan yet. She said she wanted to get through Reece's party on Saturday, open the new place next weekend, and take it from there.

The Thursday before the party Blaze called to make sure Daniel would be coming to the party, knowing he would be staying with me this weekend. Kim said she would pick up Daniel at my place as I had last minute errands to run, and I was to meet Jade at Reece's place promptly at 8 pm. I picked Daniel up at the Center on Friday morning and we headed back to the beach. Once back at the house, Daniel was surprised at how much I accomplished in just a few short weeks of living here.

"Tommy, this place is really shaping up."

"I'm glad you think so. Don't get me wrong, I love the place, but the work is harder than I thought it would be."

"What did you expect? Mr. and Mrs. Stanton hadn't done anything to this place in years and now you, one man, is taking on all of this." Daniel said, looking at the place from top to bottom. Then he addressed my love life.

"How is everything? With Jade, I mean."

"It's been good. She's been busy with the shoppe and the renovations on her new place, but now that the work is done, hopefully we'll have more time to spend together. I just gave her the choices on the cabinets I finally ordered for the kitchen. Repairs, I hadn't expected arose and the cabinets were the least of my worries."

"Did she like your choices?"

"Surprisingly, yes, especially since what I chose is in stark contrast to her place and very different from what the beach house looked like when her parents owned it."

"Have you told her yet that you bought the place?"

"No, not yet…Viv hasn't given me the go-ahead, so we're still pretending that I'm renting it, but I decided whether Viv likes it or not I'm going to tell her tonight after the party, and I'm going to talk to her about Mike and me."

"Do you think that's a good idea to tell her now? I'm not saying keep it from her, but…"

"I have to talk to her about it. We've grown so close and…I love her. I need to be honest and I need to explain it before I tell her how my feelings have changed for her. This cloud over my head weighs me down every moment I'm with her."

"What do you think her reaction will be?"

"I don't know and that's what scares the hell out of me." Losing Jade would be losing me. Life would not only be different, it wouldn't be worth living.

Brushing away the ugly thoughts swarming in my head, I looked at the time, in unison with Daniel, and I decided to get ready for Reece's party before I headed out to get my special surprise for Jade.

Daniel and I were no different when it came to deciding what to wear. We both chose white jeans, new white dress shirts, untucked. Daniel chose off-white burlap Sanuk loafers, and I went with white canvas Vans.

Jade and I had agreed to meet outside of Reece's home and walk into the party together. Reece hired a valet service to park the cars, but I opted to park outside of his driveway and wait for Jade there. There wasn't any announcement of rain in the forecast, which prompted me to leave the top down on the Camaro. Standing outside of the car, it was hard to wind down from knowing that I'd have her here with me soon. The heat of the day invaded the normal coolness of the evening just enough to make the atmosphere sultry, teetering on the fringe of romantic.

My wrist should be sore at this point based on how many times I checked my watch. The last time proved either Jade was very late or not coming at all. It wasn't like her not to call, so I called her, but it went straight to voicemail. It was useless to continue to wait outside any longer, so I got back in the car and drove up the drive to Reece's home.

The Montgomery compound sat along Long Beach Boulevard in the Harvey Cedars section of LBI. Dense pine trees hide the massive home from the main road. There was a mixture of sand and beach stones at the opening of the long driveway, its path curved up to the center hall, custom built contemporary.

At first glance, the house was sided in pure cedar—a costly addition, but I'm sure for Reece, nothing else would do. The structure boasted several entertaining areas on each floor; the very top is a rooftop deck that afforded you a 360-degree view from the ocean to the bay and back again. It had a large jacuzzi at its core. On the main living space, the outdoor area consisted of three large spaces forming one huge deck. All were covered with open cut-outs for more sensational ocean views. One area had an outdoor sauna room and swimming pool, the next held a restaurant-worthy kitchen with bar and seating area and a luxurious cream colored sectional with fire pit, and the last was a small, cozy seating place, which was secluded and seemed to appear to be off one of the main floor bedrooms.

The patio at the ocean level was beautifully designed with Italian Travertine slabs that extended its center to individual paths that led to private seating areas among the Pitch Pines that surrounded the property. I was offered a glass of Champagne as I stepped onto the deck on the main floor. As I surveyed the warmly lit space which glowed of amber and translucent orange from the fire burning to the left of me, I was greeted by Daniel and Kim.

"Tommy, what happened? I thought you were heading over here earlier?" Daniel asked.

"Did you meet up with Jade instead? Where is she?" Kim inquired, as she studied the room more closely to find her friend.

"I'm not sure, I left her a voicemail and she never called me back. I think I've been stood up, so I'm going to finish this drink, take in these amazing views, and then head back to the house if she hasn't shown by then." I had plenty of work to do, but I had myself pretty worked up and disappointed with Jade. I thought she and I were in a good place. She was fine all week, no nightmares, nothing that would explain this. My anger and concern combined, gave me plenty of new found energy to work out my frustrations on the house when I got back.

"I'm sorry, Tommy. Maybe she got caught up with something at the shoppe? You did say she was off for much of this weekend and her staff was running things. Perhaps she wanted to make sure everything was set and there were no mishaps with the long weekend ahead?" Daniel tried to play devil's advocate. Speaking of which, there came the devil himself with his offspring in tow.

"Tommy! Welcome to my home," Reece said in a happy-go-lucky voice, as he entered my personal space, put his hand on my shoulder, and clinked his drinking glass exaggeratedly with mine.

"Thank you for having me, magnificent home you have here." I raised my glass and waved it around the room. I wasn't about to let this asshole get to me.

"Thank you. I bought the place years ago, as I took advantage of the tattered housing market, and recently revived its splendor. My architect did an amazing job; well worth his weight in gold, which is basically what I had to pay him." Reece's new-found friendliness irritated me. I wasn't buying it for a second. This was his way of letting me know that he was here to gloat, on his terms, in his home, in front of his people.

I didn't take the bait, and a few seconds later... I didn't have to. Several people were leaning near the railing directly over the patio below, as they were pointing at something that turned out to be someone…my someone.

There walking up one of the paths towards the house was Jade. Adorned in an all black body-hugging dress with matching cardigan, leopard stilettos that made her already long legs even longer, and carrying a small leopard cocktail purse, Jade made her way through the guests to enter the house. Some looked appalled at Jade's rebellion of the all-white dress attire request. Some people were amused and others, mainly the men, were awestruck to see such a stunning woman…my woman.

Several minutes passed before Jade's silhouette arrived at the doorway leading out to the area we were standing in. Everyone turned and watched as Jade approached the group, kissing Blaze, Kim, and Daniel, and effectively ignoring Reece, Damien, and who I assumed was Courtney, because that blonde was tightly wrapped around Damien's arm like a vice.

Once Jade reached me, she folded her arms around my neck and kissed my mouth softly and attentively."Sorry I was late, but I couldn't find a thing to wear," She said sarcastically, as she rolled her eyes and smiled a devilishly satisfying smile. My hands went to her hips, as my eyes drank her in from head to toe and back again.

"You wear it well, baby."

"How could it be so difficult to find something white to wear, as I requested of all my guests to do?" Reece said with heightened annoyance.

Jade's smile turned grim, as she pivoted to face Reece, cocked her head to regard his statement. As it annoyed her further, she fully pressed her backside against my front and directed my hands around her waist. I obliged fully, silently and with no protest, but wondered where all of this drama was coming from.

"Who said I was wearing white? I said I couldn't find anything to wear." Jade's defiance was clear.

"I told you the night of your girls little get together that it was a white party."

"That's true you did, and you purposely phoned me two days ago after not talking to me for the entire summer to inform me that *she* and Damien weren't going to be here. Yet again another lie—I should've known. Your promise to stay out of my personal life was too good to be true." Jade singled out Courtney with her pointed index finger.

Damien and Courtney remained silent. They were apparently stunned by Jade's description of Reece's recent phone call to her. If I had to hazard a guess, Jade found out about Reece's surprise guests through Blaze and probably no earlier than today, which explained why she was late.

"Jade, originally Damien and Courtney were to come out here for only a few days and then leave for Napa, but plans change. What can I say?"

"You could have offered me the courtesy of a phone call to let me know they would still be here, and allow me the decision to decline your invitation, since you knew I didn't want to be in the same room with them, but yet again you felt it necessary to not play by the rules of simple etiquette, *and* I, in turn, am showing you that I will not play by your rules either, whether it be the clothes I choose to wear or the company I choose to keep. Do I make myself clear?"

Reece stood there, saying nothing, yet his face displayed a dismissive smirk.

"I said, do I make myself clear?" Jade roared at Reece's false ignorance and blatant disregard for her feelings. Her voice echoed throughout the house and the grounds, as people turned to look at the spectacle this event had turned into.

Again, he said nothing and lifted his glass to quench his thirst.

Damien moved forward to… I guess to apologize for his father's behavior, but Courtney tugged his jacket sleeve to pull him back into the fold before he said something that she would regret. Like the obedient puppy he seemed to be, he followed her command.

Jade laughed.

"It's funny, Reece, you got what you wanted…turmoil. And you, Damien, got what you were looking for. Interestingly, you both got what you deserve. Enjoy the rest of the evening." Jade raised her glass, took a sip, and placed a delicious kiss on my mouth.

"Let's get out of here." She whispered.

Taking her glass and placing it with mine on the nearest tray, we turned to leave.

"Not so fast!" Reece bellowed. "You can't leave before my surprise announcement."

Jade stalled, but I pulled her closer to the door to make our escape.

"Let's go, baby. He's got nothing to say that we need to hear."

Jade, still fuming, nodded and turned to go again.

"Oh, I think she'll definitely want to hear what I have to say, Mr. Conte. Especially since it involves you and your not so stellar past." Reece was superior. He lifted a champagne glass from the server closest to him and stood almost statuesque, turning to his right and then to his left before returning to center, making sure he had everyone's full attention.

Jade turned back to listen. Blaze, Kim, and Daniel stood their ground with ominous expressions blanketing their faces. Damien and Courtney moved forward. Damien appeared perplexed as if he wasn't hearing his father correctly.

"Now that I have everyone's full attention, let me explain. My dear Jade was about to fall head over heels for a man she knew very little about. I must admit, at first I thought the announcement that you and Mr. Conte had become a couple was fake, but as time has passed I see I was wrong, and I never like being wrong, but I do so relish being the one who said I told you so."

Jade snapped her hand away from mine, stalked forward to confront him.

"You son-of-a-bitch…you never mind your own damn business. So, what if Tommy and I are happy? I'm never getting back together with Damien. Do you get it yet?"

Cocking his arrogant head to one side and maliciously appeasing Jade, "Oh Jade, darling, I know you feel Damien has treated you with utter disrespect, and while it is true he ruined his chances with you by his very embarrassing indiscretions with…her, it is also a fact that your own Mr. Conte has appeared to have done the same thing to someone he loves."

Bile began to rise in my throat. My anger fueled me, as I stormed toward him to stop his insanity. Only to be held back by his security guards. I knew what he was about to say. Somehow Reece found out about my affair with Raven, my brother's ex-fiancée, and Rain's sister. I fought back to stop him. I should be the one to tell Jade, and now I was about to regret not telling her sooner.

"Right now, you're very angry with me and I'm pretty sure after what I'm about to tell you, you will be even more enraged, but not with me, with him." Reece's focus pinned in my direction as I struggled to break the hold the guards had on me."Let him go, let him go. He knows he's been discovered. There's nothing he can do about it now."

Once released, I went to Jade, wrapping my arms around her from behind. Knowing full well this may be the last time I'd ever get to hold her in my arms again. My strength building her strength as she egged Reece on.

"Go ahead, tell me, hell, I mean tell us all what you think you know." Jade's voice never shook once, but her body was trembling in my embrace.

Reece moved directly in front of us. His eyes black and vile as he looked at me. Yet, when he looked to Jade, his eyes softened with the knowledge of my personal guilt—his weapon against both of us…to destroy what we have.

"Tommy slept with his brother's fiancée. Of course, he and his brother made amends to keep up appearances, but you see his brother and his ex-soon-to-be-sister-in-law worked as attorneys for her father's very successful and high profile law firm in Manhattan, and that very same law firm had gone through a much larger controversy last year. The only reason why he and his brother talk is not to cause further scandal and damage the firm's already tarnished reputation."

"You piece of shit. You have no idea what you're talking about." I'd held my tongue long enough.

"Really? Interesting, because some of the staff at your brother's firm Kane and Medici were forthcoming with their information…very forthcoming."

Jade's body shook, her breathing was heavy and rapid as she turned with tears running down her face.

"We need to talk." It was all she said as she walked to the doorway, pausing for a moment to gain her bearings while waiting for me to follow.

Jade took me through the rooms of Reece's estate until we reached the door to an oceanfront patio where we were alone and wouldn't be seen or disturbed by the party guests.

Turning, she didn't wait. She didn't pull any punches.

"Did you sleep with her? Is Reece telling the truth?"

"Baby…"

"Don't baby me, Tommy. Did you cheat with your brother's fiancée?"

"Yes and no, they weren't together any longer, but I still shouldn't have gotten involved with Raven."

Jade turned and laughed out loud. It was humorous; it was an appalling, anger driven, heart-wrenching laugh. It cut my insides…it was about to end our tomorrows.

Then she turned back calmly and spoke.

"You know the one thing I could do all day long was my life before you. It was…it was easy. I could do that life. Now, after this summer and the beach house and the surfing accident and Lucky, I can't do that life anymore. After you, I can't do it." Jade paced, curling her fists. Lifting them to her head, then in the air, then out wide as if she didn't know what to do or how to responded or where she belonged.

"Jade, I didn't mean for you to find out like this. I wanted to talk to you about it numerous times, yet it never felt like the right time presented itself. That's why I had told you, earlier today, I had something to talk with you about after the party. I had no idea this would happen before I'd gotten the chance to set things straight."

"Tommy, can you remember what I said when we first got together? I said, 'just don't lie to me.' I said the truth…always. And what did you do? You promised. You promised. I had to hear about this bullshit from Reece, of all fucking people."

Jade paused. Not to get her bearings, not to yell or hear me out. Jade stopped to end it.

"I can't do this, Tommy. I can't," she said, looking to the ocean for an answer, for understanding, before continuing. "What's most fucked up about this is that I can't go back to that life before either, I can't, and do you know why I can't?"

I shook my head.

Here's where her anguish and her rage took over. "Because now Jimmy isn't the only memory that will be there. You, damn it, you will be the other memory that broke my heart. Everywhere I look, you'll be there. From the paint on the walls, the footprints on the floor, you and I made memories there." She stopped, to fight against the tears that kept coming.

I wanted to touch her, to comfort her. To take away her pain, yet I was the cause of it.

"Jade…"

"No, don't. I knew it. I knew we should have just stayed friends."

Now, this is where my anger took over.

"Friends? Friends? I wanted you from the beginning. I couldn't figure it out. I couldn't get enough of you. Even when I thought all we would be was friends, I wanted to see you every minute of every day. Friends? I don't want to be your fucking friend, Jade! I love you! I'm in love with you! I want to be the guy who burns your toast in the morning but makes you giggle and say it's okay. I want to be the guy who surfs with you in the sunlight and rides those same waves with you into the darkness. I want to be the man who takes your nightmares away. I want to be the man who protects you from the storm. I want to be more than your friend…I want to be your boyfriend, your lover, your hero. Remember, I was there with you making those memories…they were ours. I can't be anything less…not anymore."

Jade continued to stare off into nowhere. This was it, nothing more to do or say. I waited for a sign, anything from her that told me she would give me another chance, but it never came. She continued to look away, not acknowledging that I was there, disconnecting herself from me and the situation, once again self-protecting.

I moved in to kiss her forehead. Staying briefly, my eyes and lips ached, knowing that the hardest thing I would ever have to do was let her be. I didn't fight, instead, I let our hearts break in hopes that she would see we were better together than we would ever be apart, but then I let her know one more thing, the thing that everyone around her kept for her at arm's length.

Whispering against her temple, "I'll always love you, Jade. You weren't about a timeline to be broken, you were a surprise that I would gladly give up everything for. Yet, I didn't get it but now I do. I would have never won your heart."

She pulled away stunned. "What are you talking about?" A nuance of disgust laced her question.

"You heard me. Your heart belongs to someone, something I can't compete against. And even if I could, I'd never win. Your heart belongs to a memory…to Jimmy. I'd lose hands down."

With that, I walked away from her, from what I thought was my forever, my tomorrow…our tomorrows, to give her the time she needed. My anger hadn't cooled as I walked through Montgomery's house…passing the stares, the snickers, and the whispers. My rage could have taken me to Reece, to beat him within in an inch of his life, but what would that have proven? That he'd won…I'd never let him win.

No, the best thing to do was head back ho—head back to the beach house to grab a few things and hit the road…clear my head, let it all blow over, and if Jade still couldn't trust me, then sell the place and move on permanently.

I pulled into the driveway and hurried up the stairs to get my belongings together.

Turning the corner, I walked head-on into Viv. "Viv, I'm sorry, I didn't know you were there."

"No, of course, you didn't, you were too busy running away. Blaze called to let me know what happened," she stated, reprimanding me as if I were a child.

"Viv, listen…"

"No, you listen to me. Running is not going to solve any of this. Both you and that stubborn niece of mine need to talk and I don't mean outside of the house of a man that's a complete moron. I mean you and Jade, here, alone together!"

"Oh…Viv, I would if I thought she'd listen, but she's badly hurt by what I kept from her."

"I see. Now would you like to tell me why no one, but Daniel, knew you moved here?"

"My brother was going through some shit and it changed him. Changed how he treated me and our family, our friends and especially his fiancée. They grew apart to the point of breaking up. He was angry, mean, spiteful, and as strong as Raven was, she couldn't take it. One thing led to another, and we made the mistake of sleeping together… it didn't last, and I knew it wouldn't but that's why I decided with everything going on in my life I needed to get away. To make a fresh start, and once I was settled in I would let them know. Right now, they think I'm surfing the globe. Which might not be a bad idea at the moment."

"I don't know what to say. I wish you would just wait for Jade to cool off and perhaps you could work things out."

"Thank you, Viv, but I believe getting away for Jade's sake might be the best thing for her right now." I unlocked the door and realized I couldn't leave without finding someone who could watch Lucky for a few days. I couldn't take her with me and with all of the darkness she dealt with before I adopted her, I didn't want to uproot her from the only real home she knew.

I asked Viv if Lucky could stay in the house for a few days and if she could watch her until I get back.

"Go…I'll take care of Lucky. Tommy, Jade and I both will. Don't worry, she'll be fine while you're gone."

I smiled, kissed her cheek, and ran upstairs to grab my clothes. The door on the old dresser was jammed. The more I pulled, the more crooked it became. Finally, after one good yank, the drawer flew out and fell to the floor, spilling its contents everywhere and not just my clothes. On the floor, next to my pile of shirts, was a white envelope with Jade's name on the front. I never noticed an envelope in the drawer, and when I examined it further I realized it was taped to the back. The drawer falling to the ground must have dislodged it. I went back down the stairs after packing to give Viv instructions for Lucky and to let her know that I would have someone pick her up in a few days.

I kissed Lucky and held her to let her know I would be back for her once I found a place to stay. It was breaking my heart further to leave her there.

Viv walked me to my car, and I realized I hadn't given her the letter I found upstairs.

"Viv, could you give this to Jade?"

"Sure, what is…Oh dear God. Where did you get this?" She was stunned. Stunned may be the wrong word, frightened, like something haunted her.

"I was getting my clothes and the dresser drawer wouldn't open. I guess I pulled too hard, and when the drawer crashed to the floor, out came that letter. Viv, is something wrong? You look like you've seen a ghost."

"I may have."

"What?"

"The handwriting on this letter is Jimmy's. You're sure you found it upstairs?"

"Yes, just now? Why?"

Viv with a flurry of her hands, dismissed her thoughts. "Nothing, nothing…It's probably an old letter he never gave to Jade. I'm sure she'll treasure it."

I nodded and then kissed her cheek gently before driving away.

Now on the road, I wasn't sure where I should go. I couldn't call my family and endure the questions. I couldn't call Mike because he'd only laugh in my face and tell me it served me right, and Daniel was at the party with Kim, so I certainly couldn't ruin his evening any more than I already did. I knew who I had to call, so I pulled over to hear her voice.

"Tommy?"

"Hey, baby, what do you say I fly out to Capri and we have a longer visit?"

"I'd love that Tommy, I really would, but I'm back in the states."

"Where are you, Rain?"

"Dominick and the twins and I flew back the other day. You know how I love the end of summer on Long Beach Island, so we headed to the shore house straight from the airport. Anna and Joseph will be down tonight." Rain's explanation had me grinning from ear to ear.

"So, would you guys mind some company?"

"No, not at all, I can't wait to see you. When will you get here?"

"In about ten minutes."

"Ten minutes? Where are you, Tommy, and what's going on?" Elation and concern crossing in her question.

"Baby, it's a long story."

"Then hurry your ass up, so I can hear all about her."

I laughed, a laugh I hadn't heard in me for a long time, the old me, the not so crushed me. Rain could always bring me out of the bullshit and into the light of day. The same way Jade did, but she made it perfectly clear, she wouldn't be sharing that light with me any longer. I brushed the bad thoughts away, forcing a smile, knowing soon, I'd be back where I needed to be—with the friends and family I should never have run away from. The only family I could count on at this point.

chapter
twenty-four

Jade

THE CROWD BROKE apart, walking to the foyer, forming a line to see who could get out the door fast enough. With Reece spending his time at the top of the stairs, still with a champagne glass in his hand, his disingenuous apology spewing from his lips. The world was his stage as always, only this time the inhabitants were his captive audience.

I watched from a dark corner, making sure the last of the party-goers exited the home. I wasn't sure where the other familiar players were. There were no signs of Blaze or Daniel or Kim, not even Damien or Courtney showed their faces. The lights went down, and all but the stagehands, his after-party cleanup crew, were left. I walked out from behind the shadows and climbed the stairs to find the star of his own show.

He stood alone, poolside, his back to me, staring at the wave's whitewash and the lights twinkling in the distance off the massive body of water before him, the one thing bigger than Reece Montgomery. Still drinking from his glass, he looked down, shaking his head. Perhaps a hint of regrets? That was unlikely. Probably more disappointed that I didn't allow mine and Tommy's goodbye to be the ending scene, to play out on his deck.

This time, I took the lead. I was quiet, like a cat stalking her prey, the leftover adrenaline from the surge I got earlier from confronting Reece emboldened me. I would normally walk away and later forgive Reece. I'd make up an excuse in my mind. It was Reece being Reece or he just cared deeply for me and he didn't do "meaning well" like the rest of us, but not this time. This time he went too far. Yet, this time I needed to be different, quiet in my retort. I needed for Reece to hear me, no witty comebacks, no yelling…closure.

As my footsteps closed in on my host, he turned. Rolling his eyes, he addressed me."I suppose you're here to scream at me and tell me what a horrible person I am. Go ahead, you wouldn't be the first, and you certainly won't be the last."

Leaning on the railing, facing him, I smirked. Still the same old Reece, playing the walking wounded. As if nothing that happened here tonight was his fault. He was only trying to help.

Taking a deep cleansing breath in, I answered him. I had no idea what I was going to say, but I knew I wanted this…all of this… to end here tonight.

"Did you ever think of coming to me and telling what you found out or should I say what you went and purposely looked for?"

"Of course, but you wouldn't have listened. You were already too wrapped up with emotion for him, and so soon I might add."

"Did you ever think none of this was any of your business, then?"

"Jade, when has that ever stopped me?" This was Reece, trying to make light of a bad situation.

"Can I ask you something?"

"Always."

"Why? Was it for Damien? Because it certainly wasn't for me."

He reached out and touched my cheek. His eyes closed and the breath he'd been holding released along with his frustration.

"All of it was for you. None of it was for Damien."

"What?"

He took the last drop of drink from his glass and stilled. Bracing himself for what came next.

"Your mother and father…they left for Europe for all the wrong reasons. If they had honestly gone there for your father to pursue this contract he's working on, it would be one thing, but they did it to push you into a normal life. To make you believe that they had the strength to deal with Jimmy's death. They ran away, leaving Viv and the rest of us to watch over you. A job I would gladly do, over and over again."

"What the hell are you talking about, Reece?"

"This little plan you devised to not date after Damien's betrayal was to protect your heart, but in reality, it wasn't to protect you from going through the same thing with another man. Damien's affair with Courtney came at the most opportune time because you were protecting yourself from loss, the loss of your brother, not the loss of your relationship with my son."

"You can't be serious? You had that much time away from your business to study me and my emotions?" I was no longer feeling patient.

"I didn't need to study you. You wore your emotions on your sleeve, you always have. You're honest as the day is long and you love and care for everyone around you, but everyone around you has done you a disservice, including me."

"How's that?"

"We allowed you to wallow in your grief for three long years."

The crack from my hand to his jaw came swift, out of nowhere. The last of my adrenaline stores from earlier this evening.

"I believe I deserved that and that's my point."

"Your point…which is?"

"Other than the typical and traditional emotions and reactions to Jimmy's death, everyone— and I mean everyone— wanted you to get back to business as usual…for lack of a better term."

"I don't follow."

"You know exactly what I mean. They did their best to never say the word suicide. They did their best to indulge you in these anniversary tributes to Jimmy. They made excuses for themselves that it was good for you. That these traditions cleansed your soul. When all they really did was keep you in the same state you were in three years ago when Jimmy took his life. I watched and I admit I allowed it. But no more…"

"So, you want to be the one to save my soul, Reece?" I promised not to be sarcastic or witty, but that was an impossibility after hearing this nonsense.

"I'm sure you think this is all nonsense on my part, but hear me out. When you and Damien broke up after Jimmy died, you decided not to date for a while. A natural reaction after what you discovered. Now here we are three years later, and you've barely dated…until Mr. Conte that is."

"Again, what is your point, Reece? Because I know there has to be a point."

"Oh, but there is. Tommy Conte reminds you of your brother—the surfing, the carefree attitude, his success in business, his easy-going personality. He's just like Jimmy in many ways."

"You think I'm looking for my brother in a man? You can't be serious?"

"No, I know many of your hobbies were the same as Jimmy's, so naturally with Mr. Conte loving the same things you do, the two of you would have clicked, but it was more than that—that's where my snooping began."

"At least you admit it."

"You wanted to save him."

"Come again?"

"You couldn't save Jimmy, so with Tommy having similar attributes you decided this was your chance to save him."

"You're delusional." I turned to walk away.

"Am I, Jade? He betrayed his brother. He left his business for his partner to run. A simple phone call to his office in New York and in speaking with her told me more than I could have possibly imagined. Did you know he put a book contract on hold to run off and find himself?Miss Medici, his business partner, never said those words exactly, but it was too easy to put two and two together when she told me he was traveling on sabbatical, and yet he was actually here rebuilding an old beach house."

Listening to all of this with my back towards him, my tears rolling down my face, I realized I was the delusional one.

Perhaps, Reece of all people was right. Maybe I did want to save Tommy. I knew about his timeline, about his plan. Maybe I subconsciously felt if he didn't reach that goal and find what he was looking for, he would meet the same end as Jimmy had. No, I loved him, I wasn't delusional about that. My reactions when he touched me, his smile, his laughter…his kiss, our connection when he was inside my body. The feeling I had the night on the dance floor before I even knew who Tommy was, I was happy. That wasn't fabricated from loss or sorrow…that was all Tommy.

I turned back to set him straight when his phone rang.

"I see. We're on our way." He placed the phone in his pocket and addressed me. "It's Viv…she collapsed."

We didn't speak, we didn't argue. We ran for Reece's car, where his driver was waiting to take us to Viv. Even with the car not stopping, I jumped out and ran for her stairs. Once I reached the deck, I was confronted with EMS workers and our friends.

"What happened?" I pressed, sitting down on the ground near the chair my aunt was being examined in.

"We found her here on the deck. It appears as if she fainted, so we called 911." Daniel explained,

"And I called Reece," Blaze added.

"Everyone settle down. I'm fine."

"Viv…" It was all I could muster, taking her hand. Looking into her eyes for an answer.

"I'm just dehydrated, that's all." Touching my face, Aunt Viv gave me a soft and confident smile.

"Is she dehydrated?" Desperately trying to confirm this with the closet EMS worker.

"Yeah, from what she explained to us, she is. Now, Ms. Marshall, we're going to give you some IV fluids in the ambulance, and we'd like to take you to the hospital to be checked out."

"You'll do nothing of the sort. I'm happy to take the fluids, but I'm not going to the hospital. I'll call my doctor and let him know what occurred."

"This is not optimal. You've lived here forever, and you know how brutal the sun can be."

"I'm not that old, young man, but yes, I do know, and that is why I'm staying put."

Viv was every bit her feisty self. I knew she wouldn't budge, and I knew she was more than likely fine, but that statement about a doctor; I didn't know Viv had a doctor. She's never mentioned one. She hates going to the doctor. I wondered what it was all about. It scared me.

Once the EMS tended to Viv and finally left, I took Viv inside and the others followed.

"Tell me why you're seeing a doctor."

"It's nothing to concern yourself with, Jade. Tell me what happened between you and Tommy?"

"I am concerned, and how do you know something happened?"

"Because I was at his door dropping something off when he barreled around the corner from the stairs nearly knocking me off my feet."

"We had a fight, not really a fight, but…"

"You broke it off?"

"Yes."

"I see." She took a deep, agitated breath in and let that same breath out.

"Jade, I'm going to tell you something that I've been keeping from you and I don't want you to be angry."

"What is it?" If I thought the night couldn't get any worse, it did.

"I've been dealing with some heart issues for the last few months, nothing major, part of age, but something that needs to be addressed; that's why I've been going to Philly so frequently."

My mouth opened, my tears falling, "Why, Viv? Why didn't you say anything?" She didn't get her chance to answer, Reece did.

"Because this is what I was telling you earlier, Jade. Everyone in this room with the exception of Daniel has done nothing except protect you since Jimmy passed away."

"Don't you mean committed suicide? Can't you say it, Reece?"

"Touché, my sweet girl, touché."

"I didn't tell you, because you had been and are currently struggling with enough." Viv finally answered. "You were renovating the shoppe and you were questioning whether to begin a relationship with Tommy or not. How could I possibly throw one more thing at you?"

"By just doing it, Viv, just throw it at me, and I'll catch it and fix it, or do something, but to keep me in the dark to protect me, from what? Myself? Viv, I'm far too old for that kind of protection. Please don't keep things from me, please." Viv looked to the crowd behind me and not directly in my eyes. That meant there was more, just how much more remained to be seen.

I turned in the direction Viv was looking, in the direction of more guilty faces.

"Oh God, what the hell is going on?"

"Jade, Tommy owns the house."

"What?"

"He bought it in February and moved down the beginning of the week you met him."

"Holy shit! He lied about that too?"

"He had no other choice. I asked him to keep the sale under wraps until after I spoke with you about it. We didn't know how you would feel about the house being sold, so I made up 'the rent with the option to buy' story."

"Okay, but the realtor who had listed the house would have told me someone was inquiring about it. She never called me, not even to say that someone else made the sale. I mean…unless… Don't tell me you helped Viv and my parents sell the house?" I directed my question at the only one with the license to do so.

"Okay, I won't tell you." Blaze indirectly admitted her guilt and her role in all of this.

"I asked Blaze to help. You see, Tommy found out about the house from Daniel's parents, Anna and Joseph. Only they weren't told that he purchased it. He asked that I not say anything about where he was, or about the sale of the house should they or anyone else other than Daniel inquire, so in turn I took the opportunity to ask him not to admit that he bought the place until I had a chance to talk with you, and he agreed to help."

I walked over to the fireplace where Viv displayed pictures of Jimmy and me growing up, to gain some composure. There we stood, the two of us…the laughter, the sunshine, the surf.

"It's strange how almost yesterday now feels like a lifetime ago." Gripping the mantle to steady myself, not facing the intimate crowd in the room, my mind tried to absorb what was revealed to me.

"If it would be okay, I'd like to speak with Jade privately?" Everyone nodded and preceded to say goodbye, all except for Daniel.

"Jade, if it's all right with you I'd like to wait at Tommy's until my ride arrives."

"Sure. Stay as long as you like. I'll help you get over there and then Viv, I'll come back so we can talk."

"That won't be necessary. Daniel, I would actually like you to stay while I talk to my niece."

I nodded to let him know it was fine. Daniel rolled forward in his chair, as I pulled an ottoman up closer to Viv. Without a word, she handed me an envelope with my name written on it. The handwriting was unmistakable. It was Jimmy's.

"I don't get it. You're giving me a letter from Jimmy now?" My voice crumbled.

"I didn't know about the letter either. Tommy handed it to me tonight."

"Tommy? Where did he get it?" Daniel asked while I sat here stunned.

"Tommy had gone upstairs to pack."

"Pack?" My voice escalated.

"Yes, pack…did you think he would stay in the beach house tonight consumed by all of the memories around him, Jade?" Viv's unsympathetic tone questioned.

"Well, I didn't think he would run away."

"You mean again?"

"What?" Viv looked to Daniel, whose disheartened expression told me there was more to Tommy buying the house than starting over.

"What was Tommy running from?"

"Himself," Daniel said.

"I don't get it."

"Tommy was running away from the mundane, from the reminders of how time was passing him by and he felt he had nothing to show for it, nothing that meant anything in life."

"Tommy is a successful photographer. Why would he feel like that?"

"It wasn't the photography, Jade. It was his life in general. He wasn't where he wanted to be, so he moved here to make it better."

My head shook in unison with my body. "And now he's gone. Daniel, I didn't mean to hurt Tommy. It's just…forget it."

"It's getting late and although I feel much better, I'm not up for walking Lucky this evening. Can you take her?"

"He didn't take Lucky?" Questioning why, yet feeling a bit excited that I'd have the chance to see him again.

"No, he asked me if I could watch her for a few days until he could make arrangements to pick her up. He didn't have anywhere to take her tonight, and as I said, he couldn't stay in the house. I will tell you he was heartbroken to leave her."

I kissed Viv and made sure she was okay. Daniel said he would stay with her while he waited for his ride. I told her that after I took Lucky for her walk, we would both come back and stay with her for the night.

chapter
twenty-five

Tommy

JADE AND THE beach house were literally twenty minutes south on LBI from Dominick and Rain's shore estate in the town of Loveladies. Having to pass the Montgomery compound to get to Rain left a boiling pit of anger in my stomach. Yet, once I reached her driveway adorned with wild roses of every variety, my heart returned to my childhood in Capri…my heart returned to Rain.

The crackling swoosh of the sandstone pebbles that blanketed the drive alerted my friend to my entrance. It was late, seeing the massive two-story, shingle style estate lit from every room baked its warmth into my tired body. I sat there, enjoyed it, soaked in the quiet until Rain opened the door, leaned into the frame, arms crossed; her body tanned, her hair loose and flowing…her smile, yeah, her smile.

"Well, don't just sit there and admire the view, Tommy. Get over here."

Rain ran the steps, as I stretched out of the car bracing myself for her loving welcome. Into my arms, she jumped. It was good to be back with her.

"Oh, Tommy, I missed you so, so much." Snug and muffled, Rain held on hard.

"Baby, I missed you more."

"Liar," she stated with a crooked smile.

"Hey, what you mean liar?"

"Give me a break, Tommy, this is me you're talking to, and I repeat this has a woman written all over it."

My head shaking eye roll was my only response.

"Okay, tell me I'm wrong?" She said, waiting for my rebuttal with crossed arms and a saucy shoulder shake.

"You're not wrong, Rain." It hurt to whisper it.

"All joking aside, let's go in the house. I want to hear all of it," Taking my hand and pulling me toward the house, I barely had time to grab my bag from the backseat, as she yanked me onto the porch, to a familiar annoying grimace I knew so well…Kane.

"Conte."

"Kane."

"Trouble in paradise?"

"Mr. Kane, we had a discussion mere moments ago. Would you like me to repeat myself? It appears you've forgotten my warning." Rain kissed her menace, I mean the father of her children, teasingly cautioning his behavior.

"No, angel, I didn't forget. Yet, I humbly stand corrected."

"Good…" She continued to pull me inside and then swiftly turned to block Kane and me from entering, as she swung around and slammed her hands on each side of the doorjamb.

"Let me make myself very clear. I love you and I love you. Now, that being noted and received, I expect both of you to cool it, because I have two impressionable babies in this house that will learn from your antics and I don't want them near any part of it. So, let's leave the bullshit at the door…hmm?" We both nodded and grinned.

Rain was feisty as always.

Once inside, we went directly to the kitchen. Growing up, Rain and I always sat at the island in the kitchen in Capri. It seemed so long ago—our talks there.

"Coffee?" She asked.

"Stronger?" Dominick interrupted, holding up brandy and two snifters.

"No offense, baby, but I like what Kane's pushing."

"Suit yourself. I have a feeling it's going to be a long night and coffee will keep up the momentum."

"I can do both."

"Do you love her?" Rain, bluntly sympathetic, wanted more than yes or no. She wanted, no, she deserved an explanation after I lied to her in reference to my whereabouts the last few months. Her husband grinned proudly at his wife's directness.

"Yeah, I love her, but…"

Rain's inquisition would begin with numerous interruptions. "But what…why is there always a 'but' with you men?"

"Angel, to be fair you haven't let him finish." Rain's husband established.

"Or start, if you want to get technical about it," And I added.

"Finished? Started? You didn't even tell me you were doing any of this shit, and both of you are griping about me asking a few questions? That's rich…before we go any further, why don't you explain to me why you never said a word about what you were up to all of these months? Better yet, explain why you kept me in the dark…me, your best friend of all people?"

Dominick and I looked at each other with raised brows, pursed lips, while deeply exhaling, because it was easy to see this talk was not going to go as originally planned.

"I'm waiting," Rain demanded with arms crossed and foot tapping. It made me regret calling her.

Dominick wasn't about to be trapped with me in this mess, so he did the only thing a husband who wanted to remain in his wife's good graces could do…he bailed.

"I'll leave you to this. I need to get Daniel." He said, kissing her goodbye before heading out to get his brother.

I stopped him to ask both he and Rain a favor.

"I'm not sure if this would be a good time to ask, but I had to leave my dog Lucky at the house. Viv said she would watch her, but it's not sitting right with me. When you pick up Daniel, can she come with you?"

They looked at each other and then to me, "Sure, Conte, I'll get her. Is she friendly?"

"Very, and she loves other dogs, so I don't think there will be a concern if she's around Max." Max was Rain and Dominick's lab. Lucky was largely dog-friendly, so this arrangement was going to work out fine, what a relief. It was probably going to fair better for Lucky than for me. If Rain even lets me stay at this point.

"Now, my babies are asleep, and my Mr. Kane is on his way get his brother and your dog, so tell me, what's been going on?"

"I'll give you the shortened version and add the details in if you feel you're missing something."

"Go on."

"I wasn't surfing the globe this whole time."

"No shit." Rain's response bit through me.

"I deserved that."

"What did you expect? Why lie? There wasn't any reason to hide this from me."

"Are you joking? You are always trying to fix things, especially things that are not your job to fix. That's why I hid this from you. That and the fact that I needed this time to think."

"Yet, in this time you met someone?"

"Yeah, but as of tonight, no matter what went on between us, it's over."

"Wow…giving up that easily, huh?"

"I didn't give up on her. She gave up on me."

"Why?"

"Jade found out about Mike and Raven."

"I see."

"Yeah, she was cheated on by her fiancé, Damien Montgomery."

"Reece Montgomery's son?"

"Yes."

"I see."

"Why do you keep saying, 'I see'?"

"Now that you've mentioned the key players in all of this, it explains the phone calls."

"What phone calls?"

"Reece Montgomery called a few times inquiring about hiring us again, but was specifically interested in having you do the work."

"I see." I stated, which won me a whimsically annoyed look for my 'I see.'

"Listen, to me. I love you very, very much and you can stay here for as long as you like. You know we have to head back to Italy at the end of the week, so the house is yours and Lucky's to do with as you like, but, and yes, there is a but, you have to try to work this out with…?"

"Jade."

"Okay, you have to try to work this out with Jade. You can't fall in love this quickly and in this short a time and expect it to be rosy and easy for you. You are only just starting to date, but if you are already in love with her then your emotions are in high gear and I would suspect so are hers."

"I appreciate that. I think I'm going to take you up on this. Listen, Rain, I don't want to be far from her, but I can't go back to the beach house right now and work on it with her when she is in the state she's in. There won't be anything left between us if I press the issue. At least I can monitor things without her knowing if I stay here."

"You love her very much. I can see that," she said as her tears formed.

"I told you I did. More than I thought I could have loved another person." I admitted.

"It's not over, trust me. You'll get her back, but be careful with monitoring her even from afar. Take it from me, she won't be too thrilled if she finds out." Rain's resolve was stern. I wish I had the confidence she did with this, but I wasn't seeing it. I wished, I hoped, but my faith eroded with each passing minute.

"Come…let's get you settled in before the boys return with Lucky. In the meantime, I have something that will make you feel better."

"What's that?"

"Angel and Joseph, watching the twins sleep always puts things into perspective for me."

chapter
twenty-six

Jade

NEVER COULD I have imagined in the morning, the night would have ended as it did. I was pissed Reece caused trouble. I was pissed Tommy hadn't come to me with what happened in his past. He didn't trust me enough to think I would understand or at least hear him out. To find out the way I did is what floored me. Then to hear from my family he already owned the beach house, and they kept the information from me, because I wouldn't be able to handle it, pissed me off further.

I left Daniel with Viv to get Lucky for her evening walk along the shoreline. Her excitement calmed my chattering mind. To watch her romp happily in the surf, looking back every so often to see that I was still with her, holding onto her lead— innocent, easily grateful for these moments each day.

Lucky and I reached one of the flattened slate slabs protruding from the jetty, our shadows cast on the sand from the bright glow of the moon overhead. The swoosh of the weakened waves was all that could be heard. It was late, and most residents had settled in for the night.

The walk allowed my racing thoughts to retreat— abandoning them for a moment. Yet, as I looked at Lucky, they came rushing back.

Reliving in my mind the summer with Tommy, and with Lucky—our simple, predictable routine. I would work at the shoppe, he worked on the beach house. I would run him breakfast, he would run me lunch. We'd have dinner together, alone or with friends, followed by walks like this one every evening. Nothing fancy, but it was ours…

How could I let go of him?

I ran back with Lucky to Viv's house. At her door, I heard voices, two were familiar and one was not. Stepping inside answered my question as to who the third person was. It was unmistakable, it was Daniel's brother…Dominick. They looked exactly alike, yet different. Daniel was light, like Tommy. Dominick was dark, like Reece. He stood stoic, perhaps a glimpse of a smile, but nothing like Daniel's aura.

"Jade, I'm glad you're back. I want you to meet Dominick, my brother."

"Good to meet you, Jade." His smile toward me was warmer than expected.

"Nice to meet you," I said; taking his hand, I paused thinking how different he and Daniel were even being identical twins.

"Jade, can you get Lucky's things? Her bed and toys and such, together. Dominick will be taking her for Tommy."

"Wait! You've spoken with him?"

His crooked grin told me yes before he could answer.

"He's with my wife Rain, as we speak. He asked me if it would be okay if I picked up Lucky being I was coming to get my brother. I was happy to do it. I know how hard it is to be away from my dog for just a day, so if you can show me where her belongings are, I'll put them in my car."

"Sure, follow me." With a shaky hand, I gave Daniel Lucky's leash, leaving them with Viv, to show Dominick what he needed to take.

Needing to get this over with, I feverishly snatched up as many things as I could in one swoop, leaving them to crash at my feet. I wouldn't be defeated and tried again, only to be losing ground, having picked up one toy, to only have two more drop.The only thing to stop the repetition and give me a reprieve from my insanity was Dominick's hand at my back.

"Enough of this, let's talk, shall we?" He gestured his other hand to offer me a seat on the sofa.

I nodded.

"Do you love, Conte?" He was definitely nothing like Daniel. His forwardness held me back from answering him.

"I'll take your silence as a yes."

"Yes, I love him."

"Then why is he confiding in Rain and you're confiding in me?"

"I'm not confiding in you. You merely asked me a question and…"

"I answered it for you. Listen, I don't know you, but my brother speaks highly of you and your family, so allow me to give you some advice. You can either take it, and think about what I'm about to say, or you can tell me to go to hell, I'll leave you to decide."

"Go on."

"I'm sure Conte must have confided in you somewhat. He must have explained his dislike for me in the way in which I treated Rain when we first met."

"He didn't elaborate. He said there had been some issues, but both of you fought hard against all odds to work it out and be together."

"He said that, huh?"

"Yes."

"He's not wrong. We had to fight hard against other people, against our own idiosyncrasies, beliefs, and our pasts. At times we were our own worst enemies. Sometimes we still are, but the one constant thing we both share is our love for each other. Rain and our babies make my life whole. I could never go back to the way I was before being with Rain. She is my entire world."

"Can I ask you something?"

"Of course."

"Aren't you afraid? I mean…"

"Afraid of losing her?"

"Yes"

"Always…Jade, I'm not an easy man to live with. I want things my way much of the time. Yet, I know full well if I don't refrain from my old habits, I'll lose her, an outcome I can't live with. It's never been easy for me to compromise, but with Rain, it's almost effortless. She makes me want to be a better man, a better father…a better human being. Do you understand?"

I nodded. "Tommy doesn't have to do any of those things for me. Our relationship, once it got started, was effortless. He doesn't have to be a better man."

"Then why aren't you with him?"

His question suffocated me. It was too close to proving me wrong, to allowing my heart to give in. I was too confused to make sense of Tommy and what happened at the party. It was too soon. I need to get away, running for the door, he stopped me. Dominick's hand pressed the glass, preventing me from sliding it open.

"Don't run. Tell me what happened."

"Tommy lied about his past and why he moved here. He slept with his brother's fiancée and he knew I was hurt by mine, much in the same way. He knew I needed to know the truth and yet, he lied."

"True, but he didn't cheat on you." His statement sliced through me. "Conte and I were never friends, and I'm not condoning his actions or his past, but I've come to know him through my wife, and I can say, without a shadow of a doubt, he's loyal."

"How can you when…?"

"When he did what he did?"

"Yes."

"I don't buy into the scenario of once a cheater always a cheater…not for all people; life is far too complicated to label relationships in that way. To be fair, Michael and Raven had ended their relationship before Conte and she slept together, so although highly inappropriate, he didn't technically cheat. What he did was stupid, there's no denying that, but I don't care to analyze what led them to the connection they had. Being an outsider, Raven and Tommy used to go at it. They were two different people. I could never see him being in a relationship with her. Yet, they both had something within themselves, something which placed them together, right or wrong."

"I wish he had told me from the beginning and all of this could have been avoided."

"Do you truly believe that?"

"Of course, all he had to do was tell me the truth and this shit tonight could have been avoided."

"So, let me ask you something, does one mistake from the past wipe away a lifetime of good for the future? I think you need to ask yourself that question before going forward."

"You don't think I've already done that?"

"What have you come up with?"

"I don't know. I love him, it's true, but I'm afraid."

"You're not alone. We're all afraid of love. Something so powerful it can break you, yet something you can't live without."

"I just don't know what to do anymore."

"First stop listening to others and listen to this," Dominick advised, pointing to my heart's center.

I nodded.

"You'll figure it out. Here's my card. My cell is on there. If you need to talk or need to find Conte, call me."

"Thank you."

"You're welcome, it's late and I need to get back home. Let's load up the car together."

Dominick explained that he and his family had a home in Loveladies, here on LBI and Tommy would be staying there for the night. This put my mind at ease, knowing Tommy and Lucky would be somewhere safe and not driving around because Tommy thought he couldn't come back home.

Home.

After Daniel and Dominick left, I locked up Tommy's house and mine and walked back to Viv's. At this point it was early morning, I hadn't slept, and I couldn't sleep. I tried. I crashed on Viv's couch, but my head was spinning. I decided even though I didn't work on Sunday, there was plenty to do before the opening next week and maybe it would help me to get my mind away from everything that went on in the last twenty-four hours.

When that didn't work, I went back to Viv's, but with all of the stress I'd caused, she was fast asleep and I didn't want to disturb her and decided it would be better to sleep in my own bed. As I walked out the door, I spotted the letter from Jimmy on the table in Viv's foyer. My fingertips traced his lettering of my name.

Taking the letter, I left. Standing between my house and the beach house hurt. I wanted to be close to him, but I was afraid.

Afraid of what, Jade? He said he loved you.

I ran the stairs and unlocked the door of the beach house. This was where I needed to be. I had to feel him, even though he wasn't there. I needed his strength to read my brother's letter. I needed Tommy. Wrapping the blanket he had wrapped me in the night of Viv's dinner party, I placed myself in the corner of the couch and slowly opened the letter.

Jade,

I know if you're reading this my life on earth has ended. I also know that you're angry, mainly with me, but with yourself for not saving me.

Baby girl, it wasn't your job to save me. I didn't want to be saved.

My life was never what I wanted. It was always about living up to something I wasn't or didn't want to be. I suppose I could have carried on with the status quo and dealt with dad and his demands day in and day out. I was a man, right, a grownup.

I was tired for a very long time. So long, in fact, I can't remember where the hate for the way I was living started, but I knew where it would end.

I wasn't me any longer. I was some corporate machine. I was an image I didn't want to project. It was consuming me, eating me up alive, bit by bit, day by day...with no end in sight. That's why I decided to take the year to fulfill my bucket list. To do all of the things I'd wanted to do, but no longer had the time for. Except, I wasn't dying from any disease, I was already dead on the inside.

I started this on my birthday and knew one year to the day, if I didn't feel better or get resolve from the list itself, I would end it there, with no regrets.

I never anticipated the accident at The Mavericks would wreck my plans. Then when it did, I wondered if it was a sign to me from above, telling me I was going in the wrong direction. I shouldn't have planned on ending my life. I have more than most. I have more to accomplish. I have people who love me. I have a successful career, a beautiful family, and a sister better than any brother could ask for.

So even with the rage inside, I tried. I tried to find purpose at the Center. To take the hand I was dealt and make it better. To move forward. To move on. Jade, it wasn't working. The closer my birthday came, the more I knew exactly what had to happen. I needed to finish what I started. I needed to follow through on what I knew was right for me. No amount of counseling helped, and believe me, I tried.

Knowing that the day was coming, I had written a note, but destroyed it because I didn't want the note to be for everyone. I wanted it to be for you. I knew mom and dad loved me in their own way. I knew Viv cared about me like crazy, but I needed you to know, even though I had to go, you were the most important thing to me.

You were on my mind through all of this.

Jade, I always said that you chased away the sun so you could follow the moon. It's funny, you didn't understand, although you pretended like you did. What I meant back then was you never allowed yourself the right to shine. You always stood in the shadows, never basking in the limelight. While others who didn't want it, or deserve it, still took front and center...others like me, Courtney, Blaze, Damien, and even Reece.

Then, one day when you came back to LBI from Manhattan to say that you wanted to start your own business, I saw how happy you were. I hope you realized that dream and made that dream a reality.

I knew at that moment, how wrong I was. You didn't chase away the sun. You were the sunshine...the light that everyone wanted to bask in. You were that same light in the darkness...the only light in my dark world.

I said I had no regrets. I lied. I have only one...

You.

To not see your beautiful face every day. To not laugh with you or surf with you. To have left you behind...to have so much pain in me to know that my actions would have cut you so deeply. That's the only thing I will ever regret...hurting you.

Knowing how angry you are right now as you're reading this, I need to give you some big brother advice and I want you to listen and hear me, even if what I'm about to say doesn't make a lot of sense at the moment, it will...someday.

You need to remember your last things...

You need to savor them, the way I never could. The last great cookie you baked, your last great beach day, your last great wave, your last dance, your last hug, your last smile, your last kiss, and one day if you get married...the last time you picked up your child because he or she is now walking on their own.

Your last... I love you.

You see your lasts may be just that, so savor them. I couldn't remember any of those times. I was too consumed with being swallowed up in a life I despised.

Hold on to those memories. Keep them close to you and never take them for granted. They are all that truly matters.

You, my baby sister, are not like me. You are the sunshine, you are the moonlight. You are 'my last'...I'll always remember you.

I love you forever...until we meet again,

Jimmy

The slow-motion thumps of my heart were the only sounds my ears to could hear. Drowning out the world around me, my brother didn't take his life because of his accident, he was preparing to die before The Mavericks. He was simply preparing to die...period.

I read it and re-read it...again, again, and then some more. My body ached as if Jimmy died today, in this moment. For me, he did. He did because all of this time I'd been searching for why. Why did this have to happen? What could I have done? Did I miss something that could have saved him?

Maybe I needed to be resolved to the fact "why" will never be truly answered. Only Jimmy held the truth in his heart. It didn't matter how many times I rehashed it. I'd been doing that for three fucking years. Second guessing, wondering, questioning, feeling guilty, blaming myself, hurting for him, missing him, being angry at him, but never knowing the truth until today.

It still hurt. This letter didn't make it go away, and it didn't make it better. It did as Jimmy said, bring me clarity. Clarity on my 'lasts'...

He pressed his lips to my temple.

He said he couldn't compete with a memory.

He said he didn't want to be my fucking friend.

He said…I love you.

I remembered all of my 'lasts' with him so clearly, but especially how Tommy made me feel the last time I was with him before the party last night. We had taken Lucky to the bay, to get her to feel comfortable on the paddle board so she could be a part of the water with Tommy and me.

At first, she was frightened, scrambling to get off the board, but then, little by little she stayed, and soon she was on the board with Tommy like a pro. Eventually, she climbed onto my board, and I paddled out with her, then on our way back in, a cowboy on a jet ski created an unwelcome wake, sending Lucky and me off the board. She immediately swam to shore, but before I had the chance to follow her lead, Tommy was there holding me, taking me in.

When it first happened, I thought it odd. It wasn't like we were far from the shoreline. The bay wasn't all that deep in the area we were paddling, but to Tommy, none of those things mattered. Only I mattered…I mattered to him.

I couldn't do this…I wouldn't let the way we were now…be our 'lasts.' I needed to go to him and we needed to work this out. If 'I love you' needed to be said a million times and then a million more to fix this, then that's what I was willing to do.

I pulled out the card that Dominick gave me and I phoned him. It went to voicemail. Not leaving a message, I decided to phone Daniel. He was going with Dominick to his shore home where Tommy was staying, so he could give me the address.

"Hello."

"Hi, Daniel, it's Jade."

"Hi, Jade, how are you?"

"I need your help."

"Sure. What do you need?"

"I need you to tell me where you are, the address. I need to see Tommy, and Dominick said he was there with his wife last night."

"I'd be happy to help, but Tommy left with Lucky about ten minutes ago."

"Did he say where he was going?"

"No, in fact, I was still asleep when he left. Rain said she thought he was going to head back to the city. His place didn't sell yet and there was some furniture there he could sleep on, which he hadn't taken in the move."

"I know you're loyal to him, but would you give me his address in New York ? I could get it from Blaze, but then I'd have to deal with Reece and I don't have time for that."

"Sure, anything to help get the two of you back together." Daniel gave me Tommy's address in New York. I needed to catch up with him there and let him know how I was feeling.

I told Aunt Viv, and she wholeheartedly agreed with my decision to find Tommy and bring him back home. She inquired about the letter from Jimmy, but I told her I hadn't read it yet and that I wanted Tommy with me when I did. The words came out of my mouth and guilt hit my heart, but Viv was dealing with heart issues. No matter how small, I couldn't tell her about Jimmy's true death. I lied, and if it meant protecting Viv as she had done for me much of my life, then so be it. She didn't need to be devastated, again. She needed to remember her nephew in her own way.

When I hit the city, I found Tommy's brownstone but surveying the street, I didn't see Tommy's car. I rang the bell…no answer. He was probably watching me from one of the windows and decided to ignore me. He had to know it was me when he looked out if he was home. I drove a vintage 181, not many people have them anymore.

I tried the bell, again, to no avail and then I hit the knocker. The door opened.

Perhaps Daniel was wrong and the house was vacated.

I stepped inside to see. The foyer was a dark wash of grey, with ornate black molding starting at the large planked, light grey wood floor, rising to the ceiling. In the center was a round jet black, French provincial table. The vase it held displayed an arrangement of autumn's brilliant color palette of roses and dark cut greens. Beyond the table toward the back of the room were two doors and a massive staircase leading to the upper floors.

To the left of the foyer was a rounded doorway revealing a long living room with a fireplace. The floors, the walls, and the molding matched the entrance. Yet, glints of the morning sun filtered through the floor to ceiling windows in the room from the front of the house. A substantial, black chenille sectional, like the one at the beach house, took up much of the floor space in the room. The centerpiece, the talking point, though, was the wall over the sectional. It held a massive mural displaying a lone surfer riding the perfect wave on a perfect day…the curl of the water, the shards of sunlight hitting all the right spots.

Tommy.

I surmised from the lack of noise, the door was left unlocked.

Why should I be surprised? I was delusional to think I would find him here. That it would be so easy.

I wandered around the room of the old brownstone that Tommy called home, looking one last time at the walls, the ceiling, the floor…searching for an answer to whisper back at me.

One that never came…until his fingertips pinched my elbow.

My heart jumped, but when I spun around to face him, the beats stopped. It wasn't Tommy, but someone who resembled him.

"Not so fast…it's not every day a beautiful woman walks into my house unannounced and then silently proceeds to walk out without so much as an introduction or a hello, at the very least."

"Hello," was all I could muster, as disappointment flooded my insides, drowning my very existence. I wanted to go.

"And you are?" A friendly smile formed his expression, but his question to know me was dead serious.

"I'm Jade Stanton. I'm looking for Tommy."

"I see. I'm Michael Conte, Tommy's brother. So…Jade Stanton, are you here because my brother broke your heart?"

"No…I'm here because I broke his."

An almost pleased, yet humorous smile developed on Michael's face. It said everything, then something, then nothing at all. I didn't have time for games, I needed to find Tommy.

"Do you know where I can find him?" I pressed with a small amount of annoyance coming through.

"Tommy was here, but he left. He only stopped by to sign over the papers on this place. He had a hard time renting it and being I was staying here, and heard through the grapevine—our parents—he was selling it, I stepped in to purchased it myself."

"Why didn't you know it was up for sale? I mean you are his brother."

"Now, Miss Stanton, if you were so intimate with my brother then you already know why."

"I guess you're right. I'm sorry I took up any of your time. Should you see Tommy, can you have him call me, please?" I didn't wait for an answer as I turned and walked to the door.

Michael followed. "Ah…unfinished business, Miss Stanton?" He asked.

"Much more than that…please?"

"Please don't leave. Let's talk." Touching my elbow once more, his voice somber, Michael guided me back through the living room and then to the kitchen, where he poured each of us a cup of coffee.

"You obviously know about the discord between my brother and me, which leaves me at a disadvantage."

"A disadvantage?"

"Yes, how did you break my brother's heart?"

"Tommy moved to LBI and bought a beach house that my family owned. It had fallen into disrepair after my brother past away three years ago."

"I'm sorry." His sincerity was real, not for the sake of good manners.

"Thank you. Anyway, I wasn't looking for a relationship. Actually, the opposite was true, but then…"

"You cared for my brother."

"No, I fell in love with him, almost immediately."

"Then how did you break his heart?"

"I found out about…" Embarrassed to admit my full knowledge of his personal feud with Tommy, I stopped.

"So, you do know everything?"

"Yes, and the one thing I asked of Tommy, from the beginning, was to always tell me the truth. Although he said you and he weren't on speaking terms, I found out why, later."

"Later, as in after you two had gotten more involved?"

"Yes."

"I understand." He shook his head and sighed.

"To make a long story short, the last time we were together was a shit show and none of it was Tommy's fault."

"So you want to apologize to him?"

"Yes and no, I want…" I didn't know what to say, I didn't know how to explain this to Michael without having to go into great detail about Jimmy's letter and everything else that went on this summer.

"Michael, I'm sorry. I can't get into this. I just need to find him. Please…"

"I'm not my brother's keeper, and as you are fully aware we aren't as close as we were before. We are working on it, but I'm not sure where he was going from here. If I had my guess, I'd say he would be heading back down the shore to the beach house."

"What makes you say that?"

"Well, for one thing, he had his dog with him and for another, he didn't ask to crash here. My brother has a good head on his shoulders, for the most part, I'm sure he's not going to sleep with his dog in the car just to prove a point. He's stubborn yes, but pig-headed, no." He smiled.

Relief for the first time since watching Tommy walk away flooded my body. I thanked Michael for the coffee and hurried to leave, as a renewed sense of excitement flooded my body.

Walking to the door, I turned back to Michael.

"Thank you, I know you don't know me at all and my advice I'm sure will be somewhat strange, but please, if there is any way you and Tommy could work things out sooner rather than later, please, I hope you will do so."

"I know what you're trying to tell me, Jade."

"I'm trying to tell you— I can no longer fight with my brother or make up with him, even if I wanted to. You both have that ability. Do it now. Don't wait for tomorrow."

"Thank you, Jade Stanton, perhaps we were meant to meet."

"You're welcome."

"I hope my brother realizes what a very lucky guy he is."

I smiled, kissed Michael's cheek, and left...not waiting for tomorrow to fix this. I was determined to find Tommy now.

I headed home, sickened to not see Tommy's car parked in his usual space. I went up to fill Viv in. Disappointment showed on her face, but she tried to be practical and say that he needed time and he'd be back.

I went home...I sat, I paced back and forth, on the deck, off the deck. Numerous times leaning over the railing, thinking I heard him. Yet, I never did. My hurt grew, nothing helped...tea, soothing music, a warm bath…nothing. My thoughts immediately returned to Tommy.

I wanted him, I needed to be close to him. I wanted his strong body over mine. I did the only thing I could to get close to him without him being there, I went to the beach house. I did more than that. I placed myself in my favorite corner of his sectional…the place where Tommy washed my nightmares away. I wrapped the blanket around me, after I wrapped myself in one of his shirts…his scent lingering behind, giving me comfort. Comfort to drift off into my dreams.

chapter
twenty-seven

Tommy

CLOSURE ON THE brownstone came from none other than my brother. Mike and I weren't in a good place, but he called and asked if I was willing to sell the house to him. After several failed attempts to rent it through last winter, the house Rain and I shared, lay stagnant. Offers to buy were awful, bordering on the absurd. New York real estate wasn't booming on my street. Then Mike had called in mid-March to rent the place until he could find something he really wanted. It was a win-win.

Surprisingly, I received a phone call from him the Friday before Reece's party and didn't call him until I reached Rain's house after my failed evening with Jade. I thought about moving back, but it would have only represented another failure. Selling to Mike, instead of asking him to move or worse move in with him when things were already tense between us, was the best alternative.

I drove up early Sunday morning to discuss the buy. The conversation was less awkward than it could have been. Mike said he'd have the papers drafted during the week. Being a lawyer and being family meant no realtors or professionals had to be involved.

"So, what have you been up to?" Mike hinted at the fact it took me no time to get to him when I was supposedly halfway around the world surfing the globe.

"Nothing much really, surfing, traveling, just I like planned on doing."

"Right…don't give me that bullshit, Tommy. How is it I called on Friday, you don't get back to me until this morning, but easily arrived here three hours later?"

"I was in LBI with Rain."

"This is about a woman, isn't it?"

"If you had asked me that a week ago the answer would have been yes, but not anymore."

"Listen, I know you and me have been at each other's throats since that whole thing went down with…well you know, but if you need to get this thing you're carrying around off your chest, I'm willing to listen." A concerned grimace appeared on his face.

"Thanks, Mike, but I have to handle this one on my own."

We made small talk until there was nothing more to say and I left, confirming we would meet up next week.

The airlifted as I stepped outside with Lucky. I decided, as long as I was up north, I'd head out to see my parents before heading back to NJ. My mom and dad were thrilled to see me after months away. Although my mom appeared to be more taken with Lucky than me. I explained to them that I sold the brownstone. Their expressions turned to disappointment until they realized I sold the place to Mike. For them, the relief came in knowing the building would stay in the family, and I'm sure it also came with Mike and I being able to talk long enough to make an important decision together and to be in the same room together without fighting.

I explained the story of the beach house and, although they were hurt in my choice to keep everyone in the dark, they supported me and understood. I wanted to explain the situation with Jade, but my hurt was too new, so all I could do was explain that I met someone and had feelings for her, but we just weren't far enough into our relationship to say any more than that.

On the drive home, I felt surprisingly light. I realized by pushing everyone away made for more added stress. Now, my whereabouts were out in the open, I cleared my mind, but only in part of my life. The part with Jade was cloudy and excruciating to think about. The closer my car traveled toward the exit, the closer I got to the shore, the faster my heart began to beat. I wanted to see her. Not just in passing from our decks, but I wanted her. I wanted to soothe her, heal her worry, I wanted my body inside her body. I want to love her, make love to her. I wanted to be consumed by her, as my mind was consumed by her now.

Jade was something I never anticipated and now...

It turned out finding her was easy, letting go of her...was more than I could handle.

I pulled into my driveway, Jade's car was in hers. Her house was dark; she must be asleep. I didn't care, I couldn't wait to speak with her until morning, so I knocked and knocked and knocked. It appeared her lack of response had given me no choice; tomorrow it would have to be.

I was tense. Eager to speak with her and hopefully fix this mess between us. Unlocking the door to my home, struggling with the slider I had yet to repair, eased me. I was home and even with the non-completed projects and unfinished rooms, it finally felt like home. This place gave me the strength to keep trying. I wasn't about to give up on it or on Jade.

Lucky didn't wait for me by the door to lock it like she normally would. She immediately went to her favorite area of the couch to lie down. It was no accident, she settled there to be close to one of her favorite people. There in the corner, Jade was fast asleep, curled up under the blanket I kept over the couch for chilly evenings such as tonight and wearing what looked like one of my shirts.

Apprehensive to smile, fearing to hope, I moved closer to her. Softly, I dropped my keys on the coffee table, trying not to wake her. Lucky looked to her and to me, with a slow bounce of her tail touching Jade's invisible legs. She continued to sleep. I continued to observe her, wondering what I would say when she realized I was home. Slinking onto the sofa, Lucky stood up, eventually settling back down on my lap, allowing me to sit nearer to Jade.

Should I wake her? No, let her sleep. She'll be awake soon enough.

That's what scared me.

The more Lucky tried to make her body comfortable, the more her collar jingled with her identification tags, eventually waking my sleeping beauty. Her eyes opened, meeting mine in the darkness. Jade stilled in sleepy consciousness, her thoughts and vision waking slowly. Her senses finally catching up. Sitting up she addressed me.

"Tommy…you're home." Relief came in her whisper and over my body, releasing it from its state of imprisoned tension.

"Yes, baby, I'm home."

Then the unimaginable happened. Jade crawled out and over the blanket to me and Lucky, wrapping her arms around both of us; her lips caught mine unexpectedly. Her kiss stripped away the layers of hurt and doubt between us, replacing the worry and pain with tenderness, desire…love.

My hands, not knowing where to go, barely skimmed her face, touching then pulling back, as if this kiss, as if Jade couldn't possibly be real. Finally, coming to rest on her shoulders, my thumbs caressed her collarbone. Jade initiated and continued the assault on my mouth, her actions grounding her, me… us. Lucky jumped away, allowing Jade to straddle me, settling on top, our unbroken connection strengthening her. Her hands holding my face, her mouth kissing, then stopping, then starting again. Her thoughts played out in each press of her lips. Her actions spoke volumes without delivering a sound.

We stayed that way, lingering there until Jade, uncertain, backed up slowly to await my reaction.

"Jade, what is all this? I thought I lost you."

"I was stupid. I let fear push you away. I'm so sorry." Her cries built and then released. Her body collapsed in my arms.

"Shhh…no, baby, no, don't you dare apologize. I'm the one who's so sorry. I should have told you everything from the beginning. I was afraid of losing you, but I almost lost you because of my worry. I let my head get in the way, dreading what you would do, or how you would think of me. You trusted me, and I trusted you. I should have had more faith than that. No, I do have more, I should have let that faith carry us. I shouldn't have interfered with it, changed it, or tried to control it."

"It doesn't matter. This matters. We matter. Our today, our tomorrows, our lasts…not our pasts." She rocked forward, kissing me again.

"Our lasts? What you do mean our lasts?" I didn't understand. Jade was talking about today, tomorrow…but our lasts? The sound was so final, the end. Had I misunderstood her words, her body? Inside, I was freaking out, but outside, I was holding on to her for dear life.

Pulling back, again, Jade's face flushed, her lips plumped, swollen from our kiss, her eyes sparkled like a beacon drawing me in, telling me what she was about to explain would make everything right.

She left my lap to retrieve something beneath the blanket. It was the letter I'd given to Viv before I left the other night. Jade returned to me, the letter pressed to her heart; her eyes closed tight told me this was going to hurt.

"Tommy, my brother explained a great deal in this letter. I won't say it didn't hurt. It was as if he died again…this time it was more real than I could have imagined…more real than three years ago when we got the call."

"Baby, I'm so sorry."

"No, please don't be. If you hadn't bought the house, then perhaps I would have never gotten it."

"You know?"

A light smile brightened her already beaming face. "Yes, I know. I know all the key players in your little real estate deal." She joked.

"I'm sorry about that. I wanted to tell you, but Viv asked me to wait. In fact, that was one of the things that I had wanted to talk with you about after Reece's party. My plan was to leave the party early. I know we both agreed to go, but hell, if I was going to waste time somewhere I didn't want to be at his home and knew you didn't want to be either. I was going to take you out to Holgate, to night surf and then speak with you about Mike and me, and if you were still willing to listen, I was going to tell you about the house and give you something I had gotten made especially for you."

"Damn it! This is what we should have been doing all along."

"Yeah, but then again, if I hadn't left the party to come back here, I may have never found the letter."

Jade nodded.

"You said, it revealed more. Was it the note your family was hoping to find, so they could understand more about Jimmy's death?"

"Suicide."

"Huh?"

"I always hated to say suicide, and although we all knew what it was, everyone around me allowed me to sugar coat everything that Jimmy's death touched. This letter, his words helped me to figure out what I already knew, but kept hidden."

"Baby, death under any circumstances is hard, but your brother's..." I couldn't find the words.

"His suicide was unimaginable, right?"

I nodded with puzzled uncertainty.

"It was, but this letter confirmed what he was dealing with had been going on for years and years."

"Jade, I thought he died after he sustained an injury surfing at The Mavericks."

"Oh, he did, that's true, but the reason behind his death was more. According to his letter to me, The Mavericks and the injury from that accident was only a small part of why he killed himself. The accident only confirmed his dark intentions."

"I'm not following you."

"He planned to die before The Mavericks. Here…read it for yourself." Jade handed me the letter. Discomfort coursed through me, making me stand and move around the room until the last word was read.

"You see now?"

"I'm so sorry, Jade."

"Don't be." She stood and came to me. "Jimmy wasn't happy at times. I saw it. We all did. He was miserable working with my dad. Yet, he never tried to change it. Day in and day out, we all have shit we don't like to do, Jimmy was no different. Yet, I thought he was no different, meaning I never saw any signs Jimmy's upset was…monumental. He never acted out or expressed his emotions that way, other than the way we all did when we got pissed or disappointed. Apparently, he hid it well. I spent the last three years asking why. It took you and Jimmy to answer me. Thank you."

"Me?"

"You pressed me without pushing. You made me feel without forcing. You made me want without knowing why. You made me question my decision to be alone. You woke me from a sleep—a trance I created for myself. A place that was swallowing me up, making me disappear. You brought me back, you pulled me out. On the beach the night of Reece's party, the last thing I remembered was you walking away. It was our last moment. Jimmy said always remember your 'lasts,' but you leaving was not the kind of thing I wanted to cherish. What I wanted was to feel your last kiss, hold onto our last embrace, hear your last words, see your last smile…knowing all of it belonged to me. Those were the feelings I wanted to cherish, to own, to crave, to honor, and to have again and again. I blew it that night, and I'm sorry for that."

I placed the letter down and wrapped Jade in my arms. After what felt like forever, I lifted her up and carried her to my room…to my bed. Laying her down, I kissed her lips briefly, pulling back to drink in her beauty. Her image was one I thought I'd lost forever only forty-eight hours ago. Sure, I promised myself I would fight for her, but fighting a memory, a loss that reached the deepest part of her soul seemed an impossibility of beating.

Her, here tonight was unforeseen. Jimmy's mention of always remembering our 'lasts' not only touched Jade, but it gutted me. I remembered the last time I saw Jade—at Reece's home. Protecting herself with an invisible shield, her expression stoic. I did that to her, and I knew I never wanted to be the cause for her to look or feel like that again.

"Jade, I…" I took a chance, but she jumped first. I always thought of myself as spontaneous, but the move to the beach house taught me I was a guarded man. Much in the same way Jade guarded herself, I learned through her I was no different—living a structured life, until destiny forced me out of my comfort zone to build something, in my case rebuild something—me.

"I love you, Tommy."

Jade's soul showed in her smile, as her confident arms wrapped around my shoulders. She needed to be first. Who was I to argue? Leaning in, I kissed my girl. The world asleep around us, but I was alive…full of life. Jade's love, her words, made me realize I was drowning, not knowing I needed to be rescued. Sleeping, but I couldn't wake. Suffocating, but continued to breathe through shallow breaths. Jade saved me, without me realizing I needed to be rescued. Jade freed me without me acknowledging I was trapped.

"I love you, too, baby."

I held her. Held onto her. I was the one who needed her. I needed her strength, her love. I craved it, I desired it, and now I'd have it and I'd never let it go…let her go.

Topping her, our mouths met, dancing softly at first, then savoring our connection, our tongues stealing, touching, confirming what was in our hearts. The momentum built, entwining our bodies, Jade's danced beneath me, mine over hers. Our emotions confined behind the veil, peeking through then releasing everything we held back since we first met.

Breaking from our kiss…

"I want inside you. I need to feel you again to know this is real, to know this is forever."

Jade's hands tugged the hem of my shirt, pulling it up over my head. Her hands returned to my waist, releasing me. My mouth returning to her mouth, expelling a feral groan as she gripped my hard shaft.

I thought I would lose my mind, her hand tightening further, her jerks more deliberate. I could finish this way but denied myself that pleasure. I had to be with her, in her, part of her. Pulling back, my hand covered hers, she slowed.

"I don't want it this way, not this time. You told me you love me. Now, I need to show you, Jade."

She let go of my cock. Abandoning it to frantically slip out of her clothes. I divested from what I remained wearing, leaving a heap of mangled fabrics on the floor. With our bodies unrestricted, Jade moved to straddle my lap, taking my cock once more and guiding me into her sweet, soaked pussy.

A softy, achy moan set Jade free. Her body filled, her sex dancing uninhibited over my erection. My thrusts meet her bounce. Her head slowly dropped back, her long dark tresses fell away, revealing a pronounced pulse at the side of her neck. My mouth found the soft flesh of her breast, her nipples hardened.

Her arousal grew with mine, mine strengthening with hers. We were fluid, each action deliberate, each response to the other perfect, knowing…in sync with each other. The declaration of our love started this, our carnal wants completed it.

Her breathing escalated. Mine, tighter and restrained…wanting the sex driven by our love, our untamed need to go further, last longer.

Discreetly, I slowed, but Jade noticed and pressed harder. Her fingers caressed her clit, soothing it, calming her arousal only enough to speak.

"Don't stop. Be with me. Take me. Make me come."

Her pleas weakened me; I tried to hold back, but my body was losing with each sound from her voice, inching her closer to her release. I surrendered, taking Jade onto her back, spreading her wide. My hand held her hip in place, my other tended to her core, my thumb replaced her fingers on her swollen nub. She watched my cock drive into her, one arm over her head pressed the wall, while her fingers from her free hand were at her mouth, each being teasingly bitten.

My girl knew exactly what she was doing. Jade unabashedly met my thrusts, her eyes speaking to mine, not a word said outwardly…her focus called me, held me to task, making my body move her, move us to our release.

"Baby…"

"Tommy…"

Our breathing tattered, raw, building toward our climax. Our bodies exploded unashamed, driven by what we felt in our hearts. We made it through, we came out on the other side whole, together, there in the bed we shared, and in the love we had for each other.

Fearlessly, purposefully unhurried, we floated back and settled in. There would be no more letting go, only moving forward, joined as one…complete.

Jade's body, cocooned in white linen, rested along my side. Studying her, I smiled. She was finally mine. No hidden secrets, no trepidation, dread, or alarm. It was all replaced with compassion, truth, courage…love.

Our night was replaced with daylight, seagull calls, water lapping and receding as the tide from the Atlantic mimicked the mood in our bed…easy, peaceful, contented.

Stretching and taking in a deep breath, I wrapped myself around Jade further. She buried her face in my chest.

"Good morning, baby."

"Good morning," she said, not moving.

"Hey, we're okay, right?" A simmer of doubt rose inside me.

"We're fine. I just don't want to get up and start the day." Wrapping her arms around my waist to keep the invisible pull of life from removing her from my bed, she pressed herself tightly against me.

I chuckled. "We have all day. Isn't Monday your day off?"

"Yes, but unfortunately it's moving day."

I had forgotten, with everything going on, Summertime Sweets needed to move all the contents from the old building into the new one today. We would get it done, for Jade to be ready for the grand opening on Friday.

"Ah, yes, but you're not alone. You have me and Viv…"

"No Viv."

"No Viv? Why?"

She sat up and ran her fingers through her tangled mane. "Viv collapsed on Saturday night."

"Is she hurt? Damn it! I shouldn't have left her with that note."

"Tommy…stop! Viv fainted due to dehydration and a minor heart condition she hid from everyone. I found out when Reece got a call from Blaze during the time I was confronting him about the little stunt he pulled at his party."

"How is Viv, now?"

"Better, but not well enough to be lugging boxes between the two shoppes. Besides, I have my staff to help me."

"And me," I added.

"Yes, especially you" She grinned and leaned forward to kiss me before scooting off to start her busy day.

Pulling her back, I had a surprise I wanted to give her before we left. "Wait! I have something I meant to give you Saturday night."

I left our bed to retrieve my gift.

"Here, baby. Open it," I said, climbing back in bed, giving her a reassuring smile, as I handed her the small box.

She opened her surprise to reveal the white fisherman's rope bracelet done in thinner, multiple strands that connected with a large lobster claw clasp on the ends. Attached to that clasp was a small diamond Starfish.

"It's so special. Thank you, Tommy. I love it."

Taking the bracelet from her hand, I attached it to her wrist. "The Starfish…"

"I know." Closing her eyes, Jade cherished it already, she understood. The symbol stood for healing and renewal, a Starfish can lose its legs, have a part of them violently ripped away, only to grow back and become stronger—to heal.

Jade settled into my chest, and I lay back against the pillows. Holding her in my arms, we pushed back the events of the day for a bit longer. A short reprieve, shorter than expected as her phone began to ring and ping.

"I'll get it." Leaving Jade in bed, I went to retrieve her phone in the other room. The screen was lit up like a Christmas tree.

This wasn't going to be good.

Jade sat erect the minute she saw my face. "What is it?"

"I'm not sure, but you are one popular lady this morning."

Jade took the phone and scrolled through quickly. Curiosity turned to concern as Jade phoned one of her staff members.

"What happened? Holy Shit! I see. Was anyone hurt? Did you call the police?"

Jade was incredibly calm, but her last question got my attention. She disconnected—she didn't stand or run or scream. She put the phone on the sheets, releasing it, clutching the fabric in her fists, trying to find strength, holding onto what little composure she was losing.

"What happened, Jade?"

"I don't know, but everything is gone."

"What?"

"The boxes, the equipment that we were taking over to the new place ourselves, are missing. The only things left were in my office. It was untouched." Shaking her head, staring at the sheets, she went quiet.

"Baby, could the movers have gotten their wires crossed and come earlier than expected?"

"No, these were items we agreed to move on our own. They weren't overly large, and being I needed everything in place to create the food for Friday, we decided to unpack as we went along, so all we had to do Thursday was bake. Now it's all ruined." She wasn't moving, she didn't want to go. She put her head in her hands to hide her tears from me, but her trembling frame was a sign of Jade breaking once more.

The days that passed had been emotional ones for her…Reece's party, our fight, Jimmy's letter, Viv's collapse, and now this. I had to do something.

"Jade, let's go. We need to see what happened. A police report needs to be filed. Then we can take it from there."

She wiped her face, nodded, and shot out of bed. "From where should I take this, Tommy? Everything but my office is gone. I don't have the proper equipment to make anything. None of the things taken can be replaced quickly enough to be up and running on Friday!"

"There has to be a mistake. If someone was going to steal your stuff, wouldn't they have taken the registers, the money? Are you sure about the movers? Who steals food equipment?" I tried to lighten things up.

Her laugh quelled my worry.

"I know what we agreed on, but then again I was busy losing my boyfriend, so maybe I misunderstood what they told me."

I grinned. "Well, your boyfriend is here now, and you didn't lose him, so let's go fix this, baby." I held out my hand for her.

She nodded, taking it.

We quickly washed up and dressed. I drove Jade to the first location as she made calls to her staff and the moving company and to Viv to let her know that we were together and everything was okay. We arrived at the shoppe to a small crowd out in front with balloons in hand.

Jade looked to me, and I to her, before getting out and addressing the people in front of her old place. Walking to them, the crowd separated exposing Blaze and Reece holding the balloons.

"Surprise, sweetie!" Blaze hugged Jade before she could speak.

Reece came forward and handed Jade the balloons and a bouquet.

"These are for you."

"What's this about?" Jade asked without a 'thank you.'

"Jade, I can live with many things. I apologize to no one, but you're different. I owed you, so I called a friend of mine at the police department and we unlocked this place and had your staff and some of the people I hired work through the night to get the new place ready."

Jade looked to me, pools filled her eyes. I gave her a quick wink to settle her.

"Reece, a simple, I'm sorry, would have sufficed."

"My darling, you know I don't do simple. I did, however, leave your office untouched, as I would not want anyone rummaging through my papers."

Jade and Reece embraced. Not letting go of her, he walked to me and held out his hand.

"Mr. Conte, I apologize. I'm rarely wrong, but I was wrong in this instance."

"Apology accepted."

"Now, you have everything you need in place to make Summertime Sweets new location a complete success. Don't disappoint me."

He loved her. No matter his misgivings about Jade and me, Reece loved her. He had a funny way of showing it, but an incredible way of making it up to her.

She kissed him and Blaze before heading inside the old shoppe to collect the boxes in the office. She instructed her staff to head over to the new place while she and I stayed to clean up.

Reece's surprise could have been a disaster, but it turned into the perfect start for Jade and her week ahead.

Speaking of surprises, I had one more up my sleeve for her.

One that would have to wait until Thursday.

chapter
twenty-eight

Jade

I **LEFT EARLY** each morning to make sure the shoppe was ready for Friday and the Labor Day holiday weekend ahead.

It was Thursday, the day before the grand opening. With Tommy still sleeping in my bed, Lucky right next to him, silently, I walked to the door to leave without disturbing him. Placing my hand on the doorjamb, I spied my Starfish dangling from my wrist. Looking back, Lucky's head popped up, her tail lightly tapped the blanket. My eyes went from her to the man who rescued her…the man who rescued me.

Tommy's hair flopped over his eyes, the sheets covered the parts of him that could keep me in bed all day long. His inked arms flexed over his head as he slept through my departure. I loved him more than I could have imagined. Hesitant to leave, I whispered, "I love you," before going to work at the new place.

Today was frantic. Although we had no customers, we did have the occasional pleasant interruption of one of the locals inquiring about the opening, or one of our regulars coming by to make sure we opened on schedule, as promised. None of it was annoying, all of them showed how much they cared about our work and how they were looking forward to tomorrow.

My staff finished up. We were ready. I stayed behind to put some finishing touches on my office space, make a few calls, and of course, pay a few bills. When done, I locked the office door and walked up the hallway through the opening to the pastry area. The entrance from the back allowed me to enter from behind the cases of the displayed treats. Surveying each shelf, a wide smile formed on my face that almost hurt. I was proud, happy, excited, scared…ready.

Yeah, we're ready.

Standing up to stretch, I decided it was time to shut the shoppe down for the day and head home for dinner with Tommy. Before leaving, I noticed a cellophane package tied in teal ribbon lying on the cookie scale in the center of the case in front of me. It was odd, but it may have been left there by one of my staff members. Whatever it was, I picked it up to put back in the case, but upon closer examination, I realized it was filled with Starfish of all different sizes.

What the hell?

Then I saw the tag…Tommy.

"Hey, baby, close up and call me. Change of plans for tonight. I'm taking you on a treasure hunt."

A curious laugh escaped me. I picked up the phone to call him. It went directly to voicemail, but the message was all mine.

"Jade, right on time. Here's your first clue, go out to your car. You'll find your driver for the evening waiting there to take you on a small adventure. Remember, this is all in fun, and I love you."

Then the beep came.

"I love you, Tommy."

Coming around the front of the building revealed my driver dressed in a black tuxedo jacket with three quarter length sleeves and black short shorts, killer, knee-high patent leather boots, and a chauffeur's hat.

Blaze.

"Hey, sweetie, hop in and let's do this." Her red tresses straightened, with stripes of blonde and gold shimmering in the late day sun.

"Hey, do you know where we're going?" I was dying to find out what was going on.

"No, I haven't a clue, but Tommy did give me this card and I was told expressly not to open it until I picked you up."

Taking the small aged paper envelope from Blaze's hand, I noticed the feel of sand washed across its surface. *Jade…* written on the front, a wax seal in the shape of a scallop shell secured the flap. Opening it released more sand along with the contents…another small note.

"Your driver should take you to the beach house. The ride you will be using for the evening will be waiting there for both of you, with another clue."

"Okay, let's head over there."

The ride to the beach house was my natural route to and from work, but this time heading home offered some trepidation, as I wondered what Tommy was up to. The closer to the house Blaze and I got, the more we realized the car we would be using was my brother's Mustang. It had been tucked away in one of the garage spaces below the living quarters of the beach house. Tommy must have had it repaired, with Viv's help, I'm sure. The body and interior were in great shape, white with deep blue navy seats and huge white wall tires. The engine needed some TLC, as it hadn't been driven regularly in years.

Blaze parked my 181, and we situated ourselves in our new ride. The top was down, so I climbed into the back seat to find my next clue. Blaze discovered it first under her seat.

"Got it!" Raising her arm in the air with another small pouch in hand.

In the pouch was another note and a handful of scallop shells along with more sand.

"Drive Jade down the Boulevard. Her next clue will be visible from the car. If you get to the Causeway turn off and turn around. It means you missed it and you'll have to go back, retrace and try again."

We both stared at each other.

"What the hell is he talking about?"

I shook my head slowly. "Haven't got a clue…well, you know what I mean."

Like teenagers, we laughed and headed out to the main thoroughfare on LBI.

The traffic was heavy due to the holiday weekend approaching. This allowed us to keep a slower pace as not to miss Tommy's clue for the next leg of our tour…and there it was. We couldn't have missed it. There on 11th street was a banner overhead. It was teal in color and stretched the width of the street. It displayed the Mustang and two whimsical cartoon-like women in the car. One with red hair and one with brown. Trailing behind the car in the banner was an explosion of seashells and our directions.

"Ladies, follow your road 9.5 miles to the light, to the end of your journey together."

Again, Blaze and I looked at one another, smiling because we knew exactly where this road led. It was to the other end of the island. Where cars could no longer travel. To Old Barney, to the lighthouse on LBI's northern end. Its beacon stood for so many things, to so many people. For me, it stood for summers gone by, cherished times with Jimmy, my fear of heights, my race to the top…my childhood.

Blaze parked the car in the lot. As if in a trance, we got out and realized the parking lot was empty. How could this be? This was a popular tourist attraction. The lighthouse didn't close to visitors this early in the evening. Then I spotted it…my next clue. It was hanging on the sign at the edge of the lot where visitors would enter for the nature trails.

"There it is!" I pointed to the sign near the East End.

"If you're reading this note, then Blaze's part of the journey ends here and yours begins. Leave Blaze behind and walk the rock-lined path up to Old Barney."

Doubling back past the Mustang and past Blaze I reached the entrance to the path Tommy was referring to. I stopped at the footpath that connected to the parking lot and turned back to Blaze.

"You can't be undecided on what to do, sweetie. Go and see what this fun is all about."

I nodded and had the feeling she knew more than she was letting on. Walking the path on the right of side of the lighthouse grounds parallel to the rock jetty, nestled between me and the Atlantic Ocean, seemed odd with no other visitors taking in the amazing views. My pace was unhurried so I could find any additional clues Tommy had for me along the way.

I found one.

"Jade, continue along the path to Old Barney, no more clues are necessary except to head inside the light and climb those famous steps."

Famous…he wasn't kidding. The lighthouse beacon was first lit in 1859 and there it still stood today, 172 feet above the sea. To reach the top, I was going to have to climb those famous steps, as Tommy put it…all 217 of them.

I reached the door… emotions in my head were swirling. I took the first steps slowly, apprehensive, hesitant. Along the way, my confidence and the fun began to build. Every so many steps, I lost count, there was another note card with shells glued to it and tied to the railing. Each message was different, funny, motivating, or a whimsical drawing like two hearts intertwined, or lips perched to kiss. Winding the spiraling yellow staircase, I reached the top and went inside. It was just as I always remembered, white paneled walls, original wood flooring in a circular room sitting beneath the light, that harbored framed photographs of years gone by, telling the story of this magnificent part of Long Beach Island's history.

There was a smaller, narrow white staircase. Each of its steps exposed the old wood beneath the tattered edges, worn from overuse. The stairs curled along the one side of the top room. They rose to the light, but tonight Tommy came down those few steps from the light to greet me.

"Surprise, baby…" He said smiling, confident, something hidden in his hands.

Toe to toe with me, his breathed in my presence, as my eyes drank in his features. Strangely the questions as to why he brought me here, washed out to sea. All I could focus on was him—his strength, his conviction. The way he appeared to be looking at me as if it was for the first time. I was whole, my heart full, my worries of the past few weeks evaporated into the salty air.

Tommy's manner, quiet, he pressed his lips to mine. He was subdued. Pulling back slightly, his jaw tensely pulsed, his intent unclear, but imminent.

Taking both my hands to his mouth, then placing them over his heart, he whispered.

"Jade, I love you. I didn't know if this, us…would ever be possible. From the moment I didn't know you, but met you on the dance floor, something in my world shifted. I knew I made the right decision to move here. For the first time in a long time, life felt the way I hope it would."

"I feel exactly the same way. Even when I fought this, us, I loved you. I can't imagine going back to my old life. I can't imagine life without you."

"Good, I was hoping you'd say something like that."

"You were?"

"Yeah." Then he stopped and kneeled, lifting a small box out of his back pocket.

"Jade, I want to marry you. I want you to be mine, always. Will you?"

My smile popped, my tears fell, my breathing hitched, as I kneeled down to give him my answer.

"Yes, Tommy, I will."

He wrapped his arms around me to kiss me and stopped.

Squinting, I asked, "What's wrong?"

"You realize you broke your own promise."

Cocking my head to the side, with a perplexed smirk on my face. "What's that?"

"If I remember correctly, you distinctly said you wouldn't get married in six months."

Teasing him, "Oh, that's right, I did say that. In that case, I think I'll change my answer."

"Not a chance, baby, you said yes and yes it stays." Tommy owned my mouth once again and then took my hand and slid the most beautiful engagement ring onto my finger.

It was made of white gold. The band…there were two. They delicately resembled fisherman's rope. The braiding started along the sides and twisted up and under the base of the center stone. The jewel of the ring was a large princess cut gemstone of Aquamarine, surrounded by a square halo of smaller diamonds.

The ring was exquisite in its own right, made even more so when Tommy turned my hand over and kissed my palm, and said…

"Read it."

I did as he asked, but silently protested, as he just placed it on my hand. Yet, when I read what he had inscribed, removing it, made our day—our engagement even more poignant.

The inscription read:

Together, we will chase the sun & follow the moon…

chapter
twenty-nine

Tommy

I HELD JADE in my arms, our bodies relaxed, united. We watched the sunset on the bay from the doorway lookout on top of Old Barney. The wild seagrass appeared carved into the wetlands near the lighthouse. The water rippled from a light breeze coming from the North. The green blades of the grass rustled back and forth as a pair of Red-throated Loons weaved their way through the foliage, while a small flock of Seagulls swooped down to join in the Loons' evening meal. The clouds slowly evaporated, as the sky turned a bluish plum. The orange sphere cut in half by the horizon, its evening presence glowed white with pale yellow rays mixing into a pink and burnish red mass spreading out on three sides, its reflection glimmering on the water.

We didn't move. Held captive by our view and the nature that surrounded us, holding me and I suspected, Jade, in peaceful awe. We wanted to stay a bit longer, to not have this end just yet. To enjoy it, every minute of it—the sounds, the scents, and colors that engulfed us. To hold on to the pledge we made for a little while longer…told hold on to our 'last' as Jimmy reminded Jade in the letter— to take nothing for granted.

Eventually, Jade's hands rubbed over my arms, hinting to me she was cold and wanted to go—to get warm and confirm our connection more intimately.

"I love you, baby."

"I love you, too. Now let's go home so you can show me how much." She innocently played, but it was provocative in meaning.

We descended the long-doubled staircase; leaving the building, we walked back on the picnic area trail. I had parked my car behind the luncheonette, beyond the official lighthouse grounds so Jade and Blaze wouldn't see it when they drove up.

Jade and I returned to her place and ordered in, as we had originally planned. She had a big day tomorrow and I intended to be there with her all the way, whatever she needed from me, I would do, but tonight for us... no friends or family, no interruptions.

A light breeze rolled across my skin. The coolness had not been there earlier in the evening. It woke me to find Jade's spot vacant. She must have woken in the middle of the night and left our bed to sit on the small baloney outside her room.

"Baby, is everything okay? You're not having second thoughts, are you?" I stood in the doorway, half of my body in her room, half out in the night air. I braced myself for the worst.

"No, Tommy, I'm not having second thoughts, just the opposite." Sitting on the edge of the lounge chair, Jade scooted her feet in closer, to make room for me.

"Then why are you out here alone in the middle of the night?"

"Well, this is the last official weekend of summer. Everyone will be heading home, life will get back to the mundane for them. Hectic schedules, no time to come back down here, etc...etc."

"And...?"

"And...I want us to get married before they go home. I want to marry you in the summer, my favorite season, and I don't want to wait until next year. That's all I've done is wait my whole damn life. Do you understand?" She approached the subject of our wedding with vigor, but left some doubt, depending on what I wanted.

"Yeah. I understand, and the truth is I really want Rain there when we tie the knot, but they're going to be leaving for Italy in two weeks. I'm not sure how we can pull any of this off." Now I was the one with doubts.

"You leave that to me." She kissed my mouth chastely and pulled me back to bed.

Even with a lack of sleep, Jade and I were up bright and early to get to her shoppe.

Friday's opening of Summertime Sweets was an easy success. She had her locals, her regulars, and plenty of visitors to LBI to keep her busy. Sunday was another full day and Monday as well. Yet, at one point, while Viv and I were in the back, counting stock during a lull in the day, Jade slipped out to run some errands.

It was nearly three o'clock and Jade hadn't returned. Her staff asked if would be okay if they finished up and could leave. Viv told them to head out since all of the customers were gone and the day was winding down. Jade was still nowhere to be found. Four o'clock came, Viv and I decided to lock up.

"If she's not home when we get there, I'm calling the cops," I announced.

"Calm down. She's probably caught up in a delay of some sort, that's all."

"She didn't call, and she didn't come back to lock up. That's not like her."

"I know, but she knew it would be okay because we're here."

"I hope you're right."

"I'm sure everything will be fine."

I had less faith than Jade's aunt. This *was* so unlike her, but maybe she was running scared? She was up late the night we had gotten engaged. In fact, she hadn't slept well the entire weekend. I found her awake on Saturday and Sunday night doing paperwork at the kitchen table. She said she was trying to play catch up, but I wasn't buying it, especially now that she had gone off to parts unknown, plus she only mentioned the wedding once and then we never discussed it again. This had me thinking Jade wasn't ready for marriage after all.

I pulled down our street feeling confused, lost, and worried, but once I reached the beach house, the confusion, the loss, and the worry were replaced with anxious curiosity. Cars crowded both of our driveways. Large potted palms with white bows trimmed with raffia and strung with Starfish lights decorated each trunk. Surfing music emanated through the alleyway, reminding me of the movie Endless Summer. Exiting the car I heard voices overhead.

Looking up, I saw Blaze and Reece on Jade's deck. Blaze spotted me first and ran the stairs to stop me from coming up.

"Don't go up there."

"Why? Isn't Jade up there?"

"Yes, but you can't see her right now."

My anger bubbled to the surface. Fuck this! I needed to see her. I tried, but Blaze wasn't budging. Our staring contest turned into a shouting match, at least until Jade appeared. Then my world stopped…I mean it started again.

There, on the top step was Jade, barefoot, dressed in white jeans, a white t-shirt, holding white roses with salmon tipped petals from the rose bush I was about to cut down the day we officially met, and a mini rose halo adorning her head.

Her cheeks flushed…her tears, her happiness, and her love, all on display. Blaze moved to one side for me to get to my girl. Meeting in the middle of the staircase, our smiles reflected each other.

"You said you wanted this, too. So, I pulled it off…a summer wedding we hoped for and a summer wedding we're going to get."

"But…" She answered my question before I could ask.

"I had some help from our friends." Jade looked back to Reece, who was smiling and raising his glass of white wine in a toast.

Jade took my hand and guided me down the stairs, through the alley, and toward the beach.

"Jade, wait, I don't have anything to wear." Flattening my hands over my graphic t-shirt, feeling awkward.

"Hmm…hold these." She handed me the flowers and ran back up to the house. When she returned she was holding one of my white dress shirts.

"Take it off." Removing my t-shirt at Jade's command, she fastened each button methodically, while keeping her eyes on mine.

I took her hand and walked toward the ceremony when Jade stopped.

"Wait!" Jade tugged back.

"What?"

"You're completely overdressed." She teased.

"Huh?

"Lose the shoes, Conte."

"Oh." I laughed and kicked them off, before pulling her forward to make us official.

Over the dune and down the sand pathway to the opening for the beach, I stopped, my eyes had to be deceiving me. There in the distance were several rectangular tables dressed in white linen. They were decorated with tea light candles, shells, more roses, complete with flatware and wine glasses. A small path made of palm leaves was placed on the beach leading to our makeshift altar.

"I can't believe you did all of this for us."

Jade nodded, completely satisfied with the end result.

"Ready, baby?"

We were hand in hand to the altar, where the crowd was gathered to witness our wedding. As we got closer, I realized it was more than a crowd. It was our family and friends. Smiles and warm wishes came from all sides. On the left were my parents, Rain, and Dominick, their twins, Daniel and Daniel's parents Anna and Joseph. On the right, were Kim, Reece, Viv, and a couple who I assumed were Jade's parents, plus Jade's staff from the shoppe. They knew all along where Jade had gone.

Walking up to the altar, Jade handed Blaze her bouquet and then turned back to me.

"Jade, I don't have the rings we talked about. I hadn't ordered them yet."

"Don't worry, I took care of that." She tipped her chin, and I followed her direction to see my brother Mike walking to us on the sand. Jade did this, she got him to be here, to be part of my life again.

"Baby, thank you."

She nodded. She knew what this meant for me. She knew better than most.

"Did you think I'd let you get married without me, bro?" Michael's hand clamped down on my shoulder, as I turned to hug him.

The music softened along with the sounds from our wedding guests. Jade and I said our vows. We pledged our love and lives to each other. We promised to care and to protect one another no matter what. We spoke of the importance of family and friends, and how happy we were and honored we could share this very important part of our life with them.

Then, when we were done, Mike handed me the box with our rings.

"I just don't know how you got these rings are such short notice?"

"I didn't."

"What?"

"Open the box, Tommy." She smiled.

Inside the box were two circles made of sailor's rope, one slighter larger than the other.

"You see, I had to get creative."

I placed the small braided rope on Jade's ring finger next to the engagement ring I gave her Thursday night. She then placed mine on my ring finger where the permanent ring would go once it arrived. I kissed my bride and she kissed me back before we walked to our awaiting crowd of family and friends.

Jade's parents came forward with Viv, her mother hugging and kissing her. Her dad more stoic, yet pride emanating from his expression as he looked at his beautiful daughter's happiness on display.

Viv was next to hug Jade and me.

"Just think, this was all my doing." She proudly announced.

"Really? You are taking credit for me marrying Tommy?"

"Of course. If I hadn't sold him the house, we wouldn't be standing here right now like we are today."

We all smiled and laughed, but Viv's declaration wasn't far from the truth.

Blaze, Reece, Kim, Daniel and Daniel's parents took their turns to wish us well.

Mike, Rain, and Dominick came forward last, to congratulate us.

"Conte, Jade, I'm happy for you both. I truly hope what Rain and I found, you will have forever as well." Kane shook my hand and hugged my bride before joining Daniel and the others for drinks near the dinner table.

The only people left to wish us well were the two people I needed to hear it from the most.

"Tommy, I love you and I'm so happy for both of you." Rain's eyes pooled with tears.

Hugging her, she whispered a small secret for only my ears to hear. "We're both free now."

"I know, baby. I know."

Rain stood next to Jade, both looking on while Mike and I spoke.

"Mike, thank you."

"Don't thank me. Thank your beautiful wife. We had quite a talk the morning she came looking for you last week."

I turned, stunned by my brother's statement. Jade came looking for me?

She nodded slowly, knowing what I was thinking.

She came to find me. She didn't want to walk away, she didn't want us to end that night.

Our marriage and the people sharing it with us, was proof of that.

Once the evening began to wind down, and everyone left, Jade and I, along with Lucky went back to Jade's house. Our living arrangements, and the beach house, we could make decisions on later.

Lying in bed with Lucky at our feet, we toasted, kissed, and cuddled.

"Happy?" I asked.

"That's a silly question."

"Why?"

"It's evident. Did I or did I not say I'd make this day happen?"

"Yeah, Jade, you did, and it couldn't have been any more special."

"True…except for one thing."

"Jimmy."

"Yeah, but I'm pretty sure he was there in spirit."

"Here's to Jimmy watching over us," I lifted my glass and kissed Jade's temple.

"Here's to Jimmy, and here's to all the 'lasts' we will never forget," she added.

"I love you, baby."

"I love you, Tommy."

epilogue

Tommy

WITHIN TWO WEEKS our rings finally arrived, replacing the worn-down rope stand-ins we exchanged on our wedding day. Jade and I unanimously agreed to wait to go on our honeymoon until the holidays. With Summertime Sweets doing tremendously well this fall season, and our decision to keep the beach house, expanding on its size by building an extension which would connect to Jade's home, made it far too difficult to go on the honeymoon we wanted right then.

As for our friends and family, Jade and I were surprised by some of the plans and changes they had been making in their personal lives since they left Long Beach Island.

Rain, Dominick, and their twins headed back to Capri for the winter. Mainly for Dominick to continue his work at the law firm in Italy, but also for Rain to be closer to her twin, Raven, who was opening up a new office for the firm in France.

Blaze and Reece went back to Manhattan, and as Jade predicted, they broke off their relationship just weeks after Blaze moved into Reece's beachfront property in The Hamptons.

Look out world, Blaze and Reece are available…again.

Daniel's surprise blew us completely and excitedly out of the water. He and Kim seemed to be building quite a strong friendship…one he hoped would become more, and one which seemed to be going in that direction. He decided to follow suit and move here to LBI and not just to any available space, but to an old chapel that fell in disrepair, but one with a fully renovated cottage he could stay in until the chapel was complete. Daniel's plans would not only include living in the space, but he intended on turning the grounds into an art and community center, similar to the one he lived and worked at near Philadelphia. He felt the move would be a positive one for him, and Jade and I were glad he would be nearby.

My brother Mike and I were spending more time together. Thanks to my beautiful wife, he was going to make a major change in his life, as well. He would keep the brownstone but took a sabbatical from the law firm Rain's family owned to help me with the expansion of the beach house.

Mike had always been a true craftsman at heart when he was younger. He made many of the furniture pieces displayed in his home. He said he needed a break from corporate law and, being he had the financial means to do something he loved, he would split his time between working down the shore with me and working on a new business making custom furniture and surfboards with materials found around the world. Law—he could always go back to, but for Mike, this was a once in a lifetime chance. I understood completely. It was not unlike the chance I took moving here in the spring.

It was getting dark. I wondered where Jade was. Walking out on the deck, I spied her running with Lucky in the cool surf opposite our home. Her body bundled up in sweats and an oversized hoodie. Her long dark hair escaping its confines of the heavy cotton material as she chased our dog through the brisk salty air and low tide.

A low chuckle hit my throat. Watching them—my life before me, made me realize how far my life had come in such a short time. My life and my heart couldn't be fuller.

A year ago, loneliness crushed my very existence. I had friends and family, sure, but a crowded room for me no longer held comfort; it held emptiness...a disconnect that drove me to find something better, something for me...someone for me.

Yet, if anyone had told me I would have met Jade and married her over this past summer— me the man with the plan, I would have told them they were crazy. Yet, I did meet her, and I did marry her, and I did get everything I wanted, everything I was searching for...now no longer struggling to find that which was missing. I found my life. I found my girl—the one I dreamed of but could've lost forever.

I found a home. A beach house with a tragic story— a life which scarred my beautiful wife's past, scars which still linger today, and reappeared now and then. Scars I intended to erase so Jade could heal for her future...for our future.

None of this happened in a day, it didn't happen in a week.

But, it did happen...

Within six months.

acknowledgements

First and foremost, I want to thank my readers. Several events in my life pushed the completion of this book back far longer than I would have liked. I appreciate the support you have given me from the beginning, and the love you have for this character from the original series, Miss Taken Identity. I hope you love Tommy and Jade's story, even more.

To Mac Bros Book Stuff, for taking on the edits for this book. Thank you for working with me, and helping me to see things differently. I learned so much, including there is no such thing as London Broil in the United Kingdom.

To Stephanie Hobbs, I love what you did with the cover for Within Six Months. The colors, the fonts, the attention to detail…you nailed it, as always. Thank you!

To Michael Reh, I can't thank you enough for working with me and allowing me to have your beautiful photograph of Micah Truitt, my muse for the character Tommy. It means more than you'll ever know. It truly completes the story. Thank you so, so much!

To JM Walker, I can't thank you enough for taking on this project to format, and for making the words on the pages… beautiful.

To Samantha Talarico and Misty Goulet Yancey, my beta-readers, I appreciate the time you took out of your own busy lives to read and re-read this story. I love your suggestions and talking points…thank you for being a very important part in the making of this book.

To my family, you're always there for me, no matter what, even when I'm a little bit nuts. Get used to it, that won't change. I love you more than you'll ever know.

I'd like to give a special thank you to my husband Sal, and my sister-in-law Michele, for our conversation about… 'the last time'. That night I went home and penned the letter that Jade's brother wrote for her in the book. It was eye-opening and heart-wrenching, to think about it though, it's true. Do we really remember 'the last time'? The last time we picked up our child because now they're grown. Do we remember that day? Do we remember the last cookie we ate that our mom made from scratch? Do we even realize many small and precious moments we all take for granted, will be one day 'the last time'?

Perhaps not, but…

Thank you for that time, I won't forget it.

about the author

Cleo Scornavacca is an author of Adult Romance, a wife, a mom & a true "Jersey Girl". She was born and raised in NJ and still resides in the Garden State.

In 2012, Cleo began writing Miss Taken, her debut novel and book one of the Miss Taken Identity Series. Identity, book two, was published in 2014 and The Ties That Bind followed in 2016, which completed the series.

In addition, Cleo is currently working on several other titles which include four standalones in her new Wild Roses Series, that will feature the secondary characters from Miss Taken Identity. Within Six Months is the first book in this series.

Cleo was honored to be a part of This Beautiful Escape, Volume One. An anthology that contains her personal short story called Small Gestures. All of the proceeds to This Beautiful Escape go to the fund for Ataxia Awareness.

Cleo is a proud member of Romance Writers of America (RWA) and the New Jersey Romance Writers (NJRW) organizations. When she isn't writing, she's spending time with her family, friends, and her Dobie, Brayden. Cleo enjoys reading all types romance, books on Italy, listening to 80's metal bands, watching shows on house and garden design, movies from Hollywood's Golden Age and of course, squishing her feet in the sand down at the Jersey Shore every chance she gets.

You can follow Cleo and get updates on her books through several social media sites, including:

www.cleoscornavacca.com

www.facebook.com/cleoscornavaccabooks

https://www.bookbub.com/authors/cleo-scornavacca

https://www.goodreads.com/author/show/7242174.Cleo_Scornavacca

https://www.instagram.com/cleoscornavacca/

www.twitter.com/@cleoscornavacca

https://booksprout.co/author/482/cleo-scornavacca

An Excerpt from Miss Taken

For many readers, this may be the first time you're reading about the character Tommy Conte. But this is not the first time I've written him. Tommy was one of the original characters from my debut series, Miss Taken Identity.

Here's chapter one, from Miss Taken…

Chapter One

Capri…or so I thought

I looked at the clock…only 4:30 am. New York was barely stirring. Soon the city would be jammed with the rush of commuters ready to begin their workday. Except for Theresa, my dad's housekeeper, I might be the only one up this early in the morning. The evidence of Theresa being awake came from the aroma of fresh coffee and homemade pastries that drifted through the house and settled in my bedroom. I knew it wouldn't be long before everyone was out of bed killing the stillness I'd been enjoying at that very moment.

At the request of my (I won't take no for an answer, Rain) dad; I was sleeping over, so he could drive me to Newark Airport later that morning. My father, Victor

Medici, was a man people rarely said no to. I was headed to Capri, Italy. My home away from home. The one place in my life that made me feel free; where I was able to breathe.

I'd made the trip numerous times over the years. I didn't understand why my dad still felt the need to be so overprotective of me. Well, I understood why, but I after all of these years, I wished his view about my safety had changed.

Clearly, it hadn't.

I considered confronting him on it, but then I thought better of it. No need to leave with upset between us.

My only regret about leaving today was that Tommy, my best friend, wouldn't be going with me. Tommy Conte was a very successful, highly sought-after photographer and my business partner. His sexy charm and bad-boy looks didn't hurt his image either. Tommy's frame was 6'2 built, but not bulky, with black hair, brown eyes, and numerous tattoos.

He had a very important holiday shoot for an Italian wine distributor this week. It was August and the holidays were not far off, so it was crunch time for Tommy. He was going to meet me in Capri next week, which I was grateful for.

Tommy had always been a stable presence in my life. We grew up together, went to college together and now we lived together. There had never been a sexual relationship between us, but the emotional bond we shared went much deeper than mere childhood friends.

Tommy was my protector. He'd been there through everything. During the confinement, my parents imposed upon me due to the obsession my mother had. She constantly felt the need to keep me safe and retain control over 'my fragile life.'

My mother's words, not mine.

Tommy was there to pick up the pieces or be the buffer when life got to be too much.

I was brought out of my reverie by a sudden and sharp knocking on the door. "Rain, you up, sweetie?"

Raven, my twin sister, always knew how to silence the silence, so to speak. Raven lived next door to our dad with her fiancé Michael. He happened to be Tommy's older brother. She must have been up early for her daily run. Raven and Michael were lawyers with my dad's firm Kane and Medici.

Raven and I looked exactly alike. We both had long black hair, blue eyes and we were tall and lean. She was slightly thinner than me; I had bangs, but she didn't.

Our physical features were where our likeness ended. Raven was very strict when it came to her career and her personal life. Everything always had a schedule. I often wondered if she penciled in sex with Michael. The thought made me laugh.

I, on the other hand, didn't like to be scheduled. I was a freelance photographer, like Tommy, but I specialized in the sand, sun, and surf. I loved traveling and truly enjoyed every bit of my life…now.

"No regrets"…my words to live by.

"Rain, you up?" She sounded slightly annoyed at this point.

"Come in. I'm up," I said just loud enough to be heard through the thick door, yet trying not to wake my dad, whose room was just down the hall.

Stepping into my room, Raven notice I was still in bed. With a puzzled look on her face, she questioned me, "Don't you have to get ready for your flight?"

"It's not for several hours, but I'm getting up now," I stretched and crawled out of bed to start my day.

I had noticed she was wearing a black running suit and had her hair tied back in a severe ponytail. I was right, she was going for her run. Her routine was so predictable. I loved her with all my heart, but I could never *be* her. She craved the power of the courtroom, while I preferred to experience life in a different way. There were no mergers and acquisitions for me, just spectacular shorelines and faraway destinations. Give me a beach anywhere in the world and I'd be there photographing it, along with the people that made it come to life. I loved to live life in that way, even when it scared me. Some of that fright was left over from my so-called childhood.

No matter, the past was in the past and I had finally moved on.

Raven walked to the table by the window and thumbed through my portfolio. She partially whipped around to address me.

"These are fantastic. Are they for the show?"

"Maybe."

"Why maybe?" She asked, with a hint of annoyance.

"I have some revisions to make first. Plus I'm hoping to use some of the shots I'll be getting from this trip."

"How long will you be gone this time?"

"I'll be home for Christmas dinner," I said, grinning at her.

"CHRISTMAS! What about Thanksgiving? You're not coming home for Thanksgiving?"

"C'mon, Raven, you know as well as I do that you and Dad are never around for Thanksgiving. It's your time to clean up your cases and I'm always left hanging around the city with nothing to do."

"Rain, what if Tommy came home for Thanksgiving this year? Then would you reconsider?" she cunningly asked.

I smiled at her and replied, "Good try Raven, but contrary to popular belief, Tommy and I aren't joined at the hip. You know full well he won't be home. He always goes with Michael to their parent's house. Something you should be doing now that you and Michael are going to be man and wife. Besides, even if Tommy does come home, it doesn't mean I'm coming with him."

"Okay, but promise me you'll think about it?"

"I promise." I just smiled and shook my head. "You're a real pain in my ass."

"Good…Now let's go get some of Theresa's fabulous coffee," she said while she curled her arm around mine. Then she gave me a small, but tight squeeze as we headed out the door.

I smirked. "Wait…I thought you were going for a run?"

"Changed my mind. Coffee with my sister is so much better than exercise."

As we headed out of my room to go downstairs, our dad appeared in the hallway. He was already dressed for what looked to be a full day at the office. He was wearing a black three-piece suit, white shirt, Turquoise blue tie, and handkerchief. The suit really complemented his olive skin and white slicked back hair. My dad was very strong and very powerful. He wouldn't wear anything, but the best to showcase his power and strength.

"Good morning, ladies. Why are my girls up so early?"

"We could say the same about you," Raven spoke first.

"I had to get up for an early meeting at the office today."

I was silent but tilted my head to the side in annoyance. Why did I stay over if he wasn't taking me to the airport? I could have spent my evening with Tommy before leaving for Italy.

"Now Rain, please don't give me that look. You know if I could get out of this I would, but I have obligations, sweetie."

"Dad, its fine. I told you originally I could get to Newark by myself."

"That's my girl, but Michael is taking you to the airport. It's all been arranged."

"Dad, I don't need Michael to take me to the airport. I'm 34 years old. I think I can get myself to Italy. I've been doing it for years."

"Rain, do this for me. Let Michael take you. I'll feel better knowing you're safe. He doesn't have a case today, so it's no trouble."

I knew at this point I wouldn't win, so I just nodded. Conversation over, Victor Medici gets his way as usual.

Case closed.

We headed downstairs to the kitchen to get some much-needed coffee. It was on the first floor of the house toward the back. It was slightly on the narrow side, but very beautiful. The appliances were all professional size and stainless steel. The cabinets were an off-white French style with heavy iron pulls. The countertops were black granite and the floors, travertine. The center island had been used mainly for small family gatherings and breakfast, such as this morning. There were French doors that led out to a secluded patio and garden with a Koi-Fish Pond. It was tranquil…soothing, and one of my favorite spaces in the townhouse. When I sat out there, I hardly heard the city anymore.

Theresa prepared a wonderful spread this morning. It consisted of a large bowl of fresh berries, Greek yogurt, a small pitcher of honey, nuts, and granola. In addition, she made homemade pastries, my dad's favorite.

We were a very casual family. We weren't extravagant. It was always about being together, sharing a meal and enjoying the company we were with. It really helped during my younger years when being confined at home was, at times, unbearable—having company made those days more manageable.

I hopped up onto the counter next to where Theresa was cooking, after I grabbed my cup. Raven and my dad settled in around the island.

Just then, Michael walked in and joined us. He and Tommy had the same features; black hair, chocolate colored eyes, and a solid jaw. Michael also had tattoos, just not as many as Tommy did. I loved Mike. He easy going, and he balanced out my sister, who was anything but.

"How's my girl this morning?" Michael asked Raven, giving her a soft kiss on her cheek.   "Your girl is not happy. The caterer hasn't returned my calls. They were highly recommended and are supposed to be the best in New York but now, that remains to be seen."

Time to tease the uptight twin.

"Raven, why don't you just cut out all the bullshit and run off to Vegas and elope?" I asked, smiling at Michael. He knew exactly what I was doing and he enjoyed it just as much as me.

"ELOPE!" She shrieked, "Have you lost your fucking mind, Rain?"

Just as I was about to deal with my sister's typical outburst, my phone started to ring. It was Tommy. My day was finally improving.I raised my hand, she needed to stop her continued screaming.

Silence…finally.

"I have to take this." I went into the family room for some privacy and quiet. "Tommy?"

"Hey, baby, did you get through the evening with your dad okay?" Tommy's voice made me smile.

As I was about to tell him, I could hear he was still in bed and not alone. Why did this bother me?

"Oh my God, please don't tell me you slept with the winery owner's daughter."

"You know me better than that. I nailed his wife."

"Tommy, you are fucking crazy."

"Don't start, Rain. If you would just sleep with me, then I wouldn't sleep around like I do." He was grinning. I just knew it.

"Never going to happen."

"Never say never." Although he was joking, his voice was determined and I became silent, so he changed the subject fast.

"Okay, enough about my sex life and the lack of yours. When does your flight leave?" I ignored his last comment.

"It departs at 1 pm, so I'm leaving here around ten; Michael's driving me." I decided to inform him of the change of plans.

"What happened with your dad?"

"Don't ask. Same old shit. Again, he got his way. I wish you were coming with me now."

"Stop it, Rain."

"Stop what?" I asked, slightly confused.

"Stop pouting. You know I always know when you're doing it."

"I am not pouting!"

"Yes, you are, baby. You always do it whenever any of us ask you what your plans are or tries to help you in any way. So, what if your dad asked Mike to take you? Be glad for the company. It's not like he's escorting you to Italy, just to the airport."

I sighed out of frustration.

"Listen, Rain, I know its tough for you to accept help. I was there, remember? When all that shit with your mom went down. Sure it was bad, but its over. You make the decisions for your life now…no one else. It's just a ride to the airport. Don't make it out to be more than it is. It's not worth the aggravation you're laying on yourself."

There was a stillness over the phone because Tommy was waiting for my response. I knew he was right. Tommy had always been there when my parents, mainly my mom, controlled my every move. They were easier on me when Tommy was around *and* he'd been around a lot.

He was there when I was at my worst and at my best. He never left me. Even now when the nightmares and anxiety attacks creep up on me, he's there. He'll stay with me all night, if necessary and hold onto me to keep the past away. I don't know what I'd do without him…perhaps go insane.

"I'm sorry, Tommy. Don't be angry with me. You know I love you, but he frustrates me."

"Baby, you know I can never stay mad at you… not for very long anyway," His voice softened.

I looked at the clock.

"Tommy, I'll call you later. I have to get ready for my flight. I haven't even showered yet."

"Okay, I'll wait to hear from you. Rain, we're okay, yeah?"

"We're fine. Listen, I know you're right, but it's not that easy for me to let go of the past."

"It's been over for a long time. Try…do it for me."

"I'll try. I'll talk to you later."

Just then a warm hand came around my waist.

"I was just coming to find you. I have to leave for my meeting and wanted to say goodbye to you before I left." That was his guilt talking.

"I'm fine. Oh and that was Tommy. He'll be out at the end of next week."

"Are you going to be okay with that?"

"Dad, I'm telling you I'll be fine. Besides, I don't mind the time alone. Capri is warm and beautiful this time of the year. I'm going to work on my fading tan, start reading a new book, get some photos for the show, and spend time with Mema and Antonio. Stop worrying about me, please!"

"Sweetheart, I'll always worry about you. You're my child. That's my job to care for you.   Did   you remember to pack your shots?"

Without messing up his suit, I gave him a big hug and then smoothed out his collar. "Yes, I have my shots. And Dad…I love you."

"I love you, too." He smiled, kissed my cheek and disappeared out the front door.

I went back toward the kitchen and heard Raven screaming about something that affected her wedding plans. Something I'm sure I was going regret asking her about. Just as I passed the staircase in the hallway, she came out and stated she needed Michael to go with her to the caterers today. Her wedding was over a year away and at this rate, possibly two years because she kept changing things.

Personally, I hoped she wouldn't have to change the groom with the way she carried on.

"Rain, will you be okay getting to the airport without Michael?"

I smiled at Mike and said, "Sure, I told all of you before, I don't need a babysitter. What could possibly happen on the way to the airport?"

"Are you positive?" Michael asked, making sure it was really okay with me.

"Positive, but I need to take a shower. So can you call the car service you use and tell them to be here in about an hour and a half?"

"Absolutely," Michael gave me a grin with a quick wink; and with that, I kissed both Raven and Mike. Then headed upstairs to get ready.

Once I was done with my bathroom ritual, I decided on black leggings, a long sleeve black T-shirt and my black suede ankle boots with the silver buckles. I tended to get cold very easily, so I didn't want to be uncomfortable on the plane. I grabbed my bags, turned back and checked to make sure I wasn't missing anything before heading out the door.

It was sunny and warm in Manhattan.

This was going to be great weather to fly in.

I stepped out onto the curb in front of my dad's home. There was a large black SUV waiting with its motor idling. I hadn't asked Mike to order such a large vehicle, but perhaps it was all the car service had available on such short notice.

I checked my phone. I had plenty of time to catch my flight. Even if we came across some traffic, I'd still be okay. I tucked my cell away in the side of my boot when…

That's all I remembered before everything faded to black…

* 9 7 8 0 6 9 2 1 9 3 4 7 1 *